RESURRECTION

LEO TOLSTOY

Resurrection

Translated by Louise Maude

with an introduction by
Anthony Briggs

WORDSWORTH EDITIONS

For my husband
ANTHONY JOHN RANSON
with love from your wife, the publisher
Eternally grateful for your
unconditional love

Readers who are interested in other titles from
Wordsworth Editions are invited to visit our
website at www.wordsworth-editions.com

For our latest list and a full mail order service contact
Bibliophile Books, Unit 5 Datapoint,
South Crescent, London E16 4TL
Tel: +44 (0) 20 74 74 24 74
Fax: +44 (0) 20 74 74 85 89
orders@bibliophilebooks.com
www.bibliophilebooks.com

This edition published 2014 by Wordsworth Editions Limited
8B East Street, Ware, Hertfordshire SG12 9HJ

ISBN 978 1 84022 728 4

Wordsworth Editions is
the company founded in 1987 by
MICHAEL TRAYLER

Typeset in Great Britain by Roperford Editorial
Printed and bound by Clays Ltd, St Ives plc

CONTENTS

INTRODUCTION

Court of conscience

Imagine a courtroom, where a young prostitute is on trial for a murder, and you are a male member of the jury. Suddenly you are stunned by an instant of shocking recognition. You *know* the woman – isn't she *that girl,* the one whose virginity you took with some force – how many years ago? Could it be that your forgotten moment of self-gratification somehow set her on a downward path to where she is now – in the dock facing the most serious of all charges? Is there any way to make amends for your terrible misdeed?

This is the situation at the beginning of Leo Tolstoy's last big novel, *Resurrection* (1899), in which the hero (who is also the villain), Dmitri Nekhlyudov, will devote the next five hundred pages to a single-handed attempt to overturn multiple injustice for which he is primarily responsible. The trial itself is a thrilling piece of theatre, one of the finest courtroom dramas in all literature, and the story that follows is intensely moving.

This is not surprising. Not only is it recounted by a master of narrative prose, often described as the world's greatest novelist, but, more remarkably, the events described at the outset actually occurred in real life. At least a decade before the novel was written Tolstoy was told a true story by a friend of his, a distinguished lawyer, A. F. Koni, one of whose clients had been called to jury service only to recognize the shabby prostitute standing before him, charged with theft from a client. Years before he had seduced a reluctant sixteen-year-old house-servant and abandoned her to pregnancy and dismissal from service. The baby had been adopted, she had gone downhill, and now here she was, a wreck of a woman whose collapse had been determined by him and his young lust. After the guilty verdict, overcome with remorse, he got permission to marry the girl, but alas, she died in prison from typhus before his spiritual resurrection through expiation could begin.

This account is sure to have troubled the great writer's own conscience since he had been guilty of sexual misbehaviour just as bad and also unexpiated. (One of the sins Leo Tolstoy had forcibly reported to his new bride, half his age and a complete innocent, concerned a serf-girl still living on his estate with an illegitimate child fathered by him). At the time he had no plans to exploit the story himself. He encouraged Koni to do so, but time passed, and nothing came of it. With Koni's permission he decided to write it up as fiction himself, but the novel was nowhere near finished even ten years later. It needed a special impulse to turbo-charge the enterprise, and this came in 1898 when the moralist who repudiated the use of money as immoral was presented with a need for funding on a large scale.

But we are getting ahead of ourselves. Tolstoy's attitude to this late novel cannot be understood outside the context of his life, his other major works and the development of his moral philosophy.

A life in literature

Leo Tolstoy is an emblematic figure in the history of a nation celebrated for its cultural achievement, one of the two or three contenders for the title of Russia's greatest writer. He is famous for having written two of the world's biggest and best novels, and no fewer than fifty of his other prose works are still available in English translations. But he became known also as a religious thinker, a moral crusader, and an inspirational predecessor of pacifist protesters like Mahatma Gandhi. Tolstoy has been the subject of thousands of biographical, literary, religious and ethical studies, books and articles in every language you can think of, and yet he is still incompletely understood.

The biggest misunderstanding concerns his two novels, *War and Peace* (1864–69) and *Anna Karenina* (1873–76). The problem with them is summarised in an event during an American 'Get Smart' movie, when Agent 86 is stabbed and left for dead. Somehow he survives the attack, and explains how he did it by opening his coat to display a thick book into which a murderous knife has been plunged without doing any harm. His comment is, 'I figured nobody ever makes it all the way through *War and Peace*.' This is a good joke, and it says much for the author that his work is a household name the world over.

Unfortunately, the thickness of the book seems to confirm the idea that *War and Peace* is impenetrably long and hard to read. Many people also believe that it is stuffed with French and bogged down by the author's comments on warfare, history and the human condition. It seems to satisfy the cynical definition of a classic work as something everyone wants to have read but no one wants to read.

The truth is different in several ways. First, although Tolstoy's early versions of the novel did contain long passages in French, including the opening lines, these were excluded from his edition of 1873, and good translations now reflect this decision.

Second, the novel is certainly a long one, at something like 1400 pages, but it is conveniently broken down into four unformidable volumes, each of which runs along in small sections based on individual chapters that average out at no longer than *four-and-a-half pages* in length. There is no danger of getting lost or feeling overwhelmed. Third, to make things easier still, the author has kindly relocated his various reflections in a couple of epilogues, so that they do not clog the narrative itself. No one should be discouraged from reading this splendid and easily readable work (one-third war and two-thirds peace) because of the myths with which it is encrusted.

Even the minutely recorded life of this great man has been somewhat misrepresented. Biographers, in the grip of admiration for a distinguished writer and his noble intentions, have been rather too lenient with him as a man. (One writer, Edward Crankshaw, can be exempted from this charge – see Further Reading). It is clear that this apostle of peace and brotherly love was never able to treat those around him with any degree of sympathy or charity. At every stage of his life he was a hostile and aggressive personality. Everyone spoke of his burning, malevolent glare and attitude of vindictive severity. When the novelist Ivan Turgenev called him 'a troglodyte' in 1855 he used the term at first in a spirit of light humour, only to discover that it was taxonomically exact; anyone might have employed it, at any time. In his day-to-day dealings Leo Tolstoy had the manners of a cave-man.

His life divides into four or five distinct stages. Born in 1828, he had a warmly protected childhood despite the death of his mother when he was two and his father when he was nine. In late adolescence he moved to Kazan, where he spent the time in youthful debauchery and so little study that he left the university without graduating. Rather more productively he then followed his older brother, a soldier, down to the Caucasus, where he was launched into a military career, fighting first against the local militants in Chechnya before transferring to other theatres and eventually ending up as a combatant in the Crimean War. In all of these places he distinguished himself as a courageous officer, and learned at first hand all there was to know about the atrocities of war. Many passages in *War and Peace* could never have been written without this direct experience of survival in close combat.

But this frenzy of activity was not to last. For the next half-dozen years he retired to a relaxed and still debauched life in St Petersburg, travelled abroad in leisurely style and finally, in 1862, he got married and settled down. His long-suffering wife, Sofya, was to bear him thirteen children, six of whom died before adulthood. Despite a short period of married bliss in the 1860s, and the delight of working together on what would turn out to be the world's greatest novel, the pair soon declined into a state of bickering animosity, and their long marriage ended in a terrible story of mistrust and alienation bordering on outright hatred even though shot through by inextinguishable admiration of the wife for her husband's genius.

After the sixties (*War and Peace*) and the seventies (*Anna Karenina*) Tolstoy spent his last three eventless decades at home on his estate, sometimes writing, sometimes not. He became obsessed with a search for religious truth and moral purity, setting unattainable goals of righteousness for himself and the rest of us. The remarkable thing about this period is that it produced not only a string of instructional works about how we should live our lives – according to the precepts of Jesus Christ unencumbered by the hypocritical complications created by his church – but also a series of literary masterpieces that broke their own author's self-imposed rules by avoiding out-and-out religious teaching and following the paths of good, entertaining and challenging literature. He died in 1910 at the age of 82, world-famous as an anarchist and pacifist, though as the years went by this aspect of his writing has steadily fallen away, leaving a residue of remarkable fiction by which his name is now unforgettably honoured.

There is a painful paradox right at the heart of Leo Tolstoy and his legacy. His literary achievement is at variance with his proclaimed ideas. From an early age he was obsessed with his own weakness of character. He knew the path towards goodness, self-control, but could not follow it. As a young man he gave in to every available temptation, not least the sexual ones, becoming ever more disgusted with himself and his animal appetites. It came as a relief to discover from the writings of Rousseau (see below) that all young men were as bad as he was, but this had a devastating consequence. Suddenly he knew the full extent of human weakness and degradation, and he would devote the rest of his life, not merely to self-improvement, because whenever he tried this he never succeeded, but to exposing the obvious iniquity of humankind in general. Most of his works were originally intended as didactic illustrations of human misbehaviour, intended to awaken our conscience and improve our conduct. (Many of them, including all his greatest works, escape these limitations by taking on a life of their own based on reality rather than any well-intentioned sermonising). The fact that he could never bring himself to love anyone did not prevent Leo Tolstoy from insisting that the rest of us should build our lives on love, aiming at a kind of Christ-like selflessness. As we shall see, his actual formula for human improvement would collapse repeatedly under its burden of utopian idealism. Meanwhile we need to look at two thinkers who invaded his mind at crucial times and (it is no exaggeration to claim) took over his whole personality.

Teachers of Tolstoy

Leo Tolstoy was in his mid-teens when he came across the writings of a man who would dominate his thinking until the moment of his death: the Swiss-born French philosopher and political thinker, Jean-Jacques Rousseau (1712–78). Without some knowledge of this strange man it will be difficult to understand the life and work of the great Russian writer. Born in Geneva, Rousseau moved through Italy and Savoy before settling in France, where he made his name in 1750 with a prize essay, *A*

Discourse on the Arts and Sciences, which is now described as 'feeble and almost unreadable', though in its day it was greatly praised. His instant apotheosis as a serious thinker would one day be described by a famous French critic, Jules Lemaître, as 'one of the strongest proofs ever provided of human stupidity'. Nevertheless, this writer's main ideas became fashionable and were taken seriously by many later writers, including Leo Tolstoy. Rousseau still has a doggedly faithful following today, though mainly in France and Switzerland.

Rousseau's one big idea is that human babies are born into a natural state of goodness, only to become corrupted by education, science, art and material prosperity, a process which explains our lapses into bad behaviour and consequent unhappiness. The argument goes as follows: the corruption comes from moving from small communities into large settlements, which have encouraged the ownership of property, the rise of inequality and immorality, as well as the imposition of despotism. There can be no happiness for mankind in this direction; the only solution would be for a fortunate few people to reorganise their lives by returning to nature, and living in small moral communities. It is already too late for most of humanity to adopt this strategy. This theory is so obviously unsound (and disprovable, as history has shown) that we can only marvel at its instant popularity and stubborn endurance.

We do not have to argue this matter out in abstract terms. As generations have gone by it has been tested to destruction in the most practical way, one which has involved a contribution from Leo Tolstoy, whose endorsement of Rousseau's idea carried great weight because of his reputation as a successful novelist. At the end of the nineteenth century not a few idealists were naive enough to retreat from the distasteful world and form small agrarian communities based on co-operative living and self-sufficiency. Some of them, in Russia, America, England and almost every country in northern Europe, withdrew from society into 'Tolstoyan colonies'. The expectation was that under these narrowed circumstances the natural goodness of men and women would prevail over self-interest and immorality, resulting in a kind of contentment that would be the envy of the outside world and a model for all to follow. After all, these well-meaning people would, in the words of one historian, 'be leading simple, honest lives untainted by the evils of capitalism.' Every one of these communities broke down in short order. Another chronicler describes how, in the early summer of 1899, a visitor to the Purleigh Colony in the south of England discovered that, instead of harmony and happiness, 'argument seemed to be the farm's chief produce.' As he explains, perhaps unnecessarily, the good participants had been 'stimulated by the desire to live a perfect life in an imperfect world.'

Rousseau's (now obvious) mistake was a wrong deduction. Driven to despair by the immorality of modern, civilised life, he assumed that this was due to the processes of modernity and civilisation themselves rather than endemic in humanity's animal nature, which needed more time to evolve. Contrary to his thinking, it has been the very process of enrichment and sophistication which has led people on a huge scale out of poverty and deprivation and into multi-million communities where they rub along quite nicely. But it is a sobering thought that some of the older hymn-books in our churches still include a verse that begins,

> What though the spicy breezes
> Blow soft o'er Java's isle;
> Though every prospect pleases
> And only man is vile?

This could have been the mission statement of Jean-Jacques Rousseau, and the sentiment was shared by Leo Tolstoy; they both believed not in the natural goodness but the natural vileness of mankind. So did the only other thinker for whom Tolstoy later developed a lifelong obsession, Arthur Schopenhauer (1788–1860), famous for his systematic philosophical pessimism. This man ('dark, distrustful, misogynistic and truculent') believed not only in the nastiness of human nature, but in the total wretchedness of the entire universe and the process of life itself. The great Russian novelist warmly embraced the negative ideas of these two men and never repudiated them. When he transcended them in splendid literary works, he later regretted doing so.

The wonder is that the best of his published works travel in the opposite direction. *War and Peace* is nothing less than 'a triumphant affirmation of life', and Martin Amis captures the essence of Tolstoy in a single question: 'Who else but Tolstoy has made happiness really swing on the page?'

Despite his personal failings as a man, particularly his incapacity for love or charity, and notwithstanding his pessimistic theorising, the world's greatest novelist amazed himself by transmitting an inspiring vision of the world and its people, summarised by Russia's famous critic, Prince Dmitri Mirsky, as 'a general message of beauty, and satisfaction that the world should be so beautiful'.

The struggle between the dark moraliser and the generous lover of life raged in this writer from his earliest stories to the end of his days. It is still being waged in *Resurrection*.

Rebirth of a novelist

At the turn of the nineteenth and twentieth centuries Leo Tolstoy the novelist was reborn, having undergone a virtual death in literary terms while completing *Anna Karenina* in 1878, a time when he teetered on the brink of suicide in real life. With this novel behind him he determined never again to waste his life writing fiction. Utterly depressed and convinced of the nastiness and futility of human life, he withdrew from the trade of which he had become the supreme master. At first he was determined never to write again, but before long, finding the urge to do so irresistible, he chose to carry on with the pen while limiting his subject matter to an intellectual search for moral certainty and religious truth. There followed a string of publications and private writings of a spiritual and didactic nature, though one or two of them were so well-written that they still count among his masterpieces despite their obvious intention to inveigh and instruct. These great works include *A Confession*, *The Death of Ian Il'yich*, *The Power of Darkness* (a play), *Master and Man*, and *Hadji Murad* (published posthumously).

It was in 1895 that Tolstoy received a strong inducement to earn a lot of money quickly, needing it for a good cause. This impulse arose because of a change in the destiny of a centuries-old religious sect known as the Dukhobors (Fighters for the Spirit), who lived in Ukraine and the Caucasus. Tolstoy warmed to these people because they had come, independently of him, to a set of beliefs that closely matched his own. Despite being deeply religious they spurned the rituals and writings of the Church, they did not believe in private property, they refrained from eating animals, and, more to the point at this time in Russian history, they took their pledge of non-violence to such an extreme that they would have no truck with military service. The Tsarist government, tightening its grip following the assassination of Alexander II in 1881, began a series of reprisals against Dukhobor pacifists, whose leaders were being imprisoned and exiled. Tolstoy took up their cause, signing every letter and manifesto set before him, and by doing so he placed Nicholas II in an awkward position. The tsar could not allow pacifist insubordination to persist, but the great novelist's worldwide reputation cast a cloak of inviolability over this group of protesters.

As the pressure built up between the two camps the government came up with an ingenious compromise. The Dukhobors could not be allowed to stay on in Russia without performing their civic duties, but what they could do is leave the country *en masse* and settle down somewhere else. Land had even been found for them in North America. However, it was asking too much for the government to make such a generous exception and also pay the costs involved in transporting seven thousand adherents to a distant land. This is where Tolstoy came into the picture. Years ago he had renounced the copyright to all his literary works; now at the stroke of a pen he reasserted his rights over any new writings in order to sell them at the highest possible price at home and abroad. A publisher signed up his new novel for twelve thousand roubles, every kopeck of which went into the Dukhobor fund. It was enough to send the whole community to Canada, where, after a chequered history of troublesome nonconformity in that country too, their descendants live on to this day.

So far, so good. We begin with a good idea for a dramatic story, grounded in personal experience and the guilty consciences of three different characters, two of them real people (Koni's friend, and Leo Tolstoy himself) and one fictional, (Dmitri Nekhlyudov), who are backed up by a fictional figure in the dock also deriving from more than one real-life prototype. This shows a strong grip on reality, and augurs well for the coming narrative. Less promising is the author's mercenary motivation for writing. Worse than that, we also know that he has settled into a permanently didactic mode; with many axes to grind, he is unlikely to pass up any chance to infuse his thoughts about human behaviour into his story. All in all, the enterprise begins to look rather flaky. Novels written purely for money or directed towards the moral improvement of our species do not have a good track record. How does *Resurrection* fare under these circumstances?

Resurrection

Much better than you might think. First the action. The trial scene which we have mentioned results in a terrible miscarriage of injustice, with repercussions enough to sustain the reader's interest indefinitely. We follow the victim back into prison and become privy to its dreadful secrets, a life of unending conflict and cruelty; nothing is spared, from the nauseating stench of sewage to the vicious maltreatment of the prison population, right through to the barbaric business of a flogging so savage that it sickens even the hardened superintendent. We are taken back in time and learn all the details of Nekhlyudov's relationship with Katyusha, a beautiful boy-girl encounter to begin with but destined for a brutal consummation in sexual frenzy. Woven into the details of court and prison is the story of Nekhlyudov's past and present life, a parade of pampered luxury and idleness standing in stark contrast to the hardship described in the main story-line. His agony of spirit has been convincingly established. By the end of Part One (59 short chapters, almost half the novel) it would be a hard-hearted reader who did not feel passionately involved in this rich material and eager to go on in search of a happier resolution.

It is in this direction that the second and third parts of *Resurrection* evolve. The scope of the action becomes broader as the hero, while remaining in close contact with the prison population, extends his contacts outwards and upwards in society, calling on all possible contacts in St Petersburg and the highest government circles, for assistance with an appeal against the ill-considered judicial verdict in which he had played no little part. Alas, the goal seems to get further and further away, and eventually he finds himself travelling with a prisoners' convoy well out into Siberia (with them walking and him driving, of course) before, at long last, a resolution is achieved, though not one which results in all-round satisfaction and happiness. Narrative interest is maintained at a high level to the very end. The resolution of two major complexities is held back until the last half-dozen chapters.

The narrative method of *Resurrection* is unusual, being dependent on opposite qualities. At one and the same time the novel, like a river with boulders in it, presents a smooth-flowing story and a series of outstanding set-pieces, highly individualised occurrences that stick in the mind. A number of the scenes are as good as anything you will anywhere else in the works of this master novelist. The entire trial scene occupying several chapters; the seduction of Katyusha, and her vain attempt to catch Nekhlyudov's attention as his train stops at night in their village (Part One); the hero's sadly amusing attempts to give away his land, the rejection of the appeal (Part Two); a skirmish among the marching prisoners when a brutal guard separates a prisoner from his tiny daughter, and a double execution scene as recounted by a witness (Part Three); these are only a few of those memorable moments. At times like these it is clear that the ageing writer has not lost sight of the novelist's first duty, to transfix and engross his readers. Although events move slowly because of the inertia built into the tsarist system of government and law, a mounting sense of injustice, unease and anger creates an atmosphere of gathering impatience and importance. A novel which could have been diffuse and disconnected is unified by its central character and his obsessive purpose, which gains strength and solidity chapter by chapter even when his business is continually frustrated.

Interwoven into this tapestry of fascinating events is a broad range of characters. The action of the novel moves about a good deal, from capital to countryside, luxury to destitution, courtroom to squalid cell, high society to the dregs of humanity, government ministers in their offices to peasants in their hovels, and wherever we go we come across new people, some of whom stay with us for the duration, though a good number make a kind of guest appearance and are soon left behind. The total of them comes to over a hundred named characters. These varied people and their situations present innumerable opportunities for contrast, irony, comedy and satire. A high-court judge is seen working out with weights, totally preoccupied with his physical jerks and an assignment later that day with a little red-headed beauty, before he goes into court; a senator stuffs his prodigious beard into his mouth and champs on it; a prominent general is presented in a ridiculous situation, communing with Joan of Arc over an Ouija board.

These elevated personages, all too human in their private behaviour, provide a painful contrast with the other characters in this novel – the great majority - who are suffering. When you read about life in a Russian prison cell or on the long walk to Siberia, a flogging or an execution, you cannot forget or forgive the pampered perpetrators of injustice whose own lives are as luxurious as they are stupidly misspent. They are made to look ludicrous in order to strengthen our feeling of inequity and our understanding of Nekhlyudov's rage.

The spread of characters is completed by a small scattering of persons not at the top or the bottom of society, but right in the middle, struggling to make a decent living on the soil or at a job in town. To take one small instance, in the twelfth chapter of Part Two the hero takes a cab across the city, and his conversation with the hard-working driver is identical in every way to the conversations between London taxi-drivers and their fares in our own day. The dialogue is instantly recognisable. The driver takes pride in the new buildings that are going up and shocks Nekhlyudov by saluting them both in their own right and for the work they create for ordinary folk, rather than sharing the other man's disgust at these luxury items as symbols of exploitation; likewise, the cabby's views on immigration and the people who come in from outside, taking all the good jobs, have an amusingly strong resonance with what is said in similar circumstances in our own society fifteen hundred miles away and a hundred years on. A tiny chapter like this one proves doubly effective in broadening the scope of argument around Nekhlyudov's entire cause while slightly delaying and varying the narrative interest.

Incidentally, there is something unusual in this technique which has not been widely acknowledged. It is unTolstoyan. The famous author of *War and Peace* is generally considered to be massive and serious in subject matter and technique; in this late work he is light-footed and full of humour. The result is that a series of portraits which could have proved too near to caricature (as in much of Charles Dickens, for instance, especially in *The Pickwick Papers*) comes out as a positive feature of the novel, giving it a rich supply of contrast and irony without undermining the sense of reality.

The biggest risk taken by the author in this novel is an obvious one. He has charged it with a heavy responsibility by making his story a vehicle for a set of ideas long held and brought to completion in his full maturity. Two things are dangerous in this undertaking. One is that the ideas themselves may be wrong; the alternative is that, even if they are correct, they may weigh down the narrative and detract from its effectiveness. We cannot make a definitive judgement in either of these cases. Readers must decide for themselves, though at least we have a certain advantage of hindsight gained over more than a century. We can ask ourselves this: how have the ideas worked out during the following five or six generations of human history?

What ideas are we talking about? As we have seen, they go back, via Schopenhauer, to Rousseau, who believed that human society becomes increasingly immoral as it gathers material prosperity. Organisation into specialised groups, the process of education (some would say civilisation) and particularly the ownership of property create selfishness, greed and violence, thus producing all the evils of society with which we are too familiar. Thus in the novel Nekhyudov decides to give up his social status, his career, his prospective marriage and all of his property in order to simplify himself and live the good life, none of which he can even attempt until he has expiated the awful sexual sin of his young years. While going about his task of redemption he attacks the institutions of which he and Katyusha have fallen foul with a venomous rage that will strike some readers as excessive, since it brooks no compromise between a perceived world of evil and the possibility of gradual development into a world of greater justice and harmony. Some would say that, whereas Nekhlyudov and Leo Tolstoy have failed in their enterprise of reforming humanity and its society along the simplistic lines of a Swiss–French writer of dubious reliability, the world itself has moved on, brought material prosperity to billions of citizens and actually shown them to be far more charitable (once their basic needs are taken care of) than Rousseau or Tolstoy ever imagined to be possible.

So, in a sense, the passage of time seems to have proved these earnest reformers to have made a fundamental mistake and also got the details wrong. However, to be mistaken in strategy does not mean that the tactical aims were necessarily false and unachievable.

Some of the causes taken up by the hero of *Resurrection* are still worth fighting for. Many of the injustices outlined in this powerful novel are still with us. Wrongful arrests, torture and executions stain the modern world to a shocking degree, and even when miscarriages of justice are corrected it can take many years of bureaucratic delay and obfuscation to bring them about. Our dealings with crime, judgment and punishment are far from perfect, and the knowledge of this sad fact will remove any complacency, allowing us to sympathise with Nekhlyudov for much of the way. He is rampaging against things that still need to be put right. No reader should be put off by any suggestion (as in some critical studies of Tolstoy's writings) that this novel is debased by its passionate message of complaint. *Resurrection* is a dynamic creation, charged with enough narrative interest and unforgettable incidents, compelling characters and profound ideas to satisfy the demands of all readers. During the five generations that have passed since its publication, the appeal of this work and its challenging ideas on crime and punishment remain as fresh as ever.

A.D.P.Briggs

Visiting Research Fellow,
University of Bristol

Professor Emeritus,
University of Birmingham

SUGGESTIONS FOR FURTHER READING

Charlotte Alston, *Tolstoy and His Disciples: the History of a Radical International Movement*, London, I. B. Tauris, 2014.

John Bayley, *Tolstoy and the Novel*, London, Chatto & Windus, 1966.

Rosamund Bartlett, *Tolstoy*, London, Profile Books, 2010.

Anthony Briggs, *Leo Tolstoy*, Hesperus, Brief Lives, 2010.

T. G. S. Cain, *Tolstoy,* London and New York, Elek, 1977.

R. F. Christian, *Tolstoy: A Critical Introduction,* Cambridge University Press, 1969.

Edward Crankshaw, *The Making of a Novelist*, London, Weidenfeld & Nicolson, 1974.

Henry Gifford, *Tolstoy,* Oxford, Past Masters, 1982.

Malcolm Jones, *New Essays on Tolstoy*, Cambridge University Press, 1978.

Janko Lavrin, *Tolstoy: an Approach,* London, 1944.

Aylmer Maude, *The Life of Tolstoy*, 2 vols, London, 1908–10, reprinted, Westport, Connecticut, 1970.

Donna Tussing Orwin, *Tolstoy's Art and Thought*, Princeton, 1993.

Theodore Redpath, *Tolstoy,* London, 1960.

E. J. Simmons, *Leo Tolstoy,* Boston, 1946, reprinted New York, 1960.

Henri Troyat, *Tolstoy,* New York, W. H. Allen, 1967.

A. N. Wilson, *Tolstoy,* London 1988, Harmondsworth, 1989.

RESURRECTION

Part 1

Chapter 1

Maslova in prison

Though hundreds of thousands had done their very best to disfigure the small piece of land on which they were crowded together, by paving the ground with stones, scraping away every vestige of vegetation, cutting down the trees, turning away birds and beasts, and filling the air with the smoke of naphtha and coal, still spring was spring, even in the town.

The sun shone warm, the air was balmy; everywhere, where it did not get scraped away, the grass revived and sprang up between the paving-stones as well as on the narrow strips of lawn on the boulevards. The birches, the poplars, and the wild cherry unfolded their gummy and fragrant leaves, the limes were expanding their opening buds; crows, sparrows, and pigeons, filled with the joy of spring, were getting their nests ready; the flies were buzzing along the walls, warmed by the sunshine. All were glad, the plants, the birds, the insects, and the children. But men, grown-up men and women, did not leave off cheating and tormenting themselves and each other. It was not this spring morning men thought sacred and worthy of consideration, not the beauty of God's world, given for a joy to all creatures, this beauty which inclines the heart to peace, to harmony, and to love, but only their own devices for enslaving one another.

Thus, in the prison office of the government town, it was not the fact that men and animals had received the grace and gladness of spring that was considered sacred and important, but that a notice, numbered and with a superscription, had come the day before, ordering that on this 28th day of April, at 9 a.m., three prisoners at present detained in the prison, a man and two women (one of these women, as the chief criminal, to be conducted separately), had to appear at Court. So now, on the 28th of April, at 8 o'clock, a jailer and soon after him a woman warder with curly grey hair, dressed in a jacket with sleeves trimmed with gold, with a blue-edged belt round her waist, and having a look of suffering on her face, came into the corridor.

'You want Maslova?' she asked, coming up to the cell with the jailer who was on duty.

The jailer, rattling the iron padlock, opened the door of the cell, from which there came a whiff of air fouler even than that in the corridor, and called out, 'Maslova! to the Court', and closed the door again.

Even into the prison yard the breeze had brought the fresh vivifying air from the fields. But in the corridor the air was laden with the germs of typhoid, the smell of sewage, putrefaction, and tar; every newcomer felt sad and dejected in it. The woman warder felt this, though she was used to bad air. She had just come in from outside, and entering the corridor, she at once became sleepy.

From inside the cell came the sound of bustle and women's voices, and the patter of bare feet on the floor.

'Now, then, hurry up, Maslova, I say!' called out the jailer, and in a minute or two a small young woman with a very full bust came briskly out of the door and went up to the jailer. She had on a grey cloak over a white jacket and petticoat. On her feet she wore linen stockings and prison shoes, and round her head was tied a white kerchief, from under which a few locks of black hair were brushed over the forehead with evident intent. The face of the woman was of that whiteness peculiar to people who have lived long in confinement, and which puts one in mind of shoots of potatoes that spring up in a cellar. Her small broad hands and full neck, which showed from under the broad collar of her cloak, were of the same hue. Her black, sparkling eyes, one with a slight squint, appeared in striking contrast to the dull pallor of her face.

She carried herself very straight, expanding her full bosom.

With her head slightly thrown back, she stood in the corridor, looking straight into the eyes of the jailer, ready to comply with any order.

The jailer was about to lock the door when a wrinkled and severe-looking old woman put out her grey head and began speaking to Maslova. But the jailer closed the door, pushing the old woman's head with it. A woman's laughter was heard from the cell, and Maslova smiled, turning to the little grated opening in the cell door. The old woman pressed her face to the grating from the other side, and said, in a hoarse voice:

'Now mind, and when they begin questioning you, just repeat over the same thing, and stick to it; tell nothing that is not wanted.'

'Well, it could not be worse than it is now, anyhow; I only wish it was settled one way or another.'

'Of course, it will be settled one way or another,' said the jailer, with a superior's self-assured witticism. 'Now, then, get along! Take your places!'

The old woman's eyes vanished from the grating, and Maslova stepped out into the middle of the corridor. The warder in front, they descended the stone stairs, past the still fouler, noisy cells of the men's ward, where they were followed by eyes looking out of every one of the gratings in the doors, and entered the office, where two soldiers were waiting to escort her. A clerk who was sitting there gave one of the soldiers a paper reeking of tobacco, and pointing to the prisoner, remarked, 'Take her.'

The soldier, a peasant from Nijni Novgorod, with a red, pock-marked face, put the paper into the sleeve of his coat, winked to his companion, a broad-shouldered Chuvash, and then the prisoner and the soldiers went to the front entrance, out of the prison yard, and through the town up the middle of the roughly-paved street.

Isvostchiks,* tradespeople, cooks, workmen, and government clerks, stopped and looked curiously at the prisoner; some shook their heads and thought, 'This is what evil conduct, conduct unlike ours, leads to.' The children stopped and gazed at the robber with frightened looks; but the thought that the soldiers were preventing her from doing more harm quieted their fears. A peasant, who had sold his charcoal, and had had some tea in the town, came up, and, after crossing himself, gave her a copeck. The prisoner blushed and muttered something; she noticed that she was attracting everybody's attention, and that pleased her. The comparatively fresh air also gladdened her, but it was painful to step on the rough stones with the ill-made prison shoes on her

* Cabmen.

feet, which had become unused to walking. Passing by a corn-dealer's shop, in front of which a few pigeons were strutting about, unmolested by anyone, the prisoner almost touched a grey-blue bird with her foot; it fluttered up and flew close to her ear, fanning her with its wings. She smiled, then sighed deeply as she remembered her present position.

Chapter 2

Maslova's early life

The story of the prisoner Maslova's life was a very common one.

Maslova's mother was the unmarried daughter of a village woman, employed on a dairy farm, which belonged to two maiden ladies who were landowners. This unmarried woman had a baby every year, and, as often happens among the village people, each one of these undesired babies, after it had been carefully baptised, was neglected by its mother, whom it hindered at her work, and left to starve. Five children had died in this way. They had all been baptised and then not sufficiently fed, and just left to die. The sixth baby, whose father was a gipsy tramp, would have shared the same fate, had it not so happened that one of the maiden ladies came into the farmyard to scold the dairymaids for sending up cream that smelt of the cow. The young woman was lying in the cowshed with a fine, healthy, new-born baby. The old maiden lady scolded the maids again for allowing the woman (who had just been confined) to lie in the cowshed, and was about to go away, but seeing the baby her heart was touched, and she offered to stand godmother to the little girl, and pity for her little god-daughter induced her to give milk and a little money to the mother, so that she should feed the baby; and the little girl lived. The old ladies spoke of her as 'the saved one'. When the child was three years old, her mother fell ill and died, and the maiden ladies took the child from her old grandmother, to whom she was nothing but a burden.

The little black-eyed maiden grew to be extremely pretty, and so full of spirits that the ladies found her very entertaining.

The younger of the ladies, Sophia Ivanovna, who had stood godmother to the girl, had the kinder heart of the two sisters; Maria Ivanovna, the elder, was rather hard. Sophia Ivanovna dressed the little girl in nice clothes, and taught her to read and write, meaning to educate her like a lady. Maria Ivanovna thought the child should be brought up to work, and trained her to be a good servant. She was exacting; she punished, and, when in a bad temper, even struck the little girl. Growing up under these two different influences, the girl turned out half servant, half young lady. They called her Katusha, which sounds less refined than Katinka, but is not quite so common as Katka. She used to sew, tidy up the rooms, polish the metal cases of the icons and do other light work, and sometimes she sat and read to the ladies.

Though she had more than one offer, she would not marry. She felt that life as the wife of any of the working men who were courting her would be too hard; spoilt as she was by a life of ease.

She lived in this manner till she was sixteen, when the nephew of the old ladies, a rich young prince, and a university student, came to stay with his aunts, and Katusha, not daring to acknowledge it even to herself, fell in love with him.

Then two years later this same nephew stayed four days with his aunts before proceeding to join his regiment, and the night before he left he betrayed Katusha, and, after giving her a hundred-rouble note, went away. Five months later she knew for certain that she was to be a mother. After that everything seemed repugnant to her, her only thought being how to escape from the shame that awaited her. She began not only to serve the ladies in a half-hearted and negligent way, but once, without knowing how it happened, was very rude to them, and gave them notice, a thing she repented of later, and the ladies let her go, noticing something wrong and very dissatisfied with her. Then she got a housemaid's place in a police-officer's house, but stayed there only three months, for the police officer, a man of fifty, began to torment her, and once, when he was in a specially enterprising mood, she fired up, called him 'a fool and old devil', and gave him such a knock in the chest that he fell. She was turned out for her rudeness. It was useless to look for another situation, for the time of her confinement was drawing near, so she went to the house of a village midwife, who also sold wine.

The confinement was easy; but the midwife, who had a case
of fever in the village, infected Katusha, and her baby boy had
to be sent to the foundlings' hospital, where, according to the
words of the old woman who took him there, he at once died.
When Katusha went to the midwife she had a hundred and twenty-
seven roubles in all, twenty-seven which she had earned and a
hundred given her by her betrayer. When she left she had but six
roubles; she did not know how to keep money, but spent it on
herself, and gave to all who asked. The midwife took forty roubles
for two months' board and attendance, twenty-five went to get the
baby into the foundlings' hospital, and forty the midwife borrowed
to buy a cow with. Twenty roubles went just for clothes and
dainties. Having nothing left to live on, Katusha had to look out for
a place again, and found one in the house of a forester. The forester
was a married man, but he, too, began to annoy her from the first
day. He disgusted her, and she tried to avoid him. But he, more
experienced and cunning, besides being her master, who could
send her wherever he liked, managed to accomplish his object. His
wife found it out, and, catching Katusha and her husband in a room
all by themselves, began beating her. Katusha defended herself, and
they had a fight, and Katusha got turned out of the house without
being paid her wages.

Then Katusha went to live with her aunt in town. The aunt's
husband, a bookbinder, had once been comfortably off, but had
lost all his customers, and had taken to drink, and spent all he
could lay hands on at the public-house. The aunt kept a little
laundry, and managed to support herself, her children, and her
wretched husband. She offered Katusha the place of an assistant
laundress; but seeing what a life of misery and hardship her aunt's
assistants led, Katusha hesitated, and applied to a registry office
for a place. One was found for her with a lady who lived with her
two sons, pupils at a public day school. A week after Katusha
had entered the house the elder, a big fellow with moustaches,
threw up his studies and made love to her, continually following
her about. His mother laid all the blame on Katusha, and gave
her notice.

It so happened that, after many fruitless attempts to find a
situation, Katusha again went to the registry office, and there met
a woman with bracelets on her bare, plump arms and rings on

most of her fingers. Hearing that Katusha was badly in want of a place, the woman gave her her address, and invited her to come to her house. Katusha went. The woman received her very kindly, set cake and sweet wine before her, then wrote a note and gave it to a servant to take to somebody. In the evening a tall man, with long, grey hair and a white beard, entered the room, and sat down at once near Katusha, smiling and gazing at her with glistening eyes. He began joking with her. The hostess called him away into the next room, and Katusha heard her say, 'A fresh one from the country'. Then the hostess called Katusha aside and told her that the man was an author, and that he had a great deal of money, and that if he liked her he would not grudge her anything. He did like her, and gave her twenty-five roubles, promising to see her often. The twenty-five roubles soon went; some she paid to her aunt for board and lodging; the rest was spent on a hat, ribbons, and such like. A few days later the author sent for her, and she went. He gave her another twenty-five roubles, and offered her a separate lodging.

Next door to the lodging rented for her by the author there lived a jolly young shopman, with whom Katusha soon fell in love. She told the author, and moved to a little lodging of her own. The shopman, who promised to marry her, went to Nijni on business without mentioning it to her, having evidently thrown her up, and Katusha remained alone. She meant to continue living in the lodging by herself, but was informed by the police that in this case she would have to get a licence. She returned to her aunt. Seeing her fine dress, her hat, and mantle, her aunt no longer offered her laundry work. As she understood things, her niece had risen above that sort of thing. The question as to whether she was to become a laundress or not did not occur to Katusha, either. She looked with pity at the thin, hard-worked laundresses, some already in consumption, who stood washing or ironing with their thin arms in the fearfully hot front room, which was always full of soapy steam and draughts from the windows, and thought with horror that she might have shared the same fate.

Katusha had begun to smoke some time before, and since the young shopman had thrown her up she was getting more and more into the habit of drinking. It was not so much the flavour of wine that tempted her as the fact that it gave her a chance of forgetting the misery she suffered, making her feel more unrestrained and more confident of her own worth, which she was not when quite sober; without wine she felt sad and ashamed. Just at this time a woman came along who offered to place her in one of the largest establishments in the city, explaining all the advantages and benefits of the situation. Katusha had the choice before her of either going into service or accepting this offer – and she chose the latter. Besides, it seemed to her as though, in this way, she could revenge herself on her betrayer and the shopman and all those who had injured her. One of the things that tempted her, and was the cause of her decision, was the woman telling her she might order her own dresses – velvet, silk, satin, low-necked ball dresses, anything she liked. A mental picture of herself in a bright yellow silk trimmed with black velvet with low neck and short sleeves conquered her, and she gave up her passport. On the same evening the procuress took an *isvostchik* and drove her to the notorious house kept by Carolina Albertovna Kitaeva.

From that day a life of chronic sin against human and divine laws commenced for Katusha Maslova, a life which is led by hundreds of thousands of women, and which is not merely tolerated but sanctioned by the government, anxious for the welfare of its subjects; a life which for nine women out of ten ends in painful disease, premature decrepitude, and death.

Katusha Maslova lived this life for seven years. During these years she twice changed houses, and had once been to the hospital. In the seventh year of this life, when she was twenty-six years old, happened that for which she was put in prison and for which she was now being taken to be tried, after more than three months of confinement with thieves and murderers in the stifling air of a prison.

Chapter 3

Nekhlyudov

When Maslova, wearied out by the long walk, reached the building, accompanied by two soldiers, Prince Dmitri Ivanovitch Nekhlyudov, who had seduced her, was still lying on his high bedstead, with a feather bed on the top of the spring mattress, in a fine, clean, well-ironed linen nightshirt, smoking a cigarette, and considering what he had to do today, and what had happened yesterday.

Recalling the evening he had spent with the Korchagins, a wealthy and aristocratic family, whose daughter everyone expected he would marry, he sighed, and, throwing away the end of his cigarette, was going to take another out of the silver case; but, changing his mind, he resolutely raised his solid frame, and, putting down his smooth, white legs, stepped into his slippers, threw his silk dressing gown over his broad shoulders, and passed into his dressing-room, walking heavily and quickly. There he carefully cleaned his teeth, many of which were filled, with tooth powder, and rinsed his mouth with scented elixir. After that he washed his hands with perfumed soap, cleaned his long nails with particular care, then, from a tap fixed to his marble washstand, he let a spray of cold water run over his face and stout neck. Having finished this part of the business, he went into a third room, where a shower bath stood ready for him. Having refreshed his full, white, muscular body, and dried it with a rough bath sheet, he put on his fine undergarments and his boots, and sat down before the glass to brush his black beard and his curly hair, that had begun to get thin above the forehead. Everything he used, everything belonging to his toilet, his linen, his clothes, boots, necktie, pin, studs, was of the best quality, very quiet, simple, durable and costly.

Nekhlyudov dressed leisurely, and went into the dining-room. A table, which looked very imposing with its four legs carved in the shape of lions' paws, and a huge sideboard to match, stood in the oblong room, the floor of which had been polished by three men the day before. On the table, which was covered with a fine, starched cloth, stood a silver coffee-pot full of aromatic coffee, a sugar basin, a jug of fresh cream, and a bread basket filled with fresh rolls, rusks, and biscuits; and beside the plate lay the last number of the *Revue des Deux Mondes*, a newspaper, and several letters.

Nekhlyudov was just going to open his letters, when a stout, middle-aged woman in mourning, a lace cap covering the widening parting of her hair, glided into the room. This was Agraphena Petrovna, formerly lady's maid to Nekhlyudov's mother. Her mistress had died quite recently in this very house, and she remained with the son as his housekeeper. Agraphena Petrovna had spent nearly ten years, at different times, abroad with Nekhlyudov's mother, and had the appearance and manners of a lady. She had lived with the Nekhlyudovs from the time she was a child, and had known Dmitri Ivanovitch at the time when he was still little Mitinka.

'Good-morning, Dmitri Ivanovitch.'

'Good-morning, Agraphena Petrovna. What is it you want?' Nekhlyudov asked.

'A letter from the princess; either from the mother or the daughter. The maid brought it some time ago, and is waiting in my room,' answered Agraphena Petrovna, handing him the letter with a significant smile.

'All right! Directly!' said Nekhlyudov, taking the letter and frowning as he noticed Agraphena Petrovna's smile.

That smile meant that the letter was from the younger Princess Korchagin, whom Agraphena Petrovna expected him to marry. This supposition of hers annoyed Nekhlyudov.

'Then I'll tell her to wait?' and Agraphena Petrovna took a crumb brush which was not in its place, put it away, and sailed out of the room.

Nekhlyudov opened the perfumed note, and began reading it.

The note was written on a sheet of thick grey paper, with rough edges; the writing looked English. It said:

Having assumed the task of acting as your memory, I take the liberty of reminding you that on this the 28th day of April you have to appear at the Law Courts, as juryman, and, in consequence, can on no account accompany us and Kolosov to the picture gallery, as, with your habitual flightiness, you promised yesterday; *à moins que vous ne soyez disposé à payer la cour d'assise les 300 roubles d'amende que vous vous refusez pour votre cheval,* for not appearing in time. I remembered it last night after you were gone, so do not forget.

Princess M. Korchagin

On the other side was a postscript.

Maman vous fait dire que votre convert vous attendra jusqu'à la nuit. Venez absolument à quelle heure que celà soit.

M. K.

Nekhlyudov made a grimace. This note was a continuation of that skilful manoeuvring which the Princess Korchagin had already practised for two months in order to bind him closer and closer with invisible threads. And yet, beside the usual hesitation of men past their youth to marry unless they are very much in love, Nekhlyudov had very good reasons why, even if he did make up his mind to it, he could not propose at once. It was not that ten years previously he had betrayed and forsaken Maslova; he had quite forgotten that, and he would not have considered it a reason for not marrying. No! the reason was that he had a liaison with a married woman, and, though he considered it broken off, she did not.

Nekhlyudov was rather shy with women, and his very shyness awakened in this married woman, the unprincipled wife of the *Maréchal de Noblesse* of a district where Nekhlyudov was present at an election, the desire of vanquishing him. This woman drew him into an intimacy which entangled him more and more, while it daily became more distasteful to him. Having succumbed to the temptation, Nekhlyudov felt guilty, and had not the courage to break the tie without her consent. And this was the reason he did not feel at liberty to propose to Korchagin even if he had wished to do so. Among the letters on the table was one from this woman's husband. Seeing his writing and the postmark, Nekhlyudov flushed, and felt his energies awakening, as they always did when he was facing any kind of danger.

But his excitement passed at once. The *Maréchal de Noblesse*, of the district in which his largest estate lay, wrote only to let

Nekhlyudov know that there was to be a special meeting towards the end of May, and that Nekhlyudov was to be sure and come to '*donner un coup d'épaule*,' at the important debates concerning the schools and the roads, as a strong opposition by the reactionary party was expected.

The *Maréchal* was a liberal, and was quite engrossed in this fight, not even noticing the misfortune that had befallen him.

Nekhlyudov remembered the dreadful moments he had lived through; once when he thought that the husband had found him out and was going to challenge him, and he was making up his mind to fire into the air; also the terrible scene he had with her when she ran out into the park, and in her excitement tried to drown herself in the pond.

'Well, I cannot go now, and can do nothing until I get a reply from her,' thought Nekhlyudov. A week ago he had written her a decisive letter, in which he acknowledged his guilt, and his readiness to atone for it; but at the same time he pronounced their relations to be at an end, for her own good, as he expressed it. To this letter he had as yet received no answer. This might prove a good sign, for if she did not agree to break off their relations, she would have written at once, or even come herself, as she had done before. Nekhlyudov had heard that there was some officer who was paying her marked attention, and this tormented him by awakening jealousy, and at the same time encouraged him with the hope of escape from the deception that was oppressing him.

The other letter was from his steward. The steward wrote to tell him that a visit to his estates was necessary in order to enter into possession, and also to decide about the further management of his lands; whether it was to continue in the same way as when his mother was alive, or whether, as he had represented to the late lamented princess, and now advised the young prince, they had not better increase their stock and farm all the land now rented by the peasants themselves. The steward wrote that this would be a far more profitable way of managing the property; at the same time, he apologised for not having forwarded the three thousand roubles income due on the 1st. This money would be sent on by the next mail. The reason for the delay was that he could not get the money out of the peasants, who had grown so untrustworthy that he had to appeal to the authorities. This letter was partly disagreeable, and partly pleasant. It was pleasant to feel that he had power over so large a property, and yet disagreeable, because Nekhlyudov had been an enthusiastic admirer of Henry George and Herbert Spencer. Being himself heir to a large property, he was especially struck by the position taken up by Spencer in *Social Statics*, that justice forbids private landholding, and with the straightforward resoluteness of his age, had not merely spoken to prove that land could not be looked upon as private property, and written essays on that subject at the university, but had acted up to his convictions, and, considering it wrong to hold landed property, had given the small piece of land he had inherited from his father to the peasants. Inheriting his mother's large estates, and thus becoming a landed proprietor, he had to choose one of two things: either to give up his property, as he had given up his father's land ten years before, or silently to confess that all his former ideas were mistaken and false.

He could not choose the former because he had no means but the landed estates (he did not care to serve); moreover, he had formed luxurious habits which he could not easily give up. Besides, he had no longer the same inducements; his strong convictions, the resoluteness of youth, and the ambitious desire to do something unusual were gone. As to the second course, that of denying those clear and unanswerable proofs of the injustice of landholding, which he had drawn from Spencer's *Social Statics*, and the brilliant corroboration of which he had at a later period found in the works of Henry George, such a course was impossible to him.

Chapter 4

Missy

When Nekhlyudov had finished his coffee, he went to his study to look at the summons, and find out what time he was to appear at the court, before writing his answer to the princess. Passing through his studio, where a few studies hung on the walls and, facing the easel, stood an unfinished picture, a feeling of inability to advance in art, a sense of his incapacity, came over him. He had often had this feeling, of late, and explained it by his too finely developed aesthetic taste; still, the feeling was a very unpleasant one. Seven years before this he had given up military service, feeling sure that he had a talent for art, and had looked down with some disdain at all other activity from the height of his artistic standpoint. And now it turned out that he had no right to do so, and therefore everything that reminded him of all this was unpleasant. He looked at the luxurious fittings of the studio with a heavy heart, and it was in no cheerful mood that he entered his study, a large, lofty room fitted up with a view to comfort, convenience, and elegant appearance. He found the summons at once in a pigeon hole, labelled 'immediate', of his large writing table. He had to appear at the court at 11 o'clock.

Nekhlyudov sat down to write a note in reply to the princess, thanking her for the invitation, and promising to try and come to dinner. Having written one note, he tore it up, as it seemed too intimate. He wrote another, but it was too cold; he feared it might give offence, so he tore it up, too. He pressed the button of an electric bell, and his servant, an elderly, morose-looking man, with whiskers and shaved chin and lip, wearing a grey cotton apron, entered at the door.

'Send to fetch an *isvostchik*, please.'

'Yes, sir.'

'And tell the person who is waiting that I send thanks for the invitation, and shall try to come.'

'Yes, sir.'

'It is not very polite, but I can't write; no matter, I shall see her today,' thought Nekhlyudov, and went to get his overcoat.

When he came out of the house, an *isvostchik* he knew, with india-rubber tires to his trap, was at the door waiting for him. 'You had hardly gone away from Prince Korchagin's yesterday,' he said, turning half round, 'when I drove up, and the Swiss at the door says, "just gone".' The *isvostchik* knew that Nekhlyudov visited at the Korchagins, and called there on the chance of being engaged by him.

'Even the *isvostchiks* know of my relations with the Korchagins,' thought Nekhlyudov, and again the question whether he should not marry Princess Korchagin presented itself to him, and he could not decide it either way, any more than most of the questions that arose in his mind at this time.

It was in favour of marriage in general, that besides the comforts of hearth and home, it made a moral life possible, and chiefly that a family would, so Nekhlyudov thought, give an aim to his now empty life.

Against marriage in general was the fear, common to bachelors past their first youth, of losing freedom, and an unconscious awe before this mysterious creature, a woman.

In this particular case, in favour of marrying Missy (her name was Mary, but, as is usual among a certain set, a nickname had been given her) was that she came of good family, and differed in everything, manner of speaking, walking, laughing, from the common people, not by anything exceptional, but by her 'good breeding' – he could find no other term for this quality, though he prized it very highly – and, besides, she thought more of him than of anybody else, therefore evidently understood him. This understanding of him, i.e., the recognition of his superior merits, was to Nekhlyudov a proof of her good sense and correct judgment. Against marrying Missy in particular, was, that in all likelihood, a girl with even higher qualities could be found, that she was already twenty-seven, and that he was hardly her first love. This last idea was painful to him. His pride would not reconcile itself with the thought that she had loved someone else, even in the past. Of course, she could not have known that she should meet him, but the thought that she was capable of loving another offended him. So that he had as many reasons for marrying as against it; at any rate, they weighed equally with Nekhlyudov, who laughed at himself, and called himself the ass of the fable, remaining like that animal undecided which haycock to turn to.

'At any rate, before I get an answer from Mary Vasilievna (the *Maréchal's* wife), and finish completely with her, I can do nothing,' he said to himself. And the conviction that he might, and was even obliged to, delay his decision, was comforting. 'Well, I shall consider all that later on,' he said to himself, as the trap drove silently along the asphalt pavement up to the doors of the Court.

'Now I must fulfil my public duties conscientiously, as I am in the habit of always doing, and as I consider it right to do. Besides, they are often interesting.' And he entered the hall of the Law Courts, past the doorkeeper.

Chapter 5

The jurymen

The corridors of the Court were already full of activity. The attendants hurried, out of breath, dragging their feet along the ground without lifting them, backwards and forwards, with all sorts of messages and papers. Ushers, advocates, and law officers passed hither and thither. Plaintiffs, and those of the accused who were not guarded, wandered sadly along the walls or sat waiting.

'Where is the Law Court?' Nekhlyudov asked of an attendant.

'Which? There is the Civil Court and the Criminal Court.'

'I am on the jury.'

'The Criminal Court you should have said. Here to the right, then to the left – the second door.'

Nekhlyudov followed the direction.

Meanwhile some of the Criminal Court jurymen who were late had hurriedly passed into a separate room. At the door mentioned two men stood waiting.

One, a tall, fat merchant, a kind-hearted fellow, had evidently partaken of some refreshments and a glass of something, and was in most pleasant spirits. The other was a shopman of Jewish extraction. They were talking about the price of wool when Nekhlyudov came up and asked them if this was the jurymen's room.

'Yes, my dear sir, this is it. One of us? On the jury, are you?' asked the merchant, with a merry wink.

'Ah, well, we shall have a go at the work together,' he continued, after Nekhlyudov had answered in the affirmative. 'My name is Baklashev, merchant of the Second Guild,' he said, putting out his broad, soft, flexible hand.

'With whom have I the honour?'

Nekhlyudov gave his name and passed into the jurymen's room.

Inside the room were about ten persons of all sorts. They had come but a short while ago, and some were sitting, others walking up and down, looking at each other, and making each other's acquaintance. There was a retired colonel in uniform; some were in frock coats, others in morning coats, and only one wore a peasant's dress.

Their faces all had a certain look of satisfaction at the prospect of fulfilling a public duty, although many of them had had to leave their businesses, and most were complaining of it.

The jurymen talked among themselves about the weather, the early spring, and the business before them, some having been introduced, others just guessing who was who. Those who were not acquainted with Nekhlyudov made haste to get introduced, evidently looking upon this as an honour, and he taking it as his due, as he always did when among strangers. Had he been asked why he considered himself above the majority of people, he could not have given an answer; the life he had been living of late was not particularly meritorious. The fact of his speaking English, French, and German with a good accent, and of his wearing the best linen, clothes, ties, and studs, bought from the most expensive dealers in these goods, he quite knew would not serve as a reason for claiming superiority. At the same time he did claim superiority, and accepted the respect paid him as his due, and was hurt if he did not get it. In the jurymen's room his feelings were hurt by disrespectful treatment. Among the jury there happened to be a man whom he knew, a former teacher of his sister's children, Peter Gerasimovitch. Nekhlyudov never knew his surname, and even bragged a bit about this. This man was now a master at a public school. Nekhlyudov could not stand his familiarity, his self-satisfied laughter, his vulgarity, in short.

'Ah ha! You're also trapped.' These were the words, accompanied with boisterous laughter, with which Peter Gerasimovitch greeted Nekhlyudov. 'Have you not managed to get out of it?'

'I never meant to get out of it,' replied Nekhlyudov, gloomily, and in a tone of severity.

'Well, I call this being public-spirited. But just wait until you get hungry or sleepy; you'll sing to another tune then.'

'This son of a priest will be saying "thou" to me next,' * thought Nekhlyudov, and walked away, with such a look of sadness on his

* In Russian, as in many other languages, 'thou' is used generally among people very familiar with each other, or by superiors to inferiors.

face, as might have been natural if he had just heard of the death of all his relations. He came up to a group that had formed itself round a clean-shaven, tall, dignified man, who was recounting something with great animation. This man was talking about the trial going on in the Civil Court as of a case well known to himself, mentioning the judges and a celebrated advocate by name. He was saying that it seemed wonderful how the celebrated advocate had managed to give such a clever turn to the affair that an old lady, though she had the right on her side, would have to pay a large sum to her opponent. 'The advocate is a genius,' he said.

The listeners heard it all with respectful attention, and several of them tried to put in a word, but the man interrupted them, as if he alone knew all about it.

Though Nekhlyudov had arrived late, he had to wait a long time. One of the members of the Court had not yet come, and everybody was kept waiting.

Chapter 6

The judges

The president, who had to take the chair, had arrived early. The president was a tall, stout man, with long grey whiskers. Though married, he led a very loose life, and his wife did the same, so they did not stand in each other's way. This morning he had received a note from a Swiss girl, who had formerly been a governess in his house, and who was now on her way from South Russia to St Petersburg. She wrote that she would wait for him between five and six p.m. in the Hotel Italia. This made him wish to begin and get through the sitting as soon as possible, so as to have time to call before six p.m. on the little red-haired Clara Vasilievna, with whom he had begun a romance in the country last summer. He went into a private room, latched the door, took a pair of dumb-bells out of a cupboard, moved his arms twenty times upwards, downwards, forwards, and sideways, then holding the dumb-bells above his head, lightly bent his knees three times.

'Nothing keeps one going like a cold bath and exercise,' he said, feeling the biceps of his right arm with his left hand, on the third finger of which he wore a gold ring. He had still to do the *moulinée* movement (for he always went through those two exercises before a long sitting), when there was a pull at the door. The president quickly put away the dumb-bells and opened the door, saying, 'I beg your pardon.'

One of the members, a high-shouldered, discontented-looking man, with gold spectacles, came into the room. 'Matthew Nikitich has again not come,' he said, in a dissatisfied tone.

'Not yet?' said the president, putting on his uniform. 'He is always late.'

'It is extraordinary. He ought to be ashamed of himself,' said the member, angrily, and taking out a cigarette.

This member, a very precise man, had had an unpleasant encounter with his wife in the morning, because she had spent her allowance before the end of the month, and had asked him to give her some money in advance, but he would not give way to her, and they had a quarrel. The wife told him that if he were going to behave so, he need not expect any dinner; there would be no dinner for him at home. At this point he left, fearing that she might carry out her threat, for anything might be expected from her. 'This comes of living a good, moral life,' he thought, looking at the beaming, healthy, cheerful, and kindly president, who, with elbows far apart, was smoothing his thick grey whiskers with his fine white hands over the embroidered collar of his uniform. 'He is always contented and merry while I am suffering.'

The secretary came in and brought some document.

'Thanks, very much,' said the president, lighting a cigarette. 'Which case shall we take first, then?'

'The poisoning case, I should say,' answered the secretary, with indifference.

'All right; the poisoning case let it be,' said the president, thinking that he could get this case over by four o'clock, and then go away. 'And Matthew Nikitich; has he come?'

'Not yet.'

'And Breve?'

'He is here,' replied the secretary.

'Then if you see him, please tell him that we begin with the poisoning case.' Breve was the public prosecutor, who was to read the indictment in this case.

In the corridor the secretary met Breve, who, with uplifted shoulders, a portfolio under one arm, the other swinging with the palm turned to the front, was hurrying along the corridor, clattering with his heels.

'Michael Petrovitch wants to know if you are ready?' the secretary asked.

'Of course; I am always ready,' said the public prosecutor. 'What are we taking first?'

'The poisoning case.'

'That's quite right,' said the public prosecutor, but did not think it at all right. He had spent the night in a hotel playing cards with a friend who was giving a farewell party. Up to five in the morning they played and drank, so he had no time to look at this poisoning case, and meant to run it through now. The secretary, happening to know this, advised the president to begin with the poisoning case. The secretary was a Liberal, even a Radical, in opinion.

Breve was a Conservative; the secretary disliked him, and envied him his position.

'Well, and how about the Skoptzy?' * asked the secretary.

'I have already said that I cannot do it without witnesses, and so I shall say to the Court.'

'Dear me, what does it matter?'

'I cannot do it,' said Breve; and, waving his arm, he ran into his private room.

He was putting off the case of the Skoptzy on account of the absence of a very unimportant witness, his real reason being that if they were tried by an educated jury they might possibly be acquitted.

By an agreement with the president this case was to be tried in the coming session at a provincial town, where there would be more peasants, and, therefore, more chances of conviction.

The movement in the corridor increased. The people crowded most at the doors of the Civil Court, in which the case that the dignified man talked about was being heard.

* A religious sect.

An interval in the proceedings occurred, and the old woman came out of the court, whose property that genius of an advocate had found means of getting for his client, a person versed in law who had no right to it whatever. The judges knew all about the case, and the advocate and his client knew it better still, but the move they had invented was such that it was impossible not to take the old woman's property and not to hand it over to the person versed in law.

The old woman was stout, well dressed, and had enormous flowers on her bonnet; she stopped as she came out of the door, and spreading out her short fat arms and turning to her advocate, she kept repeating. 'What does it all mean? Just fancy!'

The advocate was looking at the flowers in her bonnet, and evidently not listening to her, but considering some question or other.

Next to the old woman, out of the door of the Civil Court, his broad, starched shirt front glistening from under his low-cut waistcoat, with a self-satisfied look on his face, came the celebrated advocate who had managed to arrange matters so that the old woman lost all she had, and the person versed in the law received more than a hundred thousand roubles. The advocate passed close to the old woman, and, feeling all eyes directed towards him, his whole bearing seemed to say: 'No expressions of deference are required.'

Chapter 7
The officials of the court

At last Matthew Nikitich also arrived, and the usher, a thin man with a long neck and a kind of sideways walk, his nether lip protruding to one side, which made him resemble a turkey, came into the jurymen's room.

This usher was an honest man, and had a university education, but could not keep a place for any length of time, as he was subject to fits of drunkenness. Three months before a certain countess, who patronised his wife, had found him this place, and he was very pleased to have kept it so long.

'Well, sirs, is everybody here?' he asked, putting his pince-nez on his nose, and looking round.

'Everybody, I think,' said the jolly merchant.

'All right; we'll soon see.' And, taking a list from his pocket, he began calling out the names, looking at the men, sometimes through and sometimes over his pince-nez.

'Councillor of State,* J. M. Nikivorov!'

'I am he,' said the dignified-looking man, well versed in the habits of the law court.

'Ivan Semionovitch Ivanov, retired colonel!'

'Here!' replied a thin man, in the uniform of a retired officer.

'Merchant of the Second Guild, Peter Baklashev!'

'Here we are, ready!' said the good-humoured merchant, with a broad smile.

'Lieutenant of the Guards, Prince Dmitri Nekhlyudov!'

'I am he,' answered Nekhlyudov.

The usher bowed to him, looking over his pince-nez, politely and pleasantly, as if wishing to distinguish him from the others.

'Captain Youri Dmitrievitch-Dantchenko, merchant; Grigori Euphimitch Kouleshov,' etc. All but two were present.

'Now please to come to the court, gentlemen,' said the usher, pointing to the door, with an amiable wave of his hand.

All moved towards the door, pausing to let each other pass. Then they went through the corridor into the court.

The court was a large, long room. At one end there was a raised platform, with three steps leading up to it, on which stood a table covered with a green cloth trimmed with a fringe of a darker shade. At the table were placed three armchairs, with high-carved oak backs; on the wall behind them hung a full-length, brightly-coloured portrait of the Emperor in uniform and ribbon, with one foot in advance, and holding a sword. In the right corner hung a case, with an image of Christ crowned with thorns, and beneath it stood a lectern, and on the same side the prosecuting attorney's desk. On the left, opposite the desk, was the secretary's table, and in front of it, nearer the public, an oak grating, with the prisoners' bench, as yet unoccupied, behind it.

* Grades such as this are common in Russia, and mean very little.

Besides all this, there were on the right side of the platform high-backed ashwood chairs for the jury, and on the floor below tables for the advocates. All this was in the front part of the court, divided from the back by a grating.

The back was all taken up by seats in tiers. Sitting on the front seats were four women, either servant or factory girls, and two working men, evidently overawed by the grandeur of the room, and not venturing to speak above a whisper.

Soon after the jury had come in the usher entered, with his sideward gait, and stepping to the front, called out in a loud voice, as if he meant to frighten those present, 'The Court is coming!' Everyone got up as the members stepped on to the platform. Among them the president, with his muscles and fine whiskers. Next came the gloomy member of the Court, who was now more gloomy than ever, having met his brother-in-law, who informed him that he had just called in to see his sister (the member's wife), and that she had told him that there would be no dinner there.

'So that, evidently, we shall have to call in at a cook shop,' the brother-in-law added, laughing.

'It is not at all funny,' said the gloomy member, and became gloomier still.

Then at last came the third member of the Court, the same Matthew Nikitich, who was always late. He was a bearded man, with large, round, kindly eyes. He was suffering from a catarrh of the stomach, and, according to his doctor's advice, he had begun trying a new treatment, and this had kept him at home longer than usual. Now, as he was ascending the platform, he had a pensive air. He was in the habit of making guesses in answer to all sorts of self-put questions by different curious means. Just now he had asked whether the new treatment would be beneficial, and had decided that it would cure his catarrh if the number of steps from the door to his chair would divide by three. He made twenty-six steps, but managed to get in a twenty-seventh just by his chair.

The figures of the president and the members in their uniforms, with gold-embroidered collars, looked very imposing. They seemed to feel this themselves, and, as if overpowered by their own grandeur, hurriedly sat down on the high-backed chairs behind the table with the green cloth, on which were a triangular article with an eagle at the top, two glass vases – something like those in which sweetmeats are kept in refreshment rooms – an inkstand, pens, clean paper, and good, newly-cut pencils of different kinds.

The public prosecutor came in with the judges. With his portfolio under one arm, and swinging the other, he hurriedly walked to his seat near the window, and was instantly absorbed in reading and looking through the papers, not wasting a single moment, in hope of being ready when the business commenced. He had been public prosecutor but a short time, and had only prosecuted four times before this. He was very ambitious, and had firmly made up his mind to get on, and therefore thought it necessary to get a conviction whenever he prosecuted. He knew the chief facts of the poisoning case, and had already formed a plan of action. He only wanted to copy out a few points which he required.

The secretary sat on the opposite side of the platform, and, having got ready all the papers he might want, was looking through an article, prohibited by the censor, which he had procured and read the day before. He was anxious to have a talk about this article with the bearded member, who shared his views, but wanted to look through it once more before doing so.

Chapter 8

Swearing in the jury

The president, having looked through some papers and put a few questions to the usher and the secretary, gave the order for the prisoners to be brought in.

The door behind the grating was instantly opened, and two gendarmes, with caps on their heads, and holding naked swords in their hands, came in, followed by the prisoners, a red-haired, freckled man, and two women. The man wore a prison cloak, which was too long and too wide for him. He stuck out his thumbs, and held his arms close to his sides, thus keeping the sleeves, which were also too long, from slipping over his hands.

Without looking at the judges he gazed steadfastly at the form, and passing to the other side of it, he sat down carefully at the very edge, leaving plenty of room for the others. He fixed his eyes on the president, and began moving the muscles of his cheeks, as if whispering something. The woman who came next was also dressed in a prison cloak, and had a prison kerchief round her head. She had a sallow complexion, no eyebrows or lashes, and very red eyes. This woman appeared perfectly calm. Having caught her cloak against something, she detached it carefully, without any haste, and sat down.

The third prisoner was Maslova.

As soon as she appeared, the eyes of all the men in the court turned her way, and remained fixed on her white face, her sparklingly-brilliant black eyes and the swelling bosom under the prison cloak. Even the gendarme whom she passed on her way to her seat looked at her fixedly till she sat down, and then, as if feeling guilty, hurriedly turned away, shook himself, and began staring at the window in front of him.

The president paused until the prisoners had taken their seats, and when Maslova was seated, turned to the secretary.

Then the usual procedure commenced: the counting of the jury, remarks about those who had not come, the fixing of the fines to be exacted from them, the decisions concerning those who claimed exemption, the appointing of reserve jurymen.

Having folded up some bits of paper and put them in one of the glass vases, the president turned up the gold-embroidered cuffs of his uniform a little way, and began drawing the lots, one by one, and opening them. Nekhlyudov was among the jurymen thus drawn. Then, having let down his sleeves, the president requested the priest to swear in the jury.

The old priest, with his puffy, red face, his brown gown, and his gold cross and little order, laboriously moving his stiff legs, came up to the lectern beneath the icon.

The jurymen got up, and crowded towards the lectern.

'Come up, please,' said the priest, pulling at the cross on his breast with his plump hand, and waiting till all the jury had drawn near. When they had all come up the steps of the platform, the priest passed his bald, grey head sideways through the greasy opening of the stole, and, having rearranged his thin hair, he again turned to the jury. 'Now, raise your right arms in this way, and put your fingers together, thus,' he said, with his tremulous old voice, lifting his fat, dimpled hand, and putting the thumb and two first fingers together, as if taking a pinch of something. 'Now, repeat after me, I promise and swear, by the Almighty God, by His holy gospels, and by the life-giving cross of our Lord, that in this work which,' he said, pausing between each sentence – 'don't let your arm down; hold it like this,' he remarked to a young man who had lowered his arm – 'that in this work which . . .'

The dignified man with the whiskers, the colonel, the merchant, and several more held their arms and fingers as the priest required of them, very high, very exactly, as if they liked doing it; others did it unwillingly and carelessly. Some repeated the words too loudly, and with a defiant tone, as if they meant to say, 'In spite of all, I will and shall speak.' Others whispered very low, and not fast enough, and then, as if frightened, hurried to catch up the priest. Some kept their fingers tightly together, as if fearing to drop the pinch of invisible something they held; others kept separating and folding theirs. Everyone save the old priest felt awkward, but he was sure he was fulfilling a very useful and important duty.

After the swearing in, the president requested the jury to choose a foreman, and the jury, thronging to the door, passed out into the debating-room, where almost all of them at once began to smoke cigarettes. Someone proposed the dignified man as foreman, and he was unanimously accepted. Then the jurymen put out their cigarettes and threw them away and returned to the court. The dignified man informed the president that he was chosen foreman, and all sat down again on the high-backed chairs.

Everything went smoothly, quickly, and not without a certain solemnity. And this exactitude, order, and solemnity evidently pleased those who took part in it: it strengthened the impression that they were fulfilling a serious and valuable public duty. Nekhlyudov, too, felt this.

As soon as the jurymen were seated, the president made a speech on their rights, obligations, and responsibilities. While speaking he kept changing his position; now leaning on his right, now on his left hand, now against the back, then on the arms of his chair, now putting the papers straight, now handling his pencil and paper-knife.

According to his words, they had the right of interrogating the prisoners through the president, to use paper and pencils, and to examine the articles put in as evidence. Their duty was to judge not falsely, but justly. Their responsibility meant that if the secrecy of their discussion were violated, or communications were established with outsiders, they would be liable to punishment. Everyone listened with an expression of respectful attention. The merchant, diffusing a smell of brandy around him, and restraining loud hiccups, approvingly nodded his head at every sentence.

Chapter 9

The trial – the prisoners questioned

When he had finished his speech, the president turned to the male prisoner.

'Simeon Kartinkin, rise.'

Simeon jumped up, his lips continuing to move nervously and inaudibly.

'Your name?'

'Simon Petrov Kartinkin,' he said, rapidly, with a cracked voice, having evidently prepared the answer.

'What class do you belong to?'

'Peasant.'

'What government, district, and parish?'

'Toula government, Krapivinskia district, Koupianovski parish, the village Borki.'

'Your age?'

'Thirty-three; born in the year one thousand eight— '

'What religion?'

'Of the Russian religion, orthodox.'

'Married?'

'Oh, no, sir.'

'Your occupation?'

'I had a place in the Hotel Mauritania.'

'Have you ever been tried before?'

'I never got tried before, because, as we used to live formerly – '

'So you never were tried before?'

'God forbid, never.'

'Have you received a copy of the indictment?'

'I have.'

'Sit down.'

'Euphemia Ivanovna Botchkova,' said the president, turning to the next prisoner.

But Simon continued standing in front of Botchkova.

'Kartinkin, sit down!' Kartinkin continued standing.

'Kartinkin, sit down!' But Kartinkin sat down only when the usher, with his head on one side, and with preternaturally wide-open eyes, ran up, and said, in a tragic whisper, 'Sit down, sit down!'

Kartinkin sat down as hurriedly as he had risen, wrapping his cloak round him, and again began moving his lips silently.

'Your name?' asked the president, with a weary sigh at being obliged to repeat the same questions, without looking at the prisoner, but glancing over a paper that lay before him. The president was so used to his task that, in order to get quicker through it all, he did two things at a time.

Botchkova was forty-three years old, and came from the town of Kalomna. She, too, had been in service at the Hotel Mauritania.

'I have never been tried before, and have received a copy of the indictment.' She gave her answers boldly, in a tone of voice as if she meant to add to each answer, 'And I don't care who knows it, and I won't stand any nonsense.'

She did not wait to be told, but sat down as soon as she had replied to the last question.

'Your name?' turning abruptly to the third prisoner. 'You will have to rise,' he added, softly and gently, seeing that Maslova kept her seat.

Maslova got up and stood, with her chest expanded, looking at the president with that peculiar expression of readiness in her smiling black eyes.

'What is your name?'

'Lubov,' she said.

Nekhlyudov had put on his pince-nez, looking at the prisoners while they were being questioned.

'No, it is impossible,' he thought, not taking his eyes off the prisoner. 'Lubov! How can it be?' he thought to himself, after hearing her answer. The president was going to continue his questions, but the member with the spectacles interrupted him, angrily whispering something. The president nodded, and turned again to the prisoner.

'How is this,' he said, 'you are not put down here as Lubov?'

The prisoner remained silent.

'I want your real name.'

'What is your baptismal name?' asked the angry member.

'Formerly I used to be called Katerina.'

'No, it cannot be,' said Nekhlyudov to himself; and yet he was now certain that this was she, that same girl, half ward, half servant to his aunts; that Katusha, with whom he had once been in love, really in love, but whom he had betrayed and then abandoned, and never again brought to mind, for the memory would have been too painful, would have convicted him too clearly, proving that he who was so proud of his integrity had treated this woman in a revolting, scandalous way.

Yes, this was she. He now clearly saw in her face that strange, indescribable individuality which distinguishes every face from all others; something peculiar, all its own, not to be found anywhere else. In spite of the unhealthy pallor and the fulness of the face, it was there, this sweet, peculiar individuality; on those lips, in the slight squint of her eyes, in the voice, particularly in the naive smile, and in the expression of readiness on the face and figure.

'You should have said so,' remarked the president, again in a gentle tone. 'Your patronymic?'

'I am illegitimate.'

'Well, were you not called by your godfather's name?'

'Yes, Mikhaelovna.'

'And what is it she can be guilty of?' continued Nekhlyudov, in his mind, unable to breathe freely.

'Your family name — your surname, I mean?' the president went on.

'They used to call me by my mother's surname, Maslova.'

'What class?'

'Meschanka.' *

* The lowest town class or grade.

'Religion — orthodox?'

'Orthodox.'

'Occupation. What was your occupation?'

Maslova remained silent.

'What was your employment?'

'You know yourself,' she said, and smiled. Then, casting a hurried look round the room, again turned her eyes on the president.

There was something so unusual in the expression of her face, so terrible and piteous in the meaning of the words she had uttered, in this smile, and in the furtive glance she had cast round the room, that the president was abashed, and for a few minutes silence reigned in the court. The silence was broken by someone among the public laughing, then somebody said 'Ssh', and the president looked up and continued:

'Have you ever been tried before?'

'Never,' answered Maslova, softly, and sighed.

'Have you received a copy of the indictment?'

'I have,' she answered.

'Sit down.'

The prisoner leant back to pick up her skirt in the way a fine lady picks up her train, and sat down, folding her small white hands in the sleeves of her cloak, her eyes fixed on the president. Her face was calm again.

The witnesses were called, and some sent away; the doctor who was to act as expert was chosen and called into the court.

Then the secretary got up and began reading the indictment. He read distinctly, though he pronounced the 'l' and 'r' alike, with a loud voice, but so quickly that the words ran into one another and formed one uninterrupted, dreary drone.

The judges bent now on one, now on the other arm of their chairs, then on the table, then back again, shut and opened their eyes, and whispered to each other. One of the gendarmes several times repressed a yawn.

The prisoner Kartinkin never stopped moving his cheeks. Botch-kova sat quite still and straight, only now and then scratching her head under the kerchief.

Maslova sat immovable, gazing at the reader; only now and then she gave a slight start, as if wishing to reply, blushed, sighed heavily, and changed the position of her hands, looked round, and again fixed her eyes on the reader.

Nekhlyudov sat in the front row on his high-backed chair, without removing his pince-nez, and looked at Maslova, while a complicated and fierce struggle was going on in his soul.

Chapter 10

The trial – the indictment

The indictment ran as follows: On the 17th of January, 18— in the lodging-house Mauritania, occurred the sudden death of the Second Guild merchant, Ferapont Emilianovich Smelkov, of Kourgan.

The local police doctor of the fourth district certified that death was due to rupture of the heart, owing to the excessive use of alcoholic liquids. The body of the said Smelkov was interred. After several days had elapsed, the merchant Timokhin, a fellow-townsman and companion of the said Smelkov, returned from St Petersburg, and hearing the circumstances that accompanied the death of the latter, notified his suspicions that the death was caused by poison, given with intent to rob the said Smelkov of his money. This suspicion was corroborated on inquiry, which proved:

1. That shortly before his death the said Smelkov had received the sum of three thousand eight hundred roubles from the bank. When an inventory of the property of the deceased was made, only three hundred and twelve roubles and sixteen copecks were found.

2. The whole day and night preceding his death the said Smelkov spent with Lubka (alias Katerina Maslova) at her home and in the lodging-house Mauritania, which she also visited at the said Smelkov's request during his absence, to get some money, which she took out of his portmanteau in the presence of the servants of the lodging-house Mauritania, Euphemia Botchkova and Simeon Kartinkin, with a key given her by the said Smelkov. In the portmanteau opened by the said Maslova, the said Botchkova and Kartinkin saw packets of hundred-rouble bank-notes.

3. On the said Smelkov's return to the lodging-house Mauritania, together with Lubka, the latter, in accordance with the attendant Kartinkin's advice, gave the said Smelkov some white powder given to her by the said Kartinkin, dissolved in brandy.

4. The next morning the said Lubka (alias Katerina Maslova) sold to her mistress, the witness Kitaeva, a brothel-keeper, a diamond ring given to her, as she alleged, by the said Smelkov.

5. The housemaid of the lodging-house Mauritania, Euphemia Botchkova, placed to her account in the local Commercial Bank one thousand eight hundred roubles. The post mortem examination of the body of the said Smelkov and the chemical analysis of his intestines proved beyond doubt the presence of poison in the organism, so that there is reason to believe that the said Smelkov's death was caused by poisoning.

When cross-examined, the accused, Maslova, Botchkova, and Kartinkin, pleaded not guilty, deposing – Maslova, that she had really been sent by Smelkov from the brothel, where she 'works', as she expresses it, to the lodging-house Mauritania to get the merchant some money, and that, having unlocked the portmanteau with a key given her by the merchant, she took out forty roubles, as she was told to do, and that she had taken nothing more; that Botchkova and Kartinkin, in whose presence she unlocked and locked the portmanteau, could testify to the truth of the statement.

She gave this further evidence – that when she came to the lodging-house for the second time she did, at the instigation of Simeon Kartinkin, give Smelkov some kind of powder, which she thought was a narcotic, in a glass of brandy, hoping he would fall asleep and that she would be able to get away from him; and that Smelkov, having beaten her, himself gave her the ring when she cried and threatened to go away.

The accused, Euphemia Botchkova, stated that she knew nothing about the missing money, that she had not even gone into Smelkov's room, but that Lubka had been busy there all by herself; that if anything had been stolen, it must have been done by Lubka when she came with the merchant's key to get his money.

At this point Maslova gave a start, opened her mouth, and looked at Botchkova. 'When,' continued the secretary, 'the receipt for eighteen hundred roubles from the bank was shown to Botchkova, and she was asked where she had obtained the money, she said that it was her own earnings for twelve years, and those of Simeon, whom she was going to marry. The accused Simeon Kartinkin, when first examined, confessed that he and Botchkova, at the instigation of Maslova, who had come with the key from the brothel, had stolen the money and divided it equally among themselves and Maslova.' Here Maslova again started, half-rose from her seat, and, blushing scarlet, began to say something, but was stopped by the usher. 'At last,' the secretary continued, reading, 'Kartinkin confessed also that he had supplied the powders in order to get Smelkov to sleep. When examined the second time he denied having had anything to do with the stealing of the money or giving Maslova the powders, accusing her of having done it alone.'

Concerning the money placed in the bank by Botchkova, he said the same as she, that is, that the money was given to them both by the lodgers in tips during twelve years' service.

The indictment concluded as follows:

In consequence of the foregoing, the peasant of the village Borki, Simeon Kartinkin, thirty-three years of age, the meschanka Euphemia Botchkova, forty-three years of age, and the meschanka Katerina Maslova, twenty-seven years of age, are accused of having on the 17th day of January, 188— jointly stolen from the said merchant, Smelkov, a ring and money, to the value of two thousand fivehundred roubles, and of having given the said merchant, Smelkov, poison to drink, with intent of depriving him of life, and thereby causing his death. This crime is provided for in clause 1,455 of the Penal Code, paragraphs 4 and 5.

Chapter 11

The trial – Maslova cross-examined

When the reading of the indictment was over, the president, after having consulted the members, turned to Kartinkin, with an expression that plainly said: Now we shall find out the whole truth down to the minutest detail.

'Peasant Simeon Kartinkin,' he said, stooping to the left.

Simeon Kartinkin got up, stretched his arms down his sides, and leaning forward with his whole body, continued moving his cheeks inaudibly.

'You are accused of having on the 17th January, 188— together with Euphemia Botchkova and Katerina Maslova, stolen money from a portmanteau belonging to the merchant Smelkov, and then, having procured some arsenic, persuaded Katerina Maslova to give it to the merchant Smelkov in a glass of brandy, which was the cause of Smelkov's death. Do you plead guilty?' said the president, stooping to the right.

'Not nohow, because our business is to attend on the lodgers, and – '

'You'll tell us that afterwards. Do you plead guilty?'

'Oh, no, sir. I only – '

'You'll tell us that afterwards. Do you plead guilty?' quietly and firmly asked the president.

'Can't do such a thing, because that – '

The usher again rushed up to Simeon Kartinkin, and stopped him in a tragic whisper.

The president moved the hand with which he held the paper and placed the elbow in a different position with an air that said: 'This is finished,' and turned to Euphemia Botchkova.

'Euphemia Botchkova, you are accused of having, on the 17th of January, 188—, in the lodging-house Mauritania, together with Simeon Kartinkin and Katerina Maslova, stolen some money and a ring out of the merchant Smelkov's portmanteau, and having shared the money among yourselves, given poison to the merchant Smelkov, thereby causing his death. Do you plead guilty?'

'I am not guilty of anything,' boldly and firmly replied the prisoner. 'I never went near the room, but when this baggage went in she did the whole business.'

'You will say all this afterwards,' the president again said, quietly and firmly. 'So you do not plead guilty?'

'I did not take the money nor give the drink, nor go into the room. Had I gone in I should have kicked her out.'

'So you do not plead guilty?'

'Never.'

'Very well.'

'Katerina Maslova,' the president began, turning to the third prisoner, 'you are accused of having come from the brothel with the key of the merchant Smelkov's portmanteau, money, and a ring.' He said all this like a lesson learned by heart, leaning towards the member on his left, who was whispering into his ear that a bottle mentioned in the list of the material evidence was missing. 'Of having stolen out of the portmanteau money and a ring,' he repeated, 'and shared it. Then, returning to the lodging house Mauritania with Smelkov, of giving him poison in his drink, and thereby causing his death. Do you plead guilty?'

'I am not guilty of anything,' she began rapidly. 'As I said before I say again, I did not take it – I did not take it; I did not take anything, and the ring he gave me himself.'

'You do not plead guilty of having stolen two thousand five hundred roubles?' asked the president.

'I've said I took nothing but the forty roubles.'

'Well, and do you plead guilty of having given the merchant Smelkov a powder in his drink?'

'Yes, that I did. Only I believed what they told me, that they were sleeping powders, and that no harm could come of them. I never thought, and never wished . . . God is my witness; I say, I never meant this,' she said.

'So you do not plead guilty of having stolen the money and the ring from the merchant Smelkov, but confess that you gave him the powder?' said the president.

'Well, yes, I do confess this, but I thought they were sleeping powders. I only gave them to make him sleep; I never meant and never thought of worse.'

'Very well,' said the president, evidently satisfied with the results gained. 'Now tell us how it all happened,' and he leaned back in his chair and put his folded hands on the table. 'Tell us all about it. A free and full confession will be to your advantage.'

Maslova continued to look at the president in silence, and blushing.

'Tell us how it happened.'

'How it happened?' Maslova suddenly began, speaking quickly. 'I came to the lodging-house, and was shown into the room. He was there, already very drunk.' She pronounced the word *he* with a look of horror in her wide-open eyes. 'I wished to go away, but he would not let me.' She stopped, as if having lost the thread, or remembered some thing else.

'Well, and then?'

'Well, what then? I remained a bit, and went home again.'

At this moment the public prosecutor raised himself a little, leaning on one elbow in an awkward manner.

'You would like to put a question?' said the president, and having received an answer in the affirmative, he made a gesture inviting the public prosecutor to speak.

'I want to ask, was the prisoner previously acquainted with Simeon Kartinkin?' said the public prosecutor, without looking at Maslova, and, having put the question, he compressed his lips and frowned.

The president repeated the question. Maslova stared at the public prosecutor, with a frightened look.

'With Simeon? Yes,' she said.

'I should like to know what the prisoner's acquaintance with Kartinkin consisted in. Did they meet often?'

'Consisted in? . . . He invited me for the lodgers; it was not an acquaintance at all,' answered Maslova, anxiously moving her eyes from the president to the public prosecutor and back to the president.

'I should like to know why Kartinkin invited only Maslova, and none of the other girls, for the lodgers?' said the public prosecutor, with half-closed eyes and a cunning, Mephistophelian smile.

'I don't know. How should I know?' said Maslova, casting a

frightened look round, and fixing her eyes for a moment on Nekhlyudov. 'He asked whom he liked.'

'Is it possible that she has recognised me?' thought Nekhlyudov, and the blood rushed to his face. But Maslova turned away without distinguishing him from the others, and again fixed her eyes anxiously on the public prosecutor.

'So the prisoner denies having had any intimate relations with Kartinkin? Very well, I have no more questions to ask.'

And the public prosecutor took his elbow off the desk, and began writing something. He was not really noting anything down, but only going over the letters of his notes with a pen, having seen the procureur and leading advocates, after putting a clever question, make a note, with which, later on, to annihilate their adversaries.

The president did not continue at once, because he was consulting the member with the spectacles, whether he was agreed that the questions (which had all been prepared beforehand and written out) should be put.

'Well! What happened next?' he then went on.

'I came home,' looking a little more boldly only at the president, 'and went to bed. Hardly had I fallen asleep when one of our girls, Bertha, woke me. "Go, your merchant has come again!" He – she again uttered the word *he* with evident horror – he kept treating our girls, and then wanted to send for more wine, but his money was all gone, and he sent me to his lodgings and told me where the money was, and how much to take. So I went.'

The president was whispering to the member on his left, but, in order to appear as if he had heard, he repeated her last words.

'So you went. Well, what next?'

'I went, and did all he told me; went into his room. I did not go alone, but called Simeon Kartinkin and her,' she said, pointing to Botchkova.

'That's a lie; I never went in,' Botchkova began, but was stopped.

'In their presence I took out four notes,' continued Maslova, frowning, without looking at Botchkova.

'Yes, but did the prisoner notice,' again asked the prosecutor, 'how much money there was when she was getting out the forty roubles?'

Maslova shuddered when the prosecutor addressed her; she did not know why it was, but she felt that he wished her evil.

'I did not count it, but only saw some hundred-rouble notes.'

'Ah! The prisoner saw hundred-rouble notes. That's all?'

'Well, so you brought back the money,' continued the president, looking at the clock.

'I did.'

'Well, and then?'

'Then he took me back with him,' said Maslova.

'Well, and how did you give him the powder? In his drink?'

'How did I give it? I put them in and gave it him.'

'Why did you give it him?'

She did not answer, but sighed deeply and heavily.

'He would not let me go,' she said, after a moment's silence, 'and I was quite tired out, and so I went out into the passage and said to Simeon, "If he would only let me go, I am so tired." And he said, "We are also sick of him; we were thinking of giving him a sleeping draught; he will fall asleep, and then you can go." So I said all right. I thought they were harmless, and he gave me the packet. I went in. He was lying behind the partition, and at once called for brandy. I took a bottle of "fine champagne" from the table, poured out two glasses, one for him and one for myself, and put the powders into his glass, and gave it him. Had I known how could I have given them to him?'

'Well, and how did the ring come into your possession?' asked the president. 'When did he give it you?'

'That was when we came back to his lodgings. I wanted to go away, and he gave me a knock on the head and broke my comb. I got angry and said I'd go away, and he took the ring off his finger and gave it to me so that I should not go,' she said.

Then the public prosecutor again slightly raised himself, and, putting on an air of simplicity, asked permission to put a few more questions, and, having received it, bending his head over his embroidered collar, he said: 'I should like to know how long the prisoner remained in the merchant Smelkov's room.'

Maslova again seemed frightened, and she again looked anxiously from the public prosecutor to the president, and said hurriedly:

'I do not remember how long.'

'Yes, but does the prisoner remember if she went anywhere else in the lodging-house after she left Smelkov?'

Maslova considered for a moment. 'Yes, I did go into an empty room next to his.'

'Yes, and why did you go in?' asked the public prosecutor, forgetting himself, and addressing her directly.

'I went in to rest a bit, and to wait for an *isvostchik*.'

'And was Kartinkin in the room with the prisoner, or not?'

'He came in.'

'Why did he come in?'

'There was some of the merchant's brandy left, and we finished it together.'

'Oh, finished it together. Very well! And did the prisoner talk to Kartinkin, and, if so, what about?'

Maslova suddenly frowned, blushed very red, and said, hurriedly, 'What about? I did not talk about anything, and that's all I know. Do what you like with me; I am not guilty, and that's all.'

'I have nothing more to ask,' said the prosecutor, and, drawing up his shoulders in an unnatural manner, began writing down, as the prisoner's own evidence, in the notes for his speech, that she had been in the empty room with Kartinkin.

There was a short silence.

'You have nothing more to say?'

'I have told everything,' she said, with a sigh, and sat down.

Then the president noted something down, and, having listened to something that the member on his left whispered to him, he announced a ten-minutes' interval, rose hurriedly, and left the court. The communication he had received from the tall, bearded member with the kindly eyes was that the member, having felt a slight stomach derangement, wished to do a little massage and to take some drops. And this was why an interval was made.

When the judges had risen, the advocates, the jury, and the witnesses also rose, with the pleasant feeling that part of the business was finished, and began moving in different directions.

Nekhlyudov went into the jury's room, and sat down by the window.

Chapter 12

Twelve years before

'Yes, this was Katusha.'

The relations between Nekhlyudov and Katusha had been the following:

Nekhlyudov first saw Katusha when he was a student in his third year at the University, and was preparing an essay on land tenure during the summer vacation, which he passed with his aunts. Until then he had always lived, in summer, with his mother and sister on his mother's large estate near Moscow. But that year his sister had married, and his mother had gone abroad to a watering-place, and he, having his essay to write, resolved to spend the summer with his aunts. It was very quiet in their secluded estate and there was nothing to distract his mind; his aunts loved their nephew and heir very tenderly, and he, too, was fond of them and of their simple, old-fashioned life.

During that summer on his aunts' estate, Nekhlyudov passed through that blissful state of existence when a young man for the first time, without guidance from anyone outside, realises all the beauty and significance of life, and the importance of the task allotted in it to man; when he grasps the possibility of unlimited advance towards perfection for one's self and for all the world, and gives himself to this task, not only hopefully, but with full conviction of attaining to the perfection he imagines. In that year, while still at the University, he had read Spencer's *Social Statics*, and Spencer's views on landholding especially impressed him, as he himself was heir to large estates. His father had not been rich, but his mother had received ten thousand acres of land for her dowry. At that time he fully realised all the cruelty and injustice of private property in land, and being one of those to whom a sacrifice to the demands of conscience gives the highest spiritual enjoyment, he decided not to retain property rights, but to give up to the peasant labourers the land he had inherited from his father. It was on this land question he wrote his essay.

He arranged his life on his aunts' estate in the following manner. He got up very early, sometimes at three o'clock, and before sunrise went through the morning mists to bathe in the river, under the hill. He returned while the dew still lay on the grass and the flowers. Sometimes, having finished his coffee, he sat down with his books of reference and his papers to write his essay, but very often, instead of reading or writing, he left home again, and wandered through the fields and the woods. Before dinner he lay down and slept somewhere in the garden. At dinner he amused and entertained his aunts with his bright spirits, then he rode on horseback or went for a row on the river, and in the evening he again worked at his essay, or sat reading or playing patience with his aunts.

His joy in life was so great that it agitated him, and kept him awake many a night, especially when it was moonlight, so that instead of sleeping he wandered about in the garden till dawn, alone with his dreams and fancies.

And so, peacefully and happily, he lived through the first month of his stay with his aunts, taking no particular notice of their half-ward, half-servant, the black-eyed, quick-footed Katusha. Then, at the age of nineteen, Nekhlyudov, brought up under his mother's wing, was still quite pure. If a woman figured in his dreams at all it was only as a wife. All the other women who, according to his ideas he could not marry, were not women for him, but human beings.

But on Ascension Day that summer, a neighbour of his aunts', and her family, consisting of two young daughters, a schoolboy, and a young artist of peasant origin who was staying with them, came to spend the day. After tea they all went to play in the meadow in front of the house, where the grass had already been mown. They played at the game of *gorelki*, and Katusha joined them. Running about and changing partners several times, Nekhlyudov caught Katusha, and she became his partner. Up to this time he had liked Katusha's looks, but the possibility of any nearer relations with her had never entered his mind.

'Impossible to catch those two,' said the merry young artist, whose turn it was to catch, and who could run very fast with his short, muscular legs.

'You! And not catch us?' said Katusha.

'One, two, three,' and the artist clapped his hands. Katusha, hardly restraining her laughter, changed places with Nekhlyudov, behind the artist's back, and pressing his large hand with her little rough one, and rustling with her starched petticoat, ran to the left. Nekhlyudov ran fast to the right, trying to escape from the artist, but when he looked round he saw the artist running after Katusha, who kept well ahead, her firm young legs moving rapidly. There was a lilac bush in front of them, and Katusha made a sign with her head to Nekhlyudov to join her behind it, for if they once clasped hands again they were safe from their pursuer, that being a rule of the game. He understood the sign, and ran behind the bush, but he did not know that there was a small ditch overgrown with nettles there. He stumbled and fell into the nettles, already wet with dew, stinging his bands, but rose immediately, laughing at his mishap.

Katusha, with her eyes black as sloes, her face radiant with joy, was flying towards him, and they caught hold of each other's hands.

'Got stung, I dare say?' she said, arranging her hair with her free hand, breathing fast and looking straight up at him with a glad, pleasant smile.

'I did not know there was a ditch here,' he answered, smiling also, and keeping her hand in his. She drew nearer to him, and he himself, not knowing how it happened, stooped towards her. She did not move away, and he pressed her hand tight and kissed her on the lips.

'There! You've done it!' she said; and, freeing her hand with a swift movement, ran away from him. Then, breaking two branches of white lilac from which the blossoms were already falling, she began fanning her hot face with them; then, with her head turned back to him, she walked away, swaying her arms briskly in front of her, and joined the other players.

After this there grew up between Nekhlyudov and Katusha those peculiar relations which often exist between a pure young man and girl who are attracted to each other.

When Katusha came into the room, or even when he saw her white apron from afar, everything brightened up in Nekhlud-ov's eyes, as when the sun appears everything becomes more interesting, more joyful, more important. The whole of life seemed full of gladness. And she felt the same. But it was not only Katusha's presence that had this effect on Nekhlyudov. The mere thought that Katusha existed (and for her that Nekhlyudov existed) had this effect.

When he received an unpleasant letter from his mother, or could not get on with his essay, or felt the unreasoning sadness that young people are often subject to, he had only to remember Katusha and that he should see her, and it all vanished. Katusha had much work to do in the house, but she managed to get a little leisure for reading, and Nekhlyudov gave her Dostoevsky and Turgenev (whom he had just read himself) to read. She liked Turgenev's *Lull* best. They had talks at moments snatched when meeting in the passage, on the veranda, or the yard, and sometimes in the room of his aunts' old servant, Matrona Pavlovna, with whom he sometimes used to drink tea, and where Katusha used to work.

These talks in Matrona Pavlovna's presence were the pleasantest. When they were alone it was worse. Their eyes at once began to say something very different and far more important than what their mouths uttered. Their lips puckered, and they felt a kind of dread of something that made them part quickly. These relations continued between Nekhlyudov and Katusha during the whole time of his first visit to his aunts'. They noticed it, and became frightened, and even wrote to Princess Elena Ivanovna, Nekhlyudov's mother. His aunt, Mary Ivanovna, was afraid Dmitri would form an intimacy with Katusha; but her fears were groundless, for Nekhlyudov, himself hardly conscious of it, loved Katusha, loved her as the pure love, and therein lay his safety – his and hers. He not only did not feel any desire to possess her, but the very thought of it filled him with horror. The fears of the more poetical Sophia Ivanovna, that Dmitri, with his thorough-going, resolute character, having fallen in love with a girl, might make up his mind to marry her, without considering either her birth or her station, had more ground.

Had Nekhlyudov at that time been conscious of his love for Katusha, and especially if he had been told that he could on no account join his life with that of a girl in her position, it might have easily happened that, with his usual straightforwardness, he would have come to the conclusion that there could be no possible reason for him not to marry any girl whatever, as long as he loved her. But his aunts did not mention their fears to him; and, when he left, he was still unconscious of his love for Katusha. He was sure that what he felt for Katusha was only one of the manifestations of the joy of life that filled his whole being, and that this sweet, merry little girl shared this joy with him. Yet, when he was going away, and Katusha stood with his aunts in the porch, and looked after him, her dark, slightly-squinting eyes filled with tears, he felt, after all, that he was leaving something beautiful, precious, something which would never reoccur. And he grew very sad.

'Goodbye, Katusha,' he said, looking across Sophia Ivanovna's cap as he was getting into the trap. 'Thank you for everything.'

'Goodbye, Dmitri Ivanovitch,' she said, with her pleasant, tender voice, keeping back the tears that filled her eyes – and ran away into the hall, where she could cry in peace.

Chapter 13

Life in the army

After that Nekhlyudov did not see Katusha for more than three years. When he saw her again he had just been promoted to the rank of officer and was going to join his regiment. On the way he came to spend a few days with his aunts, being now a very different young man from the one who had spent the summer with them three years before. He then had been an honest, un-selfish lad, ready to sacrifice himself for any good cause; now he was depraved and selfish, and thought only of his own enjoyment. Then God's world seemed a mystery which he tried enthus-iastically and joyfully to solve; now everything in life seemed clear and simple, defined by the conditions of the life he was leading. Then he had felt the importance of, and had need of intercourse with, nature, and with those who had lived and thought and felt before him – philosophers and poets. What he now considered necessary and important were human institutions and intercourse with his comrades. Then women seemed mysterious and charming – charming by the very mystery that enveloped them; now the purpose of women, all women except those of his own family and the wives of his friends, was a very definite one: women were the best means towards an already experienced enjoyment. Then money was not needed, and he did not require even one-third of what his mother allowed him; but now this allowance of fifteen hundred roubles a month did not suffice, and he had already had some unpleasant talks about it with his mother.

Then he had looked on his spirit as the I; now it was his healthy strong animal I that he looked upon as himself.

And all this terrible change had come about because he had ceased to believe himself and had taken to believing others. This he had done because it was too difficult to live believing one's self; believing one's self, one had to decide every question not in favour of one's own animal life, which is always seeking for easy gratifications, but almost in every case against it. Believing others there was nothing to decide; everything had been decided already, and decided always in favour of the animal I and against the spiritual. Nor was this all. Believing in his own self he was always exposing himself to the censure of those around him; believing others he had their approval. So, when Nekhlyudov had talked of the serious matters of life, of God, truth, riches, and poverty, all round him thought it out of place and even rather funny, and his mother and aunts called him, with kindly irony, *notre cher philosophe*. But when he read novels, told improper anecdotes, went to see funny vaudevilles in the French theatre and gaily repeated the jokes, everybody admired and encouraged him. When he considered it right to limit his needs, wore an old overcoat, took no wine, everybody thought it strange and looked upon it as a kind of showing off; but when he spent large sums on hunting, or on furnishing a peculiar and luxurious study for himself, everybody admired his taste and gave him expensive presents to encourage his hobby. While he kept pure and meant to remain so till he married his friends prayed for his health, and even his mother was not grieved but rather pleased when she found out that he had become a real man and had gained over some French woman from his friend. (As to the episode with Katusha, the princess could not without horror think that he might possibly have married her.) In the same way, when Nekhlyudov came of age, and gave the small estate he had inherited from his father to the peasants because he considered the holding of private property in land wrong, this step filled his mother and relations with dismay and served as an excuse for making fun of him to all his relatives. He was continually told that these peasants, after they had received the land, got no richer, but, on the contrary, poorer, having opened three public-houses and left off doing any work. But when Nekhlyudov entered the Guards and spent and gambled away so much with his aristocratic companions that Elena Ivanovna, his mother, had to draw on her capital, she was hardly pained, considering it quite natural and even good that wild oats should be sown at an early age and in good company, as her son was doing. At first Nekhlyudov struggled, but all that he had considered good while he had faith in himself was considered bad by others, and what he had considered evil was looked upon as good by those among whom he lived, and the struggle grew too hard. And at last Nekhlyudov gave in, i.e., left off believing himself and began believing others. At first this giving up of faith in himself was unpleasant, but it did not long continue to be so. At that time he acquired the habit of smoking, and drinking wine, and soon got over this unpleasant feeling and even felt great relief.

Nekhlyudov, with his passionate nature, gave himself thoroughly to the new way of life so approved of by all those around, and he entirely stifled the inner voice which demanded something different. This began after he moved to St Petersburg, and reached its highest point when he entered the army.

Military life in general depraves men. It places them in conditions of complete idleness, i.e., absence of all useful work; frees them of their common human duties, which it replaces by merely conventional ones to the honour of the regiment, the uniform, the flag; and, while giving them on the one hand absolute power over other men, also puts them into conditions of servile obedience to those of higher rank than themselves.

But when, to the usual depraving influence of military service with its honours, uniforms, flags, its permitted violence and murder, there is added the depraving influence of riches and nearness to and intercourse with members of the Imperial family, as is the case in the chosen regiment of the Guards in which all the officers are rich and of good family, then this depraving influence creates in the men who succumb to it a perfect mania of selfishness. And this mania of selfishness attacked Nekhlyudov from the moment he entered the army and began living in the way his companions lived. He had no occupation whatever except to dress in a uniform, splendidly made and well brushed by other people, and, with arms also made and cleaned and handed to him by others, ride to reviews on a fine horse which had been bred, broken in and fed by others. There, with other men like himself, he had to wave a sword, shoot off guns, and teach others to do the same. He had no other work, and the highly-placed persons, young and old, the Tsar and those near him, not only sanctioned his occupation but praised and thanked him for it.

After this was done, it was thought important to eat, and particularly to drink, in officers' clubs or the salons of the best restaurants, squandering large sums of money, which came from some invisible source; then theatres, ballets, women, then again riding on horseback, waving of swords and shooting, and again the squandering of money, the wine, cards, and women. This kind of life acts on military men even more depravingly than on others, because if any other than a military man lead such a life he cannot help being ashamed of it in the depth of his heart. A military man is, on the contrary, proud of a life of this kind especially at war time, and Nekhlyudov had entered the army just after war with the Turks had been declared. 'We are prepared to sacrifice our lives at the wars, and therefore a gay, reckless life is not only pardonable, but absolutely necessary for us, and so we lead it.'

Such were Nekhlyudov's confused thoughts at this period of his existence, and he felt all the time the delight of being free of the moral barriers he had formerly set himself. And the state he lived in was that of a chronic mania of selfishness. He was in this state when, after three years' absence, he came again to visit his aunts.

Chapter 14

The second meeting with Maslova

Nekhlyudov went to visit his aunts because their estate lay near the road he had to travel in order to join his regiment, which had gone forward, because they had very warmly asked him to come, and especially because he wanted to see Katusha. Perhaps in his heart he had already formed those evil designs against Katusha which his now uncontrolled animal self suggested to him, but he did not acknowledge this as his intention, but only wished to go back to the spot where he had been so happy, to see his rather funny, but dear, kind-hearted old aunts, who always, without his noticing it, surrounded him with an atmosphere of love and admiration, and to see sweet Katusha, of whom he had retained so pleasant a memory.

He arrived at the end of March, on Good Friday, after the thaw had set in. It was pouring with rain so that he had not a dry thread on him and was feeling very cold, but yet vigorous and full of spirits, as always at that time. 'Is she still with them?' he thought, as he drove into the familiar, old-fashioned courtyard, surrounded by a low brick wall, and now filled with snow off the roofs.

He expected she would come out when she heard the sledge bells but she did not. Two bare-footed women with pails and tucked-up skirts, who had evidently been scrubbing the floors, came out of the side door. She was not at the front door either, and only Tikhon, the manservant, with his apron on, evidently also busy cleaning, came out into the front porch. His aunt Sophia Ivanovna alone met him in the ante-room; she had a silk dress on and a cap on her head. Both aunts had been to church and had received communion.

'Well, this is nice of you to come,' said Sophia Ivanovna, kissing him. 'Mary is not well, got tired in church; we have been to communion.'

'I congratulate you, Aunt Sophia,'* said Nekhlyudov, kissing Sophia Ivanovna's hand. 'Oh, I beg your pardon, I have made you wet.'

'Go to your room – why you are soaking wet. Dear me, you have got moustaches! . . . Katusha! Katusha! Get him some coffee; be quick.'

'Directly,' came the sound of a well-known, pleasant voice from the passage, and Nekhlyudov's heart cried out 'She's here!' and it was as if the sun had come out from behind the clouds.

Nekhlyudov, followed by Tikhon, went gaily to his old room to change his things. He felt inclined to ask Tikhon about Katusha; how she was, what she was doing, was she not going to be married? But Tikhon was so respectful and at the same time so severe, insisted so firmly on pouring the water out of the jug for him, that Nekhlyudov could not make up his mind to ask him about Katusha, but only inquired about Tikhon's grandsons, about the old so-called 'brother's' horse, and about the dog Polkan. All were alive except Polkan, who had gone mad the summer before.

When he had taken off all his wet things and just begun to dress again, Nekhlyudov heard quick, familiar footsteps and a knock at the door. Nekhlyudov knew the steps and also the knock. No one but she walked and knocked like that.

Having thrown his wet greatcoat over his shoulders, he opened the door.

'Come in.' It was she, Katusha, the same, only sweeter than before. The slightly squinting naive black eyes looked up in the same old way. Now as then, she had on a white apron. She brought him from his aunts a piece of scented soap, with the wrapper just taken off, and two towels – one a long Russian embroidered one, the other a bath towel. The unused soap with the stamped inscription, the towels, and her own self, all were equally clean, fresh, undefiled and pleasant. The irrepressible smile of joy at the sight of him made the sweet, firm lips pucker up as of old.

'How do you do, Dmitri Ivanovitch?' she uttered with difficulty, her face suffused with a rosy blush.

'Good-morning! How do you do?' he said, also blushing. 'Alive and well?'

---

* It is usual in Russia to congratulate those who have received communion.

'Yes, the Lord be thanked. And here is your favorite pink soap and towels from your aunts,' she said, putting the soap on the table and hanging the towels over the back of a chair.

'There is everything here,' said Tikhon, defending the visitor's independence, and pointing to Nekhlyudov's open dressing case filled with brushes, perfume, *fixatoire*, a great many bottles with silver lids and all sorts of toilet appliances.

'Thank my aunts, please. Oh, how glad I am to be here,' said Nekhlyudov, his heart filling with light and tenderness as of old.

She only smiled in answer to these words, and went out. The aunts, who had always loved Nekhlyudov, welcomed him this time more warmly than ever. Dmitri was going to the war, where he might be wounded or killed, and this touched the old aunts. Nekhlyudov had arranged to stay only a day and night with his aunts, but when he had seen Katusha he agreed to stay over Easter with them and telegraphed to his friend Schönbock, whom he was to have joined in Odessa, that he should come and meet him at his aunts' instead.

As soon as he had seen Katusha Nekhlyudov's old feelings toward her awoke again. Now, just as then, he could not see her white apron without getting excited; he could not listen to her steps, her voice, her laugh, without a feeling of joy; he could not look at her eyes, black as sloes, without a feeling of tenderness, especially when she smiled; and, above all, he could not notice without agitation how she blushed when they met. He felt he was in love, but not as before, when this love was a kind of mystery to him and he would not own, even to himself, that he loved, and when he was persuaded that one could love only once; now he knew he was in love and was glad of it, and knew dimly what this love consisted of and what it might lead to, though he sought to conceal it even from himself. In Nekhlyudov, as in every man, there were two beings: one the spiritual, seeking only that kind of happiness for himself which should tend towards the happiness of all; the other, the animal man, seeking only his own happiness, and ready to sacrifice to it the happiness of the rest of the world. At this period of his mania of self-love brought on by life in Petersburg and in the army, this animal man ruled supreme and completely crushed the spiritual man in him.

But when he saw Katusha and experienced the same feelings as he had had three years before, the spiritual man in him raised its head once more and began to assert its rights. And up to Easter, during two whole days, an unconscious, ceaseless inner struggle went on in him.

He knew in the depths of his soul that he ought to go away, that there was no real reason for staying on with his aunts, knew that no good could come of it; and yet it was so pleasant, so delightful, that he did not honestly acknowledge the facts to himself and stayed on. On Easter Eve, the priest and the deacon who came to the house to say Mass had had (so they said) the greatest difficulty in getting over the three miles that lay between the church and the old ladies' house, coming across the puddles and the bare earth in a sledge.

Nekhlyudov attended the Mass with his aunts and the servants, and kept looking at Katusha, who was near the door and brought in the censers for the priests. Then having given the priests and his aunts the Easter kiss, though it was not midnight and therefore not Easter yet, he was already going to bed when he heard the old servant Matrona Pavlovna preparing to go to the church to get the *koulitch* and *paski* * blessed after the midnight service. 'I shall go too,' he thought.

The road to the church was impassable either in a sledge or on wheels, so Nekhlyudov, who behaved in his aunts' house just as he did at home, ordered the old horse, 'the brother's horse', to be saddled, and instead of going to bed he put on his gay uniform, a pair of tight-fitting riding breeches and his overcoat, and got on the old over-fed and heavy horse, which neighed continually all the way as he rode in the dark through the puddles and snow to the church.

---

* Easter cakes.

Chapter 15

The early Mass

For Nekhlyudov this early Mass remained for ever after one of the brightest and most vivid memories of his life. When he rode out of the darkness, broken only here and there by patches of white snow, into the churchyard illuminated by a row of lamps around the church, the service had already begun.

The peasants, recognising Mary Ivanovna's nephew, led his horse, which was pricking up its ears at the sight of the lights, to a dry place where he could get off, put it up for him, and showed him into the church, which was full of people. On the right stood the peasants; the old men in homespun coats, and clean white linen bands* wrapped round their legs, the young men in new cloth coats, bright-coloured belts round their waists, and top-boots.

On the left stood the women, with red silk kerchiefs on their heads, black velveteen sleeveless jackets, bright red shirt-sleeves, gay-coloured green, blue, and red skirts, and thick leather boots. The old women, dressed more quietly, stood behind them, with white kerchiefs, homespun coats, old-fashioned skirts of dark homespun material, and shoes on their feet. Gaily-dressed children, their hair well oiled, went in and out among them.

The men, making the sign of the cross, bowed down and raised their heads again, shaking back their hair.

The women, especially the old ones, fixed their eyes on an icon surrounded with candles and made the sign of the cross, firmly pressing their folded fingers to the kerchief on their foreheads, to their shoulders, and their stomachs, and, whispering something, stooped or knelt down. The children, imitating the grown-up people, prayed earnestly when they knew that they were being observed. The gilt case containing the icon glittered, illuminated on all sides by tall candles ornamented with golden spirals. The

---

* Long strips of linen are worn by the peasants instead of stockings.

candelabra was filled with tapers, and from the choir sounded most merry tunes sung by amateur choristers, with bellowing bass and shrill boys' voices among them.

Nekhlyudov passed up to the front. In the middle of the church stood the aristocracy of the place: a landed proprietor, with his wife and son (the latter dressed in a sailor's suit), the police officer, the telegraph clerk, a tradesman in top-boots, and the village elder, with a medal on his breast; and to the right of the ambo, just behind the landed proprietor's wife, stood Matrona Pavlovna in a lilac dress and fringed shawl and Katusha in a white dress with a tucked bodice, blue sash, and red bow in her black hair.

Everything seemed festive, solemn, bright, and beautiful: the priest in his silver cloth vestments with gold crosses; the deacon, the clerk and chanter in their silver and gold surplices; the amateur choristers in their best clothes, with their well-oiled hair; the merry tunes of the holiday hymns that sounded like dance music; and the continual blessing of the people by the priests, who held candles decorated with flowers, and repeated the cry of 'Christ is risen!' 'Christ is risen!' All was beautiful; but, above all, Katusha, in her white dress, blue sash, and the red bow on her black head, her eyes beaming with rapture.

Nekhlyudov knew that she felt his presence without looking at him. He noticed this as he passed her, walking up to the altar. He had nothing to tell her, but he invented something to say and whispered as he passed her: 'Aunt told me that she would break her fast after the late Mass.' The young blood rushed up to Katusha's sweet face, as it always did when she looked at him. The black eyes, laughing and full of joy, gazed naively up and remained fixed on Nekhlyudov.

'I know,' she said, with a smile.

At this moment the clerk was going out with a copper coffee-pot* of holy water in his hand, and, not noticing Katusha, brushed her with his surplice. Evidently he brushed against Katusha through wishing to pass Nekhlyudov at a respectful distance, and Nekhlyudov was surprised that he, the clerk, did not understand that everything here, yes, and in all the world, only existed for Katusha, and that everything else might remain unheeded, only not she, because she was the centre of all. For her the gold glittered round

* Coffee-pots are often used for holding holy water in Russia.

the icons; for her all these candles in candelabra and candlesticks were alight; for her were sung these joyful hymns, 'Behold the Passover of the Lord' 'Rejoice, O ye people!' All – all that was good in the world was for her. And it seemed to him that Katusha was aware that it was all for her when he looked at her well-shaped figure, the tucked white dress, the rapt, joyous expression of her face, by which he knew that just exactly the same that was singing in his own soul was also singing in hers.

In the interval between the early and the late Mass Nekhlyudov left the church. The people stood aside to let him pass, and bowed. Some knew him; others asked who he was.

He stopped on the steps. The beggars standing there came clamouring round him, and he gave them all the change he had in his purse and went down. It was dawning, but the sun had not yet risen. The people grouped round the graves in the churchyard. Katusha had remained inside. Nekhlyudov stood waiting for her.

The people continued coming out, clattering with their nailed boots on the stone steps and dispersing over the churchyard. A very old man with shaking head, his aunts' cook, stopped Nekhlyudov in order to give him the Easter kiss, his old wife took an egg, dyed yellow, out of her handkerchief and gave it to Nekhlyudov, and a smiling young peasant in a new coat and green belt also came up.

'Christ is risen,' he said, with laughing eyes, and coming close to Nekhlyudov he enveloped him in his peculiar but pleasant peasant smell, and, tickling him with his curly beard, kissed him three times straight on the mouth with his firm, fresh lips.

While the peasant was kissing Nekhlyudov and giving him a dark brown egg, the lilac dress of Matrona Pavlovna and the dear black head with the red bow appeared.

Katusha caught sight of him over the heads of those in front of her, and he saw how her face brightened up.

She had come out with Matrona Pavlovna on to the porch, and stopped there distributing alms to the beggars. A beggar with a red scab in place of a nose came up to Katusha. She gave him something, drew nearer him, and, evincing no sign of disgust, but her eyes still shining with joy, kissed him three times. And while she was doing this her eyes met Nekhlyudov's with a look as if she were asking, 'Is this that I am doing right?' 'Yes, dear, yes, it is right; everything is right, everything is beautiful. I love!'

They came down the steps of the porch, and he came up to them.

He did not mean to give them the Easter kiss, but only to be nearer to her. Matrona Pavlovna bowed her head, and said with a smile, 'Christ is risen!' and her tone implied, 'Today we are all equal.' She wiped her mouth with her handkerchief rolled into a ball and stretched her lips towards him.

'He is, indeed,' answered Nekhlyudov, kissing her. Then he looked at Katusha; she blushed, and drew nearer. 'Christ is risen, Dmitri Ivanovitch.' 'He is risen, indeed,' answered Nekhlyudov, and they kissed twice, then paused as if considering whether a third kiss were necessary, and, having decided that it was, kissed a third time and smiled.

'You are going to the priests?' asked Nekhlyudov.

'No, we shall sit out here a bit, Dmitri Ivanovitch,' said Katusha with effort, as if she had accomplished some joyous task, and, her whole chest heaving with a deep sigh, she looked straight in his face with a look of devotion, virgin purity, and love, in her very slightly squinting eyes.

In the love between a man and a woman there always comes a moment when this love has reached its zenith – a moment when it is unconscious, unreasoning, and with nothing sensual about it. Such a moment had come for Nekhlyudov on that Easter eve. When he brought Katusha back to his mind, now, this moment veiled all else; the smooth glossy black head, the white tucked dress closely fitting her graceful maidenly form, her as yet undeveloped bosom, the blushing cheeks, the tender shining black eyes with their slight squint heightened by the sleepless night, and her whole being stamped with those two marked features, purity and chaste love, love not only for him (he knew that), but for everybody and everything, not for the good alone, but for all that is in the world, even for that beggar whom she had kissed.

He knew she had that love in her because on that night and morning he was conscious of it in himself, and conscious that in this love he became one with her. Ah! if it had all stopped there, at the point it had reached that night. 'Yes, all that horrible business had not yet happened on that Easter eve!' he thought, as he sat by the window of the jurymen's room.

Chapter 16

The first step

When he returned from church Nekhlyudov broke the fast with his aunts and took a glass of spirits and some wine, having got into that habit while with his regiment, and when he reached his room fell asleep at once, dressed as he was. He was awakened by a knock at the door. He knew it was her knock, and got up, rubbing his eyes and stretching himself.

'Katusha, is it you? Come in,' said he.

She opened the door.

'Dinner is ready,' she said. She still had on the same white dress, but not the bow in her hair. She looked at him with a smile, as if she had communicated some very good news to him.

'I am coming,' he answered, as he rose, taking his comb to arrange his hair.

She stood still for a minute, and he, noticing it, threw down his comb and made a step towards her, but at that very moment she turned suddenly and went with quick light steps along the strip of carpet in the middle of the passage.

'Dear me, what a fool I am,' thought Nekhlyudov. 'Why did I not stop her?' What he wanted her for he did not know himself, but he felt that when she came into his room something should have been done, something that is generally done on such occasions, and that he had left it undone.

'Katusha, wait,' he said.

'What do you want?' she said, stopping.

'Nothing, only – ' and, with an effort, remembering how men in his position generally behave, he put his arm round her waist.

She stood still and looked into his eyes.

'Don't, Dmitri Ivanovitch, you must not,' she said, blushing to tears and pushing away his arm with her strong hard hand. Nekhlyudov let her go, and for a moment he felt not only confused and ashamed but disgusted with himself. He should now have believed himself, and then he would have known that this confusion and shame were caused by the best feelings of his soul demanding to be set free; but he thought it was only his stupidity and that he ought to behave as everyone else did. He caught her up and kissed her on the neck.

This kiss was very different from that first thoughtless kiss behind the lilac bush, and very different to the kiss this morning in the churchyard. This was a dreadful kiss, and she felt it.

'Oh, what are you doing?' she cried, in a tone as if he had irreparably broken something of priceless value, and ran quickly away.

He came into the dining-room. His aunts, elegantly dressed, their family doctor, and a neighbour were already there. Everything seemed so very ordinary, but in Nekhlyudov a storm was raging. He understood nothing of what was being said and gave wrong answers, thinking only of Katusha. The sound of her steps in the passage brought back the thrill of that last kiss and he could think of nothing else. When she came into the room he, without looking round, felt her presence with his whole being and had to force himself not to look at her.

After dinner he at once went into his bedroom and for a long time walked up and down in great excitement, listening to every sound in the house and expecting to hear her steps. The animal man inside him had now not only lifted its head, but had succeeded in trampling under foot the spiritual man of the days of his first visit, and even of that every morning. That dreadful animal man alone now ruled over him.

Though he was watching for her all day he could not manage to meet her alone. She was probably trying to evade him. In the evening, however, she was obliged to go into the room next to his. The doctor had been asked to stay the night, and she had to make his bed. When he heard her go in Nekhlyudov followed her, treading softly and holding his breath as if he were going to commit a crime.

She was putting a clean pillow-case on the pillow, holding it by two of its corners with her arms inside the pillow-case. She turned round and smiled, not a happy, joyful smile as before, but in a frightened, piteous way. The smile seemed to tell him that what he was doing was wrong. He stopped for a moment. There was still the possibility of a struggle. The voice of his real love for her, though feebly, was still speaking of her, her feelings, her life. Another voice was saying, 'Take care! Don't let the opportunity for your own happiness, your own enjoyment, slip by!' And this second voice completely stifled the first. He went up to her with determination and a terrible, ungovernable animal passion took possession of him.

With his arm round he made her sit down on the bed; and feeling that there was something more to be done he sat down beside her.

'Dmitri Ivanovitch, dear! please let me go,' she said, with a piteous voice. 'Matrona Pavlovna is coming,' she cried, tearing herself away. Someone was really coming to the door.

'Well, then, I'll come to you in the night,' he whispered. 'You'll be alone?'

'What are you thinking of? On no account. No, no!' she said, but only with her lips; the tremulous confusion of her whole being said something very different.

It was Matrona Pavlovna who had come to the door. She came in with a blanket over her arm, looked reproachfully at Nekhlyudov, and began scolding Katusha for having taken the wrong blanket.

Nekhlyudov went out in silence, but he did not even feel ashamed. He could see by Matrona Pavlovna's face that she was blaming him, he knew that she was blaming him with reason and felt that he was doing wrong, but this novel, low animal excitement, having freed itself of all the old feelings of real love for Katusha, ruled supreme, leaving room for nothing else. He went about as if demented all the evening, now into his aunts', then back into his own room, then out into the porch, thinking all the time how he could meet her alone; but she avoided him, and Matrona Pavlovna watched her closely.

Chapter 17

Nekhlyudov and Katusha

And so the evening passed and night came. The doctor went to bed. Nekhlyudov's aunts had also retired, and he knew that Matrona Pavlovna was now with them in their bedroom so that Katusha was sure to be alone in the maids' sitting-room. He again went out into the porch. It was dark, damp and warm out of doors, and that white spring mist which drives away the last snow, or is diffused by the thawing of the last snow, filled the air. From the river under the hill, about a hundred steps from the front door, came a strange sound. It was the ice breaking. Nekhlyudov came down the steps and went up to the window of the maids' room, stepping over the puddles on the bits of glazed snow. His heart was beating so fiercely in his breast that he seemed to hear it, his laboured breath came and went in a burst of long-drawn sighs. In the maids' room a small lamp was burning, and Katusha sat alone by the table, looking thoughtfully in front of her. Nekhlyudov stood a long time without moving and waited to see what she, not knowing that she was observed, would do. For a minute or two she did not move; then she lifted her eyes, smiled and shook her head as if chiding herself, then changed her pose and dropped both her arms on the table and again began gazing down in front of her. He stood and looked at her, involuntarily listening to the beating of his own heart and the strange sounds from the river. There on the river, beneath the white mist, the unceasing labour went on, and sounds as of something sobbing, cracking, dropping, being shattered to pieces, mixed with the tinkling of the thin bits of ice as they broke against each other like glass.

There he stood, looking at Katusha's serious, suffering face, which betrayed the inner struggle of her soul, and he felt pity for her; but, strange though it may seem, this pity only confirmed him in his evil intention.

He knocked at the window. She started as if she had received an electric shock, her whole body trembled, and a look of horror came into her face. Then she jumped up, approached the window and brought her face up to the pane. The look of terror did not leave her face even when, holding her hands up to her eyes like blinkers and peering through the glass, she recognised him. Her face was unusually grave; he had never seen it so before. She returned his smile, but only in submission to him; there was no smile in her soul, only fear. He beckoned her with his hand to come out into the yard to him. But she shook her head and remained by the window. He brought his face close to the pane and was going to call out to her, but at that moment she turned to the door; evidently someone inside had called her. Nekhlyudov moved away from the window. The fog was so dense that five steps from the house the windows could not be seen, but the light from the lamp shone red and huge out of a shapeless black mass. And on the river the same strange sounds went on, sobbing and rustling and cracking and tinkling. Somewhere in the fog, not far off, a cock crowed; another answered, and then others, far in the village took up the cry till the sound of the crowing blended into one, while all around was silent excepting the river. It was the second time the cocks crowed that night.

Nekhlyudov walked up and down behind the corner of the house, and once or twice got into a puddle. Then he again came up to the window. The lamp was still burning, and she was again sitting alone by the table as if uncertain what to do. He had hardly approached the window when she looked up. He knocked. Without looking who it was she at once ran out of the room, and he heard the outside door open with a snap. He waited for her near the side porch and put his arms round her without saying a word. She clung to him, put up her face, and met his kiss with her lips. Then the door again gave the same sort of snap and opened, and the voice of Matrona Pavlovna called out angrily, 'Katusha!'

She tore herself away from him and returned into the maids' room. He heard the latch click, and then all was quiet. The red light disappeared and only the mist remained, and the bustle on the river went on. Nekhlyudov went up to the window. Nobody was to be seen; he knocked, but got no answer. He went back into the house by the front door, but could not sleep. He got up and went with bare feet along the passage to her door, next Matrona Pavlovna's room. He heard Matrona Pavlovna snoring quietly, and was about to go on when she coughed and turned on her creaking bed, and his heart fell, and he stood immovable for about five minutes. When all was quiet and she began to snore peacefully again, he went on, trying to step on the boards that did not creak, and came to Katusha's door. There was no sound to be heard. She was probably awake, or else he would have heard her breathing. But as soon as he had whispered 'Katusha' she jumped up and began to persuade him, as if angrily, to go away.

'Open! Let me in just for a moment! I implore you!' He hardly knew what he was saying.

* * *

When she left him, trembling and silent, giving no answer to his words, he again went out into the porch and stood trying to understand the meaning of what had happened.

It was getting lighter. From the river below the creaking and tinkling and sobbing of the breaking ice came still louder and a gurgling sound could now also be heard. The mist had begun to sink, and from above it the waning moon dimly lighted up something black and weird.

'What was the meaning of it all? Was it a great joy or a great misfortune that had befallen him?' he asked himself.

Chapter 18

Afterwards

The next day the gay, handsome and brilliant Schönbock joined Nekhlyudov at his aunts' house, and quite won their hearts by his refined and amiable manner, his high spirits, his generosity, and his affection for Dmitri.

But though the old ladies admired his generosity it rather perplexed them, for it seemed exaggerated. He gave a rouble to some blind beggars who came to the gate, gave fifteen roubles in tips to

the servants, and when Sophia Ivanovna's pet dog hurt his paw
and it bled, he tore his hem-stitched cambric handkerchief into
strips (Sophia Ivanovna knew that such handkerchiefs cost at least
fifteen roubles a dozen) and bandaged the dog's foot. The old ladies
had never met people of this kind, and did not know that Schönbock owed two hundred thousand roubles which he was never
going to pay, and that therefore twenty-five roubles more or less
did not matter a bit to him. Schönbock stayed only one day, and he
and Nekhlyudov both left at night. They could not stay away from
their regiment any longer, for their leave was fully up.

At the stage which Nekhlyudov's selfish mania had now reached
he could think of nothing but himself. He was wondering
whether his conduct, if found out, would be blamed much or at
all, but he did not consider what Katusha was now going through,
and what was going to happen to her.

He saw that Schönbock guessed his relations to her and this
flattered his vanity.

'Ah, I see how it is you have taken such a sudden fancy
to your aunts that you have been living nearly a week with
them,' Schönbock remarked when he had seen Katusha. 'Well, I
don't wonder – should have done the same. She's charming.'
Nekhlyudov was also thinking that though it was a pity to go
away before having fully gratified the cravings of his love for her,
yet the absolute necessity of parting had its advantages because it
put a sudden stop to relations it would have been very difficult for
him to continue. Then he thought that he ought to give her some
money, not for her, not because she might need it, but because it
was the thing to do.

So he gave her what seemed to him a liberal amount, considering
his and her station. On the day of his departure, after dinner, he
went out and waited for her at the side entrance. She flushed up
when she saw him and wished to pass by, directing his attention to
the open door of the maids' room by a look, but he stopped her.

'I have come to say goodbye,' he said, crumbling in his hand an
envelope with a hundred-rouble note inside. 'There, I . . . '

She guessed what he meant, knit her brows, and shaking her
head pushed his hand away.

'Take it; oh, you must!' he stammered, and thrust the envelope
into the bib of her apron and ran back to his room, groaning and

frowning as if he had hurt himself. And for a long time he went up and down writhing as in pain, and even stamping and groaning aloud as he thought of this last scene. 'But what else could I have done? Is it not what happens to everyone? And if everyone does the same . . . well I suppose it can't be helped.' In this way he tried to get peace of mind, but in vain. The recollection of what had passed burned his conscience. In his soul – in the very depths of his soul – he knew that he had acted in a base, cruel, cowardly manner, and that the knowledge of this act of his must prevent him, not only from finding fault with anyone else, but even from looking straight into other people's eyes; not to mention the impossibility of considering himself a splendid, noble, high-minded fellow, as he did and had to do to go on living his life boldly and merrily. There was only one solution of the problem – i.e., not to think about it. He succeeded in doing so. The life he was now entering upon, the new surroundings, new friends, the war, all helped him to forget. And the longer he lived, the less he thought about it, until at last he forgot it completely.

Once only when, after the war, he went to see his aunts in hopes of meeting Katusha, and heard that soon after his last visit she had left, and that his aunts had heard she had been confined somewhere or other and had gone quite to the bad, his heart ached. According to the time of her confinement, the child might or might not have been his. His aunts said she had gone wrong, that she had inherited her mother's depraved nature, and he was pleased to hear this opinion of his aunts. It seemed to acquit him. At first he thought of trying to find her and her child, but then, just because in the depths of his soul he felt so ashamed and pained when thinking about her, he did not make the necessary effort to find her, but tried to forget his sin again and ceased to think about it. And now this strange coincidence brought it all back to his memory, and demanded from him the acknowledgment of the heartless, cruel cowardice which had made it possible for him to live these nine years with such a sin on his conscience. But he was still far from such an acknowledgment, and his only fear was that everything might now be found out, and that she or her advocate might recount it all and put him to shame before everyone present.

Chapter 19

The trial – resumption

In this state of mind Nekhlyudov left the Court and went into the jurymen's room. He sat by the window smoking all the while, and hearing what was being said around him.

The merry merchant seemed with all his heart to sympathise with Smelkov's way of spending his time. 'There, old fellow, that was something like! Real Siberian fashion! He knew what he was about, no fear! That's the sort of wench for me.'

The foreman was stating his conviction, that in some way or other the expert's conclusions were the important thing. Peter Gerasimovitch was joking about something with the Jewish clerk, and they burst out laughing. Nekhlyudov answered all the questions addressed to him in monosyllables and longed only to be left in peace.

When the usher, with his sideways gait, called the jury back to the Court, Nekhlyudov was seized with fear, as if he were not going to judge, but to be judged. In the depth of his soul he felt that he was a scoundrel, who ought to be ashamed to look people in the face, yet by sheer force of habit, he stepped on to the platform in his usual self-possessed manner, and sat down, crossing his legs and playing with his pince-nez.

The prisoners had also been led out, and were now brought in again. There were some new faces in the Court witnesses, and Nekhlyudov noticed that Maslova could not take her eyes off a very fat woman who sat in the row in front of the grating, very showily dressed in silk and velvet, a high hat with a large bow on her head, and an elegant little reticule on her arm, which was bare to the elbow. This was, as he subsequently found out, one of the witnesses, the mistress of the establishment to which Maslova had belonged.

The examination of the witnesses commenced: they were asked their names, religion, etc. Then, after some consultation as to whether the witnesses were to be sworn in or not, the old priest came in again, dragging his legs with difficulty, and, again arranging the golden cross on his breast, swore the witnesses and the expert in the same quiet manner, and with the same assurance that he was doing something useful and important.

The witnesses having been sworn, all but Kitaeva, the keeper of the house, were led out again. She was asked what she knew about this affair. Kitaeva nodded her head and the big hat at every sentence and smiled affectedly. She gave a very full and intelligent account, speaking with a strong German accent. First of all, the hotel servant Simeon, whom she knew, came to her establishment on behalf of a rich Siberian merchant, and she sent Lubov back with him. After a time Lubov returned with the merchant. The merchant was already somewhat intoxicated – she smiled as she said this – and went on drinking and treating the girls. He was short of money. He sent this same Lubov to his lodgings. He had taken a 'predilection' to her. She looked at the prisoner as she said this.

Nekhlyudov thought he saw Maslova smile here, and this seemed disgusting to him. A strange, indefinite feeling of loathing, mingled with suffering, arose in him.

'And what was your opinion of Maslova?' asked the blushing and confused applicant for a judicial post, appointed to act as Maslova's advocate.

'Zee ferry pesht,' answered Kitaeva. 'Zee yoong voman is etucated and elecant. She was prought up in a coot family and can reat French. She tid have a trop too moch sometimes, put nefer forcot herself. A ferry coot girl.'

Katusha looked at the woman, then suddenly turned her eyes on the jury and fixed them on Nekhlyudov, and her face grew serious and even severe. One of her serious eyes squinted, and those two strange eyes for some time gazed at Nekhlyudov, who in spite of the terrors that seized him, could not take his look off these squinting eyes, with their bright, clear whites.

He thought of that dreadful night, with its mist, the ice breaking on the river below, and when the waning moon, with horns turned upwards, that had risen towards morning, lit up something black and weird. These two black eyes now looking at him reminded him of this weird, black something. 'She has recognised me,' he thought, and Nekhlyudov shrank as if expecting a blow. But she had not recognised him. She sighed quietly and again looked at the president. Nekhlyudov also sighed. 'Oh, if it would only get on quicker,' he thought.

He now felt the same loathing and pity and vexation as when, out shooting, he was obliged to kill a wounded bird. The wounded bird struggles in the game bag. One is disgusted and yet feels pity, and one is in a hurry to kill the bird and forget it.

Such mixed feelings filled Nekhlyudov's breast as he sat listening to the examination of the witnesses.

Chapter 20

The trial – the medical report

But, as if to spite him, the case dragged out to a great length. After each witness had been examined separately and the expert last of all, and a great number of useless questions had been put, with the usual air of importance, by the public prosecutor and by both advocates, the president invited the jury to examine the objects offered as material evidence. They consisted of an enormous diamond ring, which had evidently been worn on the first finger, and a test tube in which the poison had been analysed. These things had seals and labels attached to them.

Just as the witnesses were about to look at these things, the public prosecutor rose and demanded that before they did this the results of the doctor's examination of the body should be read. The president, who was hurrying the business through as fast as he could in order to visit his Swiss friend, though he knew that the reading of this paper could have no other effect than that of producing weariness and putting off the dinner hour, and that the public prosecutor wanted it read simply because he knew he had a right to demand it, had no option but to express his consent.

The secretary got out the doctor's report and again began to read in his weary lisping voice, making no distinction between the 'r's and 'l's.

The external examination proved that:

'1. Ferapont Smelkov's height was six feet five inches.

'Not so bad, that. A very good size,' whispered the merchant, with interest, into Nekhlyudov's ear.

2. He looked about forty years of age.

3. The body was of a swollen appearance.

4. The flesh was of a greenish colour, with dark spots in several places.

5. The skin was raised in blisters of different sizes and in places had come off in large pieces.

6. The hair was chestnut; it was thick, and separated easily from the skin when touched.

7. The eyeballs protruded from their sockets and the cornea had grown dim.

8. Out of the nostrils, both ears, and the mouth oozed serous liquid; the mouth was half open.

9. The neck had almost disappeared, owing to the swelling of the face and chest.'

And so on and so on.

Four pages were covered with the twenty-seven paragraphs describing all the details of the external examination of the enormous, fat, swollen, and decomposing body of the merchant who had been making merry in the town. The indefinite loathing that Nekhlyudov felt was increased by the description of the corpse. Katusha's life, and the scum oozing from the nostrils of the corpse, and the eyes that protruded out of their sockets, and his own treatment of her – all seemed to belong to the same order of things, and he felt surrounded and wholly absorbed by things of the same nature.

When the reading of the report of the external examination was ended, the president heaved a sigh and raised his hand, hoping it was finished; but the secretary at once went on to the description of the internal examination. The president's head again dropped into his hand and he shut his eyes. The merchant next to Nekhlyudov could hardly keep awake, and now and then his body swayed to and fro. The prisoners and the gendarmes sat perfectly quiet.

The internal examination showed that:

1. The skin was easily detachable from the bones of the skull, and there was no coagulated blood.

2. The bones of the skull were of average thickness and in sound condition.
3. On the membrane of the brain there were two discoloured spots about four inches long, the membrane itself being of a dull white.

And so on for thirteen paragraphs more. Then followed the names and signatures of the assistants, and the doctor's conclusion showing that the changes observed in the stomach, and to a lesser degree in the bowels and kidneys, at the post mortem examination, and described in the official report, gave great probability to the conclusion that Smelkov's death was caused by poison which had entered his stomach mixed with alcohol. To decide from the state of the stomach what poison had been introduced was difficult; but it was necessary to suppose that the poison entered the stomach mixed with alcohol, since a great quantity of the latter was found in Smelkov's stomach.

'He could drink, and no mistake,' again whispered the merchant, who had just waked up.

The reading of this report had taken a full hour, but it had not satisfied the public prosecutor, for, when it had been read through and the president turned to him, saying, 'I suppose it is superfluous to read the report of the examination of the internal organs?' he answered in a severe tone, without looking at the president, 'I shall ask to have it read.'

He raised himself a little, and showed by his manner that he had a right to have this report read, and would claim this right, and that if that were not granted it would serve as a cause of appeal.

The member of the Court with the big beard, who suffered from catarrh of the stomach, feeling quite done up, turned to the president: 'What is the use of reading all this? It is only dragging it out. These new brooms do not sweep clean; they only take a long while doing it.'

The member with the gold spectacles said nothing, but only looked gloomily in front of him, expecting nothing good, either from his wife or life in general. The reading of the report commenced.

In the year 188—, on February 15th, I, the undersigned, commissioned by the medical department, made an examination, No. 638, [the secretary began again with firmness and raising the pitch of his voice as if to dispel the sleepiness that had overtaken all present], in the presence of the assistant medical inspector, of the internal organs:

1. The right lung and the heart (contained in a 6-lb. glass jar).
2. The contents of the stomach (in a 6-lb. glass jar).
3. The stomach itself (in a 6-lb. glass jar).
4. The liver, the spleen and the kidneys (in a 9-lb. glass jar).
5. The intestines (in a 9-lb. earthenware jar).

The president here whispered to one of the members, then stooped to the other, and having received their consent, he said: 'The Court considers the reading of this report superfluous.' The secretary stopped reading and folded the paper, and the public prosecutor angrily began to write down something. 'The gentlemen of the jury may now examine the articles of material evidence,' said the president. The foreman and several of the others rose and went to the table, not quite knowing what to do with their hands. They looked in turn at the glass, the test tube, and the ring. The merchant even tried on the ring.

'Ah! that was a finger,' he said, returning to his place; 'like a cucumber,' he added. Evidently the image he had formed in his mind of the gigantic merchant amused him.

Chapter 21

The trial – the prosecutor and the advocates

When the examination of the articles of material evidence was finished, the president announced that the investigation was now concluded, and immediately called on the prosecutor to proceed, hoping that as the latter was also a man, he, too, might feel inclined to smoke or dine, and show some mercy on the rest. But the public prosecutor showed mercy neither to himself nor to anyone else. He was very stupid by nature, but, besides this, he had had the misfortune of finishing school with a gold medal and of receiving a reward for his essay on 'Servitude' when studying Roman Law at the University, and was therefore self-confident and self-satisfied in the highest degree (his success with the ladies also conducing to this), and his stupidity had become extraordinary.

When the word was given to him, he got up slowly, showing the whole of his graceful figure in his embroidered uniform. Putting his hand on the desk he looked round the room, slightly bowing his head, and, avoiding the eyes of the prisoners, began to read the speech he had prepared while the reports were being read.

'Gentlemen of the jury! The business that now lies before you is, if I may so express myself, very characteristic.'

The speech of a public prosecutor, according to his views, should always have a social importance, like the celebrated speeches made by the advocates who have become distinguished. True, the audience consisted of three women – a sempstress, a cook, and Simeon's sister – and a coachman; but this did not matter. The celebrities had begun in the same way. To be always at the height of his position, i.e., to penetrate into the depths of the psychological significance of crime and to discover the wounds of society, was one of the prosecutor's principles.

'You see before you, gentlemen of the jury, a crime characteristic, if I may so express myself, of the end of our century; bearing, so to say, the specific features of that very painful phenomenon, the corruption to which those elements of our present-day society, which are, so to say, particularly exposed to the burning rays of this process, are subject.'

The public prosecutor spoke at great length, trying not to forget any of the notions he had formed in his mind, and, on the other hand, never to hesitate, and let his speech flow on for an hour and a quarter without a break.

Only once he stopped and for some time stood swallowing his saliva, but he soon mastered himself and made up for the interruption by heightened eloquence. He spoke now with a tender, insinuating accent, stepping from foot to foot and looking at the jury, now in quiet, businesslike tones, glancing into his notebook, then with a loud, accusing voice, looking from the audience to the advocates. But he avoided looking at the prisoners, who were all three fixedly gazing at him. Every new craze then in vogue among his set was alluded to in his speech; everything that then was, and some things that still are, considered to be the last words of scientific wisdom: the laws of heredity and inborn criminality, evolution and the struggle for existence, hypnotism and hypnotic influence.

According to his definition, the merchant Smelkov was of the genuine Russian type, and had perished in consequence of his generous, trusting nature, having fallen into the hands of deeply degraded individuals.

Simeon Kartinkin was the atavistic production of serfdom, a stupefied, ignorant, unprincipled man, who had not even any religion. Euphemia was his mistress, and a victim of heredity; all the signs of degeneration were noticeable in her. The chief wire-puller in this affair was Maslova, presenting the phenomenon of decadence in its lowest form. 'This woman,' he said, looking at her, 'has, as we have today heard from her mistress in this court, received an education; she cannot only read and write, but she knows French; she is illegitimate, and probably carries in her the germs of criminality. She was educated in an enlightened, noble family and might have lived by honest work, but she deserts her benefactress, gives herself up to a life of shame in which she is distinguished from her companions by her education, and chiefly, gentlemen of the jury, as you have heard from her mistress, by her power of acting on the visitors by means of that mysterious capacity lately investigated by science, especially by the school of Charcot, known by the name of hypnotic influence. By these means she gets hold of this Russian, this kind-hearted Sadko,* the rich guest, and uses his trust in order first to rob and then pitilessly to murder him.'

'Well, he is piling it on now, isn't he?' said the president with a smile, bending towards the serious member.

'A fearful blockhead!' said the serious member.

Meanwhile the public prosecutor went on with his speech. 'Gentlemen of the jury,' gracefully swaying his body, 'the fate of society is to a certain extent in your power. Your verdict will influence it. Grasp the full meaning of this crime, the danger that awaits society from those whom I may perhaps be permitted to call pathological individuals, such as Maslova. Guard it from infection; guard the innocent and strong elements of society from contagion or even destruction.'

And as if himself overcome by the significance of the expected

* Sadko, the hero of a legend.

verdict, the public prosecutor sank into his chair, highly delighted with his speech.

The sense of the speech, when divested of all its flowers of rhetoric, was that Maslova, having gained the merchant's confidence, hypnotised him and went to his lodgings with his key meaning to take all the money herself, but having been caught in the act by Simeon and Euphemia had to share it with them. Then, in order to hide the traces of the crime, she had returned to the lodgings with the merchant and there poisoned him.

After the prosecutor had spoken, a middle-aged man in swallow-tail coat and low-cut waistcoat showing a large half-circle of starched white shirt, rose from the advocates' bench and made a speech in defence of Kartinkin and Botchkova; this was an advocate engaged by them for three hundred roubles. He acquitted them both and put all the blame on Maslova. He denied the truth of Maslova's statements that Botchkova and Kartinkin were with her when she took the money, laying great stress on the point that her evidence could not be accepted, she being charged with poisoning. 'The two thousand five hundred roubles,' the advocate said, 'could have been easily earned by two honest people getting from three to five roubles per day in tips from the lodgers. The merchant's money was stolen by Maslova and given away, or even lost, as she was not in a normal state.'

The poisoning was committed by Maslova alone; therefore he begged the jury to acquit Kartinkin and Botchkova of stealing the money; or if they could not acquit them of the theft, at least to admit that it was done without any participation in the poisoning.

In conclusion the advocate remarked, with a thrust at the public prosecutor, that 'the brilliant observations of that gentleman on heredity, while explaining scientific facts concerning heredity, were inapplicable in this case, as Botchkova was of unknown parentage.' The public prosecutor put something down on paper with an angry look, and shrugged his shoulders in contemptuous surprise.

Then Maslova's advocate rose, and timidly and hesitatingly began his speech in her defence.

Without denying that she had taken part in the stealing of the money, he insisted on the fact that she had no intention of poisoning Smelkov, but had given him the powder only to make him fall asleep. He tried to go in for a little eloquence in giving a description of how Maslova was led into a life of debauchery by a man who had remained unpunished while she had to bear all the weight of her fall; but this excursion into the domain of psychology was so unsuccessful that it made everybody feel uncomfortable. When he muttered something about men's cruelty and women's helplessness, the president tried to help him by asking him to keep closer to the facts of the case. When he had finished the public prosecutor got up to reply. He defended his position against the first advocate, saying that oven if Botchkova was of unknown parentage the truth of the doctrine of heredity was thereby in no way invalidated, since the laws of heredity were so far proved by science that we can not only deduce the crime from heredity, but heredity from the crime. As to the statement made in defence of Maslova, that she was the victim of an imaginary (he laid a particularly venomous stress on the word imaginary) betrayer, he could only say that from the evidence before them it was much more likely that she had played the part of temptress to many and many a victim who had fallen into her hands. Having said this he sat down in triumph. Then the prisoners were offered permission to speak in their own defence.

Euphemia Botchkova repeated once more that she knew nothing about it and had taken part in nothing, and firmly laid the whole blame on Maslova. Simeon Kartinkin only repeated several times: 'It is your business, but I am innocent; it's unjust.' Maslova said nothing in her defence. Told she might do so by the president, she only lifted her eyes to him, cast a look round the room like a hunted animal, and, dropping her head, began to cry, sobbing aloud.

'What is the matter?' the merchant asked Nekhlyudov, hearing him utter a strange sound. This was the sound of weeping fiercely kept back. Nekhlyudov had not yet understood the significance of his present position, and attributed the sobs he could hardly keep back and the tears that filled his eyes to the weakness of his nerves. He put on his pince-nez in order to hide the tears, then got out his handkerchief and began blowing his nose.

Fear of the disgrace that would befall him if everyone in the court knew of his conduct stifled the inner working of his soul. This fear was, during this first period, stronger than all else.

Chapter 22

The trial — the summing up

After the last words of the prisoners had been heard, the form in which the questions were to be put to the jury was settled, which also took some time. At last the questions were formulated, and the president began the summing up.

Before putting the case to the jury, he spoke to them for some time in a pleasant, homely manner, explaining that burglary was burglary and theft was theft, and that stealing from a place which was under lock and key was stealing from a place under lock and key. While he was explaining this, he looked several times at Nekhludov as if wishing to impress upon him these important facts, in hopes that having understood it, Nekhludov would make his fellow-jurymen also understand it. When he considered that the jury were sufficiently imbued with these facts, he proceeded to enunciate another truth – namely, that a murder is an action which has the death of a human being as its consequence, and that poisoning could therefore also be termed murder. When, according to his opinion, this truth had also been received by the jury, he went on to explain that if theft and murder had been committed at the same time, the combination of the crimes was theft with murder.

Although he was himself anxious to finish as soon as possible, although he knew that his Swiss friend would be waiting for him, he had grown so used to his occupation that, having begun to speak, he could not stop himself, and therefore he went on to impress on the jury with much detail that if they found the prisoners guilty, they would have the right to give a verdict of guilty; and if they found them not guilty, to give a verdict of not guilty; and if they found them guilty of one of the crimes and not of the other, they might give a verdict of guilty on the one count and of not guilty on the other. Then he explained that though this right was given them they should use it with reason.

He was going to add that if they gave an affirmative answer to any question that was put to them they would thereby affirm everything included in the question, so that if they did not wish to affirm the whole of the question they should mention the part of the question they wished to be excepted. But, glancing at the clock, and seeing it was already five minutes to three, he resolved to trust to their being intelligent enough to understand this without further comment.

'The facts of this case are the following,' began the president, and repeated all that had already been said several times by the advocates, the public prosecutor and the witnesses.

The president spoke, and the members on each side of him listened with deeply-attentive expressions, but looked from time to time at the clock, for they considered the speech too long though very good – i.e., such as it ought to be. The public prosecutor, the lawyers, and, in fact, everyone in the court, shared the same impression. The president finished the summing up. Then he found it necessary to tell the jury what they all knew, or might have found out by reading it up – i.e., how they were to consider the case, count the votes, in case of a tie to acquit the prisoners, and so on.

Everything seemed to have been told; but no, the president could not forego his right of speaking as yet. It was so pleasant to hear the impressive tones of his own voice, and therefore he found it necessary to say a few words more about the importance of the rights given to the jury, how carefully they should use the rights and how they ought not to abuse them, about their being on their oath, that they were the conscience of society, that the secrecy of the debating-room should be considered sacred, etc.

From the time the president commenced his speech, Maslova watched him without moving her eyes as if afraid of losing a single word; so that Nekhlyudov was not afraid of meeting her eyes and kept looking at her all the time. And his mind passed through those phases in which a face which we have not seen for many years first strikes us with the outward changes brought about during the time of separation, and then gradually becomes more and more like its old self, when the changes made by time seem to disappear, and before our spiritual eyes rises only the principal expression of one exceptional, unique individuality. Yes, though dressed in a prison cloak, and in spite of the developed figure, the fullness of the bosom and lower part of the face, in spite of a few wrinkles on the forehead and temples and the swollen eyes, this was certainly the same Katusha who, on that Easter eve, had so innocently looked up to him whom she loved, with her fond, laughing eyes full of joy and life.

'What a strange coincidence that after ten years, during which I never saw her, this case should have come up today when I am on the jury, and that it is in the prisoners' dock that I see her again! And how will it end? Oh, dear, if they would only get on quicker.'

Still he would not give in to the feelings of repentance which began to arise within him. He tried to consider it all as a coincidence, which would pass without infringing his manner of life. He felt himself in the position of a puppy, when its master, taking it by the scruff of its neck, rubs its nose in the mess it has made. The puppy whines, draws back and wants to get away as far as possible from the effects of its misdeed, but the pitiless master does not let go.

And so Nekhlyudov, feeling all the repulsiveness of what he had done, felt also the powerful hand of the Master, but he did not feel the whole significance of his action yet and would not recognise the Master's hand. He did not wish to believe that it was the effect of his deed that lay before him, but the pitiless hand of the Master held him and he felt he could not get away. He was still keeping up his courage and sat on his chair in the first row in his usual self-possessed pose, one leg carelessly thrown over the other, and playing with his pince-nez. Yet all the while, in the depths of his soul, he felt the cruelty, cowardice and baseness, not only of this particular action of his but of his whole self-willed, depraved, cruel, idle life; and that dreadful veil which had in some unaccountable manner hidden from him this sin of his and the whole of his subsequent life was beginning to shake, and he caught glimpses of what was covered by that veil.

Chapter 23

The trial – the verdict

At last the president finished his speech, and lifting the list of
questions with a graceful movement of his arm he handed it to the
foreman, who came up to take it. The jury, glad to be able to
get into the debating-court, got up one after the other and left
the room, looking as if a bit ashamed of themselves and again not
knowing what to do with their hands. As soon as the door was
closed behind them a gendarme came up to it, pulled his sword
out of the scabbard, and, holding it up against his shoulder, stood
at the door. The judges got up and went away. The prisoners were
also led out. When the jury came into the debating-room the first
thing they did was to take out their cigarettes, as before, and begin
smoking. The sense of the unnaturalness and falseness of their
position, which all of them had experienced while sitting in their
places in the court, passed when they entered the debating-room
and started smoking, and they settled down with a feeling of relief
and at once began an animated conversation.

' 'Tisn't the girl's fault. She's got mixed up in it,' said the kindly
merchant. 'We must recommend her to mercy.'

'That's just what we are going to consider,' said the foreman.
'We must not give way to our personal impressions.'

'The president's summing up was good,' remarked the colonel.

'Good? Why, it nearly sent me to sleep!'

'The chief point is that the servants could have known nothing
about the money if Maslova had not been in accord with them,'
said the clerk of Jewish extraction.

'Well, do you think that it was she who stole the money?' asked
one of the jury.

'I will never believe it,' cried the kindly merchant; 'it was all
that red-eyed hag's doing.'

'They are a nice lot, all of them,' said the colonel.

'But she says she never went into the room.'

'Oh, believe her by all means.'

'I should not believe that jade, not for the world.'

'Whether you believe her or not does not settle the question,' said the clerk.

'The girl had the key,' said the colonel.

'What if she had?' retorted the merchant.

'And the ring?'

'But didn't she say all about it?' again cried the merchant. 'The fellow had a temper of his own, and had had a drop too much besides, and gave the girl a licking; what could be simpler? Well, then he's sorry – quite naturally. "There, never mind," says he; "take this." Why, I heard them say he was six foot five high; I should think he must have weighed about twenty stones.'

'That's not the point,' said Peter Gerasimovitch. 'The question is, whether she was the instigator and inciter in this affair, or the servants?'

'It was not possible for the servants to do it alone; she had the key.'

This kind of random talk went on for a considerable time. At last the foreman said: 'I beg your pardon, gentlemen, but had we not better take our places at the table and discuss the matter? Come, please.' And he took the chair.

The questions were expressed in the following manner.

1. Is the peasant of the village Borki, Krapivinskia district, Simeon Petrov Kartinkin, thirty-three years of age, guilty of having, in agreement with other persons, given the merchant Smelkov, on the 17th January, 188—, in the town of N— —, with intent to deprive him of life, for the purpose of robbing him, poisoned brandy, which caused Smelkov's death, and of having stolen from him about two thousand five hundred roubles in money and a diamond ring?

2. Is the meschanka Euphemia Ivanovna Botchkova, forty-three years of age, guilty of the crimes described above?

3. Is the meschanka Katerina Michaelovna Maslova, twenty-seven years of age, guilty of the crimes described in the first question?

4. If the prisoner Euphemia Botchkova is not guilty according to the first question, is she guilty of having, on the 17th January, in the town of N— —, while in service at the hotel Mauritania, stolen from a locked portmanteau, belonging to the merchant

Smelkov, a lodger in that hotel, and which was in the room occupied by him, two thousand five hundred roubles, for which object she unlocked the portmanteau with a key she brought and fitted to the lock?

The foreman read the first question.

'Well, gentlemen, what do you think?' This question was quickly answered. All agreed to say 'Guilty', as if convinced that Kartinkin had taken part both in the poisoning and the robbery. An old *artelshik*,* whose answers were all in favour of acquittal, was the only exception.

The foreman thought he did not understand, and began to point out to him that everything tended to prove Kartinkin's guilt. The old man answered that he did understand, but still thought it better to have pity on him. 'We are not saints ourselves,' and he kept to his opinion.

The answer to the second question concerning Botchkova was, after much dispute and many exclamations, answered by the words, 'Not guilty', there being no clear proofs of her having taken part in the poisoning – a fact her advocate had strongly insisted on. The merchant, anxious to acquit Maslova, insisted that Botchkova was the chief instigator of it all. Many of the jury shared this view, but the foreman, wishing to be in strict accord with the law, declared they had no grounds to consider her as an accomplice in the poisoning. After much disputing the foreman's opinion triumphed.

To the fourth question concerning Botchkova the answer was 'Guilty'. But on the *artelshik*'s insistence she was recommended to mercy.

The third question, concerning Maslova, raised a fierce dispute. The foreman maintained she was guilty both of the poisoning and the theft, to which the merchant would not agree. The colonel, the clerk and the old *artelshik* sided with the merchant, the rest seemed shaky, and the opinion of the foreman began to gain ground, chiefly because all the jurymen were getting tired, and preferred to take up the view that would bring them sooner to a decision and thus liberate them.

From all that had passed, and from his former knowledge of Maslova, Nekhlyudov was certain that she was innocent of both

* Member of an artel, an association of workmen, in which the members share profits and liabilities.

the theft and the poisoning. And he felt sure that all the others would come to the same conclusion. When he saw that the merchant's awkward defence (evidently based on his physical admiration for her, which he did not even try to hide) and the foreman's insistence, and especially everybody's weariness, were all tending to her condemnation, he longed to state his objections, yet dared not, lest his relations with Maslova should be discovered. He felt he could not allow things to go on without stating his objection; and, blushing and growing pale again, was about to speak when Peter Gerasimovitch, irritated by the authoritative manner of the foreman, began to raise his objections and said the very things Nekhlyudov was about to say.

'Allow me one moment,' he said. 'You seem to think that her having the key proves she is guilty of the theft; but what could be easier than for the servants to open the portmanteau with a false key after she was gone?'

'Of course, of course,' said the merchant.

'She could not have taken the money, because in her position she would hardly know what to do with it.'

'That's just what I say,' remarked the merchant.

'But it is very likely that her coming put the idea into the servants' heads and that they grasped the opportunity and shoved all the blame on her.' Peter Gerasimovitch spoke so irritably that the foreman became irritated too, and went on obstinately defending the opposite views; but Peter Gerasimovitch spoke so convincingly that the majority agreed with him, and decided that Maslova was not guilty of stealing the money and that the ring was given her.

But when the question of her having taken part in the poisoning was raised, her zealous defender, the merchant, declared that she must be acquitted, because she could have no reason for the poisoning. The foreman, however, said that it was impossible to acquit her, because she herself had pleaded guilty to having given the powder.

'Yes, but thinking it was opium,' said the merchant.

'Opium can also deprive one of life,' said the colonel, who was fond of wandering from the subject, and he began telling how his brother-in-law's wife would have died of an overdose of opium if there had not been a doctor near at hand to take

the necessary measures. The colonel told his story so impressively, with such self-possession and dignity, that no one had
the courage to interrupt him. Only the clerk, infected by his
example, decided to break in with a story of his own: 'There are
some who get so used to it that they can take forty drops. I have
a relative – ' but the colonel would not stand the interruption,
and went on to relate what effects the opium had on his brother-
in-law's wife.

'But, gentlemen, do you know it is getting on towards five
o'clock?' said one of the jury.

'Well, gentlemen, what are we to say, then?' inquired the
foreman. 'Shall we say she is guilty, but without intent to rob?
And without stealing any property? Will that do?' Peter Gerasimovitch, pleased with his victory, agreed.

'But she must be recommended to mercy,' said the merchant.

All agreed; only the old *artelshik* insisted that they should say
'Not guilty'.

'It comes to the same thing,' explained the foreman; 'without
intent to rob, and without stealing any property. Therefore, "Not
guilty", that's evident.'

'All right; that'll do. And we recommend her to mercy,' said the
merchant, gaily.

They were all so tired, so confused by the discussions, that
nobody thought of saying that she was guilty of giving the
powder but without the intent of taking life. Nekhlyudov was
so excited that he did not notice this omission, and so the
answers were written down in the form agreed upon and taken
to the court.

Rabelais says that a lawyer who was trying a case quoted all sorts
of laws, read twenty pages of judicial senseless Latin, and then
proposed to the judges to throw dice, and if the numbers proved
odd the defendant would be right, if not, the plaintiff.

It was much the same in this case. The resolution was taken,
not because everybody agreed upon it, but because the president,
who had been summing up at such length, omitted to say what
he always said on such occasions, that the answer might be, 'Yes,
guilty, but without the intent of taking life'; because the colonel
had related the story of his brother-in-law's wife at such great
length; because Nekhlyudov was too excited to notice that the

proviso 'without intent to take life' had been omitted, and thought that the words 'without intent' nullified the conviction; because Peter Gerasimovitch had retired from the room while the questions and answers were being read, and chiefly because, being tired, and wishing to get away as soon as possible, all were ready to agree with the decision which would bring matters to an end soonest.

The jurymen rang the bell. The gendarme who had stood outside the door with his sword drawn put the sword back into the scabbard and stepped aside. The judges took their seats and the jury came out one by one.

The foreman brought in the paper with an air of solemnity and handed it to the president, who looked at it, and, spreading out his hands in astonishment, turned to consult his companions. The president was surprised that the jury, having put in a proviso – without intent to rob – did not put in a second proviso – without intent to take life. From the decision of the jury it followed that Maslova had not stolen, nor robbed, and yet poisoned a man without any apparent reason.

'Just see what an absurd decision they have come to,' he whispered to the member on his left. 'This means penal servitude in Siberia, and she is innocent.'

'Surely you do not mean to say she is innocent?' answered the serious member.

'Yes, she is positively innocent. I think this is a case for putting Article 817 into practice.' (Article 817 states that if the Court considers the decision of the jury unjust it may set it aside.)

'What do you think?' said the president, turning to the other member. The kindly member did not answer at once. He looked at the number on a paper before him and added up the figures; the sum would not divide by three. He had settled in his mind that if it did divide by three he would agree to the president's proposal, but though the sum would not so divide his kindness made him agree all the same.

'I, too, think it should be done,' he said.

'And you?' asked the president, turning to the serious member.

'On no account,' he answered, firmly. 'As it is, the papers accuse the jury of acquitting prisoners. What will they say if the Court does it? I shall not agree to that on any account.'

The president looked at his watch. 'It is a pity, but what's to be done?' and handed the questions to the foreman to read out. All got up, and the foreman, stepping from foot to foot, coughed, and read the questions and the answers. All the Court, secretary, advocates, and even the public prosecutor, expressed surprise. The prisoners sat impassive, evidently not understanding the meaning of the answers. Everybody sat down again, and the president asked the prosecutor what punishments the prisoners were to be subjected to.

The prosecutor, glad of his unexpected success in getting Maslova convicted, and attributing the success entirely to his own eloquence, looked up the necessary information, rose and said: 'With Simeon Kartinkin I should deal according to Statute 1,452 paragraph 93. Euphemia Botchkova according to Statute . . . etc. Katerina Maslova according to Statute . . . etc.'

All three punishments were the heaviest that could be inflicted.

'The Court will adjourn to consider the sentence,' said the president, rising. Everybody rose after him, and with the pleasant feeling of a task well done began to leave the room or move about in it.

'D'you know, sirs, we have made a shameful hash of it?' said Peter Gerasimovitch, approaching Nekhlyudov, to whom the foreman was relating something. 'Why, we've got her to Siberia.'

'What are you saying?' exclaimed Nekhlyudov. This time he did not notice the teacher's familiarity.

'Why, we did not put in our answer "Guilty, but without intent of causing death." The secretary just told me the public prosecutor is for condemning her to fifteen years' penal servitude.'

'Well, but it was decided so,' said the foreman.

Peter Gerasimovitch began to dispute this, saying that since she did not take the money it followed naturally that she could not have had any intention of committing murder.

'But I read the answer before going out,' said the foreman, defending himself, 'and nobody objected.'

'I had just then gone out of the room,' said Peter Gerasimovitch, turning to Nekhlyudov, 'and your thoughts must have been wool-gathering to let the thing pass.'

'I never imagined this,' Nekhlyudov replied.

'Oh, you didn't?'

'Oh, well, we can get it put right,' said Nekhlyudov.

'Oh dear, no; it's finished.'

Nekhlyudov looked at the prisoners. They whose fate was being decided still sat motionless behind the grating in front of the soldiers. Maslova was smiling. Another feeling stirred in Nekhlyudov's soul. Up to now, expecting her acquittal and thinking she would remain in the town, he was uncertain how to act towards her. Any kind of relations with her would be so very difficult. But Siberia and penal servitude at once cut off every possibility of any kind of relations with her. The wounded bird would stop struggling in the game-bag, and no longer remind him of its existence.

Chapter 24

The trial – the sentence

Peter Gerasimovitch's assumption was correct. The president came back from the debating room with a paper, and read as follows: 'April 28th, 188—. By His Imperial Majesty's ukase No. —. The Criminal Court, on the strength of the decision of the jury, in accordance with Section 3 of Statute 771, Section 3 of Statutes 770 and 777, decrees that the peasant, Simeon Kartinkin, thirty-three years of age, and the meschanka Katerina Maslova, twenty-seven years of age, are to be deprived of all property rights and to be sent to penal servitude in Siberia, Kartinkin for eight, Maslova for four years, with the consequences stated in Statute 25 of the code. The meschanka Botchkova, forty-three years of age, to be deprived of all special personal and acquired rights, and to be imprisoned for three years with consequences in accord with Statute 48 of the code. The costs of the case to be borne equally by the prisoners; and, in the case of their being without sufficient property, the costs to be transferred to the Treasury. Articles of material evidence to be sold, the ring to be returned, the phials destroyed.' Botchkova was condemned to prison, Simeon Kartinken and Katerina Maslova to the loss of all special rights and privileges and to penal servitude in Siberia, he for eight and she for four years.

Kartinkin stood holding his arms close to his sides and moving his lips. Botchkova seemed perfectly calm. Maslova, when she heard the sentence, blushed scarlet. 'I'm not guilty, not guilty!' she suddenly cried, so that it resounded through the room. 'It is a sin! I am not guilty! I never wished – I never thought! It is the truth I am saying – the truth!' and sinking on the bench she burst into tears and sobbed aloud. When Kartinkin and Botchkova went out she still sat crying, so that a gendarme had to touch the sleeve of her cloak.

'No; it is impossible to leave it as it is,' said Nekhlyudov to himself, utterly forgetting his bad thoughts. He did not know why he wished to look at her once more, but hurried out into the corridor. There was quite a crowd at the door. The advocates and jury were going out, pleased to have finished the business, and he was obliged to wait a few seconds, and when he at last got out into the corridor she was far in front. He hurried along the corridor after her, regardless of the attention he was arousing, caught her up, passed her, and stopped. She had ceased crying and only sobbed, wiping her red, discoloured face with the end of the kerchief on her head. She passed without noticing him. Then he hurried back to see the president. The latter had already left the court, and Nekhlyudov followed him into the lobby and went up to him just as he had put on his light grey overcoat and was taking the silver-mounted walking-stick which an attendant was handing him.

'Sir, may I have a few words with you concerning some business I have just decided upon?' said Nekhlyudov. 'I am one of the jury.'

'Oh, certainly, Prince Nekhlyudov. I shall be delighted. I think we have met before,' said the president, pressing Nekhlyudov's hand and recalling with pleasure the evening when he first met Nekhlyudov, and when he had danced so gaily, better than all the young people. 'What can I do for you?'

'There is a mistake in the answer concerning Maslova. She is not guilty of the poisoning and yet she is condemned to penal servitude,' said Nekhlyudov, with a preoccupied and gloomy air.

'The Court passed the sentence in accordance with the answers you yourselves gave,' said the president, moving towards the front door; 'though they did not seem to be quite in accord.' And he remembered that he had been going to explain to the jury that a verdict of 'guilty' meant guilty of intentional murder unless the words 'without intent to take life' were added, but had, in his hurry to get the business over, omitted to do so.

'Yes, but could not the mistake be rectified?'

'A reason for an appeal can always be found. You will have to speak to an advocate,' said the president, putting on his hat a little to one side and continuing to move towards the door.

'But this is terrible.'

'Well, you see, there were two possibilities before Maslova,' said the president, evidently wishing to be as polite and pleasant to Nekhlyudov as he could. Then, having arranged his whiskers over his coat collar, he put his hand lightly under Nekhlyudov's elbow, and, still directing his steps towards the front door, he said, 'You are going, too?'

'Yes,' said Nekhlyudov, quickly getting his coat, and following him.

They went out into the bright, merry sunlight, and had to raise their voices because of the rattling of the wheels on the pavement.

'The situation is a curious one, you see,' said the president; 'what lay before this Maslova was one of two things: either to be almost acquitted and only imprisoned for a short time or, taking the preliminary confinement into consideration, perhaps not at all – or Siberia. There is nothing between. Had you but added the words, "without intent to cause death", she would have been acquitted.'

'Yes, it was inexcusable of me to omit that,' said Nekhlyudov.

'That's where the whole matter lies,' said the president, with a smile, and looked at his watch. He had only three-quarters of an hour left before the time appointed by his Clara would elapse.

'Now, if you like to speak to the advocates you'll have to find a reason for an appeal; that can be easily done.' Then, turning to an *isvostchik*, he called out, 'To the Dvoryanskaya thirty copecks; I never give more.' 'All right, your honour; here you are.'

'Good afternoon. If I can be of any use, my address is House Dvornikov, on the Dvoryanskaya; it's easy to remember.' And he bowed in a friendly manner as he got into the trap and drove off.

Chapter 25

Nekhlyudov consults an advocate

His conversation with the president and the fresh air quieted Nekhlyudov a little. He now thought that the feelings experienced by him had been exaggerated by the unusual surroundings in which he had spent the whole of the morning, and by that wonderful and startling coincidence. Still, it was absolutely necessary to take some steps to lighten Maslova's fate, and to take them quickly. 'Yes, at once! It will be best to find out here in the court where the advocate Fanarin or Mikishin lives.' These were two well-known advocates whom Nekhlyudov called to mind. He returned to the court, took off his overcoat, and went upstairs. In the first corridor he met Fanarin himself. He stopped him, and told him that he was just going to look him up on a matter of business.

Fanarin knew Nekhlyudov by sight and name, and said he would be very glad to be of service to him.

'Though I am rather tired, still, if your business will not take very long, perhaps you might tell me what it is now. Will you step in here?' And he led Nekhlyudov into a room, probably some judge's cabinet. They sat down by the table.

'Well, and what is your business?'

'First of all, I must ask you to keep the business private. I do not want it known that I take an interest in the affair.'

'Oh, that of course. Well?'

'I was on the jury today, and we have condemned a woman to Siberia, an innocent woman. This bothers me very much.' Nekhlyudov, to his own surprise, blushed and became confused. Fanarin glanced at him rapidly, and looked down again, listening.

'Well?'

'We have condemned a woman, and I should like to appeal to a higher court.'

'To the Senate, you mean,' said Fanarin, correcting him.

'Yes, and I should like to ask you to take the case in hand.' Nekhlyudov wanted to get the most difficult part over, and added, 'I shall take the costs of the case on myself, whatever they may be.'

'Oh, we shall settle all that,' said the advocate, smiling with condescension at Nekhlyudov's inexperience in these matters. 'What is the case?'

Nekhlyudov stated what had happened.

'All right. I shall look the case through tomorrow or the day after – no, better on Thursday. If you will come to me at six o'clock I will give you an answer. Well, and now let us go; I have to make a few inquiries here.'

Nekhlyudov took leave of him and went out. This talk with the advocate, and the fact that he had taken measures for Maslova's defence, quieted him still further. He went out into the street. The weather was beautiful, and he joyfully drew in a long breath of spring air. He was at once surrounded by *isvostchiks* offering their services, but he went on foot. A whole swarm of pictures and memories of Katusha and his conduct to her began whirling in his brain, and he felt depressed and everything appeared gloomy. 'No, I shall consider all this later on; I must now get rid of all these disagreeable impressions,' he thought to himself.

He remembered the Korchagin's dinner and looked at his watch. It was not yet too late to get there in time. He heard the ring of a passing tramcar, ran to catch it, and jumped on. He jumped off again when they got to the market-place, took a good *isvostchik*, and ten minutes later was at the entrance of the Korchagins' big house.

Chapter 26

The house of Korchagin

'Please to walk in, your excellency,' said the friendly, fat door-keeper of the Korchagins' big house, opening the door, which moved noiselessly on its patent English hinges. 'You are expected. They are at dinner. My orders were to admit only you.' The doorkeeper went as far as the staircase and rang.

'Are there any strangers?' asked Nekhlyudov, taking off his overcoat.

'Mr Kolosov and Michael Sergeivitch only, besides the family.'

A very handsome footman with whiskers, in a swallow-tail coat and white gloves, looked down from the landing.

'Please to walk up, your excellency,' he said. 'You are expected.'

Nekhlyudov went up and passed through the splendid large dancing-room, which he knew so well, into the dining-room. There the whole Korchagin family – except the mother, Sophia Vasilievna, who never left her cabinet – were sitting round the table. At the head of the table sat old Korchagin; on his left the doctor, and on his right, a visitor, Ivan Ivanovitch Kolosov, a former *Maréchal de Noblesse*, now a bank director, Korchagin's friend and a Liberal. Next on the left side sat Miss Rayner, the governess of Missy's little sister, and the four-year-old girl herself. Opposite them, Missy's brother, Petya, the only son of the Korchagins, a public-school boy of the Sixth Class. It was because of his examinations that the whole family were still in town. Next to him sat a University student who was coaching him, and Missy's cousin, Michael Sergeyevitch Telegin, generally called Misha; opposite him, Katerina Alexeyevna, a forty-year-old maiden lady, a Slavophil; and at the foot of the table sat Missy herself, with an empty place by her side.

'Ah! that's right! Sit down. We are still at the fish,' said old Korchagin with difficulty, chewing carefully with his false teeth, and lifting his bloodshot eyes (which had no visible lids to them) to Nekhlyudov.

'Stephen!' he said, with his mouth full, addressing the stout, dignified butler, and pointing with his eyes to the empty place. Though Nekhlyudov knew Korchagin very well, and had often seen him at dinner, today this red face with the sensual smacking lips, the fat neck above the napkin stuck into his waistcoat, and the whole over-fed military figure, struck him very disagreeably. Then Nekhlyudov remembered, without wishing to, what he knew of the cruelty of this man, who, when in command, used to have men flogged, and even hanged, without rhyme or reason, simply because he was rich and had no need to curry favour.

'Immediately, your excellency,' said Stephen, getting a large soup ladle out of the sideboard, which was decorated with a number of silver vases. He made a sign with his head to the handsome footman, who began at once to arrange the untouched knives and forks and the napkin, elaborately folded with the embroidered family crest uppermost, in front of the empty place next to Missy. Nekhlyudov went round shaking hands with everyone, and all, except old Korchagin and the ladies, rose when he approached. And this walk round the table, this shaking the hands of people, with many of whom he never talked, seemed unpleasant and odd. He excused himself for being late, and was about to sit down between Missy and Katerina Alexeyevna, but old Korchagin insisted that if he would not take a glass of vodka he should at least take a bit of something to whet his appetite, at the side table, on which stood small dishes of lobster, caviare, cheese, and salt herrings. Nekhlyudov did not know how hungry he was until he began to eat, and then, having taken some bread and cheese, he went on eating eagerly.

'Well, have you succeeded in undermining the basis of society?' asked Kolosov, ironically quoting an expression used by a retrograde newspaper in attacking trial by jury. 'Acquitted the culprits and condemned the innocent, have you?'

'Undermining the basis – undermining the basis,' repeated Prince Korchagin, laughing. He had a firm faith in the wisdom and learning of his chosen friend and companion.

At the risk of seeming rude, Nekhlyudov left Kolosov's question unanswered, and sitting down to his steaming soup, went on eating.

'Do let him eat,' said Missy, with a smile. The pronoun him she used as a reminder of her intimacy with Nekhlyudov. Kolosov went on in a loud voice and lively manner to give the contents of the article against trial by jury which had aroused his indignation. Missy's cousin, Michael Sergeivitch, endorsed all his statements, and related the contents of another article in the same paper. Missy was, as usual, very *distinguée*, and well, unobtrusively well, dressed.

'You must be terribly tired,' she said, after waiting until Nekhlyudov had swallowed what was in his mouth.

'Not particularly. And you? Have you been to look at the pictures?' he asked.

'No, we put that off. We have been playing tennis at the Salamatovs'. It is quite true, Mr Crooks plays remarkably well.'

Nekhlyudov had come here in order to distract his thoughts, for he used to like being in this house, both because its refined luxury had a pleasant effect on him and because of the atmosphere of tender flattery that unobtrusively surrounded him. But today everything in the house was repulsive to him – everything: beginning with the doorkeeper, the broad staircase, the flowers, the footman, the table decorations, up to Missy herself, who today seemed unattractive and affected. Kolosov's self-assured, trivial tone of liberalism was unpleasant, as was also the sensual, self-satisfied, bull-like appearance of old Korchagin, and the French phrases of Katerina Alexeyevna, the Slavophil. The constrained looks of the governess and the student were unpleasant, too, but most unpleasant of all was the pronoun *him* that Missy had used. Nekhlyudov had long been wavering between two ways of regarding Missy; sometimes he looked at her as if by moonlight, and could see in her nothing but what was beautiful, fresh, pretty, clever and natural; then suddenly, as if the bright sun shone on her, he saw her defects and could not help seeing them. This was such a day for him. Today he saw all the wrinkles of her face, knew which of her teeth were false, saw the way her hair was crimped, the sharpness of her elbows, and, above all, how large her thumb-nail was and how like her father's.

'Tennis is a dull game,' said Kolosov; 'we used to play *lapta* when we were children. That was much more amusing.'

'Oh, no, you never tried it; it's awfully interesting,' said Missy, laying, it seemed to Nekhlyudov, a very affected stress on the word 'awfully'. Then a dispute arose in which Michael Serge-yevitch, Katerina Alexeyevna and all the others took part, except the governess, the student and the children, who sat silent and wearied.

'Oh, these everlasting disputes!' said old Korchagin, laughing, and he pulled the napkin out of his waistcoat, noisily pushed back his chair, which the footman instantly caught hold of, and left the table.

Everybody rose after him, and went up to another table on which stood glasses of scented water. They rinsed their mouths, then resumed the conversation, interesting to no one.

'Don't you think so?' said Missy to Nekhlyudov, calling for a confirmation of the statement that nothing shows up a man's character like a game. She noticed that preoccupied and, as it seemed to her, dissatisfied look which she feared, and she wanted to find out what had caused it.

'Really, I can't tell; I have never thought about it,' Nekhlyudov answered.

'Will you come to mamma?' asked Missy.

'Yes, yes,' he said, in a tone which plainly proved that he did not want to go, and took out a cigarette.

She looked at him in silence, with a questioning look, and he felt ashamed. 'To come into a house and give the people the dumps,' he thought about himself; then, trying to be amiable, said that he would go with pleasure if the princess would admit him.

'Oh, yes! Mamma will be pleased. You may smoke there; and Ivan Ivanovitch is also there.'

The mistress of the house, Princess Sophia Vasilievna, was a recumbent lady. It was the eighth year that, when visitors were present, she lay in lace and ribbons, surrounded with velvet, gilding, ivory, bronze, lacquer and flowers, never going out, and only, as she put it, receiving intimate friends, i.e., those who according to her idea stood out from the common herd.

Nekhlyudov was admitted into the number of these friends because he was considered clever, because his mother had been an intimate friend of the family, and because it was desirable that Missy should marry him.

Sophia Vasilievna's room lay beyond the large and the small drawing-rooms. In the large drawing-room, Missy, who was in front of Nekhlyudov, stopped resolutely, and taking hold of the back of a small green chair, faced him.

Missy was very anxious to get married, and as he was a suitable match and she also liked him, she had accustomed herself to the thought that he should be hers (not she his). To lose him would be very mortifying. She now began talking to him in order to get him to explain his intentions.

'I see something has happened,' she said. 'Tell me, what is the matter with you?'

He remembered the meeting in the law court, and frowned and blushed.

'Yes, something has happened,' he said, wishing to be truthful; 'a very unusual and serious event.'

'What is it, then? Can you not tell me what it is?' She was pursuing her aim with that unconscious yet obstinate cunning often observable in the mentally diseased.

'Not now. Please do not ask me to tell you. I have not yet had time fully to consider it,' and he blushed still more.

'And so you will not tell me?' A muscle twitched in her face and she pushed back the chair she was holding. 'Well then, come!' She shook her head as if to expel useless thoughts, and, faster than usual, went on in front of him.

He fancied that her mouth was unnaturally compressed in order to keep back the tears. He was ashamed of having hurt her, and yet he knew that the least weakness on his part would mean disaster, i.e., would bind him to her. And today he feared this more than anything, and silently followed her to the princess's cabinet.

Chapter 27

Missy's mother

Princess Sophia Vasilievna, Missy's mother, had finished her very elaborate and nourishing dinner. (She had it always alone, that no one should see her performing this unpoetical function.) By her couch stood a small table with her coffee, and she was smoking a *pachitos*. Princess Sophia Vasilievna was a long, thin woman, with dark hair, large black eyes and long teeth, and still pretended to be young.

Her intimacy with the doctor was being talked about. Nekhlyudov had known that for some time; but when he saw the doctor sitting by her couch, his oily, glistening beard parted in the middle, he not only remembered the rumours about them, but felt greatly disgusted. By the table, on a low, soft, easy chair, next to Sophia Vasilievna, sat Kolosov, stirring his coffee. A glass of liqueur stood on the table. Missy came in with Nekhlyudov, but did not remain in the room.

'When mamma gets tired of you and drives you away, then come to me,' she said, turning to Kolosov and Nekhlyudov, speaking as if nothing had occurred; then she went away, smiling merrily and stepping noiselessly on the thick carpet.

'How do you do, dear friend? Sit down and talk,' said Princess Sophia Vasilievna, with her affected but very naturally-acted smile, showing her fine, long teeth – a splendid imitation of what her own had once been. 'I hear that you have come from the Law Courts very much depressed. I think it must be very trying to a person with a heart,' she added in French.

'Yes, that is so,' said Nekhlyudov. 'One often feels one's own de – one feels one has no right to judge.' [check]

'*Comme c'est vrai*,' she cried, as if struck by the truth of this remark. She was in the habit of artfully flattering all those with whom she conversed. 'Well, and what of your picture? It does interest me so. If I were not such a sad invalid I should have been to see it long ago,' she said.

'I have quite given it up,' Nekhlyudov replied drily. The falseness of her flattery seemed as evident to him today as her age, which she was trying to conceal, and he could not put himself into the right state to behave politely.

'Oh, that *is* a pity! Why, he has a real talent for art; I have it from Repin's own lips,' she added, turning to Kolosov.

'Why is it she is not ashamed of lying so?' Nekhlyudov thought, and frowned.

When she had convinced herself that Nekhlyudov was in a bad temper and that one could not get him into an agreeable and clever conversation, Sophia Vasilievna turned to Kolosov, asking his opinion of a new play. She asked it in a tone as if Kolosov's opinion would decide all doubts, and each word of this opinion be worthy of being immortalised. Kolosov found fault both with the play and its author, and that led him to express his views on art. Princess Sophia Vasilievna, while trying at the same time to defend the play, seemed impressed by the truth of his arguments, either giving in at once, or at least modifying her opinion. Nekhlyudov looked and listened, but neither saw nor heard what was going on before him.

Listening now to Sophia Vasilievna, now to Kolosov, Nekhlyudov noticed that neither he nor she cared anything about the play or each other, and that if they talked it was only to gratify the

physical desire to move the muscles of the throat and tongue after
having eaten; and that Kolosov, having drunk vodka, wine and
liqueur, was a little tipsy. Not tipsy like the peasants who drink
seldom, but like people to whom drinking wine has become a
habit. He did not reel about or talk nonsense, but he was in a state
that was not normal; excited and self-satisfied. Nekhlyudov also
noticed that during the conversation Princess Sophia Vasilievna
kept glancing uneasily at the window, through which a slanting
ray of sunshine, which might vividly light up her aged face, was
beginning to creep up.

'How true,' she said in reference to some remark of Kolosov's,
touching the button of an electric bell by the side of her couch.
The doctor rose, and, like one who is at home, left the room
without saying anything. Sophia Vasilievna followed him with her
eyes and continued the conversation.

'Please, Philip, draw these curtains,' she said, pointing to the
window, when the handsome footman came in answer to the bell.
'No; whatever you may say, there is some mysticism in him;
without mysticism there can be no poetry,' she said, with one of
her black eyes angrily following the footman's movements as he
was drawing the curtains. 'Without poetry, mysticism is superstition; without mysticism, poetry is – prose,' she continued, with
a sorrowful smile, still not losing sight of the footman and the
curtains. 'Philip, not that curtain; the one on the large window,'
she exclaimed, in a suffering tone. Sophia Vasilievna was evidently
pitying herself for having to make the effort of saying these words;
and, to soothe her feelings, she raised to her lips a scented,
smoking cigarette with her jewel-bedecked fingers.

The broad-chested, muscular, handsome Philip bowed slightly,
as if begging pardon; and stepping lightly across the carpet with his
broad-calved, strong, legs, obediently and silently went to the
other window, and, looking at the princess, carefully began to
arrange the curtain so that not a single ray dared fall on her. But
again he did not satisfy her, and again she had to interrupt the
conversation about mysticism, and correct in a martyred tone the
unintelligent Philip, who was tormenting her so pitilessly. For a
moment a light flashed in Philip's eyes.

' "The devil take you! What do you want?" was probably what
he said to himself,' thought Nekhlyudov, who had been observing

all this scene. But the strong, handsome Philip at once managed to conceal the signs of his impatience, and went on quietly carrying out the orders of the worn, weak, false Sophia Vasilievna.

'Of course, there is a good deal of truth in Lombroso's teaching,' said Kolosov, lolling back in the low chair and looking at Sophia Vasilievna with sleepy eyes; 'but he overstepped the mark. Oh, yes.'

'And you? Do you believe in heredity?' asked Sophia Vasilievna, turning to Nekhlyudov, whose silence annoyed her. 'In heredity?' he asked. 'No, I don't.' At this moment his whole mind was taken up by strange images that in some unaccountable way rose up in his imagination. By the side of this strong and handsome Philip he seemed at this minute to see the nude figure of Kolosov as an artist's model; with his stomach like a melon, his bald head, and his arms without muscle, like pestles. In the same dim way the limbs of Sophia Vasilievna, now covered with silks and velvets, rose up in his mind as they must be in reality; but this mental picture was too horrid and he tried to drive it away.

'Well, you know Missy is waiting for you,' she said. 'Go and find her. She wants to play a new piece by Grieg to you; it is most interesting.'

'She did not mean to play anything; the woman is simply lying, for some reason or other,' thought Nekhlyudov, rising and pressing Sophia Vasilievna's transparent and bony, ringed hand.

Katerina Alexeyevna met him in the drawing-room, and at once began, in French, as usual:

'I see the duties of a juryman act depressingly upon you.'

'Yes; pardon me, I am in low spirits today, and have no right to weary others by my presence,' said Nekhlyudov.

'Why are you in low spirits?'

'Allow me not to speak about that,' he said, looking round for his hat.

'Don't you remember how you used to say that we must always tell the truth? And what cruel truths you used to tell us all! Why do you not wish to speak out now? Don't you remember, Missy?' she said, turning to Missy, who had just come in.

'We were playing a game then,' said Nekhlyudov, seriously; 'one may tell the truth in a game, but in reality we are so bad – I mean I am so bad – that I, at least, cannot tell the truth.'

'Oh, do not correct yourself, but rather tell us why *we* are so bad,' said Katerina Alexeyevna, playing with her words and pretending not to notice how serious Nekhlyudov was.

'Nothing is worse than to confess to being in low spirits,' said Missy. 'I never do it, and therefore am always in good spirits.'

Nekhlyudov felt as a horse must feel when it is being caressed to make it submit to having the bit put in its mouth and be harnessed, and today he felt less than ever inclined to draw.

'Well, are you coming into my room? We will try to cheer you up.'

He excused himself, saying he had to be at home, and began taking leave. Missy kept his hand longer than usual.

'Remember that what is important to you is important to your friends,' she said. 'Are you coming tomorrow?'

'I hardly expect to,' said Nekhlyudov; and feeling ashamed, without knowing whether for her or for himself, he blushed and went away.

'What is it? *Comme celà m'intrigue,*' said Katerina Alexeyevna. 'I must find it out. I suppose it is some *affaire d'amour propre; il est très susceptible, notre cher Mitya.*'

'*Plutôt une affaire d'amour sale,*' Missy was going to say, but stopped and looked down with a face from which all the light had gone – a very different face from the one with which she had looked at him. She would not mention to Katerina Alexeyevna even, so vulgar a pun, but only said, 'We all have our good and our bad days.'

'Is it possible that he, too, will deceive?' she thought; 'after all that has happened it would be very bad of him.'

If Missy had had to explain what she meant by 'after all that has happened', she could have said nothing definite, and yet she knew that he had not only excited her hopes but had almost given her a promise. No definite words had passed between them – only looks and smiles and hints; and yet she considered him as her own, and to lose him would be very hard.

Chapter 28

The awakening

'Shameful and stupid, horrid and shameful!' Nekhlyudov kept saying to himself, as he walked home along the familiar streets. The depression he had felt whilst speaking to Missy would not leave him. He felt that, looking at it externally, as it were, he was in the right, for he had never said anything to her that could be considered binding, never made her an offer; but he knew that in reality he had bound himself to her, had promised to be hers. And yet today he felt with his whole being that he could not marry her.

'Shameful and horrid, horrid and shameful!' he repeated to himself, with reference not only to his relations with Missy but also to the rest. 'Everything is horrid and shameful,' he muttered, as he stepped into the porch of his house. 'I am not going to have any supper,' he said to his manservant Corney, who followed him into the dining-room, where the cloth was laid for supper and tea. 'You may go.'

'Yes, sir,' said Corney, yet he did not go, but began clearing the supper off the table. Nekhlyudov looked at Corney with a feeling of ill-will. He wished to be left alone, and it seemed to him that everybody was bothering him in order to spite him. When Corney had gone away with the supper things, Nekhlyudov moved to the tea urn and was about to make himself some tea, but hearing Agraphena Petrovna's footsteps, he went hurriedly into the drawing-room, to avoid being seen by her, and shut the door after him. In this drawing-room his mother had died three months before. On entering the room, in which two lamps with reflectors were burning, one lighting up his father's and the other his mother's portrait, he remembered what his last relations with his mother had been. And they also seemed shameful and horrid. He remembered how, during the latter period of her illness, he had simply wished her to die. He had said to himself that he wished it for her sake, that she might be released from her suffering, but in reality he wished to be released from the sight of her sufferings for his own sake.

Trying to recall a pleasant image of her, he went up to look at her portrait, painted by a celebrated artist for eight hundred roubles. She was depicted in a very low-necked black velvet dress. There was something very revolting and blasphemous in this representation of his mother as a half-nude beauty. It was all the more disgusting because three months ago, in this very room, lay this same woman, dried up to a mummy. And he remembered how a few days before her death she clasped his hand with her bony, discoloured fingers, looked into his eyes, and said: 'Do not judge me, Mitya, if I have not done what I should,' and how the tears came into her eyes, grown pale with suffering.

'Ah, how horrid!' he said to himself, looking up once more at the half-naked woman, with the splendid marble shoulders and arms, and the triumphant smile on her lips. 'Oh, how horrid!' The bared shoulders of the portrait reminded him of another, a young woman, whom he had seen exposed in the same way a few days before. It was Missy, who had devised an excuse for calling him into her room just as she was ready to go to a ball, so that he should see her in her ball dress. It was with disgust that he remembered her fine shoulders and arms. 'And that father of hers, with his doubtful past and his cruelties, and the *bel-esprit* her mother, with her doubtful reputation.' All this disgusted him, and also made him feel ashamed. 'Shameful and horrid; horrid and shameful!'

'No, no,' he thought; 'freedom from all these false relations with the Korchagins and Mary Vasilievna and the inheritance and from all the rest must be got. Oh, to breathe freely, to go abroad, to Rome and work at my picture!' He remembered the doubts he had about his talent for art. 'Well, never mind; only just to breathe freely. First Constantinople, then Rome. Only just to get through with this jury business, and arrange with the advocate first.'

Then suddenly there arose in his mind an extremely vivid picture of a prisoner with black, slightly-squinting eyes, and how she began to cry when the last words of the prisoners had been heard; and he hurriedly put out his cigarette, pressing it into the ash-pan, lit another, and began pacing up and down the room. One after another the scenes he had lived through with her rose in his mind. He recalled that last interview with her. He remembered the white dress and blue sash, the early Mass. 'Why, I loved her, really loved her with a good, pure love, that night; I loved her even before: yes, I loved her when I lived with my aunts the first time and was writing my composition.' And he remembered himself as he had been then. A breath of that freshness, youth and fulness of life seemed to touch him, and he grew painfully sad. The difference between what he had been then and what he was now, was enormous – just as great, if not greater than the difference between Katusha in church that night, and the prostitute who had been carousing with the merchant and whom they judged this morning. Then he was free and fearless, and innumerable possibilities lay ready to open before him; now he felt himself caught in the meshes of a stupid, empty, valueless, frivolous life, out of which he saw no means of extricating himself even if he wished to, which he hardly did. He remembered how proud he was at one time of his straightforwardness, how he had made a rule of always speaking the truth, and really had been truthful; and how he was now sunk deep in lies: in the most dreadful of lies – lies considered as the truth by all who surrounded him. And, as far as he could see, there was no way out of these lies. He had sunk in the mire, got used to it, indulged himself in it.

How was he to break off his relations with Mary Vasilievna and her husband in such a way as to be able to look him and his children in the eyes? How disentangle himself from Missy? How choose between the two opposites – the recognition that holding land was unjust and the heritage from his mother? How atone for his sin against Katusha? This last, at any rate, could not be left as it was. He could not abandon a woman he had loved, and satisfy himself by paying money to an advocate to save her from hard labour in Siberia. She had not even deserved hard labour. Atone for a fault by paying money? Had he not then, when he gave her the money, thought he was atoning for his fault?

And he clearly recalled to mind that moment when, having caught her up in the passage, he thrust the money into her bib and ran away. 'Oh, that money!' he thought with the same horror and disgust he had then felt. 'Oh, dear! oh, dear! how disgusting,' he cried aloud as he had done then. 'Only a scoundrel, a knave, could do such a thing. And I am that knave, that scoundrel!' He went on aloud: 'But is it possible?' – he stopped and stood still – 'is it possible that I am really a scoundrel? . . . Well, who but I?' he answered himself. 'And then, is this the only thing?' he went on, convicting himself. 'Was not my conduct towards Mary Vasilievna and her husband base and disgusting? And my position with regard to money? To use riches considered by me unlawful on the plea that they are inherited from my mother? And the whole of my idle, detestable life? And my conduct towards Katusha to crown all? Knave and scoundrel! Let men judge me as they like. I can deceive them; but myself I cannot deceive.'

And, suddenly, he understood that the aversion he had lately, and particularly today, felt for everybody – the Prince and Sophia Vasilievna and Corney and Missy – was an aversion for himself. And, strange to say, in this acknowledgement of his baseness there was something painful yet joyful and quieting.

More than once in Nekhlyudov's life there had been what he called a 'cleansing of the soul'. By 'cleansing of the soul' he meant a state of mind in which, after a long period of sluggish inner life, a total cessation of its activity, he began to clear out all the rubbish that had accumulated in his soul, and was the cause of the cessation of the true life. His soul needed cleansing as a watch does. After such an awakening Nekhlyudov always made some rules for himself which he meant to follow forever after, wrote his diary, and began afresh a life which he hoped never to change again. 'Turning over a new leaf,' he called it to himself in English. But each time the temptations of the world entrapped him, and without noticing it he fell again, often lower than before.

Thus he had several times in his life raised and cleansed himself. The first time this happened was during the summer he spent with his aunts; that was his most vital and rapturous awakening, and its effects had lasted some time. Another awakening was when he gave up civil service and joined the army at war time, ready to sacrifice his life. But here the choking-up process was soon accomplished. Then an awakening came when he left the army and went abroad, devoting himself to art.

From that time until this day a long period had elapsed without any cleansing, and therefore the discord between the demands of his conscience and the life he was leading was greater than it had ever been before. He was horror-struck when he saw how great the divergence was. It was so great and the defilement so complete that he despaired of the possibility of getting cleansed. 'Have you not tried before to perfect yourself and become better, and nothing has come of it?' whispered the voice of the tempter within. 'What is the use of trying any more? Are you the only one? – All are alike, such is life,' whispered the voice. But the free spiritual being, which alone is true, alone powerful, alone eternal, had already awakened in Nekhlyudov, and he could not but believe it. Enormous though the distance was between what he wished to be and what he was, nothing appeared insurmountable to the newly-awakened spiritual being.

'At any cost I will break this lie which binds me and confess everything, and will tell everybody the truth, and act the truth,' he said resolutely, aloud. 'I shall tell Missy the truth, tell her I am a profligate and cannot marry her, and have only uselessly upset her. I shall tell Mary Vasilievna . . . Oh, there is nothing to tell her. I shall tell her husband that I, scoundrel that I am, have been deceiving him. I shall dispose of the inheritance in such a way as to acknowledge the truth. I shall tell her, Katusha, that I am a scoundrel and have sinned towards her, and will do all I can to ease her lot. Yes, I will see her, and will ask her to forgive me.

'Yes, I will beg her pardon, as children do . . . ' He stopped – 'will marry her if necessary.' He stopped again, folded his hands in front of his breast as he used to do when a little child, lifted his eyes, and said, addressing someone: 'Lord, help me, teach me, come enter within me and purify me of all this abomination.'

He prayed, asking God to help him, to enter into him and cleanse him; and what he was praying for had happened already: the God within him had awakened his consciousness. He felt himself one with Him, and therefore felt not only the freedom, fullness and joy of life, but all the power of righteousness. All, all the best that a man could do he felt capable of doing.

His eyes filled with tears as he was saying all this to himself, good and bad tears: good because they were tears of joy at the awakening of the spiritual being within him, the being which had been asleep all these years; and bad tears because they were tears of tenderness to himself at his own goodness.

He felt hot, and went to the window and opened it. The window opened into a garden. It was a moonlit, quiet, fresh night; a vehicle rattled past, and then all was still. The shadow of a tall poplar fell on the ground just opposite the window, and all the intricate pattern of its bare branches was clearly defined on the clean swept gravel. To the left the roof of a coach-house shone white in the moonlight, in front the black shadow of the garden wall was visible through the tangled branches of the trees.

Nekhlyudov gazed at the roof, the moonlit garden, and the shadows of the poplar, and drank in the fresh, invigorating air.

'How delightful, how delightful; oh, God, how delightful,' he said, meaning that which was going on in his soul.

Chapter 29

Maslova in prison

Maslova reached her cell only at six in the evening, tired and footsore, having, unaccustomed as she was to walking, gone ten miles on the stony road that day. She was crushed by the unexpectedly severe sentence and tormented by hunger. During the first interval of her trial, when the soldiers were eating bread and hard-boiled eggs in her presence, her mouth watered and she realised she was hungry, but considered it beneath her dignity to beg of them. Three hours later the desire to eat had passed, and she felt only weak. It was then she received the unexpected sentence. At first she thought she had made a mistake; she could not imagine herself as a convict in Siberia, and could not believe what she heard. But seeing the quiet, businesslike faces of judges and jury, who heard this news as if it were perfectly natural and expected, she grew indignant, and proclaimed loudly to the whole Court that she was not guilty. Finding that her cry was also taken as something natural and expected, and feeling incapable of altering matters, she was horror-struck and began to weep in despair, knowing that she must submit to the cruel and surprising injustice that had been done her. What astonished her most was that young men – or, at any rate, not old men – the same men who always looked so approvingly at her (one of them, the public prosecutor, she had seen in quite a different humour) had condemned her. While she was sitting in the prisoners' room before the trial and during the intervals, she saw these men looking in at the open door pretending they had to pass there on some business, or enter the room and gaze on her with approval. And then, for some unknown reason, these same men had condemned her to hard labour, though she was innocent of the charge laid against her. At first she cried, but then quieted down and sat perfectly stunned in the prisoners' room, waiting to be led back. She wanted only two things now – tobacco and strong drink. In this state Botchkova and Kartinkin found her when they were led into the same room after being sentenced. Botchkova began at once to scold her, and call her a 'convict'.

'Well! What have you gained? Justified yourself, have you? What you have deserved, that you've got. Out in Siberia you'll give up your finery, no fear!'

Maslova sat with her hands inside her sleeves, hanging her head and looking in front of her at the dirty floor without moving, only saying: 'I don't bother you, so don't you bother me. I don't bother you, do I?' she repeated this several times, and was silent again. She did brighten up a little when Botchkova and Kartinkin were led away and an attendant brought her three roubles.

'Are you Maslova?' he asked. 'Here you are; a lady sent it you,' he said, giving her the money.

'A lady – what lady?'

'You just take it. I'm not going to talk to you.'

This money was sent by Kitaeva, the keeper of the house in which she used to live. As she was leaving the court she turned to the usher with the question whether she might give Maslova a little money. The usher said she might. Having got permission, she removed the three-buttoned Swedish kid glove from her plump, white hand, and from an elegant purse brought from the back folds of her silk skirt took a pile of coupons,* just cut off from the interest-bearing papers which she had earned in her establishment, chose one worth two roubles and fifty copecks, added two twenty- and one ten-copeck coins, and gave all this to

* In Russia coupons cut off interest-bearing papers are often used as money.

the usher. The usher called an attendant, and in his presence gave the money.

'Belease to giff it accurately,' said Carolina Albertovna Kitaeva.

The attendant was hurt by her want of confidence, and that was why he treated Maslova so brusquely. Maslova was glad of the money, because it could give her the only thing she now desired. 'If I could but get cigarettes and take a whiff!' she said to herself, and all her thoughts centred on the one desire to smoke and drink. She so longed for spirits that she tasted them and felt the strength they would give her; and she greedily breathed in the air when the fumes of tobacco reached her from the door of a room that opened into the corridor. But she had to wait long, for the secretary, who should have given the order for her to go, forgot about the prisoners while talking and even disputing with one of the advocates about the article forbidden by the censor.

At last, about five o'clock, she was allowed to go, and was led away through the back door by her escort, the Nijni man and the Chuvash. Then, still within the entrance to the Law Courts, she gave them fifty copecks, asking them to get her two rolls and some cigarettes. The Tchoovash laughed, took the money, and said, 'All right; I'll get 'em,' and really got her the rolls and the cigarettes and honestly returned the change. She was not allowed to smoke on the way, and, with her craving unsatisfied, she continued her way to the prison. When she was brought to the gate of the prison, a hundred convicts who had arrived by rail were being led in. The convicts, bearded, clean-shaven, old, young, Russians, foreigners, some with their heads shaved and rattling with the chains on their feet, filled the anteroom with dust, noise and an acid smell of perspiration. Passing Maslova, all the convicts looked at her, and some came up to her and brushed her as they passed.

'Ay, here's a wench – a fine one,' said one.

'My respects to you, miss,' said another, winking at her. One dark man with a moustache, the rest of his face and the back of his head clean shaved, rattling with his chains and catching her feet in them, sprang near and embraced her.

'What! don't you know your chum? Come, come; don't give yourself airs,' showing his teeth and his eyes glittering when she pushed him away.

'You rascal! what are you up to?' shouted the inspector's assistant, coming in from behind. The convict shrank back and jumped away. The assistant assailed Maslova.

'What are you here for?'

Maslova was going to say she had been brought back from the Law Courts, but she was so tired that she did not care to speak.

'She has returned from the Law Courts, sir,' said one of the soldiers, coming forward with his fingers lifted to his cap.

'Well, hand her over to the chief warder. I won't have this sort of thing.'

'Yes, sir.'

'Sokolov, take her in!' shouted the assistant inspector.

The chief warder came up, gave Maslova a slap on the shoulder, and making a sign with his head for her to follow led her into the corridor of the women's ward. There she was searched, and as nothing prohibited was found on her (she had hidden her box of cigarettes inside a roll) she was led to the cell she had left in the morning.

Chapter 30

The cell

The cell in which Maslova was imprisoned was a large room twenty-one feet long and ten feet broad; it had two windows and a large stove. Two-thirds of the space were taken up by shelves used as beds. The planks they were made of had warped and shrunk. Opposite the door hung a dark-coloured icon with a wax candle sticking to it and a bunch of everlastings hanging down from it. By the door to the right there was a dark spot on the floor on which stood a stinking tub. The inspection had taken place and the women were locked up for the night.

The occupants of this room were fifteen persons, including three children. It was still quite light. Only two of the women were lying down: a consumptive woman imprisoned for theft, and an idiot who spent most of her time in sleep and who was arrested because she had no passport. The consumptive woman was not asleep, but lay with wide open eyes, her cloak folded under her head, trying to keep back the phlegm that irritated her throat, and not to cough.

Some of the other women, most of whom had nothing on but coarse brown holland chemises, stood looking out of the window at the convicts down in the yard, and some sat sewing. Among the latter was the old woman, Korableva, who had seen Maslova off in the morning. She was a tall, strong, gloomy-looking woman; her fair hair, which had begun to turn grey on the temples, hung down in a short plait. She was sentenced to hard labour in Siberia because she had killed her husband with an axe for making up to their daughter. She was at the head of the women in the cell, and found means of carrying on a trade in spirits with them. Beside her sat another woman sewing a coarse canvas sack. This was the wife of a railway watchman,* imprisoned for three months because she did not come out with the flags to meet a train that was passing, and an accident had occurred. She was a short, snub-nosed woman, with small, black eyes; kind and talkative. The third of the women who were sewing was Theodosia, a quiet young girl, white and rosy, very pretty, with bright child's eyes, and long fair plaits which she wore twisted round her head. She was in prison for attempting to poison her husband. She had done this immediately after her wedding (she had been given in marriage without her consent at the age of sixteen) because her husband would give her no peace. But in the eight months during which she had been let out on bail, she had not only made it up with her husband, but come to love him, so that when her trial came they were heart and soul to one another. Although her husband, her father-in-law, but especially her mother-in-law, who had grown very fond of her, did all they could to get her acquitted, she was sentenced to hard labour in Siberia. The kind, merry, ever-smiling Theodosia had a place next Maslova's on the shelf bed, and had grown so fond of her that she took it upon herself as a duty to attend and wait on her. Two other women were sitting without any work at the other end of the shelf bedstead. One was a woman of about forty, with a pale,

---

* There are small watchmen's cottages at distances of about one mile from each other along the Russian railways, and the watchmen or their wives have to meet every train.

thin face, who once probably had been very handsome. She sat with her baby at her thin, white breast. The crime she had committed was that when a recruit was, according to the peasants' view, unlawfully taken from their village, and the people stopped the police officer and took the recruit away from him, she (an aunt of the lad unlawfully taken) was the first to catch hold of the bridle of the horse on which he was being carried off. The other, who sat doing nothing, was a kindly, grey-haired old woman, hunchbacked and with a flat bosom. She sat behind the stove on the bedshelf, and pretended to catch a fat four-year-old boy, who ran backwards and forwards in front of her, laughing gaily. This boy had only a little shirt on and his hair was cut short. As he ran past the old woman he kept repeating, 'There, haven't caught me!' This old woman and her son were accused of incendiarism. She bore her imprisonment with perfect cheerfulness, but was concerned about her son, and chiefly about her 'old man', who she feared would get into a terrible state with no one to wash for him. Besides these seven women, there were four standing at one of the open windows, holding on to the iron bars. They were making signs and shouting to the convicts whom Maslova had met when returning to prison, and who were now passing through the yard. One of these women was big and heavy, with a flabby body, red hair, and freckles on her pale yellow face, her hands, and her fat neck. She shouted something in a loud, raucous voice, and laughed hoarsely. This woman was serving her term for theft. Beside her stood an awkward, dark little woman, no bigger than a child of ten, with a long waist and very short legs, a red, blotchy face, thick lips which did not hide her long teeth, and eyes too far apart. She broke by fits and starts into screeching laughter at what was going on in the yard. She was to be tried for stealing and incendiarism. They called her Khoroshavka. Behind her, in a very dirty grey chemise, stood a thin, miserable-looking pregnant woman, who was to be tried for concealment of theft. This woman stood silent, but kept smiling with pleasure and approval at what was going on below. With these stood a peasant woman of medium height, the mother of the boy who was playing with the old woman and of a seven-year-old girl. These were in prison with her because she had no one to leave them with. She was serving her term of imprisonment for illicit sale of spirits. She stood a little further from the window knitting a stocking, and though she listened to the other prisoners' words she shook her head disapprovingly, frowned, and closed her eyes. But her seven-year-old daughter stood in her little chemise, her flaxen hair done up in a little pigtail, her blue eyes fixed, and holding the red-haired woman by the skirt, attentively listened to the words of abuse that the women and the convicts flung at each other, and repeated them softly, as if learning them by heart. The twelfth prisoner, who paid no attention to what was going on, was a very tall, stately girl, the daughter of a deacon, who had drowned her baby in a well. She went about with bare feet, wearing only a dirty chemise. The thick, short plait of her fair hair had come undone and hung down dishevelled, and she paced up and down the free space of the cell, not looking at anyone, turning abruptly every time she came up to the wall.

Chapter 31

The prisoners

When the padlock rattled and the door opened to let Maslova into the cell, all turned towards her. Even the deacon's daughter stopped for a moment and looked at her with lifted brows before resuming her steady striding up and down.

Korableva stuck her needle into the brown sacking and looked questioningly at Maslova through her spectacles. 'Eh, eh, deary me, so you have come back. And I felt sure they'd acquit you. So you've got it?' She took off her spectacles and put her work down beside her on the shelf bed.

'And here have I and the old lady been saying, "Why, it may well be they'll let her go free at once." Why, it happens, ducky, they'll even give you a heap of money sometimes, that's sure,' the watchman's wife began, in her singing voice: 'Yes, we were wondering, "Why's she so long?" And now just see what it is. Well, our guessing was no use. The Lord willed otherwise,' she went on in musical tones.

'Is it possible? Have they sentenced you?' asked Theodosia, with concern, looking at Maslova with her bright blue, child-like eyes; and her merry young face changed as if she were going to cry.

Maslova did not answer, but went on to her place, the second from the end, and sat down beside Korableva.

'Have you eaten anything?' said Theodosia, rising and coming up to Maslova.

Maslova gave no reply, but putting the rolls on the bedstead, took off her dusty cloak, the kerchief off her curly black head, and began pulling off her shoes. The old woman who had been playing with the boy came up and stood in front of Maslova. 'Tz, tz, tz,' she clicked with her tongue, shaking her head pityingly. The boy also came up with her, and, putting out his upper lip, stared with wide open eyes at the roll Maslova had brought. When Maslova saw the sympathetic faces of her fellow-prisoners, her lips trembled and she felt inclined to cry, but she succeeded in restraining herself until the old woman and the boy came up. When she heard the kind, pitying clicking of the old woman's tongue, and met the boy's serious eyes turned from the roll to her face, she could bear it no longer; her face quivered and she burst into sobs.

'Didn't I tell you to insist on having a proper advocate?' said Norableva. 'Well, what is it? Exile?'

Maslova could not answer, but took from inside the roll a box of cigarettes, on which was a picture of a lady with hair done up very high and dress cut low in front, and passed the box to Korableva. Korableva looked at it and shook her head, chiefly because she did not approve of Maslova's putting her money to such bad use; but still she took out a cigarette, lit it at the lamp, took a puff, and almost forced it into Maslova's hand. Maslova, still crying, began greedily to inhale the tobacco smoke. 'Penal servitude,' she muttered, blowing out the smoke and sobbing.

'Don't they fear the Lord, the cursed soul-slayers,' muttered Korableva, 'sentencing the lass for nothing?' At this moment the sound of loud, coarse laughter came from the women who were still at the window. The little girl also laughed, and her childish treble mixed with the hoarse and screeching laughter of the others. One of the convicts outside had done something that produced this effect on the onlookers.

'Lawks! see the shaved hound, what he's doing,' said the red-haired woman, her whole fat body shaking with laughter; and leaning against the grating she shouted meaningless obscene words.

'Ugh, the fat fright's cackling,' said Korableva, who disliked the red-haired woman. Then, turning to Maslova again, she asked: 'How many years?'

'Four,' said Maslova, and the tears ran down her cheeks in such profusion that one fell on the cigarette. Maslova crumpled it up angrily and took another.

Though the watchman's wife did not smoke she picked up the cigarette Maslova had thrown away and began straightening it out, talking unceasingly.

'There, now, ducky, so it's true,' she said. 'Truth's gone to the dogs and they do what they please, and here we were guessing that you'd go free. Norableva says, "She'll go free." I say, "No," say I. "No, dear, my heart tells me they'll give it her." And so it's turned out,' she went on, evidently listening with pleasure to her own voice.

The women who had been standing by the window now also came up to Maslova, the convicts who had amused them having gone away. The first to come up were the woman imprisoned for illicit trade in spirits, and her little girl. 'Why such a hard sentence?' asked the woman, sitting down by Maslova and knitting fast.

'Why so hard? Because there's no money. That's why! Had there been money, and had a good lawyer that's up to their tricks been hired, they'd have acquitted her, no fear,' said Korableva. 'There's what's-his-name – that hairy one with the long nose. He'd bring you out clean from pitch, mum, he would. Ah, if we'd only had him!'

'Him, indeed,' said Khoroshavka. 'Why, he won't spit at you for less than a thousand roubles.'

'Seems you've been born under an unlucky star,' interrupted the old woman who was imprisoned for incendiarism. 'Only think, to entice the lad's wife and lock him up himself to feed vermin, and me, too, in my old days – ' she began to retell her story for the hundredth time. 'If it isn't the beggar's staff it's the prison. Yes, the beggar's staff and the prison don't wait for an invitation.'

'Ah, it seems that's the way with all of them,' said the spirit trader; and after looking at her little girl she put down her knitting, and drawing the child between her knees, began to search her head with deft fingers. 'Why do you sell spirits?' she went on. 'Why? But what's one to feed the children on?'

These words brought back to Maslova's mind her craving for drink.

'A little vodka,' she said to Korableva, wiping the tears with her sleeve and sobbing less frequently.

'All right, fork out,' said Korableva.

Chapter 32

A prison quarrel

Maslova got the money, which she had also hidden in a roll, and passed the coupon to Korableva. Korableva accepted it, though she could not read, trusting to Khoroshavka, who knew everything, and who said that the slip of paper was worth two roubles fifty copecks, then climbed up to the ventilator, where she had hidden a small flask of vodka. Seeing this, the women whose places were further off went away. Meanwhile Maslova shook the dust out of her cloak and kerchief, got up on the bedstead, and began eating a roll.

'I kept your tea for you,' said Theodosia, getting down from the shelf a mug and a tin teapot wrapped in a rag, 'but I'm afraid it is quite cold.' The liquid was quite cold and tasted more of tin than of tea, yet Maslova filled the mug and began drinking it with her roll. 'Finashka, here you are,' she said, breaking off a bit of the roll and giving it to the boy, who stood looking at her mouth.

Meanwhile Korableva handed the flask of vodka and a mug to Maslova, who offered some to her and to Khoroshavka. These prisoners were considered the aristocracy of the cell because they had some money, and shared what they possessed with the others.

In a few moments Maslova brightened up and related merrily what had happened at the court, and what had struck her most, i.e., how all the men had followed her wherever she went. In the court they all looked at her, she said, and kept coming into the prisoners' room while she was there.

'One of the soldiers even says, "It's all to look at you that they come." One would come in, "Where is such a paper?" or something, but I see it is not the paper he wants; he just devours me with his eyes,' she said, shaking her head. 'Regular artists.'

'Yes, that's so,' said the watchman's wife, and ran on in her musical strain, 'they're like flies after sugar.'

'And here, too,' Maslova interrupted her, 'the same thing. They can do without anything else. But the likes of them will go without bread sooner than miss that! Hardly had they brought me back when in comes a gang from the railway. They pestered me so, I did not know how to rid myself of them. Thanks to the assistant, he turned them off. One bothered so, I hardly got away.'

'What's he like?' asked Khoroshevka.

'Dark, with moustaches.'

'It must be him.'

'Him – who?'

'Why, Scheglov; him as has just gone by.'

'What's he, this Scheglov?'

'What, she don't know Scheglov? Why, he ran twice from Siberia. Now they've got him, but he'll run away. The warders themselves are afraid of him,' said Khoroshavka, who managed to exchange notes with the male prisoners and knew all that went on in the prison. 'He'll run away, that's flat.'

'If he does go away you and I'll have to stay,' said Korableva, turning to Maslova, 'but you'd better tell us now what the advocate says about petitioning. Now's the time to hand it in.'

Maslova answered that she knew nothing about it.

At that moment the red-haired woman came up to the 'aristocracy' with both freckled hands in her thick hair, scratching her head with her nails.

'I'll tell you all about it, Katerina,' she began. 'First and foremost, you'll have to write down you're dissatisfied with the sentence, then give notice to the procureur.'

'What do you want here?' said Korableva angrily; 'smell the vodka, do you? Your chatter's not wanted. We know what to do without your advice.'

'No one's speaking to you; what do you stick your nose in for?'

'It's vodka you want; that's why you come wriggling yourself in here.'

'Well, offer her some,' said Maslova, always ready to share anything she possessed with anybody.

'I'll offer her something.'

'Come on then,' said the red-haired one, advancing towards Korableva. 'Ah! think I'm afraid of such as you?'

'Convict fright!'

'That's her as says it.'

'Slut!'

'I? A slut? Convict! Murderess!' screamed the red-haired one.

'Go away, I tell you,' said Korableva gloomily, but the red-haired one came nearer and Korableva struck her in the chest. The red-haired woman seemed only to have waited for this, and with a sudden movement caught hold of Korableva's hair with one hand and with the other struck her in the face. Korableva seized this hand, and Maslova and Khoroshavka caught the red-haired woman by her arms, trying to pull her away, but she let go the old woman's hair with her hand only to twist it round her fist. Korableva, with her head bent to one side, was dealing out blows with one arm and trying to catch the red-haired woman's hand with her teeth, while the rest of the women crowded round, screaming and trying to separate the fighters; even the consumptive one came up and stood coughing and watching the fight. The children cried and huddled together. The noise brought the woman warder and a jailer. The fighting women were separated; and Korableva, taking out the bits of torn hair from her head, and the red-haired one, holding her torn chemise together over her yellow breast, began loudly to complain.

'I know, it's all the vodka. Wait a bit; I'll tell the inspector tomorrow. He'll give it you. Can't I smell it? Mind, get it all out of the way, or it will be the worse for you,' said the warder. 'We've no time to settle your disputes. Get to your places and be quiet.'

But quiet was not soon re-established. For a long time the women went on disputing and explaining to one another whose fault it all was. At last the warder and the jailer left the cell, the women grew quieter and began going to bed, and the old woman went to the icon and commenced praying.

'The two jailbirds have met,' the red-haired woman suddenly called out in a hoarse voice from the other end of the shelf beds, accompanying every word with frightfully vile abuse.

'Mind you don't get it again,' Korableva replied, also adding words of abuse, and both were quiet again.

'Had I not been stopped I'd have pulled your damned eyes out,' again began the red-haired one, and an answer of the same kind followed from Korableva. Then again a short interval and more abuse. But the intervals became longer and longer, as when a thunder-cloud is passing, and at last all was quiet.

All were in bed, some began to snore; and only the old woman, who always prayed a long time, went on bowing before the icon, and the deacon's daughter, who had got up after the warder left, was pacing up and down the room again. Maslova kept thinking that she was now a convict condemned to hard labour, and had twice been reminded of this – once by Botchkova and once by the red-haired woman – and she could not reconcile herself to the thought. Korableva, who lay next to her, turned over in her bed.

'There now,' said Maslova in a low voice; 'who would have thought it? See what others do and get nothing for it.'

'Never mind, girl. People manage to live in Siberia. As for you, you'll not be lost there either,' Korableva said, trying to comfort her.

'I know I'll not be lost; still it is hard. It's not such a fate I want – I, who am used to a comfortable life.'

'Ah, one can't go against God,' said Korableva, with a sigh. 'One can't, my dear.'

'I know, granny. Still, it's hard.'

They were silent for a while.

'Do you hear that baggage?' whispered Korableva, drawing Maslova's attention to a strange sound proceeding from the other end of the room.

This sound was the smothered sobbing of the red-haired woman. The red-haired woman was crying because she had been abused and had not got any of the vodka she wanted so badly; also because she remembered how all her life she had been abused, mocked at, offended, beaten. Remembering this, she pitied herself, and, thinking no one heard her, began crying as children cry, sniffing with her nose and swallowing the salt tears.

'I'm sorry for her,' said Maslova.

'Of course one is sorry,' said Korableva, 'but she shouldn't come bothering.'

Chapter 33

The leaven at work – Nekhlyudov's domestic changes

The next morning Nekhlyudov awoke, conscious that something had happened to him, and even before he had remembered what it was he knew it to be something important and good.

'Katusha – the trial!' Yes, he must stop lying and tell the whole truth.

By a strange coincidence on that very morning he received the long-expected letter from Mary Vasilievna, the wife of the *Maréchal de Noblesse*, the very letter he particularly needed. She gave him full freedom, and wished him happiness in his intended marriage.

'Marriage!' he repeated with irony. 'How far I am from all that at present.'

And he remembered the plans he had formed the day before, to tell the husband everything, to make a clean breast of it, and express his readiness to give him any kind of satisfaction. But this morning this did not seem so easy as the day before. And, then, also, why make a man unhappy by telling him what he does not know? Yes, if he came and asked, he would tell him all, but to go purposely and tell – no! that was unnecessary.

And telling the whole truth to Missy seemed just as difficult this morning. Again, he could not begin to speak without offence. As in many worldly affairs, something had to remain unexpressed. Only one thing he decided on, i.e., not to visit there, and to tell the truth if asked.

But in connection with Katusha, nothing was to remain unspoken. 'I shall go to the prison and shall tell her everything, and ask her to forgive me. And if need be – yes, if need be, I shall marry her,' he thought.

This idea, that he was ready to sacrifice all on moral grounds, and marry her, again made him feel very tender towards himself.

Concerning money matters he resolved this morning to arrange them in accord with his conviction, that the holding of landed property was unlawful. Even if he should not be strong enough to give up everything, he would still do what he could, not deceiving himself or others.

It was long since he had met the coming day with so much energy. When Agraphena Petrovna came in, he told her, with more firmness than he thought himself capable of, that he no longer needed this lodging nor her services. There had been a tacit understanding that he was keeping up so large and expensive an establishment because he was thinking of getting married. The giving up of the house had, therefore, a special meaning. Agraphena Petrovna looked at him in surprise.

'I thank you very much, Agraphena Petrovna, for all your care for me, but I no longer require so large a house nor so many servants. If you wish to help me, be so good as to settle about the things, put them away as it used to be done during mamma's life, and when Natasha comes she will see to everything.' Natasha was Nekhlyudov's sister.

Agraphena Petrovna shook her head. 'See about the things? Why, they'll be required again,' she said.

'No, they won't, Agraphena Petrovna; I assure you they won't be required,' said Nekhlyudov, in answer to what the shaking of her head had expressed. 'Please tell Corney also that I shall pay him two months' wages, but shall have no further need of him.'

'It is a pity, Dmitri Ivanovitch, that you should think of doing this,' she said. 'Well, supposing you go abroad, still you'll require a place of residence again.'

'You are mistaken in your thoughts, Agraphena Petrovna; I am not going abroad. If I go on a journey, it will be to quite a different place.' He suddenly blushed very red. 'Yes, I must tell her,' he thought; 'no hiding; everybody must be told.'

'A very strange and important thing happened to me yesterday. Do you remember my Aunt Mary Ivanovna's Katusha?'

'Oh, yes. Why, I taught her how to sew.'

'Well, this Katusha was tried in the Court and I was on the jury.'

'Oh, Lord! What a pity!' cried Agraphena Petrovna. 'What was she being tried for?'

'Murder; and it is I have done it all.'

'Well, now this is very strange; how could you do it all?'

'Yes, I am the cause of it all; and it is this that has altered all my plans.'

'What difference can it make to you?'

'This difference: that I, being the cause of her getting on to that path, must do all I can to help her.'

'That is just according to your own good pleasure; you are not particularly in fault there. It happens to everyone, and if one's reasonable, it all gets smoothed over and forgotten,' she said, seriously and severely. 'Why should you place it to your account? There's no need. I had already heard before that she had strayed from the right path. Well, whose fault is it?'

'Mine! That's why I want to put it right.'

'It is hard to put right.'

'That is my business. But if you are thinking about yourself, then I will tell you that, as mamma expressed the wish – '

'I am not thinking about myself. I have been so bountifully treated by the dear defunct, that I desire nothing. Lisenka' (her married niece) 'has been inviting me, and I shall go to her when I am not wanted any longer. Only it is a pity you should take this so to heart; it happens to everybody.'

'Well, I do not think so. And I still beg that you will help me let this lodging and put away the things. And please do not be angry with me. I am very, very grateful to you for all you have done.'

And, strangely, from the moment Nekhlyudov realised that it was he who was so bad and disgusting to himself, others were no longer disgusting to him; on the contrary, he felt a kindly respect for Agraphena Petrovna, and for Corney.

He would have liked to go and confess to Corney also, but Corney's manner was so insinuatingly deferential that he had not the resolution to do it.

On the way to the Law Courts, passing along the same streets with the same *isvostchik* as the day before, he was surprised what a different being he felt himself to be. The marriage with Missy, which only yesterday seemed so probable, appeared quite impossible now. The day before he felt it was for him to choose, and had no doubts that she would be happy to marry him; today he felt himself unworthy not only of marrying, but even of being intimate with her. 'If she only knew what I am, nothing would induce her to receive me. And only yesterday I was finding fault with her because she flirted with N— . Anyhow, even if she consented to marry me, could I be, I won't say happy, but at peace, knowing that the other was here in prison, and would today or tomorrow he taken to Siberia with a gang of other prisoners, while I accepted congratulations and made calls with my young wife; or while I count the votes at the meetings, for and against the motion brought forward by the rural inspection, etc., together with the *Maréchal de Noblesse*, whom I abominably deceive, and afterwards make appointments with his wife (how abominable!) or while I continue to work at my picture, which will certainly never get finished? Besides, I have no business to waste time on such things. I can do nothing of the kind now,' he continued to himself, rejoicing at the change he felt within himself. 'The first thing now is to see the advocate and find out his decision, and then . . . then go and see her and tell her everything.'

And when he pictured to himself how he would see her, and tell her all, confess his sin to her, and tell her that he would do all in his power to atone for his sin, he was touched at his own goodness, and the tears came to his eyes.

Chapter 34

The absurdity of law – reflections of a juryman

On coming into the Law Courts Nekhlyudov met the usher of yesterday, who today seemed to him much to be pitied, in the corridor, and asked him where those prisoners who had been sentenced were kept, and to whom one had to apply for permission to visit them. The usher told him that the condemned prisoners were kept in different places, and that, until they received their sentence in its final form, the permission to visit them depended on the president. 'I'll come and call you myself, and take you to the president after the session. The president is not even here at present. After the session! And now please come in; we are going to commence.'

Nekhlyudov thanked the usher for his kindness, and went into the jurymen's room. As he was approaching the room, the other jurymen were just leaving it to go into the court. The merchant had again partaken of a little refreshment, and was as merry as the day before, and greeted Nekhlyudov like an old friend. And today Peter Gerasimovitch did not arouse any unpleasant feelings in Nekhlyudov by his familiarity and his loud laughter. Nekhlyudov would have liked to tell all the jurymen about his relations to yesterday's prisoner. 'By rights,' he thought, 'I ought to have got up yesterday during the trial and disclosed my guilt.'

He entered the court with the other jurymen, and witnessed the same procedure as the day before.

'The judges are coming,' was again proclaimed, and again three men, with embroidered collars, ascended the platform, and there was the same settling of the jury on the high-backed chairs, the same gendarmes, the same portraits, the same priest, and Nekhlyudov felt that, though he knew what he ought to do, he could not interrupt all this solemnity. The preparations for the trials were just the same as the day before, excepting that the swearing in of the jury and the president's address to them were omitted.

The case before the Court this day was one of burglary. The prisoner, guarded by two gendarmes with naked swords, was a thin, narrow-chested lad of twenty, with a bloodless, sallow face, dressed in a grey cloak. He sat alone in the prisoner's dock. This boy was accused of having, together with a companion, broken the lock of a shed and stolen several old mats valued at three roubles and sixty-seven copecks. According to the indictment, a policeman had stopped this boy as he was passing with his companion, who was carrying the mats on his shoulder. The boy and his companion confessed at once, and were both imprisoned. The boy's companion, a locksmith, died in prison, and so the boy was being tried alone. The old mats were lying on the table as the objects of material evidence. The business was conducted just in the same manner as the day before, with the whole armoury of evidence, proofs, witnesses, swearing in, questions, experts, and cross-examinations. In answer to every question put to him by the president, the prosecutor, or the advocate, the policeman (one of the witnesses) invariably ejected the words: 'Just so,' or 'Can't tell.' Yet, in spite of his being stupefied, and rendered a mere machine by military discipline, his reluctance to speak about the arrest of this prisoner was evident. Another witness, an old house proprietor, and owner of the mats, evidently a rich old man, when asked whether the mats were his, reluctantly identified them as such. When the public prosecutor asked him what he meant to do with these mats, what use they were to him, he got angry, and answered: 'The devil take those mats; I don't want them at all. Had I known there would be all this bother about them I should not have gone looking for them, but would rather have added a ten-rouble note or two to them, only not to be dragged here and pestered with questions. I have spent a lot on *isvostchiks*. Besides, I am not well. I have been suffering from rheumatism for the last seven years.' It was thus the witness spoke.

The accused himself confessed everything, and looking round stupidly, like an animal that is caught, related how it had all happened. Still the public prosecutor, drawing up his shoulders as he had done the day before, asked subtle questions calculated to catch a cunning criminal.

In his speech he proved that the theft had been committed from a dwelling-place, and a lock had been broken; and that the boy, therefore, deserved a heavy punishment. The advocate appointed by the Court proved that the theft was not committed from a dwelling-place, and that, though the crime was a serious one, the prisoner was not so very dangerous to society as the prosecutor stated. The president assumed the role of absolute neutrality in the same way as he had done on the previous day, and impressed on the jury facts which they all knew and could not help knowing. Then came an interval, just as the day before, and they smoked; and again the usher called out 'The judges are coming,' and in the same way the two gendarmes sat trying to keep awake and threatening the prisoner with their naked weapons.

The proceedings showed that this boy was apprenticed by his father at a tobacco factory, where he remained five years. This year he had been discharged by the owner after a strike, and, having lost his place, he wandered about the town without any work, drinking all he possessed. In a *traktir*[*] he met another like himself, who had lost his place before the prisoner had, a locksmith by trade and a drunkard. One night, those two, both drunk, broke the lock of a shed and took the first thing they happened to lay hands on. They confessed all and were put in prison, where the locksmith died while awaiting the trial. The boy was now being tried as a dangerous creature, from whom society must be protected.

'Just as dangerous a creature as yesterday's culprit,' thought Nekhlyudov, listening to all that was going on before him. 'They are dangerous, and we who judge them? I, a rake, an adulterer, a deceiver. We are not dangerous. But, even supposing that this boy is the most dangerous of all that are here in the court, what should be done from a common-sense point of view when he has been caught? It is clear that he is not an exceptional evil-doer, but a most ordinary boy; everyone sees it – and that he has become what he is simply because he got into circumstances that create such characters, and, therefore, to prevent such a boy from going wrong the circumstances that create these unfortunate beings must be done away with.

'But what do we do? We seize one such lad who happens to get caught, knowing well that there are thousands like him whom we have not caught, and send him to prison, where idleness, or most unwholesome, useless labour is forced on him, in company of others weakened and ensnared by the lives they have led. And then we send him, at the public expense, from the Moscow to the Irkoutsk government, in company with the most depraved of men.

'But we do nothing to destroy the conditions in which people like these are produced; on the contrary, we support the establishments where they are formed. These establishments are well known: factories, mills, workshops, public-houses, gin-shops, brothels. And we do not destroy these places, but, looking at them as necessary, we support and regulate them. We educate in this way not one, but millions of people, and then catch one of them and imagine that we have done something, that we have guarded ourselves, and nothing more can be expected of us. Have we not sent him from the Moscow to the Irkoutsk government?' Thus thought Nekhlyudov

[*] Cheap restaurant.

with unusual clearness and vividness, sitting in his high-backed chair next to the colonel, and listening to the different intonations of the advocates', prosecutor's, and president's voices, and looking at their self-confident gestures. 'And how much and what hard effort this pretence requires,' continued Nekhlyudov in his mind, glancing round the enormous room, the portraits, lamps, armchairs, uniforms, the thick walls and large windows; and picturing to himself the tremendous size of the building, and the still more ponderous dimensions of the whole of this organisation, with its army of officials, scribes, watchmen, messengers, not only in this place, but all over Russia, who receive wages for carrying on this comedy which no one needs. 'Supposing we spent one-hundredth of these efforts helping these castaways, whom we now only regard as hands and bodies, required by us for our own peace and comfort. Had someone chanced to take pity on him and given some help at the time when poverty made them send him to town, it might have been sufficient,' Nekhlyudov thought, looking at the boy's piteous face. 'Or even later, when, after twelve hours' work at the factory, he was going to the public-house, led away by his companions, had someone then come and said, "Don't go, Vanya; it is not right," he would not have gone, nor got into bad ways, and would not have done any wrong.

'But no; no one who would have taken pity on him came across this apprentice in the years he lived like a poor little animal in the town, and with his hair cut close so as not to breed vermin, and ran errands for the workmen. No, all he heard and saw, from the older workmen and his companions, since he came to live in town, was that he who cheats, drinks, swears, who gives another a thrashing, who goes on the loose, is a fine fellow. Ill, his constitution undermined by unhealthy labour, drink, and debauchery – bewildered as in a dream, knocking aimlessly about town, he gets into some sort of a shed, and takes from there some old mats, which nobody needs – and here we, all of us educated people, rich or comfortably off, meet together, dressed in good clothes and fine uniforms, in a splendid apartment, to mock this unfortunate brother of ours whom we ourselves have ruined.

'Terrible! It is difficult to say whether the cruelty or the absurdity is greater, but the one and the other seem to reach their climax.'

Nekhlyudov thought all this, no longer listening to what was going on, and he was horror-struck by that which was being revealed to him. He could not understand why he had not been able to see all this before, and why others were unable to see it.

Chapter 35

The procureur – Nekhlyudov refuses to serve

During an interval Nekhlyudov got up and went out into the corridor, with the intention of not returning to the court. Let them do what they liked with him, he could take no more part in this awful and horrid tomfoolery.

Having inquired where the procureur's cabinet was he went straight to him. The attendant did not wish to let him in, saying that the procureur was busy, but Nekhlyudov paid no heed and went to the door, where he was met by an official. He asked to be announced to the procureur, saying he was on the jury and had a very important communication to make.

His title and good clothes were of assistance to him. The official announced him to the procureur, and Nekhlyudov was let in. The procureur met him standing, evidently annoyed at the persistence with which Nekhlyudov demanded admittance.

'What is it you want?' the procureur asked, severely.

'I am on the jury; my name is Nekhlyudov, and it is absolutely necessary for me to see the prisoner Maslova,' Nekhlyudov said, quickly and resolutely, blushing, and feeling that he was taking a step which would have a decisive influence on his life.

The procureur was a short, dark man, with short, grizzly hair, quick, sparkling eyes, and a thick beard cut close on his projecting lower jaw.

'Maslova? Yes, of course, I know. She was accused of poisoning,' the procureur said, quietly. 'But why do you want to see her?' And then, as if wishing to tone down his question, he added, 'I cannot give you the permission without knowing why you require it.'

'I require it for a particularly important reason.'

'Yes?' said the procureur, and, lifting his eyes, looked attentively at Nekhlyudov. 'Has her case been heard or not?'

'She was tried yesterday, and unjustly sentenced; she is innocent.'

'Yes? If she was sentenced only yesterday,' went on the procureur, paying no attention to Nekhlyudov's statement concerning Maslova's innocence, 'she must still he in the preliminary detention prison until the sentence is delivered in its final form. Visiting is allowed there only on certain days; I should advise you to inquire there.'

'But I must see her as soon as possible,' Nekhlyudov said, his jaw trembling as he felt the decisive moment approaching.

'Why must you?' said the procureur, lifting his brows with some agitation.

'Because I betrayed her and brought her to the condition which exposed her to this accusation.'

'All the same, I cannot see what it has to do with visiting her.'

'This: that whether I succeed or not in getting the sentence changed I want to follow her, and – marry her,' said Nekhlyudov, touched to tears by his own conduct, and at the same time pleased to see the effect he produced on the procureur.

'Really! Dear me!' said the procureur. 'This is certainly a very exceptional case. I believe you are a member of the Krasnoporsk rural administration?' he asked, as if he remembered having heard before of this Nekhlyudov, who was now making so strange a declaration.

'I beg your pardon, but I do not think that has anything to do with my request,' answered Nekhlyudov, flushing angrily.

'Certainly not,' said the procureur, with a scarcely perceptible smile and not in the least abashed; 'only your wish is so extraordinary and so out of the common.'

'Well; but can I get the permission?'

'The permission? Yes, I will give you an order of admittance directly. Take a seat.'

He went up to the table, sat down, and began to write. 'Please sit down.'

Nekhlyudov continued to stand.

Having written an order of admittance, and handed it to Nekhlyudov, the procureur looked curiously at him.

'I must also state that I can no longer take part in the sessions.'

'Then you will have to lay valid reasons before the Court, as you, of course, know.'

'My reasons are that I consider all judging not only useless, but immoral.'

'Yes,' said the procureur, with the same scarcely perceptible smile, as if to show that this kind of declaration was well known to him and belonged to the amusing sort. 'Yes, but you will certainly understand that I as procureur, cannot agree with you on this point. Therefore, I should advise you to apply to the Court, which will consider your declaration, and find it valid or not valid, and in the latter case will impose a fine. Apply, then, to the Court.'

'I have made my declaration, and shall apply nowhere else,' Nekhlyudov said, angrily.

'Well, then, good-afternoon,' said the procureur, bowing his head, evidently anxious to be rid of this strange visitor.

'Who was that you had here?' asked one of the members of the Court, as he entered, just after Nekhlyudov left the room.

'Nekhlyudov, you know; the same that used to make all sorts of strange statements at the Krasnoporsk rural meetings. Just fancy! He is on the jury, and among the prisoners there is a woman or girl sentenced to penal servitude, whom he says he betrayed, and now he wants to marry her.'

'You don't mean to say so.'

'That's what he told me. And in such a strange state of excitement!'

'There is something abnormal in the young men of today.'

'Oh, but he is not so very young.'

'Yes. But how tiresome your famous Ivoshenka was. He carries the day by wearying one out. He talked and talked without end.'

'Oh, that kind of people should be simply stopped, or they will become real obstructionists.'

Chapter 36

Nekhlyudov endeavours to visit Maslova

From the procureur Nekhlyudov went straight to the preliminary detention prison. However, no Maslova was to be found there, and the inspector explained to Nekhlyudov that she would probably be in the old temporary prison. Nekhlyudov went there.

Yes, Katerina Maslova was there.

The distance between the two prisons was enormous, and Nekhlyudov only reached the old prison towards evening. He was going up to the door of the large, gloomy building, but the sentinel stopped him and rang. A warder came in answer to the bell. Nekhlyudov showed him his order of admittance, but the warder said he could not let him in without the inspector's permission. Nekhlyudov went to see the inspector. As he was going up the stairs he heard distant sounds of some complicated bravura, played on the piano. When a cross servant girl, with a bandaged eye, opened the door to him, those sounds seemed to escape from the room and to strike his ear. It was a rhapsody of Liszt's, that everybody was tired of, splendidly played but only to one point. When that point was reached the same thing was repeated. Nekhlyudov asked the bandaged maid whether the inspector was in. She answered that he was not in.

'Will he return soon?'

The rhapsody again stopped and recommenced loudly and brilliantly again up to the same charmed point.

'I will go and ask,' and the servant went away.

'Tell him he is not in and won't be today; he is out visiting. What do they come bothering for?' came the sound of a woman's voice from behind the door, and again the rhapsody rattled on and stopped, and the sound of a chair pushed back was heard. It was plain the irritated pianist meant to rebuke the tiresome visitor, who had come at an untimely hour. 'Papa is not in,' a pale girl with crimped hair said, crossly, coming out into the ante-room, but, seeing a young man in a good coat, she softened.

'Come in, please . . . What is it you want?'

'I want to see a prisoner in this prison.'

'A political one, I suppose?'

'No, not a political one. I have a permission from the procureur.'

'Well, I don't know, and papa is out; but come in, please,' she said, again, 'or else speak to the assistant. He is in the office at present; apply there. What is your name?'

'I thank you,' said Nekhlyudov, without answering her question, and went out.

The door was not yet closed after him when the same lively tones recommenced. In the courtyard Nekhlyudov met an officer with bristly moustaches, and asked for the assistant-inspector. It was the assistant himself. He looked at the order of admittance, but said that he could not decide to let him in with a pass for the preliminary prison. Besides, it was too late. 'Please to come again tomorrow. To morrow at 10, everybody is allowed to go in. Come then, and the inspector himself will be at home. Then you can have the interview either in the common room or, if the inspector allows it, in the office.'

And so Nekhlyudov did not succeed in getting an interview that day, and returned home. As he went along the streets, excited at the idea of meeting her, he no longer thought about the Law Courts, but recalled his conversations with the procureur and the inspector's assistant. The fact that he had been seeking an interview with her, and had told the procureur, and had been in two prisons, so excited him that it was long before he could calm down. When he got home he at once fetched out his diary, that had long remained untouched, read a few sentences out of it, and then wrote as follows:

For two years I have not written anything in my diary, and thought I never should return to this childishness. Yet it is not childishness, but converse with my own self, with this real divine self which lives in every man. All this time that I slept there was no one for me to converse with. I was awakened by an extraordinary event on the 28th of April, in the Law Court, when I was on the jury. I saw her in the prisoners' dock, the

Katusha betrayed by me, in a prisoner's cloak, condemned to penal servitude through a strange mistake, and my own fault. I have just been to the procureur's and to the prison, but I was not admitted. I have resolved to do all I can to see her, to confess to her, and to atone for my sin, even by a marriage. God help me. My soul is at peace and I am full of joy.

Chapter 37

Maslova recalls the past

That night Maslova lay awake a long time with her eyes open looking at the door, in front of which the deacon's daughter kept passing. She was thinking that nothing would induce her to go to the island of Sakhalin and marry a convict, but would arrange matters somehow with one of the prison officials, the secretary, a warder, or even a warder's assistant. 'Aren't they all given that way? Only I must not get thin, or else I am lost.'

She thought of how the advocate had looked at her, and also the president, and of the men she met, and those who came in on purpose at the court. She recollected how her companion, Bertha, who came to see her in prison, had told her about the student whom she had 'loved' while she was with Kitaeva, and who had inquired about her, and pitied her very much. She recalled many to mind, only not Nekhlyudov. She never brought back to mind the days of her childhood and youth, and her love to Nekhlyudov. That would have been too painful. These memories lay untouched somewhere deep in her soul; she had forgotten him, and never recalled and never even dreamt of him. Today, in the court, she did not recognise him, not only because when she last saw him he was in uniform, without a beard, and had only a small moustache and thick, curly, though short hair, and now was bald and bearded, but because she never thought about him. She had buried his memory on that terrible dark night when he, returning from the army, had passed by on the railway without stopping to call on his aunts. Katusha then knew her condition. Up to that night she did not consider the child that lay beneath her heart a burden. But on that night everything changed, and the child became nothing but a weight.

His aunts had expected Nekhlyudov, had asked him to come and see them in passing, but he had telegraphed that he could not come, as he had to be in Petersburg at an appointed time. When Katusha heard this she made up her mind to go to the station and see him. The train was to pass by at two o'clock in the night. Katusha having helped the old ladies to bed, and persuaded a little girl, the cook's daughter, Mashka, to come with her, put on a pair of old boots, threw a shawl over her head, gathered up her dress, and ran to the station.

It was a warm, rainy, and windy autumn night. The rain now pelted down in warm, heavy drops, now stopped again. It was too dark to see the path across the field, and in the wood it was pitch black, so that although Katusha knew the way well, she got off the path, and got to the little station where the train stopped for three minutes, not before, as she had hoped, but after the second bell had been rung. Hurrying up the platform, Katusha saw him at once at the windows of a first-class carriage. Two officers sat opposite each other on the velvet-covered seats, playing cards. This carriage was very brightly lit up; on the little table between the seats stood two thick, dripping candles. He sat in his close-fitting breeches on the arm of the seat, leaning against the back, and laughed. As soon as she recognised him she knocked at the carriage window with her benumbed hand, but at that moment the last bell rang, and the train first gave a backward jerk, and then gradually the carriages began to move forward. One of the players rose with the cards in his hand, and looked out. She knocked again, and pressed her face to the window, but the carriage moved on, and she went alongside looking in. The officer tried to lower the window, but could not. Nekhlyudov pushed him aside and began lowering it himself. The train went faster, so that she had to walk quickly. The train went on still faster and the window opened. The guard pushed her aside, and jumped in. Katusha ran on, along the wet boards of the platform, and when she came to the end she could hardly stop herself from falling as she ran down the steps of the platform. She was running by the side of the railway, though the first-class carriage had long passed her, and the second-class carriages were gliding by faster, and at last the third-class carriages still faster. But she ran on, and when the last carriage with the lamps at the back had gone by, she had already reached the tank which fed the engines, and was un-sheltered from the wind, which was blowing her shawl about and making her skirt cling round her legs. The shawl flew off her head, but still she ran on.

'Katerina Michaelovna, you've lost your shawl!' screamed the little girl, who was trying to keep up with her.

Katusha stopped, threw back her head, and catching hold of it with both hands sobbed aloud. 'Gone!' she screamed.

'He is sitting in a velvet armchair and joking and drinking, in a brightly lit carriage, and I, out here in the mud, in the darkness, in the wind and the rain, am standing and weeping,' she thought to herself; and sat down on the ground, sobbing so loud that the little girl got frightened, and put her arms round her, wet as she was.

'Come home, dear,' she said.

'When a train passes – then under a carriage, and there will be an end,' Katusha was thinking, without heeding the girl.

And she made up her mind to do it, when, as it always happens, when a moment of quiet follows great excitement, he, the child – his child – made himself known within her. Suddenly all that a moment before had been tormenting her, so that it had seemed impossible to live, all her bitterness towards him, and the wish to revenge herself, even by dying, passed away; she grew quieter, got up, put the shawl on her head, and went home.

Wet, muddy, and quite exhausted, she returned, and from that day the change which brought her where she now was began to operate in her soul. Beginning from that dreadful night, she ceased believing in God and in goodness. She had herself believed in God, and believed that other people also believed in Him; but after that night she became convinced that no one believed, and that all that was said about God and His laws was deception and untruth. He whom she loved, and who had loved her – yes, she knew that – had thrown her away; had abused her love. Yet he was the best of all the people she knew. All the rest were still worse. All that afterwards happened to her strengthened her in this belief at every step. His aunts, the pious old ladies, turned her out when she could no longer serve them as she used to. And of all those she met, the women used her as a means of getting money, the men, from the old police officer down to the warders of the prison, looked at her as on an object for pleasure. And no one in the world cared for aught but pleasure. In this belief the old author with whom she had come together in the second year of her life of independence had strengthened her. He had told her outright that it was this that constituted the happiness of life, and he called it poetical and aesthetic.

Everybody lived for himself only, for his pleasure, and all the talk concerning God and righteousness was deception. And if sometimes doubts arose in her mind and she wondered why everything was so ill arranged in the world that all hurt each other, and made each other suffer, she thought it best not to dwell on it, and if she felt melancholy she could smoke, or better still, drink, and it would pass.

Chapter 38

Sunday in prison – preparing for Mass

On Sunday morning at five o'clock, when a whistle sounded in the corridor of the women's ward of the prison, Korableva, who was already awake, called Maslova.

'Oh, dear! life again,' thought Maslova, with horror, involuntarily breathing in the air that had become terribly noisome towards the morning. She wished to fall asleep again, to enter into the region of oblivion, but the habit of fear overcame sleepiness, and she sat up and looked round, drawing her feet under her. The women had all got up; only the elder children were still asleep. The spirit-trader was carefully drawing a cloak from under the children, so as not to wake them. The watchman's wife was hanging up the rags to dry that served the baby as swaddling clothes, while the baby was screaming desperately in Theodosia's arms, who was trying to quiet it. The consumptive woman was coughing with her hands pressed to her chest, while the blood rushed to her face, and she sighed loudly, almost screaming, in the intervals of coughing. The fat, red-haired woman was lying on her back, with knees drawn up, and loudly relating a dream. The old woman accused of incendiarism was standing in front of the image, crossing herself and bowing, and repeating the same words over and over again. The deacon's daughter sat on the bedstead, looking before her, with a dull, sleepy face. Khoroshavka was twisting her black, oily, coarse hair round her fingers. The sound of slipshod feet was heard in the passage, and the door opened to let in two convicts, dressed in jackets and grey trousers that did not reach to their ankles. With serious, cross faces they lifted the stinking tub and carried it out of the cell. The women went out to the taps in the corridor to wash. There the red-haired woman again began a quarrel with a woman from another cell.

'Is it the solitary cell you want?' shouted an old jailer, slapping the red-haired woman on her bare, fat back, so that it sounded through the corridor. 'You be quiet.'

'Lawks! the old one's playful,' said the woman, taking his action for a caress.

'Now, then, be quick; get ready for the Mass.' Maslova had hardly time to do her hair and dress when the inspector came with his assistants.

'Come out for inspection,' cried a jailer.

Some more prisoners came out of other cells and stood in two rows along the corridor; each woman had to place her hand on the shoulder of the woman in front of her. They were all counted.

After the inspection the woman warder led the prisoners to church. Maslova and Theodosia were in the middle of a column of over a hundred women, who had come out of different cells. All were dressed in white skirts, white jackets, and wore white kerchiefs on their heads, except a few who had their own coloured clothes on. These were wives who, with their children, were following their convict husbands to Siberia. The whole flight of stairs was filled by the procession. The patter of softly-shod feet mingled with the voices and now and then a laugh. When turning, on the landing, Maslova saw her enemy, Botch-kova, in front, and pointed out her angry face to Theodosia. At the bottom of the stairs the women stopped talking. Bowing and crossing themselves, they entered the empty church, which glistened with gilding. Crowding and pushing one another, they took their places on the right.

After the women came the men condemned to banishment, those serving their term in the prison, and those exiled by their communes; and, coughing loudly, they took their stand, crowding the left side and the middle of the church.

On one side of the gallery above stood the men sentenced to penal servitude in Siberia, who had been let into the church before the others. Each of them had half his head shaved, and their presence was indicated by the clanking of the chains on their feet. On the other side of the gallery stood those in preliminary confinement, without chains, their heads not shaved.

The prison church had been rebuilt and ornamented by a rich merchant, who spent several tens of thousands of roubles on it, and it glittered with gay colours and gold. For a time there was silence in the church, and only coughing, blowing of noses, the crying of babies, and now and then the rattling of chains, was heard. But at last the convicts that stood in the middle moved, pressed against each other, leaving a passage in the centre of the church, down which the prison inspector passed to take his place in front of everyone in the nave.

Chapter 39

The prison church – blind leaders of the blind

The service began.

It consisted of the following. The priest, having dressed in a strange and very inconvenient garb, made of gold cloth, cut and arranged little bits of bread on a saucer, and then put them into a cup with wine, repeating at the same time different names and prayers. Meanwhile the deacon first read Slavonic prayers, difficult to understand in themselves, and rendered still more incomprehensible by being read very fast, and then sang them turn and turn about with the convicts. The contents of the prayers were chiefly the desire for the welfare of the Emperor and his family. These petitions were repeated many times, separately and together with other prayers, the people kneeling. Besides this, several verses from the *Acts of the Apostles* were read by the deacon in a peculiarly strained voice, which made it impossible to understand what he read, and then the priest read very distinctly a part of the *Gospel according to St Mark*, in which it said that Christ, having risen from the dead before flying up to heaven to sit down at His Father's right hand, first showed Himself to Mary Magdalene, out of whom He had driven seven devils, and then to eleven of His disciples, and ordered them to preach the Gospel to the whole creation; and the priest added that if anyone did not believe this he would perish, but he that believed it and was baptised should be saved, and should besides drive out devils and cure people by laying his hands on them, should talk in strange tongues, should take up serpents, and if he drank poison should not die, but remain well.

The essence of the service consisted in the supposition that the bits cut up by the priest and put by him into the wine, when manipulated and prayed over in a certain way, turned into the flesh and blood of God.

These manipulations consisted in the priest's regularly lifting and holding up his arms, though hampered by the gold cloth sack he had on, then, sinking on to his knees and kissing the table and all that was on it, but chiefly in his taking a cloth by two of its corners and waving it regularly and softly over the silver saucer and golden cup. It was supposed that, at this point, the bread and the wine turned into flesh and blood; therefore, this part of the service was performed with the greatest solemnity.

'Now, to the blessed, most pure, and most holy Mother of God,' the priest cried from the golden partition which divided part of the church from the rest, and the choir began solemnly to sing that it was very right to glorify the Virgin Mary, who had borne Christ without losing her virginity, and was therefore worthy of greater honour than some kind of cherubim, and greater glory than some kind of seraphim. After this the trans-formation was considered accomplished, and the priest having taken the napkin off the saucer, cut the middle bit of bread in four, and put it into the wine, and then into his mouth. He was supposed to have eaten a bit of God's flesh and swallowed a little of His blood. Then the priest drew a curtain, opened the middle door in the partition, and, taking the gold cup in his hands, came out of the door, inviting those who wished to do so also to come and eat some of God's flesh and blood that was contained in the cup. A few children appeared to wish to do so.

After having asked the children their names, the priest carefully took out of the cup, with a spoon, and shoved a bit of bread soaked in wine deep into the mouth of each child in turn, and the deacon, while wiping the children's mouths, sang, in a merry voice, that the children were eating the flesh and drinking the blood of God. After this the priest carried the cup back behind the partition, and there drank all the remaining blood and ate up all the bits of flesh, and after having carefully sucked his moustaches and wiped his mouth, he stepped briskly from behind the partition, the soles of his calfskin boots creaking. The principal part of this Christian service was now finished, but the priest, wishing to comfort the unfortunate prisoners, added to the ordinary service another. This consisted of his going up to the gilt hammered-out image (with black face and hands) supposed to represent the very God he had been eating, illuminated by a dozen wax candles, and proceeding, in a strange, discordant voice, to hum or sing the following words:

'Jesu sweetest, glorified of the Apostles, Jesu lauded by the martyrs, almighty Monarch, save me, Jesu my Saviour. Jesu, most beautiful, have mercy on him who cries to Thee, Saviour Jesu. Born of prayer Jesu, all thy saints, all thy prophets, save and find them worthy of the joys of heaven. Jesu, lover of men.'

Then he stopped, drew breath, crossed himself, bowed to the ground, and everyone did the same – the inspector, the warders, the prisoners; and from above the clinking of the chains sounded more uninterruptedly. Then he continued: 'Of angels the Creator and Lord of powers, Jesu most wonderful, the angels' amazement, Jesu most powerful, of our forefathers the Redeemer. Jesu sweetest, of patriarchs the praise. Jesu most glorious, of kings the strength. Jesu most good, of prophets the fulfilment. Jesu most amazing, of martyrs the strength. Jesu most humble, of monks the joy. Jesu most merciful, of priests the sweetness. Jesu most charitable, of the fasting the continence. Jesu most sweet, of the just the joy. Jesu most pure, of the celibates the chastity. Jesu before all ages of sinners the salvation. Jesu, son of God, have mercy on me.'

Every time he repeated the word 'Jesu' his voice became more and more wheezy. At last he came to a stop, and holding up his silk-lined cassock, and kneeling down on one knee, he stooped down to the ground and the choir began to sing, repeating the words, 'Jesu, Son of God, have mercy on me', and the convicts fell down and rose again, shaking back the hair that was left on their heads, and rattling with the chains that were bruising their thin ankles.

This continued for a long time. First came the glorification, which ended with the words, 'Have mercy on me.' Then more glorifications, ending with 'Alleluia!' And the convicts made the sign of the cross, and bowed, first at each sentence, then after every two and then after three, and all were very glad when the glorification ended, and the priest shut the book with a sigh of relief and retired behind the partition. One last act remained. The priest took a large, gilt cross, with enamel medallions at the ends, from a table, and came out into the centre of the church with it. First the inspector came up and kissed the cross, then the jailers, then the convicts, pushing and abusing each other in whispers. The priest, talking to the inspector, pushed the cross and his hand now against the mouths and now against the noses of the convicts, who were trying to kiss both the cross and the hand of the priest. And thus ended the Christian service, intended for the comfort and the teaching of these strayed brothers.

Chapter 40

The husks of religion

And none of those present, from the inspector down to Maslova, seemed conscious of the fact that this Jesus, whose name the priest repeated such a great number of times, and whom he praised with all these curious expressions, had forbidden the very things that were being done there; that He had prohibited not only this meaningless much-speaking and the blasphemous incantation over the bread and wine, but had also, in the clearest words, forbidden men to call other men their master, and to pray in temples; and had ordered that everyone should pray in solitude, had forbidden to erect temples, saying that He had come to destroy them, and that one should worship, not in a temple, but in spirit and in truth; and, above all, that He had forbidden not only to judge, to imprison, to torment, to execute men, as was being done here, but had prohibited any kind of violence, saying that He had come to give freedom to the captives.

No one present seemed conscious that all that was going on here was the greatest blasphemy and a supreme mockery of that same Christ in whose name it was being done. No one seemed to realise that the gilt cross with the enamel medallions at the ends, which the priest held out to the people to be kissed, was nothing but the emblem of that gallows on which Christ had been executed for denouncing just what was going on here. That these priests, who imagined they were eating and drinking the body and blood of Christ in the form of bread and wine, did in reality eat and drink His flesh and His blood, but not as wine and bits of bread, but by ensnaring 'these little ones' with whom He identified Himself, by depriving them of the greatest blessings and submitting them to most cruel torments, and by hiding from men the tidings of great joy which He had brought. That thought did not enter into the mind of anyone present.

The priest did his part with a quiet conscience, because he was brought up from childhood to consider that the only true faith was the faith which had been held by all the holy men of olden times and was still held by the Church, and demanded by the State authorities. He did not believe that the bread turned into flesh, that it was useful for the soul to repeat so many words, or that he had actually swallowed a bit of God. No one could believe this, but he believed that one ought to hold this faith. What strengthened him most in this faith was the fact that, for fulfilling the demands of this faith, he had for the last fifteen years been able to draw an income, which enabled him to keep his family, send his son to a gymnasium and his daughter to a school for the daughters of the clergy. The deacon believed in the same manner, and even more firmly than the priest, for he had forgotten the substance of the dogmas of this faith, and knew only that the prayers for the dead, the masses, with and without the *acathistus*, all

had a definite price, which real Christians readily paid, and therefore he called out his 'have mercy, have mercy' very willingly, and
read and said what was appointed with the same quiet certainty
of its being necessary to do so with which other men sell faggots,
flour, or potatoes. The prison inspector and the warders, though
they had never understood or gone into the meaning of these
dogmas and of all that went on in church, believed that they must
believe, because the higher authorities and the Tsar himself
believed in it. Besides, though faintly (and themselves unable
to explain why), they felt that this faith defended their cruel
occupations. If this faith did not exist it would have been more
difficult, perhaps impossible, for them to use all their powers to
torment people, as they were now doing, with a quiet conscience.
The inspector was such a kind-hearted man that he could not have
lived as he was now living unsupported by his faith. Therefore, he
stood motionless, bowed and crossed himself zealously, tried to
feel touched when the song about the cherubims was being sung,
and when the children received communion he lifted one of
them, and held him up to the priest with his own hands.

The great majority of the prisoners believed that there lay a
mystic power in these gilt images, these vestments, candles, cups,
crosses, and this repetition of incomprehensible words, 'Jesu
sweetest' and 'have mercy' – a power through which might be
obtained much convenience in this and in the future life. Only a
few clearly saw the deception that was practised on the people
who adhered to this faith, and laughed at it in their hearts; but the
majority, having made several attempts to get the conveniences
they desired, by means of prayers, masses, and candles, and not
having got them (their prayers remaining unanswered), were
each of them convinced that their want of success was accidental,
and that this organisation, approved by the educated and by
archbishops, is very important and necessary, if not for this, at
any rate for the next life.

Maslova also believed in this way. She felt, like the rest, a mixed
sensation of piety and dullness. She stood at first in a crowd
behind a railing, so that she could see no one but her companions;
but when those to receive communion moved on, she and
Theodosia stepped to the front, and they saw the inspector, and
behind him, standing among the warders, a little peasant with a

very light beard and fair hair. This was Theodosia's husband, and he was gazing with fixed eyes at his wife. During the *acathistus* Maslova occupied herself in scrutinising him and talking to Theodosia in whispers, and bowed and made the sign of the cross only when everyone else did.

Chapter 41

Visiting day – the men's ward

Nekhlyudov left home early. A peasant from the country was still driving along the side street and calling out in a voice peculiar to his trade, 'Milk! milk! milk!'

The first warm spring rain had fallen the day before, and now wherever the ground was not paved the grass shone green. The birch trees in the gardens looked as if they were strewn with green fluff, the wild cherry and the poplars unrolled their long, balmy buds, and in shops and dwelling-houses the double window-frames were being removed and the windows cleaned.

In the Tolkoochi* market, which Nekhlyudov had to pass on his way, a dense crowd was surging along the row of booths, and tattered men walked about selling top-boots, which they carried under their arms, and renovated trousers and waistcoats, which hung over their shoulders.

Men in clean coats and shining boots, liberated from the factories, it being Sunday, and women with bright silk kerchiefs on their heads and cloth jackets trimmed with jet, were already thronging at the door of the *traktir*. Policemen, with yellow cords to their uniforms and carrying pistols, were on duty, looking out for some disorder which might distract the *ennui* that oppressed them. On the paths of the boulevards and on the newly-revived grass, children and dogs ran about, playing, and the nurses sat merrily chattering on the benches. Along the streets, still fresh and damp on the shady side, but dry in the middle, heavy carts rumbled unceasingly, cabs rattled and tramcars passed ringing by.

---

* Literally, jostling market, where second-hand clothes and all sorts of cheap goods are sold.

The air vibrated with the pealing and clanging of church bells, that were calling the people to attend to a service like that which was now being conducted in the prison. And the people, dressed in their Sunday best, were passing on their way to their different parish churches.

The *isvostchik* did not drive Nekhlyudov up to the prison itself, but to the last turning that led to the prison.

Several persons – men and women – most of them carrying small bundles, stood at this turning, about a hundred steps from the prison. To the right there were several low wooden buildings; to the left, a two-storeyed house with a signboard. The huge brick building, the prison proper, was just in front, and the visitors were not allowed to come up to it. A sentinel was pacing up and down in front of it, and shouted at anyone who tried to pass him.

At the gate of the wooden buildings, to the right, opposite the sentinel, sat a warder on a bench, dressed in uniform, with gold cords, a notebook in his hands. The visitors came up to him, and named the persons they wanted to see, and he put the names down. Nekhlyudov also went up, and named Katerina Maslova. The warder wrote down the name.

'Why – don't they admit us yet?' asked Nekhlyudov.

'The service is going on. When the Mass is over, you'll be admitted.'

Nekhlyudov stepped aside from the waiting crowd. A man in tattered clothes, crumpled hat, with bare feet and red stripes all over his face, detached himself from the crowd, and turned towards the prison.

'Now, then, where are you going?' shouted the sentinel with the gun.

'And you hold your row,' answered the tramp, not in the least abashed by the sentinel's words, and turned back. 'Well, if you'll not let me in, I'll wait. But, no! must needs shout, as if he were a general.'

The crowd laughed approvingly. The visitors were, for the greater part, badly-dressed people; some were ragged, but there were also some respectable-looking men and women. Next to Nekhlyudov stood a clean-shaven, stout, and red-cheeked man, holding a bundle, apparently containing under-garments. This was the doorkeeper of a bank; he had come to see his brother, who was arrested for forgery. The good-natured fellow told Nekhlyudov the whole story of his life, and was going to question him in turn, when their attention was aroused by a student and a veiled lady, who drove up in a trap, with rubber tyres, drawn by a large thoroughbred horse. The student was holding a large bundle. He came up to Nekhlyudov, and asked if and how he could give the rolls he had brought in alms to the prisoners. His fiancée wished it (this lady was his fiancée), and her parents had advised them to take some rolls to the prisoners.

'I myself am here for the first time,' said Nekhlyudov, 'and don't know; but I think you had better ask this man,' and he pointed to the warder with the gold cords and the book, sitting on the right.

As they were speaking, the large iron door with a window in it opened, and an officer in uniform, followed by another warder, stepped out. The warder with the notebook proclaimed that the admittance of visitors would now commence. The sentinel stepped aside, and all the visitors rushed to the door as if afraid of being too late; some even ran. At the door there stood a warder who counted the visitors as they came in, saying aloud, 16, 17, and so on. Another warder stood inside the building and also counted the visitors as they entered a second door, touching each one with his hand, so that when they went away again not one visitor should be able to remain inside the prison and not one prisoner might get out. The warder, without looking at whom he was touching, slapped Nekhlyudov on the back, and Nekhlyudov felt hurt by the touch of the warder's hand; but remembering what he had come about, he felt ashamed of feeling dissatisfied and taking offence.

The first apartment behind the entrance doors was a large vaulted room with iron bars to the small windows. In this room, which was called the meeting-room, Nekhlyudov was startled by the sight of a large picture of the Crucifixion.

'What's that for?' he thought, his mind involuntarily connecting the subject of the picture with liberation and not with imprisonment.

He went on, slowly letting the hurrying visitors pass before, and experiencing a mingled feeling of horror at the evil-doers locked up in this building, compassion for those who, like Katusha and the boy they tried the day before, must be here though guiltless, and shyness and tender emotion at the thought of the interview before him. The warder at the other end of the meeting-room said something as they passed, but Nekhlyudov, absorbed by his own thoughts, paid no attention to him, and continued to follow the majority of the visitors, and so got into the men's part of the prison instead of the women's.

Letting the hurrying visitors pass before him, he was the last to get into the interviewing-room. As soon as Nekhlyudov opened the door of this room, he was struck by the deafening roar of a hundred voices shouting at once, the reason of which he did not at once understand. But when he came nearer to the people, he saw that they were all pressing against a net that divided the room in two, like flies settling on sugar, and he understood what it meant. The two halves of the room, the windows of which were opposite the door he had come in by, were separated, not by one, but by two nets reaching from the floor to the ceiling. The wire nets were stretched seven feet apart, and soldiers were walking up and down the space between them. On the further side of the nets were the prisoners, on the nearer, the visitors. Between them was a double row of nets and a space of seven feet wide, so that they could not hand anything to one another, and anyone whose sight was not very good could not even distinguish the face on the other side. It was also difficult to talk; one had to scream in order to be heard.

On both sides were faces pressed close to the nets, faces of wives, husbands, fathers, mothers, children, trying to see each other's features and to say what was necessary in such a way as to be understood.

But as each one tried to be heard by the one he was talking to, and his neighbour tried to do the same, they did their best to drown each other's voices, and that was the cause of the din and shouting which struck Nekhlyudov when he first came in. It was impossible to understand what was being said and what were the relations between the different people. Next to Nekhlyudov an old woman with a kerchief on her head stood trembling, her chin pressed close to the net, and shouting something to a young fellow, half of whose head was shaved, who listened attentively with raised brows. By the side of the old woman was a young man in a peasant's coat, who listened, shaking his head, to a boy very like himself. Next stood a man in rags, who shouted, waving his arm and laughing. Next to him a woman, with a good woollen shawl on her shoulders, sat on the floor holding a baby in her lap and crying bitterly. This was apparently the first time she saw the grey-headed man on the other side in prison clothes, and with his head shaved. Beyond her was the doorkeeper, who had spoken to Nekhlyudov outside; he was shouting with all his might to a grey-haired convict on the other side.

When Nekhlyudov found that he would have to speak in similar conditions, a feeling of indignation against those who were able to make and enforce these conditions arose in him; he was surprised that, placed in such a dreadful position, no one seemed offended at this outrage on human feelings. The soldiers, the inspector, the prisoners themselves, acted as if acknowledging all this to be necessary.

Nekhlyudov remained in this room for about five minutes, feeling strangely depressed, conscious of how powerless he was, and at variance with all the world. He was seized with a curious moral sensation like seasickness.

Chapter 42

Visiting day – the women's ward

'Well, but I must do what I came here for,' he said, trying to pick up courage. 'What is to be done now?' He looked round for an official, and seeing a thin little man in the uniform of an officer going up and down behind the people, he approached him.

'Can you tell me, sir,' he said, with exceedingly strained politeness of manner, 'where the women are kept, and where one is allowed to interview them?'

'Is it the women's ward you want to go to?'

'Yes, I should like to see one of the women prisoners,' Nekhlyudov said, with the same strained politeness.

'You should have said so when you were in the hall. Who is it, then, that you want to see?'

'I want to see a prisoner called Katerina Maslova.'

'Is she a political one?'

'No, she is simply . . . '

'What! Is she sentenced?'

'Yes; the day before yesterday she was sentenced,' meekly answered Nekhlyudov, fearing to spoil the inspector's good humour, which seemed to incline in his favour.

'If you want to go to the women's ward please to step this way,' said the officer, having decided from Nekhlyudov's appearance that he was worthy of attention. 'Siderov, conduct the gentleman to the women's ward,' he said, turning to a moustached corporal with medals on his breast.

'Yes, sir.'

At this moment heart-rending sobs were heard coming from someone near the net.

Everything here seemed strange to Nekhlyudov; but strangest of all was that he should have to thank and feel obligation towards the inspector and the chief warders, the very men who were performing the cruel deeds that were done in this house.

The corporal showed Nekhlyudov through the corridor, out of the men's into the women's interviewing-room.

This room, like that of the men, was divided by two wire nets; but it was much smaller, and there were fewer visitors and fewer prisoners, so that there was less shouting than in the men's room. Yet the same thing was going on here, only, between the nets instead of soldiers there was a woman warder, dressed in a blue-edged uniform jacket, with gold cords on the sleeves, and a blue belt. Here also, as in the men's room, the people were pressing close to the wire netting on both sides; on the nearer side, the townspeople in varied attire; on the further side, the prisoners, some in white prison clothes, others in their own coloured dresses. The whole length of the net was taken up by the people standing close to it. Some rose on tiptoe to be heard across the heads of others; some sat talking on the floor.

The most remarkable of the prisoners, both by her piercing screams and her appearance, was a thin, dishevelled gipsy. Her kerchief had slipped off her curly hair, and she stood near a post in the middle of the prisoner's division, shouting something, accompanied by quick gestures, to a gipsy man in a blue coat, girdled tightly below the waist. Next to the gipsy man, a soldier sat on the ground talking to a prisoner; next to the soldier, leaning close to the net, stood a young peasant, with a fair beard and a flushed face, keeping back his tears with difficulty. A pretty, fair-haired prisoner, with bright blue eyes, was speaking to him. These two were Theodosia and her husband. Next to them was a tramp, talking to a broad-faced woman; then two women, then a man, then again a woman, and in front of each a prisoner. Maslova was not among them. But someone stood by the window behind the prisoners, and Nekhlyudov knew it was she. His heart began to beat faster, and his breath stopped. The decisive moment was approaching. He went up to the part of the net where he could see the prisoner, and recognised her at once. She stood behind the blue-eyed Theodosia, and smiled, listening to what Theodosia was saying. She did not wear the prison cloak now, but a white dress, tightly drawn in at the waist by a belt, and very full in the bosom. From under her kerchief appeared the black ringlets of her fringe, just the same as in the court.

'Now, in a moment it will be decided,' he thought. 'How shall I call her? Or will she come herself?'

She was expecting Bertha; that this man had come to see her never entered her head.

'Whom do you want?' said the warder who was walking between the nets, coming up to Nekhlyudov.

'Katerina Maslova,' Nekhlyudov uttered, with difficulty.

'Katerina Maslova, someone to see you,' cried the warder.

Chapter 43

Nekhlyudov visits Maslova

Maslova looked round, and with head thrown back and expanded chest, came up to the net with that expression of readiness which he well knew, pushed in between two prisoners, and gazed at Nekhlyudov with a surprised and questioning look. But, concluding from his clothing he was a rich man, she smiled.

'Is it me you want?' she asked, bringing her smiling face, with the slightly squinting eyes, nearer the net.

'I, I – I wished to see – ' Nekhlyudov did not know how to address her. 'I wished to see you – I – ' He was not speaking louder than usual.

'No; nonsense, I tell you!' shouted the tramp who stood next to him. 'Have you taken it or not?'

'Dying, I tell you; what more do you want?' someone else was screaming at his other side. Maslova could not hear what Nekhlyudov was saying, but the expression of his face as he was speaking reminded her of him. She did not believe her own eyes; still the smile vanished from her face and a deep line of suffering appeared on her brow.

'I cannot hear what you are saying,' she called out, wrinkling her brow and frowning more and more.

'I have come,' said Nekhlyudov. 'Yes, I am doing my duty – I am confessing,' thought Nekhlyudov; and at this thought the tears came in his eyes, and he felt a choking sensation in his throat, and holding on with both hands to the net, he made efforts to keep from bursting into tears.

'I say, why do you shove yourself in where you're not wanted?' someone shouted at one side of him.

'God is my witness; I know nothing,' screamed a prisoner from the other side.

Noticing his excitement, Maslova recognised him.

'You're like . . . but no; I don't know you,' she shouted, without looking at him, and blushing, while her face grew still more stern.

'I have come to ask you to forgive me,' he said, in a loud but monotonous voice, like a lesson learnt by heart. Having said these words he became confused; but immediately came the thought that, if he felt ashamed, it was all the better; he had to bear this shame, and he continued in a loud voice:

'Forgive me; I have wronged you terribly.'

She stood motionless and without taking her squinting eyes off him.

He could not continue to speak, and stepping away from the net he tried to suppress the sobs that were choking him.

The inspector, the same officer who had directed Nekhlyudov to the women's ward, and whose interest he seemed to have aroused, came into the room, and, seeing Nekhlyudov not at the net, asked him why he was not talking to her whom he wanted to see. Nekhlyudov blew his nose, gave himself a shake, and, trying to appear calm, said:

'It's so inconvenient through these nets; nothing can be heard.'

Again the inspector considered for a moment.

'Ah, well, she can be brought out here for a while. Mary Karlovna,' turning to the warder, 'lead Maslova out.'

A minute later Maslova came out of the side door. Stepping softly, she came up close to Nekhlyudov, stopped, and looked up at him from under her brows. Her black hair was arranged in ringlets over her forehead in the same way as it had been two days ago; her face, though unhealthy and puffy, was attractive, and looked perfectly calm, only the glittering black eyes glanced strangely from under the swollen lids.

'You may talk here,' said the inspector, and shrugging his shoulders he stepped aside with a look of surprise. Nekhlyudov moved towards a seat by the wall.

Maslova cast a questioning look at the inspector, and then, shrugging her shoulders in surprise, followed Nekhlyudov to the bench, and having arranged her skirt, sat down beside him.

'I know it is hard for you to forgive me,' he began, but stopped. His tears were choking him. 'But though I can't undo the past, I shall now do what is in my power. Tell me – '

'How have you managed to find me?' she said, without answering his question, neither looking away from him nor quite at him, with her squinting eyes.

'O God, help me! Teach me what to do,' Nekhlyudov thought, looking at her changed face. 'I was on the jury the day before yesterday,' he said. 'You did not recognise me?'

'No, I did not; there was not time for recognitions. I did not even look,' she said.

'There was a child, was there not?' he asked.

'Thank God! he died at once,' she answered, abruptly and viciously.

'What do you mean? Why?'

'I was so ill myself, I nearly died,' she said, in the same quiet voice, which Nekhlyudov had not expected and could not understand.

'How could my aunts have let you go?'

'Who keeps a servant that has a baby? They sent me off as soon as they noticed. But why speak of this? I remember nothing. That's all finished.'

'No, it is not finished; I wish to redeem my sin.'

'There's nothing to redeem. What's been has been and is passed,' she said; and, what he never expected, she looked at him and smiled in an unpleasantly luring, yet piteous, manner.

Maslova never expected to see him again, and certainly not here and not now; therefore, when she first recognised him, she could not keep back the memories which she never wished to revive. In the first moment she remembered dimly that new, wonderful world of feeling and of thought which had been opened to her by the charming young man who loved her and whom she loved, and then his incomprehensible cruelty and the whole string of humiliations and suffering which flowed from and followed that magic joy. This gave her pain, and, unable to understand it, she did what she was always in the habit of doing, she got rid of these memories by enveloping them in the mist of a depraved life. In the first moment, she associated the man now sitting beside her with the lad she had loved; but feeling that this gave her pain, she dissociated them again. Now, this well-dressed, carefully-got-up gentleman with perfumed beard was no longer the Nekhlyudov whom she had loved but only one of the people who made use of creatures like herself when they needed them, and whom creatures like herself had to make use of in their turn as profitably as they could; and that is why she looked at him with a luring smile and considered silently how she could best make use of him.

'That's all at an end,' she said. 'Now I'm condemned to Siberia,' and her lip trembled as she was saying this dreadful word.

'I knew; I was certain you were not guilty,' said Nekhlyudov.

'Guilty! of course not; as if I could be a thief or a robber.' She stopped, considering in what way she could best get something out of him.

'They say here that all depends on the advocate,' she began. 'A petition should be handed in, only they say it's expensive.'

'Yes, most certainly,' said Nekhlyudov. 'I have already spoken to an advocate.'

'No money ought to be spared; it should be a good one,' she said.

'I shall do all that is possible.'

They were silent, and then she smiled again in the same way.

'And I should like to ask you . . . a little money if you can . . . not much; ten roubles, I do not want more,' she said, suddenly.

'Yes, yes,' Nekhlyudov said, with a sense of confusion, and felt for his purse.

She looked rapidly at the inspector, who was walking up and down the room. 'Don't give it in front of him; he'd take it away.'

Nekhlyudov took out his purse as soon as the inspector had turned his back; but had no time to hand her the note before the inspector faced them again, so he crushed it up in his hand.

'This woman is dead,' Nekhlyudov thought, looking at this once sweet, and now defiled, puffy face, lit up by an evil glitter in the black, squinting eyes which were now glancing at the hand in which he held the note, then following the inspector's movements, and for a moment he hesitated. The tempter that had been speaking to him in the night again raised its voice, trying to lead him out of the realm of his inner into the realm of his outer life, away from the question of what he should do to the question of what the consequences would be, and what would be practical.

'You can do nothing with this woman,' said the voice; 'you will only tie a stone round your neck, which will help to drown you and hinder you from being useful to others.

'Is it not better to give her all the money that is here, say goodbye, and finish with her forever?' whispered the voice.

But here he felt that now, at this very moment, something most important was taking place in his soul – that his inner life was, as it were, wavering in the balance, so that the slightest effort would make it sink to this side or the other. And he made this effort by calling to his assistance that God whom he had felt in his soul the day before, and that God instantly responded. He resolved to tell her everything now – at once.

'Katusha, I have come to ask you to forgive me, and you have given me no answer. Have you forgiven me? Will you ever forgive me?' he asked.

She did not listen to him, but looked at his hand and at the inspector, and when the latter turned she hastily stretched out her hand, grasped the note, and hid it under her belt.

'That's odd, what you are saying there,' she said, with a smile of contempt, as it seemed to him.

Nekhlyudov felt that there was in her soul one who was his enemy and who was protecting her, such as she was now, and preventing him from getting at her heart. But, strange to say, this did not repel him, but drew him nearer to her by some fresh, peculiar power. He knew that he must waken her soul, that this was terribly difficult, but the very difficulty attracted him. He now felt towards her as he had never felt towards her or anyone else before. There was nothing personal in this feeling: he wanted nothing from her for himself, but only wished that she might not remain as she now was, that she might awaken and become again what she had been.

'Katusha, why do you speak like that? I know you; I remember you – and the old days in Papovo.'

'What's the use of recalling what's past?' she remarked, drily.

'I am recalling it in order to put it right, to atone for my sin, Katusha,' and he was going to say that he would marry her, but, meeting her eyes, he read in them something so dreadful, so coarse, so repellent, that he could not go on.

At this moment the visitors began to go. The inspector came up to Nekhlyudov and said that the time was up.

'Goodbye; I have still much to say to you, but you see it is impossible to do so now,' said Nekhlyudov, and held out his hand. 'I shall come again.'

'I think you have said all.'

She took his hand but did not press it.

'No; I shall try to see you again, somewhere where we can talk, and then I shall tell you what I have to say – something very important.'

'Well, then, come; why not?' she answered, and smiled with that habitual, inviting, and promising smile which she gave to the men whom she wished to please.

'You are more than a sister to me,' said Nekhlyudov.

'That's odd,' she said again, and went behind the grating.

Chapter 44

Maslova's view of life

Before the first interview, Nekhlyudov thought that when she saw him and knew of his intention to serve her, Katusha would be pleased and touched, and would be Katusha again; but, to his horror, he found that Katusha existed no more, and there was Maslova in her place. This astonished and horrified him.

What astonished him most was that Katusha was not ashamed of her position – not the position of a prisoner (she was ashamed of that), but her position as a prostitute. She seemed satisfied, even proud of it. And, yet, how could it be otherwise? Everybody, in order to be able to act, has to consider his occupation important and good. Therefore, in whatever position a person is, he is certain to form such a view of the life of men in general which will make his occupation seem important and good.

It is usually imagined that a thief, a murderer, a spy, a prostitute, acknowledging his or her profession as evil, is ashamed of it. But the contrary is true. People whom fate and their sin-mistakes have placed in a certain position, however false that position may be, form a view of life in general which makes their position seem good and admissible. In order to keep up their view of life, these people instinctively keep to the circle of those people who share their views of life and their own place in it. This surprises us, where the persons concerned are thieves, bragging about their dexterity, prostitutes vaunting their depravity, or murderers boasting of their cruelty. This surprises us only because the circle, the atmosphere in which these people live, is limited, and we are outside it. But can we not observe the same phenomenon when the rich boast of their wealth, i.e., robbery; the commanders in the army pride themselves on victories, i.e., murder; and those in high places vaunt their power, i.e., violence? We do not see the perversion in the views of life held by these people, only because the circle formed by them is more extensive, and we ourselves are moving inside of it.

And in this manner Maslova had formed her views of life and of her own position. She was a prostitute condemned to Siberia, and yet she had a conception of life which made it possible for her to be satisfied with herself, and even to pride herself on her position before others.

According to this conception, the highest good for all men without exception − old, young, schoolboys, generals, educated and uneducated, was connected with the relation of the sexes; therefore, all men, even when they pretended to be occupied with other things, in reality took this view. She was an attractive woman, and therefore she was an important and necessary person. The whole of her former and present life was a confirmation of the correctness of this conception.

With such a view of life, she was by no means the lowest, but a very important person. And Maslova prized this view of life more than anything; she could not but prize it, for, if she lost the importance that such a view of life gave her among men, she would lose the meaning of her life. And, in order not to lose the meaning of her life, she instinctively clung to the set that looked at life in the same way as she did. Feeling that Nekhlyudov wanted to lead her out into another world, she resisted him, foreseeing that she would have to lose her place in life, with the self-possession and self-respect it gave her. For this reason she drove from her the recollections of her early youth and her first relations with Nekhlyudov. These recollections did not correspond with her present conception of the world, and were therefore quite rubbed out of her mind, or, rather, lay somewhere buried and untouched, closed up and plastered over so that they should not escape, as when bees, in order to protect the result of their labour, will sometimes plaster a nest of worms. Therefore, the present Nekhlyudov was not the man she had once loved with a pure love, but only a rich gentleman whom she could, and must, make use of, and with whom she could only have the same relations as with men in general.

'No, I could not tell her the chief thing,' thought Nekhlyudov, moving towards the front doors with the rest of the people. 'I did not tell her that I would marry her; I did not tell her so, but I will,' he thought.

The two warders at the door let out the visitors, counting them
again, and touching each one with their hands, so that no extra
person should go out, and none remain within. The slap on his
shoulder did not offend Nekhlyudov this time; he did not even
notice it.

Chapter 45

Fanarin, the advocate – the petition

Nekhlyudov meant to rearrange the whole of his external life, to
let his large house and move to an hotel, but Agraphena Petrovna
pointed out that it was useless to change anything before the
winter. No one would rent a town house for the summer; anyhow, he would have to live and keep his things somewhere. And
so all his efforts to change his manner of life (he meant to live
more simply: as the students live) led to nothing. Not only did
everything remain as it was, but the house was suddenly filled with
new activity. All that was made of wool or fur was taken out to be
aired and beaten. The gate-keeper, the boy, the cook, and Corney
himself took part in this activity. All sorts of strange furs, which no
one ever used, and various uniforms were taken out and hung on a
line, then the carpets and furniture were brought out, and the
gate-keeper and the boy rolled their sleeves up their muscular
arms and stood beating these things, keeping strict time, while the
rooms were filled with the smell of naphthaline.

When Nekhlyudov crossed the yard or looked out of the window and saw all this going on, he was surprised at the great number
of things there were, all quite useless. Their only use, Nekhlyudov
thought, was the providing of exercise for Agraphena Petrovna,
Corney, the gate-keeper, the boy, and the cook.

'But it's not worth while altering my manner of life now,' he
thought, 'while Maslova's case is not decided. Besides, it is too
difficult. It will alter of itself when she will be set free or exiled,
and I follow her.'

On the appointed day Nekhlyudov drove up to the advocate
Fanarin's own splendid house, which was decorated with huge

palms and other plants, and wonderful curtains; in fact, with all
the expensive luxury witnessing to the possession of much idle
money, i.e., money acquired without labour, which only those
possess who grow rich suddenly. In the waiting-room, just as in a
doctor's waiting-room, he found many dejected-looking people
sitting round several tables, on which lay illustrated papers meant
to amuse them, awaiting their turns to be admitted to the
advocate. The advocate's assistant sat in the room at a high desk,
and having recognised Nekhlyudov, he came up to him and said
he would go and announce him at once. But the assistant had not
reached the door before it opened and the sounds of loud,
animated voices were heard; the voice of a middle-aged, sturdy
merchant, with a red face and thick moustaches, and the voice of
Fanarin himself. Fanarin was also a middle-aged man of medium
height, with a worn look on his face. Both faces bore the
expression which you see on the faces of those who have just
concluded a profitable but not quite honest transaction.

'Your own fault, you know, my dear sir,' Fanarin said, smiling.

'We'd all be in 'eaven were it not for hour sins.'

'Oh. yes, yes; we all know that,' and both laughed unnaturally.

'Oh, Prince Nekhlyudov! Please to step in,' said Fanarin,
seeing him, and, nodding once more to the merchant, he led
Nekhlyudov into his business cabinet, furnished in a severely
correct style.

'Won't you smoke?' said the advocate, sitting down opposite
Nekhlyudov and trying to conceal a smile, apparently still excited
by the success of the accomplished transaction.

'Thanks; I have come about Maslova's case.'

'Yes, yes; directly! But oh, what rogues these fat money bags
are!' he said. 'You saw this here fellow. Why, he has about twelve
million roubles, and he cannot speak correctly; and if he can get a
twenty-five rouble note out of you he'll have it, if he's to wrench
it out with his teeth.'

'He says " 'eaven" and "hour", and you say "this here fellow",'
Nekhlyudov thought, with an insurmountable feeling of aversion
towards this man who wished to show by his free and easy manner
that he and Nekhlyudov belonged to one and the same camp,
while his other clients belonged to another.

'He has worried me to death – a fearful scoundrel. I felt I must relieve my feelings,' said the advocate, as if to excuse his speaking about things that had no reference to business. 'Well, how about your case? I have read it attentively, but do not approve of it. I mean that greenhorn of an advocate has left no valid reason for an appeal.'

'Well, then, what have you decided?'

'One moment. Tell him,' he said to his assistant, who had just come in, 'that I keep to what I have said. If he can, it's all right; if not, no matter.'

'But he won't agree.'

'Well, no matter,' and the advocate frowned.

'There now, and it is said that we advocates get our money for nothing,' he remarked, after a pause. 'I have freed one insolvent debtor from a totally false charge, and now they all flock to me. Yet every such case costs enormous labour. Why, don't we, too, "lose bits of flesh in the inkstand"? as some writer or other has said. Well, as to your case, or, rather, the case you are taking an interest in. It has been conducted abominably. There is no good reason for appealing. Still,' he continued, 'we can but try to get the sentence revoked. This is what I have noted down.' He took up several sheets of paper covered with writing, and began to read rapidly, slurring over the uninteresting legal terms and laying particular stress on some sentences. 'To the Court of Appeal, criminal department, etc., etc. According to the decisions, etc., the verdict, etc., So-and-so Maslova pronounced guilty of having caused the death through poison of the merchant Smelkov, and has, according to Statute 1454 of the penal code, been sentenced to Siberia,' etc., etc. He stopped. Evidently, in spite of his being so used to it, he still felt pleasure in listening to his own productions. 'This sentence is the direct result of the most glaring judicial perversion and error,' he continued, impressively, 'and there are grounds for its revocation. Firstly, the reading of the medical report of the examination of Smelkov's intestines was interrupted by the president at the very beginning. This is point one.'

'But it was the prosecuting side that demanded this reading,' Nekhlyudov said, with surprise.

'That does not matter. There might have been reasons for the defence to demand this reading, too.'

'Oh, but there could have been no reason whatever for that.'

'It is a ground for appeal, though. To continue: "Secondly," he went on reading, "when Maslova's advocate, in his speech for the defence, wishing to characterise Maslova's personality, referred to the causes of her fall, he was interrupted by the president calling him to order for the alleged deviation from the direct subject. Yet, as has been repeatedly pointed out by the Senate, the elucidation of the criminal's characteristics and his or her moral standpoint in general has a significance of the first importance in criminal cases, even if only as a guide in the settling of the question of imputation." That's point two,' he said, with a look at Nekhlyudov.

'But he spoke so badly that no one could make anything of it,' Nekhlyudov said, still more astonished.

'The fellow's quite a fool, and of course could not be expected to say anything sensible,' Fanarin said, laughing; 'but, all the same, it will do as a reason for appeal. Thirdly: "The president, in his summing up, contrary to the direct decree of section 1, statute 801, of the criminal code, omitted to inform the jury what the judicial points are that constitute guilt; and did not mention that having admitted the fact of Maslova having administered the poison to Smelkov, the jury had a right not to impute the guilt of murder to her, since the proofs of wilful intent to deprive Smelkov of life were absent, and only to pronounce her guilty of carelessness resulting in the death of the merchant, which she did not desire." This is the chief point.'

'Yes; but we ought to have known that ourselves. It was our mistake.'

'And now the fourth point,' the advocate continued. 'The form of the answer given by the jury contained an evident contradiction. Maslova is accused of wilfully poisoning Smelkov, her one object being that of cupidity, the only motive to commit murder she could have had. The jury in their verdict acquit her of the intent to rob, or participation in the stealing of valuables, from which it follows that they intended also to acquit her of the intent to murder, and only through a misunderstanding, which arose from the incompleteness of the president's summing up, omitted to express it in due form in their answer. Therefore an answer of this kind by the jury absolutely demanded the application of statutes 816 and 808 of the criminal code of procedure, i.e., an explanation by the president to the jury of the mistake made by them, and another debate on the question of the prisoner's guilt.'

'Then why did the president not do it?'

'I, too, should like to know why,' Fanarin said, laughing.

'Then the Senate will, of course, correct this error?'

'That will all depend on who will preside there at the time. Well, now, there it is. I have further said,' he continued, rapidly, 'a verdict of this kind gave the Court no right to condemn Maslova to be punished as a criminal, and to apply section 3, statute 771 of the penal code to her case. This is a decided and gross violation of the basic principles of our criminal law. In view of the reasons stated, I have the honour of appealing to you, etc., etc., the refutation, according to 909, 910, and section 2, 912 and 928 statute of the criminal code, etc., etc. . . . to carry this case before another department of the same Court for a further examination. There; all that can be done is done, but, to be frank, I have little hope of success, though, of course, it all depends on what members will be present at the Senate. If you have any influence there you can but try.'

'I do know some.'

'All right; only be quick about it. Else they'll all go off for a change of air; then you may have to wait three months before they return. Then, in case of failure, we have still the possibility of appealing to His Majesty. This, too, depends on the private influence you can bring to work. In this case, too, I am at your service; I mean as to the working of the petition, not the influence.'

'Thank you. Now as to your fees?'

'My assistant will hand you the petition and tell you.'

'One thing more. The procureur gave me a pass for visiting this person in prison, but they tell me I must also get a permission from the governor in order to get an interview at another time and in another place than those appointed. Is this necessary?'

'Yes, I think so. But the governor is away at present; a vice-governor is in his place. And he is such an impenetrable fool that you'll scarcely be able to do anything with him.'

'Is it Maslennikov?'

'Yes.'

'I know him,' said Nekhlyudov, and got up to go. At this

moment a horribly ugly little bony, snub-nosed, yellow-faced woman flew into the room. It was the advocate's wife, who did not seem to be in the least bit troubled by her ugliness. She was attired in the most original manner; she seemed enveloped in something made of velvet and silk, something yellow and green, and her thin hair was crimped.

She stepped out triumphantly into the ante-room, followed by a tall, smiling man, with a greenish complexion, dressed in a coat with silk facings, and a white tie. This was an author. Nekhlyudov knew him by sight.

She opened the cabinet door and said, 'Anatole, you must come to me. Here is Simeon Ivanovitch, who will read his poems, and you must absolutely come and read about Garshin.'

Nekhlyudov noticed that she whispered something to her husband, and, thinking it was something concerning him, wished to go away, but she caught him up and said: 'I beg your pardon, Prince, I know you, and, thinking an introduction superfluous, I beg you to stay and take part in our literary matinée. It will be most interesting. M. Fanarin will read.'

'You see what a lot I have to do,' said Fanarin, spreading out his hands and smilingly pointing to his wife, as if to show how impossible it was to resist so charming a creature.

Nekhlyudov thanked the advocate's wife with extreme politeness for the honour she did him in inviting him, but refused the invitation with a sad and solemn look, and left the room.

'What an affected fellow!' said the advocate's wife, when he had gone out.

In the ante-room the assistant handed him a ready-written petition, and said that the fees, including the business with the Senate and the commission, would come to a thousand roubles, and explained that M. Fanarin did not usually undertake this kind of business, but did it only to oblige Nekhlyudov.

'And about this petition. Who is to sign it?'

'The prisoner may do it herself, or if this is inconvenient, M. Fanarin can, if he gets a power of attorney from her.'

'Oh, no. I shall take the petition to her and get her to sign it,' said Nekhlyudov, glad of the opportunity of seeing her before the appointed day.

Chapter 46

A prison flogging

At the usual time the jailer's whistle sounded in the corridors of the prison, the iron doors of the cells rattled, bare feet pattered, heels clattered, and the prisoners who acted as scavengers passed along the corridors, filling the air with disgusting smells. The prisoners washed, dressed, and came out for revision, then went to get boiling water for their tea.

The conversation at breakfast in all the cells was very lively. It was all about two prisoners who were to be flogged that day. One, Vasiliev, was a young man of some education, a clerk, who had killed his mistress in a fit of jealousy. His fellow-prisoners liked him because he was merry and generous and firm in his behaviour with the prison authorities. He knew the laws and insisted on their being carried out. Therefore he was disliked by the authorities. Three weeks before a jailer struck one of the scavengers who had spilt some soup over his new uniform. Vasiliev took the part of the scavenger, saying that it was not lawful to strike a prisoner.

'I'll teach you the law,' said the jailer, and gave Vasiliev a scolding. Vasiliev replied in like manner, and the jailer was going to hit him, but Vasiliev seized the jailer's hands, held them fast for about three minutes, and, after giving the hands a twist, pushed the jailer out of the door. The jailer complained to the inspector, who ordered Vasiliev to be put into a solitary cell.

The solitary cells were a row of dark closets, locked from outside, and there were neither beds, nor chairs, nor tables in them, so that the inmates had to sit or lie on the dirty floor, while the rats, of which there were a great many in those cells, ran across them. The rats were so bold that they stole the bread from the prisoners, and even attacked them if they stopped moving. Vasiliev said he would not go into the solitary cell, because he had not done anything wrong; but they used force. Then he began struggling, and two other prisoners helped him to free himself from the jailers. All the jailers assembled, and among them was Petrov, who was distinguished for his strength. The prisoners got thrown down and pushed into the solitary cells.

The governor was immediately informed that something very like a rebellion had taken place. And he sent back an order to flog the two chief offenders, Vasiliev and the tramp, Nepomnishy, giving each thirty strokes with a birch rod. The flogging was appointed to take place in the women's interviewing-room.

All this was known in the prison since the evening, and it was being talked about with animation in all the cells.

Korableva, Khoroshevka, Theodosia, and Maslova sat together in their corner, drinking tea, all of them flushed and animated by the vodka they had drunk, for Maslova, who now had a constant supply of vodka, freely treated her companions to it.

'He's not been a-rioting, or anything,' Korableva said, referring to Vasiliev, as she bit tiny pieces off a lump of sugar with her strong teeth. 'He only stuck up for a chum, because it's not lawful to strike prisoners nowadays.'

'And he's a fine fellow, I've heard say,' said Theodosia, who sat bareheaded, with her long plaits round her head, on a log of wood opposite the shelf bedstead on which the teapot stood.

'There, now, if you were to ask *him*,' the watchman's wife said to Maslova (by him she meant Nekhlyudov).

'I shall tell him. He'll do anything for me,' Maslova said, tossing her head, and smiling.

'Yes, but when is he coming? And they've already gone to fetch them,' said Theodosia. 'It is terrible,' she added, with a sigh.

'I once did see how they flogged a peasant in the village. Father-in-law, he sent me once to the village elder. Well, I went, and there . . . ' The watchman's wife began her long story, which was interrupted by the sound of voices and steps in the corridor above them.

The women were silent, and sat listening.

'There they are, hauling him along, the devils!' Khoroshavka said. 'They'll do him to death, they will. The jailers are so enraged with him because he never would give in to them.'

All was quiet again upstairs, and the watchman's wife finished her story of how she was that frightened when she went into the barn

and saw them flogging a peasant, her inside turned at the sight, and
so on. Khoroshevka related how Scheglov had been flogged, and
never uttered a sound. Then Theodosia put away the tea things,
and Korableva and the watchman's wife took up their sewing.
Maslova sat down on the bedstead, with her arms round her knees,
dull and depressed. She was about to lie down and try to sleep,
when the woman warder called her into the office to see a visitor.

'Now, mind, and don't forget to tell him about us,' the old
woman (Menshova) said, while Maslova was arranging the kerchief on her head before the dim looking-glass. 'We did not set
fire to the house, but he himself, the fiend, did it; his workman
saw him do it, and will not damn his soul by denying it. You just
tell to ask to see my Mitri. Mitri will tell him all about it, as plain
as can be. Just think of our being locked up in prison when we
never dreamt of any ill, while he, the fiend, is enjoying himself at
the pub, with another man's wife.'

'That's not the law,' remarked Korableva.

'I'll tell him – I'll tell him,' answered Maslova. 'Suppose I have
another drop, just to keep up courage,' she added, with a wink;
and Korableva poured out half a cup of vodka, which Maslova
drank. Then, having wiped her mouth and repeating the words
'just to keep up courage', tossing her head and smiling gaily, she
followed the warder along the corridor.

Chapter 47

Nekhlyudov again visits Maslova

Nekhlyudov had to wait in the hall for a long time. When he had
arrived at the prison and rung at the entrance door, he handed the
permission of the procureur to the jailer on duty who met him.

'No, no,' the jailer on duty said hurriedly, 'the inspector is
engaged.'

'In the office?' asked Nekhlyudov.

'No, here in the interviewing-room.'

'Why, is it a visiting day today?'

'No; it's special business.'

'I should like to see him. What am I to do?' said Nekhlyudov.

'When the inspector comes out you'll tell him – wait a bit,' said the jailer.

At this moment a sergeant-major, with a smooth, shiny face and moustaches impregnated with tobacco smoke, came out of a side door, with the gold cords of his uniform glistening, and addressed the jailer in a severe tone.

'What do you mean by letting anyone in here? The office . . . .'

'I was told the inspector was here,' said Nekhlyudov, surprised at the agitation he noticed in the sergeant-major's manner.

At this moment the inner door opened, and Petrov came out, heated and perspiring.

'He'll remember it,' he muttered, turning to the sergeant major. The latter pointed at Nekhlyudov by a look, and Petrov knitted his brows and went out through a door at the back.

'Who will remember it? Why do they all seem so confused? Why did the sergeant-major make a sign to him?' Nekhlyudov thought.

The sergeant-major, again addressing Nekhlyudov, said: 'You cannot meet here; please step across to the office.' And Nekhlyudov was about to comply when the inspector came out of the door at the back, looking even more confused than his subordinates, and sighing continually. When he saw Nekhlyudov he turned to the jailer.

'Fedotov, have Maslova, cell 5, women's ward, taken to the office.'

'Will you come this way, please,' he said, turning to Nekhlyudov. They ascended a steep staircase and entered a little room with one window, a writing-table, and a few chairs in it. The inspector sat down.

'Mine are heavy, heavy duties,' he remarked, again addressing Nekhlyudov, and took out a cigarette.

'You are tired, evidently,' said Nekhlyudov.

'Tired of the whole of the service – the duties are very trying. One tries to lighten their lot and only makes it worse; my only thought is how to get away. Heavy, heavy duties!'

Nekhlyudov did not know what the inspector's particular difficulties were, but he saw that today he was in a peculiarly dejected and hopeless condition, calling for pity.

'Yes, I should think the duties were heavy for a kind-hearted man,' he said. 'Why do you serve in this capacity?'

'I have a family.'

'But, if it is so hard – '

'Well, still you know it is possible to be of use in some measure; I soften down all I can. Another in my place would conduct the affairs quite differently. Why, we have more than two thousand persons here. And what persons! One must know how to manage them. It is easier said than done, you know. After all, they are also men; one cannot help pitying them.' The inspector began telling Nekhlyudov of a fight that had lately taken place among the convicts, which had ended by one man being killed.

The story was interrupted by the entrance of Maslova, who was accompanied by a jailer.

Nekhlyudov saw her through the doorway before she had noticed the inspector. She was following the warder briskly, smiling and tossing her head. When she saw the inspector she suddenly changed, and gazed at him with a frightened look; but, quickly recovering, she addressed Nekhlyudov boldly and gaily.

'How d'you do?' she said, drawling out her words, and smilingly took his hand and shook it vigorously, not like the first time.

'Here, I've brought you a petition to sign,' said Nekhlyudov, rather surprised by the boldness with which she greeted him today. 'The advocate has written out a petition which you will have to sign, and then we shall send it to Petersburg.'

'All right! That can be done. Anything you like,' she said, with a wink and a smile.

And Nekhlyudov drew a folded paper from his pocket and went up to the table.

'May she sign it here?' asked Nekhlyudov, turning to the inspector.

'It's all right, it's all right! Sit down. Here's a pen; you can write?' said the inspector.

'I could at one time,' she said; and, after arranging her skirt and the sleeves of her jacket, she sat down at the table, smiled awkwardly, took the pen with her small, energetic hand, and glanced at Nekhlyudov with a laugh.

Nekhlyudov told her what to write and pointed out the place where to sign.

Sighing deeply as she dipped her pen into the ink, and carefully shaking some drops off the pen, she wrote her name.

'Is it all?' she asked, looking from Nekhlyudov to the inspector, and putting the pen now on the inkstand, now on the papers.

'I have a few words to tell you,' Nekhlyudov said, taking the pen from her.

'All right; tell me,' she said. And suddenly, as if remembering something, or feeling sleepy, she grew serious.

The inspector rose and left the room, and Nekhlyudov remained with her.

Chapter 48

Maslova refuses to marry

The jailer who had brought Maslova in sat on a windowsill at some distance from them.

The decisive moment had come for Nekhlyudov. He had been incessantly blaming himself for not having told her the principal thing at the first interview, and was now determined to tell her that he would marry her. She was sitting at the further side of the table. Nekhlyudov sat down opposite her. It was light in the room, and Nekhlyudov for the first time saw her face quite near. He distinctly saw the crows' feet round her eyes, the wrinkles round her mouth, and the swollen eyelids. He felt more sorry than before. Leaning over the table so as not to be beard by the jailer – a man of Jewish type with grizzly whiskers, who sat by the window – Nekhlyudov said: 'Should this petition come to nothing we shall appeal to the Emperor. All that is possible shall be done.'

'There, now, if we had had a proper advocate from the first,' she interrupted. 'My defendant was quite a silly. He did nothing but pay me compliments,' she said, and laughed. 'If it had then been known that I was acquainted with you, it would have been another matter. They think everyone's a thief.'

'How strange she is today,' Nekhlyudov thought, and was just going to say what he had on his mind when she began again:

'There's something I want to say. We have here an old woman; such a fine one, d'you know, she just surprises everyone; she is imprisoned for nothing, and her son, too, and everybody knows they are innocent, though they are accused of having set fire to a house. D'you know, hearing I was acquainted with you, she says: "Tell him to ask to see my son; he'll tell him all about it." ' Thus spoke Maslova, turning her head from side to side, and glancing at Nekhlyudov. 'Their name's Menshov. Well, will you do it? Such a fine old thing, you know; you can see at once she's innocent. You'll do it, there's a dear,' and she smiled, glanced up at him, and then cast down her eyes.

'All right. I'll find out about them,' Nekhlyudov said, more and more astonished by her free-and-easy manner. 'But I was going to speak to you about myself. Do you remember what I told you last time?'

'You said a lot last time. What was it you told me?' she said, continuing to smile and to turn her head from side to side.

'I said I had come to ask you to forgive me,' he began.

'What's the use of that? Forgive, forgive, where's the good of – '

'To atone for my sin, not by mere words, but in deed. I have made up my mind to marry you.'

An expression of fear suddenly came over her face. Her squinting eyes remained fixed on him, and yet seemed not to be looking at him.

'What's that for?' she said, with an angry frown.

'I feel that it is my duty before God to do it.'

'What God have you found now? You are not saying what you ought to. God, indeed! What God? You ought to have remembered God then,' she said, and stopped with her mouth open. It was only now that Nekhlyudov noticed that her breath smelled of spirits, and that he understood the cause of her excitement.

'Try and be calm,' he said.

'Why should I be calm?' she began, quickly, flushing scarlet. 'I am a convict, and you are a gentleman and a prince. There's no need for you to soil yourself by touching me. You go to your princesses; my price is a ten-rouble note.'

'However cruelly you may speak, you cannot express what I myself am feeling,' he said, trembling all over; 'you cannot imagine to what extent I feel myself guilty towards you.'

'Feel yourself guilty?' she said, angrily mimicking him. 'You did not feel so then, but threw me a hundred roubles. That's your price.'

'I know, I know; but what is to be done now?' said Nekhlyudov. 'I have decided not to leave you, and what I have said I shall do.'

'And I say you shan't,' she said, and laughed aloud.

'Katusha' he said, touching her hand.

'You go away. I am a convict and you a prince, and you've no business here,' she cried, pulling away her hand, her whole appearance transformed by her wrath. 'You've got pleasure out of me in this life, and want to save yourself through me in the life to come. You are disgusting to me – your spectacles and the whole of your dirty fat mug. Go, go!' she screamed, starting to her feet.

The jailer came up to them.

'What are you kicking up this row for?' That won't – '

'Let her alone, please,' said Nekhlyudov.

'She must not forget herself,' said the jailer.

'Please wait a little,' said Nekhlyudov, and the jailer returned to the window.

Maslova sat down again, dropping her eyes and firmly clasping her small hands.

Nekhlyudov stooped over her, not knowing what to do.

'You do not believe me?' he said.

'That you mean to marry me? It will never be. I'll rather hang myself. So there!'

'Well, still I shall go on serving you.'

'That's your affair, only I don't want anything from you. I am telling you the plain truth,' she said. 'Oh, why did I not die then?' she added, and began to cry piteously.

Nekhlyudov could not speak; her tears infected him.

She lifted her eyes, looked at him in surprise, and began to wipe her tears with her kerchief.

The jailer came up again and reminded them that it was time to part.

Maslova rose.

'You are excited. If it is possible, I shall come again tomorrow; you think it over,' said Nekhlyudov.

She gave him no answer and, without looking up, followed the jailer out of the room.

'Well, lass, you'll have rare times now,' Korableva said, when Maslova returned to the cell. 'Seems he's mighty sweet on you; make the most of it while he's after you. He'll help you out. Rich people can do anything.'

'Yes, that's so,' remarked the watchman's wife, with her musical voice. 'When a poor man thinks of getting married, there's many a slip 'twixt the cup and the lip; but a rich man need only make up his mind and it's done. We knew a toff like that, duckie. What d'you think he did?'

'Well, have you spoken about my affairs?' the old woman asked.

But Maslova gave her fellow-prisoners no answer; she lay down on the shelf bedstead, her squinting eyes fixed on a corner of the room, and lay there until the evening.

A painful struggle went on in her soul. What Nekhlyudov had told her called up the memory of that world in which she had suffered and which she had left without having understood, hating it. She now feared to wake from the trance in which she was living. Not having arrived at any conclusion when evening came, she again bought some vodka and drank with her companions.

Chapter 49

Vera Doukhova

'So this is what it means, this,' thought Nekhlyudov as he left the prison, only now fully understanding his crime. If he had not tried to expiate his guilt he would never have found out how great his crime was. Nor was this all; she, too, would never have felt the whole horror of what had been done to her. He only now saw what he had done to the soul of this woman; only now she saw and understood what had been done to her.

Up to this time Nekhlyudov had played with a sensation of self-admiration, had admired his own remorse; now he was simply filled with horror. He knew he could not throw her up now, and yet he could not imagine what would come of their relations to one another.

Just as he was going out, a jailer, with a disagreeable, insinuating countenance, and a cross and medals on his breast, came up and handed him a note with an air of mystery.

'Here is a note from a certain person, your honour,' he said to Nekhlyudov as he gave him the envelope.

'What person?'

'You will know when you read it. A political prisoner. I am in that ward, so she asked me; and though it is against the rules, still feelings of humanity – ' The jailer spoke in an unnatural manner.

Nekhlyudov was surprised that a jailer of the ward where political prisoners were kept should pass notes inside the very prison walls, and almost within sight of everyone; he did not then know that this was both a jailer and a spy. However, he took the note and read it on coming out of the prison.

The note was written in a bold hand, and ran as follows:

Having heard that you visit the prison, and are interested in the case of a criminal prisoner, the desire of seeing you arose in me. Ask for a permission to see me. I can give you a good deal of information concerning your *protegée*, and also our group. –
> Yours gratefully,
>> Vera Doukhova

Vera Doukhova had been a school-teacher in an out-of-the-way village of the Novgorod government, where Nekhlyudov and some friends of his had once put up while bear hunting. Nekhlyudov gladly and vividly recalled those old days, and his acquaintance with Doukhova. It was just before Lent, in an isolated spot, forty miles from the railway. The hunt had been successful; two bears had been killed; and the company were having dinner before starting on their return journey, when the master of the hut where they were putting up came in to say that the deacon's daughter wanted to speak to Prince Nekhlyudov. 'Is she pretty?' someone asked. 'None of that, please,' Nekhlyudov said, and rose with a serious look on his face. Wiping his mouth, and wondering what the deacon's daughter might want of him, he went into the host's private hut.

There he found a girl with a felt hat and a warm cloak on – a sinewy, ugly girl; only her eyes with their arched brows were beautiful.

'Here, miss, speak to him,' said the old housewife; 'this is the prince himself. I shall go out meanwhile.'

'In what way can I be of service to you?' Nekhlyudov asked.

'I – I – I see you are throwing away your money on such nonsense – on hunting,' began the girl, in great confusion. 'I know – I only want one thing – to be of use to the people, and I can do nothing because I know nothing – ' Her eyes were so truthful, so kind, and her expression of resoluteness and yet bashfulness was so touching, that Nekhlyudov, as it often happened to him, suddenly felt as if he were in her position, understood, and sympathised.

'What can I do, then?'

'I am a teacher, but should like to follow a course of study; and I am not allowed to do so. That is, not that I am not allowed to; they'd allow me to, but I have not got the means. Give them to me, and when I have finished the course I shall repay you. I am thinking the rich kill bears and give the peasants drink; all this is bad. Why should they not do good? I only want eighty roubles. But if you don't wish to, never mind,' she added, gravely.

'On the contrary, I am very grateful to you for this opportunity. . . . I will bring it at once,' said Nekhlyudov.

He went out into the passage, and there met one of his comrades, who had been overhearing his conversation. Paying no heed to his chaffing, Nekhlyudov got the money out of his bag and took it to her.

'Oh, please, do not thank me; it is I who should thank you,' he said.

It was pleasant to remember all this now; pleasant to remember that he had nearly had a quarrel with an officer who tried to make an objectionable joke of it, and how another of his comrades had taken his part, which led to a closer friendship between them. How successful the whole of that hunting expedition had been, and how happy he had felt when returning to the railway station that night. The line of sledges, the horses in tandem, glide quickly along the narrow road that lies through the forest, now between high trees, now between low firs weighed down by the snow, caked in heavy lumps on their branches. A red light flashes in the dark, someone lights an aromatic cigarette. Joseph, a bear driver, keeps running from sledge to sledge, up to his knees in snow, and while putting things to rights he speaks about the elk which are now going about on the deep snow and gnawing the bark off the aspen trees, of the bears that are lying asleep in their deep hidden dens, and his breath comes warm through the opening in the sledge cover. All this came back to Nekhlyudov's mind; but, above all, the joyous sense of health, strength, and freedom from care: the lungs breathing in the frosty air so deeply that the fur cloak is drawn tightly on his chest, the fine snow drops off the low branches on to his face, his body is warm, his face feels fresh, and his soul is free from care, self-reproach, fear, or desire. How beautiful it was. And now, O God! what torment, what trouble!

Evidently Vera Doukhova was a revolutionist and imprisoned as such. He must see her, especially as she promised to advise him how to lighten Maslova's lot.

Chapter 50

The vice-governor of the prison

Awaking early the next morning, Nekhlyudov remembered what he had done the day before, and was seized with fear.

But in spite of this fear, he was more determined than ever to continue what he had begun.

Conscious of a sense of duty, he left the house and went to see Maslennikov in order to obtain from him a permission to visit Maslova in prison, and also the Menshovs – mother and son – about whom Maslova had spoken to him. Nekhlyudov had known this Maslennikov a long time; they had been in the regiment together. At that time Maslennikov was treasurer to the regiment.

He was a kind-hearted and zealous officer, knowing and wishing to know nothing beyond the regiment and the Imperial family. Now Nekhlyudov saw him as an administrator, who had exchanged the regiment for an administrative office in the government where he lived. He was married to a rich and energetic woman, who had forced him to exchange military for civil service. She laughed at him, and caressed him, as if he were her own pet animal. Nekhlyudov had been to see them once during the winter, but the couple were so uninteresting to him that he had not gone again.

At the sight of Nekhlyudov Maslennikov's face beamed all over. He had the same fat red face, and was as corpulent and as well dressed as in his military days. Then, he used to be always dressed in a well-brushed uniform, made according to the latest fashion, tightly fitting his chest and shoulders; now, it was a civil service uniform he wore, and that, too, tightly fitted his well-fed body and showed off his broad chest, and was cut according to the latest fashion. In spite of the difference in age (Maslennikov was forty), the two men were very familiar with one another.

'Halloo, old fellow! How good of you to come! Let us go and see my wife. I have just ten minutes to spare before the meeting. My chief is away, you know. I am at the head of the government administration,' he said, unable to disguise his satisfaction.

'I have come on business.'

'What is it?' said Maslennikov, in an anxious and severe tone, putting himself at once on his guard.

'There is a person, whom I am very much interested in, in prison,' (at the word 'prison' Maslennikov's face grew stern) 'and I should like to have an interview in the office, and not in the common visiting-room. I have been told it depended on you.'

'Certainly, *mon cher*,' said Maslennikov, putting both hands on Nekhlyudov's knees, as if to tone down his grandeur; 'but remember, I am monarch only for an hour.'

'Then will you give me an order that will enable me to see her?'

'It's a woman?'

'Yes.'

'What is she there for?'

'Poisoning, but she has been unjustly condemned.'

'Yes, there you have it, your justice administered by jury, *ils n'en font point d'autres*,' he said, for some unknown reason in French. 'I know you do not agree with me, but it can't be helped, *c'est mon opinion bien arretée*,' he added, giving utterance to an opinion he had for the last twelve months been reading in the retrograde Conservative paper. 'I know you are a Liberal.'

'I don't know whether I am a Liberal or something else,' Nekhlyudov said, smiling; it always surprised him to find himself ranked with a political party and called a Liberal, when he maintained that a man should be heard before he was judged, that before being tried all men were equal, that nobody at all ought to be ill-treated and beaten, but especially those who had not yet been condemned by law. 'I don't know whether I am a Liberal or not; but I do know that however bad the present way of conducting a trial is, it is better than the old.'

'And whom have you for an advocate?'

'I have spoken to Fanarin.'

'Dear me, Fanarin!' said Maslennikov, with a grimace, recollecting how this Fanarin had examined him as a witness at a trial the year before and had, in the politest manner, held him up to ridicule for half an hour.

'I should not advise you to have anything to do with him. *Fanarin est un homme taré.*'

'I have one more request to make,' said Nekhlyudov, without answering him. 'There's a girl whom I knew long ago, a teacher; she is a very pitiable little thing, and is now also imprisoned, and would like to see me. Could you give me a permission to visit her?'

Maslennikov bent his head on one side and considered.

'She's a political one?'

'Yes, I have been told so.'

'Well, you see, only relatives get permission to visit political prisoners. Still, I'll give you an open order. *Je sais que vous n'abuserez pas.* What's the name of your *protegée*? Doukhova? *Elle est jolie?*'

'*Hideuse.*'

Maslennikov shook his head disapprovingly, went up to the table, and wrote on a sheet of paper, with a printed heading: 'The bearer, Prince Dmitri Ivanovitch Nekhlyudov, is to be allowed to interview in the prison office the meschanka Maslova, and also the medical assistant, Doukhova,' and he finished with an elaborate flourish.

'Now you'll be able to see what order we have got there. And it is very difficult to keep order, it is so crowded, especially with people condemned to exile; but I watch strictly, and love the work. You will see they are very comfortable and contented. But one must know how to deal with them. Only a few days ago we had a little trouble — insubordination; another would have called it mutiny, and would have made many miserable, but with us it all passed quietly. We must have solicitude on one hand, firmness and power on the other,' and he clenched the fat, white, turquoise-ringed fist, which issued out of the starched cuff of his shirt sleeve, fastened with a gold stud. 'Solicitude and firm power.'

'Well, I don't know about that,' said Nekhlyudov. 'I went there twice, and felt very much depressed.'

'Do you know, you ought to get acquainted with the Countess Passek,' continued Maslennikov, growing talkative. 'She has given herself up entirely to this sort of work. *Elle fait beaucoup de bien.* Thanks to her — and, perhaps I may add without false modesty, to me — everything has been changed, changed in such a way that the former horrors no longer exist, and they are really quite comfortable there. Well, you'll see. There's Fanarin. I do not know him personally; besides, my social position keeps our ways apart; but he is positively a bad man, and besides, he takes the liberty of saying such things in the court — such things!'

'Well, thank you,' Nekhlyudov said, taking the paper, and without listening further he bade good-day to his former comrade.

'And won't you go in to see my wife?'

'No, pray excuse me; I have no time now.'

'Dear me, why she will never forgive me,' said Maslennikov, accompanying his old acquaintance down to the first landing, as he was in the habit of doing to persons of not the greatest, but the second greatest importance, with whom he classed Nekhlyudov; 'now do go in, if only for a moment.'

But Nekhlyudov remained firm; and while the footman and the door-keeper rushed to give him his stick and overcoat, and opened the door, outside of which there stood a policeman, Nekhlyudov repeated that he really could not come in.

'Well, then; on Thursday, please. It is her "At-Home". I will tell her you will come,' shouted Maslennikov from the stairs.

Chapter 51

The cells

Nekhlyudov drove that day straight from Maslennikov's to the prison, and went to the inspector's lodging, which he now knew. He was again struck by the sounds of the same piano of inferior quality; but this time it was not a rhapsody that was being played, but exercises by Clementi, again with the same vigour, distinctness, and quickness. The servant with the bandaged eye said the inspector was in, and showed Nekhlyudov to a small drawing-room, in which there stood a sofa and, in front of it, a table, with a large lamp, which stood on a piece of crochet work, and the paper shade of which was burnt on one side. The chief inspector entered, with his usual sad and weary look.

'Take a seat, please. What is it you want?' he said, buttoning up the middle button of his uniform.

'I have just been to the vice-governor's, and got this order from him. I should like to see the prisoner Maslova.'

'Markova?' asked the inspector, unable to bear distinctly because of the music.

'Maslova!'

'Well, yes.' The inspector got up and went to the door whence proceeded Clementi's *roulades*.

'Mary, can't you stop just a minute?' he said, in a voice that showed that this music was the bane of his life. 'One can't hear a word.'

The piano was silent, but one could hear the sound of reluctant steps, and someone looked in at the door.

The inspector seemed to feel eased by the interval of silence, lit a thick cigarette of weak tobacco, and offered one to Nekhlyudov. Nekhlyudov refused.

'What I want is to see Maslova.'

'Oh, yes, that can be managed. Now, then, what do you want?'

he said, addressing a little girl of five or six, who came into the room and walked up to her father with her head turned towards Nekhlyudov, and her eyes fixed on him.

'There, now, you'll fall down,' said the inspector, smiling, as the little girl ran up to him, and, not looking where she was going, caught her foot in a little rug.

'Well, then, if I may, I shall go.'

'It's not very convenient to see Maslova today,' said the inspector.

'How's that?'

'Well, you know, it's all your own fault,' said the inspector, with a slight smile. 'Prince, give her no money into her hands. If you like, give it me. I will keep it for her. You see, you gave her some money yesterday; she got some spirits (it's an evil we cannot manage to root out), and today she is quite tipsy, even violent.'

'Can this be true?'

'Oh, yes, it is. I have even been obliged to have recourse to severe measures, and to put her into a separate cell. She is a quiet woman in an ordinary way. But please do not give her any money. These people are so – ' What had happened the day before came vividly back to Nekhlyudov's mind, and again he was seized with fear.

'And Doukhova, a political prisoner; might I see her?'

'Yes, if you like,' said the inspector. He embraced the little girl, who was still looking at Nekhlyudov, got up, and, tenderly motioning her aside, went into the ante-room. Hardly had he got into the overcoat which the maid helped him to put on, and before he had reached the door, the distinct sounds of Clementi's *roulades* again began.

'She entered the Conservatoire, but there is such disorder there. She has a great gift,' said the inspector, as they went down the stairs. 'She means to play at concerts.'

The inspector and Nekhlyudov arrived at the prison. The gates were instantly opened as they appeared. The jailers, with their fingers lifted to their caps, followed the inspector with their eyes. Four men, with their heads half-shaved, who were carrying tubs filled with something, cringed when they saw the inspector. One of them frowned angrily, his black eyes glaring.

'Of course a talent like that must be developed; it would not do to bury it, but in a small lodging, you know, it is rather hard.' The inspector went on with the conversation, taking no notice of the prisoners.

'Who is it you want to see?'

'Doukhova.'

'Oh, she's in the tower. You'll have to wait a little,' he said.

'Might I not meanwhile see the prisoners Menshov, mother and son, who are accused of incendiarism?'

'Oh, yes. Cell No. 21. Yes, they can be sent for.'

'But might I not see Menshov in his cell?'

'Oh, you'll find the waiting-room more pleasant.'

'No. I should prefer the cell. It is more interesting.'

'Well, you have found something to be interested in!'

Here the assistant, a smartly-dressed officer, entered the side door.

'Here, see the Prince into Menshov's cell, No. 21,' said the inspector to his assistant, 'and then take him to the office. And I'll go and call – what's her name? Vera Doukhova.'

The inspector's assistant was young, with dyed moustaches, and diffusing the smell of eau-de-cologne. 'This way, please,' he said to Nekhlyudov, with a pleasant smile. 'Our establishment interests you?'

'Yes, it does interest me; and, besides, I look upon it as a duty to help a man who I heard was confined here, though innocent.'

The assistant shrugged his shoulders. 'Yes, that may happen,' he said quietly, politely stepping aside to let the visitor enter, the stinking corridor first. 'But it also happens that they lie. Here we are.'

The doors of the cells were open, and some of the prisoners were in the corridor. The assistant nodded slightly to the jailers, and cast a side glance at the prisoners, who, keeping close to the wall, crept back to their cells, or stood like soldiers, with their arms at their sides, following the official with their eyes. After passing through one corridor, the assistant showed Nekhlyudov into another to the left, separated from the first by an iron door. This corridor was darker, and smelt even worse than the first. The corridor had doors on both sides, with little holes in them about an inch in diameter. There was only an old jailer, with an unpleasant face, in this corridor.

'Where is Menshov?' asked the inspector's assistant.

'The eighth cell to the left.'

'And these? Are they occupied?' asked Nekhlyudov.

'Yes, all but one.'

Chapter 52

No. 21

'May I look in?' asked Nekhlyudov.

'Oh, certainly,' answered the assistant, smiling, and turned to the jailer with some question.

Nekhlyudov looked into one of the little holes, and saw a tall young man pacing up and down the cell. When the man heard someone at the door he looked up with a frown, but continued walking up and down.

Nekhlyudov looked into another hole. His eye met another large eye looking out of the hole at him, and he quickly stepped aside. In the third cell he saw a very small man asleep on the bed, covered, head and all, with his prison cloak. In the fourth a broad-faced man was sitting with his elbows on his knees and his head low down. At the sound of footsteps this man raised his head and looked up. His face, especially his large eyes, bore the expression of hopeless dejection. One could see that it did not even interest him to know who was looking into his cell. Whoever it might be, he evidently hoped for nothing good from him. Nekhlyudov was seized with dread, and went to Menshov's cell, No. 21, without stopping to look through any more holes. The jailer unlocked the door and opened it. A young man, with long neck, well-developed muscles, a small head, and kind, round eyes, stood by the bed, hastily putting on his cloak, and looking at the newcomers with a frightened face. Nekhlyudov was specially struck by the kind, round eyes that were throwing frightened and inquiring glances in turns at him, at the jailer, and at the assistant, and back again.

'Here's a gentleman wants to inquire into your affair.'

'Thank you kindly.'

'Yes, I was told about you,' Nekhlyudov said, going through the cell up to the dirty grated window, 'and I should like to hear all about it from yourself.'

Menshov also came up to the window, and at once started telling his story, at first looking shyly at the inspector's assistant, but growing gradually bolder. When the assistant left the cell and went into the corridor to give some order the man grew quite bold. The story was told with the accent and in the manner common to a most ordinary good peasant lad. To hear it told by a prisoner dressed in this degrading clothing, and inside a prison, seemed very strange to Nekhlyudov. Nekhlyudov listened, and at the same time kept looking around him – at the low bedstead with its straw mattress, the window and the dirty, damp wall, and the piteous face and form of this unfortunate, disfigured peasant in his prison cloak and shoes, and he felt sadder and sadder, and would have liked not to believe what this good-natured fellow was saying. It seemed too dreadful to think that men could do such a thing as to take a man, dress him in convict clothes, and put him in this horrible place without any reason only because he himself had been injured. And yet the thought that this seemingly true story, told with such a good-natured expression on the face, might be an invention and a lie was still more dreadful. This was the story: the village public-house keeper had enticed the young fellow's wife. He tried to get justice by all sorts of means. But everywhere the public-house keeper managed to bribe the officials, and was acquitted. Once, he took his wife back by force, but she ran away next day. Then he came to demand her back, but though he saw her when he came in, the public-house keeper told him she was not there, and ordered him to go away. He would not go, so the public-house keeper and his servant beat him so that they drew blood. The next day a fire broke out in the public-house, and the young man and his mother were accused of having set the house on fire. He had not set it on fire, but was visiting a friend at the time.

'And it is true that you did not set it on fire?'

'It never entered my head to do it, sir. It must be my enemy that did it himself. They say he had only just insured it. Then they said it was mother and I that did it, and that we had threatened him. It is true I once did go for him, my heart couldn't stand it any longer.'

'Can this be true?'

'God is my witness it is true. Oh, sir, be so good – ' and Nekhlyudov had some difficulty to prevent him from bowing down to the ground. 'You see I am perishing without any reason.' His face quivered and he turned up the sleeve of his cloak and began to cry, wiping the tears with the sleeve of his dirty shirt.

'Are you ready?' asked the assistant.

'Yes. Well, cheer up. We will consult a good lawyer, and will do what we can,' said Nekhlyudov, and went out. Menshov stood close to the door, so that the jailer knocked him in shutting it, and while the jailer was locking it he remained looking out through the little hole.

Chapter 53

Victims of government

Passing back along the broad corridor (it was dinner time, and the cell doors were open), among the men dressed in their light yellow cloaks, short, wide trousers, and prison shoes, who were looking eagerly at him, Nekhlyudov felt a strange mixture of sympathy for them, and horror and perplexity at the conduct of those who put and kept them here, and besides, he felt, he knew not why, ashamed of himself calmly examining it all.

In one of the corridors, someone ran, clattering with his shoes, in at the door of a cell. Several men came out from here, and stood in Nekhlyudov's way, bowing to him.

'Please, your honour (we don't know what to call you), get our affair settled somehow.'

'I am not an official. I know nothing about it.'

'Well, anyhow, you come from outside; tell somebody – one of the authorities, if need be,' said an indignant voice. 'Show some pity on us, as a human being. Here we are suffering the second month for nothing.'

'What do you mean? Why?' said Nekhlyudov.

'Why? We ourselves don't know why, but are sitting here the second month.'

'Yes, it's quite true, and it is owing to an accident,' said the inspector. 'These people were taken up because they had no passports, and ought to have been sent back to their native government; but the prison there is burnt, and the local authorities have written, asking us not to send them on. So we have sent all the other passportless people to their different governments, but are keeping these.'

'What! for no other reason than that?' Nekhlyudov exclaimed, stopping at the door.

A crowd of about forty men, all dressed in prison clothes, surrounded him and the assistant, and several began talking at once. The assistant stopped them.

'Let some one of you speak.'

A tall, good-looking peasant, a stone-mason, of about fifty, stepped out from the rest. He told Nekhlyudov that all of them had been ordered back to their homes and were now being kept in prison because they had no passports, yet they had passports which were only a fortnight overdue. The same thing had happened every year; they had many times omitted to renew their passports till they were overdue, and nobody had ever said anything; but this year they had been taken up and were being kept in prison the second month, as if they were criminals.

'We are all masons, and belong to the same *artel*. We are told that the prison in our government is burnt, but this is not our fault. Do help us.'

Nekhlyudov listened, but hardly understood what the good-looking old man was saying, because his attention was riveted to a large, dark-grey, many-legged louse that was creeping along the good-looking man's cheek.

'How's that? Is it possible for such a reason?' Nekhlyudov said, turning to the assistant.

'Yes, they should have been sent off and taken back to their homes,' calmly said the assistant, 'but they seem to have been forgotten or something.'

Before the assistant had finished, a small, nervous man, also in prison dress, came out of the crowd, and, strangely contorting his mouth, began to say that they were being ill-used for nothing.

'Worse than dogs,' he began.

'Now, now; not too much of this. Hold your tongue, or you know – '

'What do I know?' screamed the little man, desperately. 'What is our crime?'

'Silence!' shouted the assistant, and the little man was silent.

'But what is the meaning of all this?' Nekhlyudov thought to himself as he came out of the cell, while a hundred eyes were fixed upon him through the openings of the cell doors and from the prisoners that met him, making him feel as if he were running the gauntlet.

'Is it really possible that perfectly innocent people are kept here?' Nekhlyudov uttered when they left the corridor.

'What would you have us do? They lie so. To hear them talk they are all of them innocent,' said the inspector's assistant. 'But it does happen that some are really imprisoned for nothing.'

'Well, these have done nothing.'

'Yes, we must admit it. Still, the people are fearfully spoilt. There are such types – desperate fellows, with whom one has to look sharp. Today two of that sort had to be punished.'

'Punished? How?'

'Flogged with a birch-rod, by order.'

'But corporal punishment is abolished.'

'Not for such as are deprived of their rights. They are still liable to it.'

Nekhlyudov thought of what he had seen the day before while waiting in the hall, and now understood that the punishment was then being inflicted, and the mixed feeling of curiosity, depression, perplexity, and moral nausea, that grew into physical sickness, took hold of him more strongly than ever before.

Without listening to the inspector's assistant, or looking round, he hurriedly left the corridor, and went to the office. The inspector was in the office, occupied with other business, and had forgotten to send for Doukhova. He only remembered his promise to have her called when Nekhlyudov entered the office.

'Sit down, please. I'll send for her at once,' said the inspector.

Chapter 54

Prisoners and friends

The office consisted of two rooms. The first room, with a large, dilapidated stove and two dirty windows, had a black measure for measuring the prisoners in one corner, and in another corner hung a large image of Christ, as is usual in places where they torture people. In this room stood several jailers. In the next room sat about twenty persons, men and women in groups and in pairs, talking in low voices. There was a writing table by the window.

The inspector sat down by the table, and offered Nekhlyudov a chair beside him. Nekhlyudov sat down, and looked at the people in the room.

The first who drew his attention was a young man with a pleasant face, dressed in a short jacket, standing in front of a middle-aged woman with dark eyebrows, and he was eagerly telling her something and gesticulating with his hands. Beside them sat an old man, with blue spectacles, holding the hand of a young woman in prisoner's clothes, who was telling him something. A schoolboy, with a fixed, frightened look on his face, was gazing at the old man. In one corner sat a pair of lovers. She was quite young and pretty, and had short, fair hair, looked energetic, and was elegantly dressed; he had fine features, wavy hair, and wore a rubber jacket. They sat in their corner and seemed stupefied with love. Nearest to the table sat a grey-haired woman dressed in black, evidently the mother of a young, consumptive-looking fellow, in the same kind of jacket. Her head lay on his shoulder. She was trying to say something, but the tears prevented her from speaking; she began several times, but had to stop. The young man held a paper in his hand, and, apparently not knowing what to do, kept folding and pressing it with an angry look on his face.

Beside them was a short-haired, stout, rosy girl, with very prominent eyes, dressed in a grey dress and a cape; she sat beside the weeping mother, tenderly stroking her. Everything about this girl was beautiful; her large, white hands, her short, wavy hair, her firm nose and lips, but the chief charm of her face lay in her kind, truthful hazel eyes. The beautiful eyes turned away from the mother for a moment when Nekhlyudov came in, and met his look. But she turned back at once and said something to the mother.

Not far from the lovers a dark, dishevelled man, with a gloomy face, sat angrily talking to a beardless visitor, who looked as if he belonged to the *scoptsy* sect.

At the very door stood a young man in a rubber jacket, who seemed more concerned about the impression he produced on the onlooker than about what he was saying. Nekhlyudov, sitting by the inspector's side, looked round with strained curiosity. A little boy with closely-cropped hair came up to him and addressed him in a thin little voice.

'And whom are you waiting for?'

Nekhlyudov was surprised at the question, but looking at the boy, and seeing the serious little face with its bright, attentive eyes fixed on him, answered him seriously that he was waiting for a woman of his acquaintance.

'Is she, then, your sister?' the boy asked.

'No, not my sister,' Nekhlyudov answered in surprise.

'And with whom are you here?' he inquired of the boy.

'I? With mamma; she is a political one,' he replied.

'Mary Pavlovna, take Kolya!' said the inspector, evidently considering Nekhlyudov's conversation with the boy illegal.

Mary Pavlovna, the beautiful girl who had attracted Nekhlyudov's attention, rose tall and erect, and with firm, almost manly steps, approached Nekhlyudov and the boy.

'What is he asking you? Who you are?' she inquired with a slight smile, and looking straight into his face with a trustful look in her kind, prominent eyes, and as simply as if there could be no doubt whatever that she was and must be on sisterly terms with everybody.

'He likes to know everything,' she said, looking at the boy with so sweet and kind a smile that both the boy and Nekhlyudov were obliged to smile back.

'He was asking me whom I have come to see.'

'Mary Pavlovna, it is against the rules to speak to strangers. You know it is,' said the inspector.

'All right, all right,' she said, and went back to the consumptive lad's mother, holding Kolya's little hand in her large, white one, while he continued gazing up into her face.

'Whose is this little boy?' Nekhlyudov asked of the inspector.

'His mother is a political prisoner, and he was born in prison,' said the inspector, in a pleased tone, as if glad to point out how exceptional his establishment was.

'Is it possible?'

'Yes, and now he is going to Siberia with her.'

'And that young girl?'

'I cannot answer your question,' said the inspector, shrugging his shoulders. 'Besides, here is Doukhova.'

Chapter 55

Vera Doukhova explains

Through a door, at the back of the room, entered, with a wriggling gait, the thin, yellow Vera Doukhova, with her large, kind eyes.

'Thanks for having come,' she said, pressing Nekhlyudov's hand. 'Do you remember me? Let us sit down.'

'I did not expect to see you like this.'

'Oh, I am very happy. It is so delightful, so delightful, that I desire nothing better,' said Vera Doukhova, with the usual expression of fright in the large, kind, round eyes fixed on Nekhlyudov, and twisting the terribly thin, sinewy neck, surrounded by the shabby, crumpled, dirty collar of her bodice. Nekhlyudov asked her how she came to be in prison.

In answer she began relating all about her affairs with great animation. Her speech was intermingled with a great many long words, such as propaganda, disorganisation, social groups, sections and sub-sections, about which she seemed to think everybody knew, but which Nekhlyudov had never heard of.

She told him all the secrets of the Nardovolstvo,* evidently convinced that he was pleased to hear them. Nekhlyudov looked at her miserable little neck, her thin, unkempt hair, and wondered why she had been doing all these strange things, and why she was now telling all this to him. He pitied her, but not as he had pitied Menshov, the peasant, kept for no fault of his own in the stinking prison. She was pitiable because of the confusion that filled her mind. It was clear that she considered herself a heroine, and was ready to give her life for a cause, though she could hardly have explained what that cause was and in what its success would lie.

The business that Vera Doukhova wanted to see Nekhlyudov about was the following: a friend of hers, who had not even belonged to their 'sub-group', as she expressed it, had been arrested with her about five months before, and imprisoned in the Petropavlovsky fortress because some prohibited books and papers (which she had been asked to keep) had been found in her possession. Vera Doukhova felt herself in some measure to blame for her friend's arrest, and implored Nekhlyudov, who had connections among influential people, to do all he could in order to set this friend free.

Besides this, Doukhova asked him to try and get permission for another friend of hers, Gourkevitch (who was also imprisoned in the Petropavlovsky fortress), to see his parents, and to procure some scientific books which he required for his studies. Nekhlyudov promised to do what he could when he went to Petersburg.

As to her own story, this is what she said: having finished a course of midwifery, she became connected with a group of adherents to the Nardovolstvo, and made up her mind to agitate in the revolutionary movement. At first all went on smoothly. She wrote proclamations and occupied herself with propaganda work in the factories; then, an important member having been arrested, their papers were seized and all concerned were arrested. 'I was also arrested, and shall be exiled. But what does it matter? I feel perfectly happy.' She concluded her story with a piteous smile.

Nekhlyudov made some inquiries concerning the girl with the prominent eyes. Vera Doukhova told him that this girl was the

---

* Literally, 'People's Freedom', a revolutionary movement.

daughter of a general, and had been long attached to the revolutionary party, and was arrested because she had pleaded guilty to having shot a gendarme. She lived in a house with some conspirators, where they had a secret printing press. One night, when the police came to search this house, the occupiers resolved to defend themselves, put out the light, and began destroying the things that might incriminate them. The police forced their way in, and one of the conspirators fired, and mortally wounded a gendarme. When an inquiry was instituted, this girl said that it was she who had fired, although she had never had a revolver in her hands, and would not have hurt a fly. And she kept to it, and was now condemned to penal servitude in Siberia.

'An altruistic, fine character,' said Vera Doukhova, approvingly.

The third business that Vera Doukhova wanted to talk about concerned Maslova. She knew, as everybody does know in prison, the story of Maslova's life and his connection with her, and advised him to take steps to get her removed into the political prisoner's ward, or into the hospital to help to nurse the sick, of which there were very many at that time, so that extra nurses were needed.

Nekhlyudov thanked her for the advice, and said he would try to act upon it.

Chapter 56

Nekhlyudov and the prisoners

Their conversation was interrupted by the inspector, who said that the time was up, and the prisoners and their friends must part. Nekhlyudov took leave of Vera Doukhova and went to the door, where he stopped to watch what was going on.

The inspector's order called forth only heightened animation among the prisoners in the room, but no one seemed to think of going. Some rose and continued to talk standing, some went on talking without rising. A few began crying and taking leave of each other. The mother and her consumptive son seemed especially pathetic. The young fellow kept twisting his bit of paper and his face seemed angry, so great were his efforts not to be infected by his mother's emotion. The mother, hearing that it was time to part, put her head on his shoulder and sobbed and sniffed aloud.

The girl with the prominent eyes – Nekhlyudov could not help watching her – was standing opposite the sobbing mother, and was saying something to her in a soothing tone. The old man with the blue spectacles stood holding his daughter's hand and nodding in answer to what she said. The young lovers rose, and, holding each other's hands, looked silently into one another's eyes.

'These are the only two who are merry,' said a young man with a short coat who stood by Nekhlyudov's side, also looking at those who were about to part, and pointed to the lovers. Feeling Nekhlyudov's and the young man's eyes fixed on them, the lovers – the young man with the rubber coat and the pretty girl – stretched out their arms, and with their hands clasped in each other's, danced round and round again. 'Tonight they are going to be married here in prison, and she will follow him to Siberia,' said the young man.

'What is he?'

'A convict, condemned to penal servitude. Let those two at least have a little joy, or else it is too painful,' the young man added, listening to the sobs of the consumptive lad's mother.

'Now, my good people! Please, please do not oblige me to have recourse to severe measures,' the inspector said, repeating the same words several times over. 'Do, please,' he went on in a weak, hesitating manner. 'It is high time. What do you mean by it? This sort of thing is quite impossible. I am now asking you for the last time,' he repeated wearily, now putting out his cigarette and then lighting another.

It was evident that, artful, old and common as were the devices enabling men to do evil to others without feeling responsible for it, the inspector could not but feel conscious that he was one of those who were guilty of causing the sorrow which manifested itself in this room. And it was apparent that this troubled him sorely. At length the prisoners and their visitors began to go – the first out of the inner, the latter out of the outer door. The man with the rubber jacket passed out among them, and the consumptive youth and the dishevelled man. Mary Pavlovna went out with the boy born in prison.

The visitors went out too. The old man with the blue spectacles, stepping heavily, went out, followed by Nekhlyudov.

'Yes, a strange state of things this,' said the talkative young man, as if continuing an interrupted conversation, as he descended the stairs side by side with Nekhlyudov. 'Yet we have reason to be grateful to the inspector who does not keep strictly to the rules, kind-hearted fellow. If they can get a talk it does relieve their hearts a bit, after all!'

While talking to the young man, who introduced himself as Medinzev, Nekhlyudov reached the hall. There the inspector came up to them with weary step.

'If you wish to see Maslova,' he said, apparently desiring to be polite to Nekhlyudov, 'please come tomorrow.'

'Very well,' answered Nekhlyudov, and hurried away, experiencing more than ever that sensation of moral nausea which he always felt on entering the prison.

The sufferings of the evidently innocent Menshov seemed terrible, and not so much his physical suffering as the perplexity, the distrust in the good and in God which he must feel, seeing the cruelty of the people who tormented him without any reason.

Terrible were the disgrace and sufferings cast on these hundreds of guiltless people simply because something was not written on paper as it should have been. Terrible were the brutalised jailers, whose occupation is to torment their brothers, and who were certain that they were fulfilling an important and useful duty; but most terrible of all seemed this sickly, elderly, kind-hearted inspector, who was obliged to part mother and son, father and daughter, who were just the same sort of people as he and his own children.

'What is it all for?' Nekhlyudov asked himself, and could not find an answer.

Chapter 57

The vice-governor's 'At-Home'

The next day Nekhlyudov went to see the advocate, and spoke to him about the Menshovs' case, begging him to undertake their defence. The advocate promised to look into the case, and if it turned out to be as Nekhlyudov said he would in all probability undertake the defence free of charge. Then Nekhlyudov told him of the hundred and thirty men who were kept in prison owing to a mistake. 'On whom did it depend? Whose fault was it?'

The advocate was silent for a moment, evidently anxious to give a correct reply.

'Whose fault is it? No one's,' he said, decidedly. 'Ask the procureur, he'll say it is the governor's; ask the governor, he'll say it is the procureur's fault. No one is in fault.'

'I am just going to see the vice-governor. I shall tell him.'

'Oh, that's quite useless,' said the advocate, with a smile. 'He is such a – he is not a relation or friend of yours? – such a blockhead, if I may say so, and yet a crafty animal at the same time.'

Nekhlyudov remembered what Maslennikov had said about the advocate, and did not answer, but took leave and went on to Maslennikov's. He had to ask Maslennikov two things: about Maslova's removal to the prison hospital, and about the hundred and thirty passportless men innocently imprisoned. Though it was very hard to petition a man whom he did not respect, and by whose orders men were flogged, yet it was the only means of gaining his end, and he had to go through with it.

As he drove up to Maslennikov's house Nekhlyudov saw a number of different carriages by the front door, and remembered that it was Maslennikov's wife's 'At-Home' day, to which he had been invited. At the moment Nekhlyudov drove up there was a carriage in front of the door, and a footman in livery, with a cockade in his hat, was helping a lady down the doorstep. She was holding up her train, and showing her thin ankles, black stockings, and slippered feet. Among the carriages was a closed landau, which he knew to be the Korchagins'.

The grey-haired, red-checked coachman took off his hat and bowed in a respectful yet friendly manner to Nekhlyudov, as to a gentleman he knew well. Nekhlyudov had not had time to inquire for Maslennikov, when the latter appeared on the carpeted stairs, accompanying a very important guest not only to the first landing but to the bottom of the stairs. This very important visitor, a military man, was speaking in French about a lottery for the benefit of children's homes that were to be founded in the city, and expressed the opinion that this was a good occupation for the ladies. 'It amuses them, and the money comes.'

'*Qu'elles s'amusent et que le bon dieu les bénisse.* M. Nekhlyudov! How d'you do? How is it one never sees you?' he greeted Nekhlyudov. '*Allez presenter vos devoirs à Madame.* And the Korchagins are here, and Nadine Bukshevden. *Toutes les jolies femmes de la ville,*' said the important guest, slightly raising his uniformed shoulders as he presented them to his own richly liveried servant to have his military overcoat put on. '*Au revoir, mon cher.*' And he pressed Maslennikov's hand.

'Now, come up; I am so glad,' said Maslennikov, grasping Nekhlyudov's hand. In spite of his corpulency Maslennikov hurried quickly up the stairs. He was in particularly good spirits, owing to the attention paid him by the important personage. Every such attention gave him the same sense of delight as is felt by an affectionate dog when its master pats it, strokes it, or scratches its ears. It wags its tail, cringes, jumps about, presses its ears down, and madly rushes about in a circle. Maslennikov was ready to do the same. He did not notice the serious expression on Nekhlyudov's face, paid no heed to his words, but pulled him irresistibly towards the drawing-room, so that it was impossible for Nekhlyudov not to follow. 'Business afterwards. I shall do whatever you want,' said Maslennikov, as he drew Nekhlyudov through the dancing hall. 'Announce Prince Nekhlyudov,' he said to a footman, without stopping on his way. The footman started off at a trot and passed them.

'*Vous n'avez qu' à ordonner.* But you must see my wife. As it is, I got it for letting you go without seeing her last time.'

By the time they reached the drawing-room the footman had already announced Nekhlyudov, and from between the bonnets and heads that surrounded it the smiling face of Anna Ignatievna, the vice-governor's wife, beamed on Nekhlyudov. At the other end of the drawing-room several ladies were seated round the tea-table, and some military men and some civilians stood near them. The clatter of male and female voices went on unceasingly.

'*Enfin*! you seem to have quite forgotten us. How have we offended?' With these words, intended to convey an idea of intimacy which had never existed between herself and Nekhlyudov, Anna Ignatievna greeted the newcomer.

'You are acquainted? – Madam Tilyaevsky, M. Chernov. Sit down a bit nearer. Missy, *venez donc à notre table. On vous apportera votre thé* . . . And you,' she said, having evidently forgotten his name, to an officer who was talking to Missy, 'do come here. A cup of tea, Prince?'

'I shall never, never agree with you. It's quite simple; she did not love,' a woman's voice was heard saying.

'But she loved tarts.'

'Oh, your eternal silly jokes!' put in, laughingly, another lady resplendent in silks, gold, and jewels.

'*C'est excellent*, these little biscuits, and so light. I think I'll take another.'

'Well, are you moving soon?'

'Yes, this is our last day. That's why we have come. Yes, it must be lovely in the country; we are having a delightful spring.'

Missy, with her hat on, in a dark-striped dress of some kind that fitted her like a skin, was looking very handsome. She blushed when she saw Nekhlyudov.

'And I thought you had left,' she said to him.

'I am on the point of leaving. Business is keeping me in town, and it is on business I have come here.'

'Won't you come to see mamma? She would like to see you,' she said, and knowing that she was saying what was not true, and that he knew it also, she blushed still more.

'I fear I shall scarcely have time,' Nekhlyudov said gloomily, trying to appear as if he had not noticed her blush. Missy frowned angrily, shrugged her shoulders, and turned towards an elegant officer, who grasped the empty cup she was holding, and knocking his sword against the chairs, manfully carried the cup across to another table.

'You must contribute towards the Home fund.'

'I am not refusing, but only wish to keep my bounty fresh for the lottery. There I shall let it appear in all its glory.'

'Well, look out for yourself,' said a voice, followed by an evidently feigned laugh.

Anna Ignatievna was in raptures; her 'At-Home' had turned out a brilliant success. 'Micky tells me you are busying yourself with prison work. I can understand you so well,' she said to Nekhlyudov. 'Micky (she meant her fat husband, Maslennikov) may have other defects, but you know how kind-hearted he is. All these miserable prisoners are his children. He does not regard them in any other light. *Il est d'une bonté –* ' and she stopped, finding no words to do justice to this *bonté* of his, and quickly turned to a shrivelled old woman with bows of lilac ribbon all over, who came in just then.

Having said as much as was absolutely necessary, and with as little meaning as conventionality required, Nekhlyudov rose and went up to Maslennikov. 'Can you give me a few minutes' hearing, please?'

'Oh, yes. Well, what is it?'

'Let us come in here.'

They entered a small Japanese sitting-room, and sat down by the window.

Chapter 58

The vice-governor suspicious

'Well? *Je suis à vous*. Will you smoke? But wait a bit; we must be careful and not make a mess here,' said Maslennikov, and brought an ashpan. 'Well?'

'There are two matters I wish to ask you about.'

'Dear me!'

An expression of gloom and dejection came over Maslennikov's countenance, and every trace of the excitement, like that of the dog's whom its master has scratched behind the ears, vanished completely. The sound of voices reached them from the drawing-room. A woman's voice was heard, saying, '*Jamais je ne croirais*,' and a man's voice from the other side relating something in which the names of *la Comtesse* Voronzov and Victor Apraksine kept recurring. A hum of voices, mixed with laughter, came from another side. Maslennikov tried to listen to what was going on in the drawing-room and to what Nekhlyudov was saying at the same time.

'I am again come about that same woman,' said Nekhlyudov.

'Oh, yes; I know. The one innocently condemned.'

'I would like to ask that she should be appointed to serve in the prison hospital. I have been told that this could be arranged.'

Maslennikov compressed his lips and meditated. 'That will be scarcely possible,' he said. 'However, I shall see what can be done, and shall wire you an answer tomorrow.'

'I have been told that there were many sick, and help was needed.'

'All right, all right. I shall let you know in any case.'

'Please do,' said Nekhlyudov.

The sound of a general and even a natural laugh came from the drawing-room.

'That's all that Victor. He is wonderfully sharp when he is in the right vein,' said Maslennikov.

'The next thing I wanted to tell you,' said Nekhlyudov, 'is that a hundred and thirty persons are imprisoned only because their passports are overdue. They have been kept here a month.'

And he related the circumstances of the case.

'How have you come to know of this?' said Maslennikov, looking uneasy and dissatisfied.

'I went to see a prisoner, and these men came and surrounded me in the corridor, and asked . . .'

'What prisoner did you go to see?'

'A peasant who is kept in prison, though innocent. I have put his case into the hands of a lawyer. But that is not the point. Is it possible that people who have done no wrong are imprisoned only because their passports are overdue? And . . .'

'That's the procureur's business,' Maslennikov interrupted, angrily. 'There, now, you see what it is you call a prompt and just

form of trial. It is the business of the Public Prosecutor to visit the
prison and to find out if the prisoners are kept there lawfully. But
that set play cards; that's all they do.'

'Am I to understand that you can do nothing?' Nekhlyudov
said, despondently, remembering that the advocate had foretold
that the governor would put the blame on the procureur.

'Oh, yes, I can. I shall see about it at once.'

'So much the worse for her. *C'est un souffre-douleur,*' came the
voice of a woman, evidently indifferent to what she was saying,
from the drawing-room.

'So much the better. I shall take it also,' a man's voice was heard
to say from the other side, followed by the playful laughter of a
woman, who was apparently trying to prevent the man from
taking something away from her.

'No, no; not on any account,' the woman's voice said.

'All right, then. I shall do all this,' Maslennikov repeated, and
put out the cigarette he held in his white, turquoise-ringed hand.
'And now let us join the ladies.'

'Wait a moment,' Nekhlyudov said, stopping at the door of the
drawing-room. 'I was told that some men had received corporal
punishment in the prison yesterday. Is this true?'

Maslennikov blushed.

'Oh, that's what you are after? No, *mon cher*, decidedly it won't
do to let you in there; you want to get at everything. Come,
come; Anna is calling us,' he said, catching Nekhlyudov by the
arm, and again becoming as excited as after the attention paid
him by the important person, only now his excitement was not
joyful, but anxious.

Nekhlyudov pulled his arm away, and without taking leave
of anyone and without saying a word, he passed through the
drawing-room with a dejected look, went down into the hall,
past the footman, who sprang towards him, and out at the street
door.

'What is the matter with him? What have you done to him?'
asked Anna of her husband.

'This is *à la Française*,' remarked someone.

'*À la Française*, indeed – it is *à la Zoulou*.'

'Oh, but he's always been like that.'

Someone rose, someone came in, and the clatter went on its

course. The company used this episode with Nekhlyudov as a convenient topic of conversation for the rest of the 'At-Home'.

On the day following his visit to Maslennikov, Nekhlyudov received a letter from him, written in a fine, firm hand, on thick, glazed paper, with a coat-of-arms, and sealed with sealing-wax. Maslennikov said that he had written to the doctor concerning Maslova's removal to the hospital, and hoped Nekhlyudov's wish would receive attention. The letter was signed, 'Your affectionate elder comrade', and the signature ended with a large, firm, and artistic flourish. 'Fool!' Nekhlyudov could not refrain from saying, especially because in the word 'comrade' he felt Maslennikov's condescension towards him, i.e., while Maslennikov was filling this position, morally most dirty and shameful, he still thought himself a very important man, and wished, if not exactly to flatter Nekhlyudov, at least to show that he was not too proud to call him comrade.

Chapter 59

Nekhlyudov's third interview with Maslova in prison

One of the most widespread superstitions is that every man has his own special, definite qualities; that a man is kind, cruel, wise, stupid, energetic, apathetic, etc. Men are not like that. We may say of a man that he is more often kind than cruel, oftener wise than stupid, oftener energetic than apathetic, or the reverse; but it would be false to say of one man that he is kind and wise, of another that he is wicked and foolish. And yet we always classify mankind in this way. And this is untrue. Men are like rivers: the water is the same in each, and alike in all; but every river is narrow here, is more rapid there, here slower, there broader, now clear, now cold, now dull, now warm. It is the same with men. Every man carries in himself the germs of every human quality, and sometimes one manifests itself, sometimes another, and the man often becomes unlike himself, while still remaining the same man, In some people these changes are very rapid, and Nekhlyudov was such a man. These changes in him were due to physical and to spiritual causes. At this time he experienced such a change.

That feeling of triumph and joy at the renewal of life which he had experienced after the trial and after the first interview with Katusha, vanished completely, and after the last interview fear and revulsion took the place of that joy. He was determined not to leave her, and not to change his decision of marrying her, if she wished it; but it seemed very hard, and made him suffer.

On the day after his visit to Maslennikov, he again went to the prison to see her.

The inspector allowed him to speak to her, only not in the advocate's room nor in the office, but in the women's visiting-room. In spite of his kindness, the inspector was more reserved with Nekhlyudov than hitherto.

An order for greater caution had apparently been sent, as a result of his conversation with Maslennikov.

'You may see her,' the inspector said; 'but please remember what I said as regards money. And as to her removal to the hospital, that his excellency wrote to me about, it can be done; the doctor would agree. Only she herself does not wish it. She says, "Much need have I to carry out the slops for the scurvy beggars." You don't know what these people are, Prince,' he added.

Nekhlyudov did not reply, but asked to have the interview. The inspector called a jailer, whom Nekhlyudov followed into the women's visiting-room, where there was no one but Maslova waiting. She came from behind the grating, quiet and timid, close up to him, and said, without looking at him:

'Forgive me, Dmitri Ivanovitch, I spoke hastily the day before yesterday.'

'It is not for me to forgive you,' Nekhlyudov began.

'But all the same, you must leave me,' she interrupted, and in the terribly squinting eyes with which she looked at him Nekhlyudov read the former strained, angry expression.

'Why should I leave you?'

'So.'

'But why so?'

She again looked up, as it seemed to him, with the same angry look.

'Well, then, thus it is,' she said. 'You must leave me. It is true what I am saying. I cannot. You just give it up altogether.' Her lips trembled and she was silent for a moment. 'It is true. I'd rather hang myself.'

Nekhlyudov felt that in this refusal there was hatred and unforgiving resentment, but there was also something besides, something good. This confirmation of the refusal in cold blood at once quenched all the doubts in Nekhlyudov's bosom, and brought back the serious, triumphant emotion he had felt in relation to Katusha.

'Katusha, what I have said I will again repeat,' he uttered, very seriously. 'I ask you to marry me. If you do not wish it, and for as long as you do not wish it, I shall only continue to follow you, and shall go where you are taken.'

'That is your business. I shall not say anything more,' she answered, and her lips began to tremble again.

He, too, was silent, feeling unable to speak.

'I shall now go to the country, and then to Petersburg,' he said, when he was quieter again. 'I shall do my utmost to get your – our case, I mean, reconsidered, and by the help of God the sentence may be revoked.'

'And if it is not revoked, never mind. I have deserved it, if not in this case, in other ways,' she said, and he saw how difficult it was for her to keep down her tears.

'Well, have you seen Menshov?' she suddenly asked, to hide her emotion. 'It's true they are innocent, isn't it?'

'Yes, I think so.'

'Such a splendid old woman,' she said.

There was another pause.

'Well, and as to the hospital?' she suddenly said, and looking at him with her squinting eyes. 'If you like, I will go, and I shall not drink any spirits, either.'

Nekhlyudov looked into her eyes. They were smiling.

'Yes, yes, she is quite a different being,' Nekhlyudov thought. After all his former doubts, he now felt something he had never before experienced – the certainty that love is invincible.

When Maslova returned to her noisome cell after this interview, she took off her cloak and sat down in her place on the shelf bedstead with her hands folded on her lap. In the cell were only the consumptive woman, the Vladimir woman with her baby,

Menshov's old mother, and the watchman's wife. The deacon's daughter had the day before been declared mentally diseased and removed to the hospital. The rest of the women were away, washing clothes. The old woman was asleep, the cell door stood open, and the watchman's children were in the corridor outside. The Vladimir woman, with her baby in her arms, and the watchman's wife, with the stocking she was knitting with deft fingers, came up to Maslova. 'Well, have you had a chat?' they asked. Maslova sat silent on the high bedstead, swinging her legs, which did not reach to the floor.

'What's the good of snivelling?' said the watchman's wife. 'The chief thing's not to go down into the dumps. Eh, Katusha? Now, then!' and she went on, quickly moving her fingers.

Maslova did not answer.

'And our women have all gone to wash,' said the Vladimir woman. 'I heard them say much has been given in alms today. Quite a lot has been brought.'

'Finashka,' called out the watchman's wife, 'where's the little imp gone to?'

She took a knitting needle, stuck it through both the ball and the stocking, and went out into the corridor.

At this moment the sound of women's voices was heard from the corridor, and the inmates of the cell entered, with their prison shoes, but no stockings on their feet. Each was carrying a roll, some even two. Theodosia came at once up to Maslova.

'What's the matter; is anything wrong?' Theodosia asked, looking lovingly at Maslova with her clear, blue eyes. 'This is for our tea,' and she put the rolls on a shelf.

'Why, surely he has not changed his mind about marrying?' asked Korableva.

'No, he has not, but I don't wish to,' said Maslova, 'and so I told him.'

'More fool you!' muttered Korableva in her deep tones.

'If one's not to live together, what's the use of marrying?' said Theodosia.

'There's your husband – he's going with you,' said the watchman's wife.

'Well, of course, we're married,' said Theodosia. 'But why should he go through the ceremony if he is not to live with her?'

'Why, indeed! Don't be a fool! You know if he marries her she'll roll in wealth,' said Korableva.

'He says, "Wherever they take you, I'll follow," ' said Maslova. 'If he does, it's well; if he does not, well also. I am not going to ask him to. Now he is going to try and arrange the matter in Petersburg. He is related to all the Ministers there. But, all the same, I have no need of him,' she continued.

'Of course not,' suddenly agreed Korableva, evidently thinking about something else as she sat examining her bag. 'Well, shall we have a drop?'

'You have some,' replied Maslova. 'I won't.'

Part 2

Chapter 1

Property in land

It was possible for Maslova's case to come before the Senate in a fortnight, at which time Nekhlyudov meant to go to Petersburg, and, if need be, to appeal to the Emperor (as the advocate who had drawn up the petition advised) should the appeal be disregarded (and, according to the advocate, it was best to be prepared for that, since the causes for appeal were so slight). The party of convicts, among whom was Maslova, would very likely leave in the beginning of June. In order to be able to follow her to Siberia, as Nekhlyudov was firmly resolved to do, he was now obliged to visit his estates, and settle matters there. Nekhlyudov first went to the nearest, Kousminski, a large estate that lay in the black earth district, and from which he derived the greatest part of his income.

He had lived on that estate in his childhood and youth, and had been there twice since, and once, at his mother's request, he had taken a German steward there, and had with him verified the accounts. The state of things there and the peasants' relations to the management, i.e., the landlord, had therefore been long known to him. The relations of the peasants to the administration were those of utter dependence on that management. Nekhlyudov knew all this when, still a university student, he had confessed and preached Henry Georgeism, and, on the basis of that teaching, had given the land inherited from his father to the peasants. It is true that after entering the army, when he got into the habit of spending twenty thousand roubles a year, those former occupations ceased to be regarded as a duty, and were forgotten, and he not only left off asking himself where the money his mother allowed him came from, but even avoided thinking about it. But his mother's death, the coming into the property, and the necessity of managing it, again raised the question as to what his position in reference to private property in land was. A month before Nekhlyudov would have answered that he had not the strength to alter the existing order of things; that it was not he who was administering the estate; and would one way or another have eased his conscience, continuing to live far from his estates, and having the money sent him. But now he decided that he could not leave things to go on as they were, but would have to alter them in a way unprofitable to himself, even though he had all these complicated and difficult relations with the prison world which made money necessary, as well as a probable journey to Siberia before him. Therefore he decided not to farm the land, but to let it to the peasants at a low rent, to enable them to cultivate it without depending on a landlord. More than once, when comparing the position of a landowner with that of an owner of serfs, Nekhlyudov had compared the renting of land to the peasants instead of cultivating it with hired labour, to the old system by which serf proprietors used to exact a money payment from their serfs in place of labour. It was not a solution of the problem, and yet a step towards the solution; it was a movement towards a less rude form of slavery. And it was in this way he meant to act.

Nekhlyudov reached Kousminski about noon. Trying to simplify his life in every way, he did not telegraph, but hired a cart and pair at the station. The driver was a young fellow in a nankeen coat, with a belt below his long waist. He was glad to talk to the gentleman, especially because while they were talking his broken-winded white horse and the emaciated spavined one could go at a foot-pace, which they always liked to do.

The driver spoke about the steward at Kousminski without knowing that he was driving 'the master'. Nekhlyudov had purposely not told him who he was.

'That ostentatious German,' said the driver (who had been to town and read novels) as he sat sideways on the box, passing his hand from the top to the bottom of his long whip, and trying to show off his accomplishments – 'that ostentatious German has procured three light bays, and when he drives out with his lady – oh, my! At Christmas he had a Christmas-tree in the big house. I drove some of the visitors there. It had 'lectric lights; you could not see the like of it in the whole of the government. What's it to him, he has cribbed a heap of money. I heard say he has bought an estate.'

Nekhlyudov had imagined that he was quite indifferent to the way the steward managed his estate, and what advantages the steward derived from it. The words of the long-waisted driver, however, were not pleasant to hear.

A dark cloud now and then covered the sun; the larks were soaring above the fields of winter corn; the forests were already covered with fresh young green; the meadows speckled with grazing cattle and horses. The fields were being ploughed, and Nekhlyudov enjoyed the lovely day. But every now and then he had an unpleasant feeling, and, when he asked himself what it was caused by, he remembered what the driver had told him about the way the German was managing Kousminski. When he got to his estate and set to work this unpleasant feeling vanished.

Looking over the books in the office, and a talk with the foreman, who naively pointed out the advantages to be derived from the facts that the peasants had very little land of their own and that it lay in the midst of the landlord's fields, made Nekhlyudov more than ever determined to leave off farming and to let his land to the peasants.

From the office books and his talk with the foreman, Nekhlyudov found that two-thirds of the best of the cultivated land was still being tilled with improved machinery by labourers receiving fixed wages, while the other third was tilled by the peasants at the rate of five roubles per *desiatin*.* So that the peasants had to plough each *desiatin* three times, harrow it three times, sow and mow the corn, make it into sheaves, and deliver it on the threshing ground for five roubles, while the same amount of work done by wage labour came to at least ten roubles. Everything the peasants got from the office they paid for in labour at a very high price. They paid in labour for the use of the meadows, for wood, for potato-stalks, and were nearly all of them in debt to the office. Thus, for the land that lay beyond the cultivated fields, which the peasants hired, four times the price that its value would bring in if invested at five per cent was taken from the peasants.

Nekhlyudov had known all this before, but he now saw it in a new light, and wondered how he and others in his position could help seeing how abnormal such conditions are. The steward's arguments that if the land were let to the peasants the agricultural

* About two and three-quarter acres.

implements would fetch next to nothing, as it would be impossible to get even a quarter of their value for them, and that the
peasants would spoil the land, and how great a loser Nekhlyudov
would be, only strengthened Nekhlyudov in the opinion that
he was doing a good action in letting the land to the peasants and
thus depriving himself of a large part of his income. He decided
to settle this business now, at once, while he was there. The
reaping and selling of the corn he left for the steward to manage
in due season, and also the selling of the agricultural implements
and useless buildings. But he asked his steward to call the peasants
of the three neighbouring villages that lay in the midst of his estate
(Kousminski) to a meeting, at which he would tell them of his
intentions and arrange about the price at which they were to rent
the land.

With the pleasant sense of the firmness he had shown in the face
of the steward's arguments, and his readiness to make a sacrifice,
Nekhlyudov left the office, thinking over the business before him,
and strolled round the house, through the neglected flower-
garden – this year the flowers were planted in front of the
steward's house – over the tennis ground, now overgrown with
dandelions, and along the lime-tree walk, where he used to smoke
his cigar, and where he had flirted with the pretty Kirimova, his
mother's visitor. Having briefly prepared in his mind the speech
he was going to make to the peasants, he again went in to the
steward, and, after tea, having once more arranged his thoughts,
he went into the room prepared for him in the big house, which
used to be a spare bedroom.

In this clean little room, with pictures of Venice on the walls,
and a mirror between the two windows, there stood a clean bed
with a spring mattress, and by the side of it a small table, with a
decanter of water, matches, and an extinguisher. On a table by
the looking-glass lay his open portmanteau, with his dressing-
case and some books in it: a Russian book, *The Investigation of the
Laws of Criminality*, and a German and an English book on the
same subject, which he meant to read while travelling in the
country. But it was too late to begin today, and he began
preparing to go to bed.

An old-fashioned inlaid mahogany armchair stood in the corner of the room, and this chair, which Nekhlyudov remembered

standing in his mother's bedroom, suddenly raised a perfectly
unexpected sensation in his soul. He was suddenly filled with
regret at the thought of the house that would tumble to ruin, and
the garden that would run wild, and the forest that would be cut
down, and all these farmyards, stables, sheds, machines, horses,
cows which he knew had cost so much effort, though not to
himself, to acquire and to keep. It had seemed easy to give up all
this, but now it was hard, not only to give up this, but even to let
the land and lose half his income. And at once a consideration,
which proved that it was unreasonable to let the land to the
peasants, and thus to destroy his property, came to his service. 'I
must not hold property in land. If I possess no property in land, I
cannot keep up the house and farm. And, besides, I am going to
Siberia, and shall not need either the house or the estate,' said
one voice. 'All this is so,' said another voice, 'but you are not
going to spend all your life in Siberia. You may marry and have
children, and must hand the estate on to them in as good a
condition as you received it. There is a duty to the land, too. To
give up, to destroy everything is very easy; to acquire it very
difficult. Above all, you must consider your future life, and what
you will do with yourself, and you must dispose of your property
accordingly. And are you really firm in your resolve? And then,
are you really acting according to your conscience, or are you
acting in order to be admired of men?' Nekhlyudov asked
himself all this, and had to acknowledge that he was influenced
by the thought of what people would say about him. And the
more he thought about it the more questions arose, and the more
unsolvable they seemed.

In hopes of ridding himself of these thoughts by falling asleep,
and solving them in the morning when his head would be fresh,
he lay down on his clean bed. But it was long before he could
sleep. Together with the fresh air and the moonlight, the croaking
of the frogs entered the room, mingling with the trills of a couple
of nightingales in the park and one close to the window in a bush
of lilacs in bloom. Listening to the nightingales and the frogs,
Nekhlyudov remembered the inspector's daughter and her music,
and the inspector; that reminded him of Maslova, and how her
lips trembled, like the croaking of the frogs, when she said, 'You
must just leave it.' Then the German steward began going down

to the frogs, and had to be held back, but he not only went down but turned into Maslova, who began reproaching Nekhlyudov, saying, 'You are a prince, and I am a convict.' 'No, I must not give in,' thought Nekhlyudov, waking up, and again asking himself, 'Is what I am doing right? I do not know, and no matter, no matter, I must only fall asleep now.' And he began himself to descend where he had seen the inspector and Maslova climbing down to, and there it all ended.

Chapter 2

Efforts at land restoration

The next day Nekhlyudov awoke at nine o'clock. The young office clerk who attended on 'the master' brought him his boots, shining as they had never shone before, and some cold, beautifully clear spring water, and informed him that the peasants were already assembling.

Nekhlyudov jumped out of bed, and collected his thoughts. Not a trace of yesterday's regret at giving up and thus destroying his property remained now. He remembered this feeling of regret with surprise; he was now looking forward with joy to the task before him, and could not help being proud of it. He could see from the window the old tennis ground, overgrown with dandelions, on which the peasants were beginning to assemble. The frogs had not croaked in vain the night before; the day was dull. There was no wind; a soft warm rain had begun falling in the morning, and hung in drops on leaves, twigs, and grass. Besides the smell of the fresh vegetation, the smell of damp earth, asking for more rain, entered in at the window. While dressing, Nekhlyudov several times looked out at the peasants gathered on the tennis ground. One by one they came, took off their hats or caps to one another, and took their places in a circle, leaning on their sticks. The steward, a stout, muscular, strong young man, dressed in a short pea-jacket, with a green stand-up collar, and enormous buttons, came to say that all had assembled, but that they might wait until Nekhlyudov had finished his breakfast – tea and coffee, whichever he pleased; both were ready.

'No, I think I had better go and see them at once,' said Nekhlyudov, with an unexpected feeling of shyness and shame at the thought of the conversation he was going to have with the peasants. He was going to fulfil a wish of the peasants, the fulfilment of which they did not even dare to hope for – to let the land to them at a low price, i.e., to confer a great boon; and yet he felt ashamed of something. When Nekhlyudov came up to the peasants, and the fair, the curly, the bald, the grey heads were bared before him, he felt so confused that he could say nothing. The rain continued to come down in small drops, that remained on the hair, the beards, and the fluff of the men's rough coats. The peasants looked at 'the master', waiting for him to speak, and he was so abashed that he could not speak. This confused silence was broken by the sedate, self-assured German steward, who considered himself a good judge of the Russian peasant, and who spoke Russian remarkably well. This strong, over-fed man, and Nekhlyudov himself, presented a striking contrast to the peasants, with their thin, wrinkled faces and the shoulder blades protruding beneath their coarse coats.

'Here's the Prince wanting to do you a favour, and to let the land to you; only you are not worthy of it,' said the steward.

'How are we not worthy of it, Vasili Karlovitch? Don't we work for you? We were well satisfied with the deceased lady – God have mercy on her soul – and the young Prince will not desert us now. Our thanks to him,' said a red-haired, talkative peasant.

'Yes, that's why I have called you together. I should like to let you have all the land, if you wish it.'

The peasants said nothing, as if they did not understand or did not believe it.

'Let's see. Let us have the land? What do you mean?' asked a middle-aged man.

'To let it to you, that you might have the use of it, at a low rent.'

'A very agreeable thing,' said an old man.

'If only the pay is such as we can afford,' said another.

'There's no reason why we should not rent the land.'

'We are accustomed to live by tilling the ground.'

'And it's quieter for you, too, that way. You'll have to do

nothing but receive the rent. Only think of all the sin and worry now!' several voices were heard saying.

'The sin is all on your side,' the German remarked. 'If only you did your work, and were orderly.'

'That's impossible for the likes of us,' said a sharp-nosed old man. 'You say, "Why do you let the horse get into the corn?" just as if I let it in. Why, I was swinging my scythe, or something of the kind, the livelong day, till the day seemed as long as a year, and so I fell asleep while watching the herd of horses at night, and it got into your oats, and now you're skinning me.'

'And you should keep order.'

'It's easy for you to talk about order, but it's more than our strength will bear,' answered a tall, dark, hairy middle-aged man.

'Didn't I tell you to put up a fence?'

'You give us the wood to make it of,' said a short, plain-looking peasant. 'I was going to put up a fence last year, and you put me to feed vermin in prison for three months. That was the end of that fence.'

'What is it he is saying?' asked Nekhlyudov, turning to the steward.

'*Der erste Dieb im Dorfe*,'* answered the steward in German. 'He is caught stealing wood from the forest every year.' Then turning to the peasant, he added, 'You must learn to respect other people's property.'

'Why, don't we respect you?' said an old man. 'We are obliged to respect you. Why, you could twist us into a rope; we are in your hands.'

'Eh, my friend, it's impossible to do you. It's you who are ever ready to do us,' said the steward.

'Do you, indeed. Didn't you smash my jaw for me, and I got nothing for it? No good going to law with the rich, it seems.'

'You should keep to the law.'

A tournament of words was apparently going on without those who took part in it knowing exactly what it was all about; but it was noticeable that there was bitterness on one side, restricted by fear, and on the other a consciousness of importance and power. It was very trying to Nekhlyudov to listen to all this, so he returned to the question of arranging the amount and the terms of the rent.

* The greatest thief in the village.

'Well, then, how about the land? Do you wish to take it, and what price will you pay if I let you have the whole of it?'

'The property is yours: it is for you to fix the price.' Nekhlyudov named the price. Though it was far below that paid in the neighbourhood, the peasants declared it too high, and began bargaining, as is customary among them. Nekhlyudov thought his offer would be accepted with pleasure, but no signs of pleasure were visible.

One thing only showed Nekhlyudov that his offer was a profitable one to the peasants. The question as to who would rent the land, the whole commune or a special society, was put, and a violent dispute arose among those peasants who were in favour of excluding the weak and those not likely to pay the rent regularly, and the peasants who would have to be excluded on that score. At last, thanks to the steward, the amount and the terms of the rent were fixed, and the peasants went down the hill towards their villages, talking noisily, while Nekhlyudov and the steward went into the office to make up the agreement. Everything was settled in the way Nekhlyudov wished and expected it to be. The peasants had their land thirty per cent. cheaper than they could have got it anywhere in the district, the revenue from the land was diminished by half, but was more than sufficient for Nekhlyudov, especially as there would be money coming in for a forest he sold, as well as for the agricultural implements, which would be sold, too. Everything seemed excellently arranged, yet he felt ashamed of something. He could see that the peasants, though they spoke words of thanks, were not satisfied, and had expected something greater. So it turned out that he had deprived himself of a great deal, and yet not done what the peasants had expected.

The next day the agreement was signed, and accompanied by several old peasants, who had been chosen as deputies, Nekhlyudov went out, got into the steward's elegant equipage (as the driver from the station had called it), said 'goodbye' to the peasants, who stood shaking their heads in a dissatisfied and disappointed manner, and drove off to the station. Nekhlyudov was dissatisfied with himself without knowing why, but all the time he felt sad and ashamed of something.

Chapter 3

Old associations

From Kousminski Nekhlyudov went to the estate he had inherited
from his aunts, the same where he first met Katusha. He meant to
arrange about the land there in the way he had done in Kousminski.
Besides this, he wished to find out all he could about Katusha and
her baby, and when and how it had died. He got to Panovo early
one morning, and the first thing that struck him when he drove up
was the look of decay and dilapidation that all the buildings bore,
especially the house itself. The iron roofs, which had once been
painted green, looked red with rust, and a few sheets of iron were
bent back, probably by a storm. Some of the planks which covered
the house from outside were torn away in several places; these were
easier to get at by breaking the rusty nails that held them. Both
porches, but especially the side porch he remembered so well, were
rotten and broken; only the banister remained. Some of the windows were boarded up, and the building in which the foreman
lived, the kitchen, the stables – all were grey and decaying. Only
the garden had not decayed, but had grown, and was in full bloom;
from over the fence the cherry, apple, and plum trees looked like
white clouds. The lilac bushes that formed the hedge were in full
bloom, as they had been when, fourteen years ago, Nekhlyudov
had played *gorelki* with the fifteen-year-old Katusha, and had fallen
and got his hand stung by the nettles behind one of those lilac
bushes. The larch that his aunt Sophia had planted near the house,
which then was only a short stick, had grown into a tree, the trunk
of which would have made a beam, and its branches were covered
with soft yellow green needles as with down. The river, now within
its banks, rushed noisily over the mill dam. The meadow the other
side of the river was dotted over by the peasants' mixed herds. The
foreman, a student, who had left the seminary without finishing the
course, met Nekhlyudov in the yard, with a smile on his face, and

still smiling, asked him to come into the office, and as if promising something exceptionally good by this smile, he went behind a partition. For a moment some whispering was heard behind the partition. The *isvostchik* who had driven Nekhlyudov from the station, drove away after receiving a tip, and all was silent. Then a barefooted girl passed the window; she had on an embroidered peasant blouse, and long earrings in her ears; then a man walked past, clattering with his nailed boots on the trodden path.

Nekhlyudov sat down by the little casement, and looked out into the garden and listened. A soft, fresh spring breeze, smelling of newly-dug earth, streamed in through the window, playing with the hair on his damp forehead and the papers that lay on the window-sill, which was all cut about with a knife.

'Tra-pa-trop, tra-pa-trop,' comes a sound from the river, as the women who were washing clothes there slapped them in regular measure with their wooden bats, and the sound spread over the glittering surface of the mill pond, while the rhythmical sound of the falling water came from the mill, and a frightened fly suddenly flew loudly buzzing past his ear.

And all at once Nekhlyudov remembered how, long ago, when he was young and innocent, he had heard the women's wooden bats slapping the wet clothes above the rhythmical sound from the mill, and in the same way the spring breeze had blown about the hair on his wet forehead and the papers on the window-sill, which was all cut about with a knife, and just in the same way a fly had buzzed loudly past his ear.

It was not exactly that he remembered himself as a lad of fifteen, but he seemed to feel himself the same as he was then, with the same freshness and purity, and full of the same grand possibilities for the future, and at the same time, as it happens in a dream, he knew that all this could be no more, and he felt terribly sad. 'At what time would you like something to eat?' asked the foreman, with a smile.

'When you like; I am not hungry. I shall go for a walk through the village.'

'Would you not like to come into the house? Everything is in order there. Have the goodness to look in. If the outside – '

'Not now; later on. Tell me, please, have you got a woman here called Matrona Kharina?' (This was Katusha's aunt, the village midwife.)

'Oh, yes; in the village she keeps a secret pot-house. I know she does, and I accuse her of it and scold her; but as to taking her up, it would be a pity. An old woman, you know; she has grand-children,' said the foreman, continuing to smile in the same manner, partly wishing to be pleasant to the master, and partly because he was convinced that Nekhlyudov understood all these matters just as well as he did himself.

'Where does she live? I shall go across and see her.'

'At the end of the village; the further side, the third from the end. To the left there is a brick cottage, and her hut is beyond that. But I'd better see you there,' the foreman said with a graceful smile.

'No, thanks, I shall find it; and you be so good as to call a meeting of the peasants, and tell them that I want to speak to them about the land,' said Nekhlyudov, with the intention of coming to the same agreement with the peasants here as he had done in Kousminski, and, if possible, that same evening.

Chapter 4

The peasants' lot

When Nekhlyudov came out of the gate he met the girl with the long earrings on the well-trodden path that lay across the pasture ground, overgrown with dock and plantain leaves. She had a long, brightly-coloured apron on, and was quickly swinging her left arm in front of herself as she stepped briskly with her fat, bare feet. With her right arm she was pressing a fowl to her stomach. The fowl, with red comb shaking, seemed perfectly calm; he only rolled up his eyes and stretched out and drew in one black leg, clawing the girl's apron. When the girl came nearer to 'the master', she began moving more slowly, and her run changed into a walk. When she came up to him she stopped, and, after a backward jerk with her head, bowed to him; and only when he had passed did she recommence to run homeward with the cock. As he went down towards the well, he met an old woman, who had a coarse dirty blouse on, carrying two pails full of water, that hung on a yoke across her bent back. The old woman carefully put down the pails and bowed, with the same backward jerk of her head.

After passing the well Nekhlyudov entered the village. It was a bright, hot day, and oppressive, though only ten o'clock. At intervals the sun was hidden by the gathering clouds. An unpleasant, sharp smell of manure filled the air in the street. It came from carts going up the hillside, but chiefly from the disturbed manure heaps in the yards of the huts, by the open gates of which Nekhlyudov had to pass. The peasants, barefooted, their shirts and trousers soiled with manure, turned to look at the tall, stout gentleman with the glossy silk ribbon on his grey hat who was walking up the village street, touching the ground every other step with a shiny, bright-knobbed walking-stick. The peasants returning from the fields at a trot and jolting in their empty carts, took off their hats, and, in their surprise, followed with their eyes the extraordinary man who was walking up their street. The women came out of the gates or stood in the porches of their huts, pointing him out to each other and gazing at him as he passed.

When Nekhlyudov was passing the fourth gate, he was stopped by a cart that was coming out, its wheels creaking, loaded high with manure, which was pressed down, and was covered with a mat to sit on. A six-year-old boy, excited by the prospect of a drive, followed the cart. A young peasant, with shoes plaited out of bark on his feet, led the horse out of the yard. A long-legged colt jumped out of the gate; but, seeing Nekhlyudov, pressed close to the cart, and scraping its legs against the wheels, jumped forward, past its excited, gently-neighing mother, as she was dragging the heavy load through the gateway. The next horse was led out by a barefooted old man, with protruding shoulder-blades, in a dirty shirt and striped trousers.

When the horses got out on to the hard road, strewn over with bits of dry, grey manure, the old man returned to the gate, and bowed to Nekhlyudov.

'You are our ladies' nephew, aren't you?'

'Yes, I am their nephew.'

'You've kindly come to look us up, eh?' said the garrulous old man.

'Yes, I have. Well, how are you getting on?'

'How do we get on? We get on very badly,' the old man drawled, as if it gave him pleasure.

'Why so badly?' Nekhlyudov asked, stepping inside the gate.

'What is our life but the very worst life?' said the old man, following Nekhlyudov into that part of the yard which was roofed over.

Nekhlyudov stopped under the roof.

'I have got twelve of them there,' continued the old man, pointing to two women on the remainder of the manure heap, who stood perspiring with forks in their hands, the kerchiefs tumbling off their heads, with their skirts tucked up, showing the calves of their dirty, bare legs. 'Not a month passes but I have to buy six *poods** of corn, and where's the money to come from?'

'Have you not got enough corn of your own?'

'My own?' repeated the old man, with a smile of contempt; 'why I have only got land for three, and last year we had not enough to last till Christmas.'

'What do you do then?'

'What do we do? Why, I hire out as a labourer; and then I borrowed some money from your honour. We spent it all before Lent, and the tax is not paid yet.'

'And how much is the tax?'

'Why, it's seventeen roubles for my household. Oh, Lord, such a life! One hardly knows one's self how one manages to live it.'

'May I go into your hut?' asked Nekhlyudov, stepping across the yard over the yellow-brown layers of manure that had been raked up by the forks, and were giving off a strong smell.

'Why not? Come in,' said the old man, and stepping quickly with his bare feet over the manure, the liquid oozing between his toes, he passed Nekhlyudov and opened the door of the hut.

The women arranged the kerchiefs on their heads and let down their skirts, and stood looking with surprise at the clean gentleman with gold studs to his sleeves who was entering their house. Two little girls, with nothing on but coarse chemises, rushed out of the hut. Nekhlyudov took off his hat, and, stooping to get through the low door, entered through a passage into the dirty, narrow hut, that smelt of sour food, and where much space was taken up by two weaving looms. In the hut an old

* A *pood* is 36 English pounds.

woman was standing by the stove, with the sleeves rolled up over her thin, sinewy brown arms.

'Here is our master come to see us,' said the old man.

'I'm sure he's very welcome,' said the old woman, kindly.

'I would like to see how you live.'

'Well, you see how we live. The hut is coming down, and might kill one any day; but my old man he says it's good enough, and so we live like kings,' said the brisk old woman, nervously jerking her head. 'I'm getting the dinner; going to feed the workers.'

'And what are you going to have for dinner?'

'Our food is very good. First course, bread and *kvas*;* second course, *kvas* and bread,' said the old woman, showing her teeth, which were half worn away.

'No, seriously, let me see what you are going to eat.'

'To eat?' said the old man, laughing. 'Ours is not a very cunning meal. You just show him, wife.'

'Want to see our peasant food? Well, you are an inquisitive gentleman, now I come to look at you. He wants to know everything. Did I not tell you bread and *kvas* and then we'll have soup. A woman brought us some fish, and that's what the soup is made of, and after that, potatoes.'

'Nothing more?'

'What more do you want? We'll also have a little milk,' said the old woman, looking towards the door. The door stood open, and the passage outside was full of people – boys, girls, women with babies – thronged together to look at the strange gentleman who wanted to see the peasants' food. The old woman seemed to pride herself on the way she behaved with a gentleman.

'Yes, it's a miserable life, ours; that goes without saying, sir,' said the old man. 'What are you doing there?' he shouted to those in the passage. 'Well, goodbye,' said Nekhlyudov, feeling ashamed and uneasy, though unable to account for the feeling.

'Thank you kindly for having looked us up,' said the old man.

The people in the passage pressed closer together to let Nekhlyudov pass, and he went out and continued his way up the street.

Two barefooted boys followed him out of the passage, the elder in a shirt that had once been white, the other in a worn and faded pink one. Nekhlyudov looked back at them.

* *Kvas* is a kind of sour, non-intoxicant beer made of rye.

'And where are you going now?' asked the boy with the white shirt. Nekhlyudov answered: 'To Matrona Kharina. Do you know her?' The boy with the pink shirt began laughing at something; but the elder asked, seriously:

'What Matrona is that? Is she old?'

'Yes, she is old.'

'Oh – oh,' he drawled; 'that one; she's at the other end of the village; we'll show you. Yes, Fedka, we'll go with him. Shall we?'

'Yes, but the horses?'

'They'll be all right, I dare say.'

Fedka agreed, and all three went up the street.

Chapter 5

Maslova's aunt

Nekhlyudov felt more at ease with the boys than with the grown-up people, and he began talking to them as they went along. The little one with the pink shirt stopped laughing, and spoke as sensibly and as exactly as the elder one.

'Can you tell me who are the poorest people you have got here?' asked Nekhlyudov.

'The poorest? Michael is poor, Simon Makhrov, and Martha, she is very poor.'

'And Anisia, she is still poorer; she's not even got a cow. They go begging,' said little Fedka.

'She's not got a cow, but they are only three persons, and Martha's family are five,' objected the elder boy.

'But the other's a widow,' the pink boy said, standing up for Anisia.

'You say Anisia is a widow, and Martha is no better than a widow,' said the elder boy; 'she's also no husband.'

'And where is her husband?' Nekhlyudov asked.

'Feeding vermin in prison,' said the elder boy, using this expression, common among the peasants.

'A year ago he cut down two birch trees in the landlord's forest,' the little pink boy hurried to say, 'so he was locked up; now he's sitting the sixth month there, and the wife goes begging. There are three children and a sick grandmother,' he went on with his detailed account.

'And where does she live?' Nekhlyudov asked.

'In this very house,' answered the boy, pointing to a hut, in front of which, on the footpath along which Nekhlyudov was walking, a tiny, flaxen-headed infant stood balancing himself with difficulty on his rickety legs.

'Vaska! Where's the little scamp got to?' shouted a woman, with a dirty grey blouse, and a frightened look, as she ran out of the house; and, rushing forward, seized the baby before Nekhlyudov came up to it, and carried it in, just as if she were afraid that Nekhlyudov would hurt her child.

This was the woman whose husband was imprisoned for Nekhlyudov's birch trees.

'Well, and this Matrona, is she also poor?' Nekhlyudov asked, as they came up to Matrona's house.

'She poor? No. Why, she sells spirits,' the thin, pink little boy answered decidedly.

When they reached the house Nekhlyudov left the boys outside and went through the passage into the hut. The hut was fourteen feet long. The bed that stood behind the big stove was not long enough for a tall person to stretch out on. 'And on this very bed,' Nekhlyudov thought, 'Katusha bore her baby and lay ill afterwards.' The greater part of the hut was taken up by a loom, on which the old woman and her eldest granddaughter were arranging the warp when Nekhlyudov came in, striking his forehead against the low doorway. Two other grandchildren came rushing in after Nekhlyudov, and stopped, holding on to the lintels of the door.

'Whom do you want?' asked the old woman, crossly. She was in a bad temper because she could not manage to get the warp right, and, besides, carrying on an illicit trade in spirits, she was always afraid when any stranger came in.

'I am – the owner of the neighbouring estates, and should like to speak to you.'

'Dear me; why, it's you, my honey; and I, fool, thought it was just some passer-by. Dear me, you – it's you, my precious,' said the old woman, with simulated tenderness in her voice.

'I should like to speak to you alone,' said Nekhlyudov, with a glance towards the door, where the children were standing, and behind them a woman holding a wasted, pale baby, with a sickly smile on its face, who had a little cap made of different bits of stuff on its head.

'What are you staring at? I'll give it you. Just hand me my crutch,' the old woman shouted to those at the door.

'Shut the door, will you.' The children went away, and the woman closed the door.

'And I was thinking, who's that? And it's "the master" himself. My jewel, my treasure. Just think,' said the old woman, 'where he has deigned to come. Sit down here, your honour,' she said, wiping the seat with her apron. 'And I was thinking what devil is it coming in, and it's your honour, "the master" himself, the good gentleman, our benefactor. Forgive me, old fool that I am; I'm getting blind.'

Nekhlyudov sat down, and the old woman stood in front of him, leaning her cheek on her right hand, while the left held up the sharp elbow of her right arm.

'Dear me, you have grown old, your honour; and you used to be as fresh as a daisy. And now! Cares also, I expect?'

'This is what I have come about: Do you remember Katusha Maslova?'

'Katerina? I should think so. Why, she is my niece. How could I help remembering; and the tears I have shed because of her. Why, I know all about it. Eh, sir, who has not sinned before God? Who has not offended against the Tsar? We know what youth is. You used to be drinking tea and coffee, so the devil got hold of you. He is strong at times. What's to be done? Now, if you had chucked her; but no, just see how you rewarded her, gave her a hundred roubles. And she? What has she done? Had she but listened to me, she might have lived all right. I must say the truth, though she is my niece: that girl's no good. What a good place I found her! She would not submit, but abused her master. Is it for the likes of us to scold gentlefolk? Well, she was sent away. And then at the forester's. She might have lived there; but no, she would not.'

'I want to know about the child. She was confined at your house, was she not? Where's the child?'

'As to the child, I considered that well at the time. She was so bad I never thought she would get up again. Well, so I christened the baby quite properly, and we sent it to the Foundlings'. Why should one let an innocent soul languish when the mother is dying? Others do like this: they just leave the baby, don't feed it, and it wastes away. But, thinks I, no; I'd rather take some trouble, and send it to the Foundlings'. There was money enough, so I sent it off.'

'Did you not get its registration number from the Foundlings' Hospital?'

'Yes, there was a number, but the baby died,' she said. 'It died as soon as she brought it there.'

'Who is she?'

'That same woman who used to live in Skorodno. She made a business of it. Her name was Malania. She's dead now. She was a wise woman. What do you think she used to do? They'd bring her a baby, and she'd keep it and feed it; and she'd feed it until she had enough of them to take to the Foundlings'. When she had three or four, she'd take them all at once. She had such a clever arrange-ment, a sort of big cradle – a double one she could put them in one way or the other. It had a handle. So she'd put four of them in, feet to feet and the heads apart, so that they should not knock against each other. And so she took four at once. She'd put some pap in a rag into their mouths to keep 'em silent, the pets.'

'Well, go on.'

'Well, she took Katerina's baby in the same way, after keeping it a fortnight, I believe. It was in her house it began to sicken.'

'And was it a fine baby?' Nekhlyudov asked.

'Such a baby, that if you wanted a finer you could not find one. Your very image,' the old woman added, with a wink.

'Why did it sicken? Was the food bad?'

'Eh, what food? Only just a pretence of food. Naturally, when it's not one's own child. Only enough to get it there alive. She said she just managed to get it to Moscow, and there it died. She brought a certificate – all in order. She was such a wise woman.'

That was all Nekhlyudov could find out concerning his child.

Chapter 6

Reflections of a landlord

Again striking his head against both doors, Nekhlyudov went out into the street, where the pink and the white boys were waiting for him. A few newcomers were standing with them. Among the women, of whom several had babies in their arms, was the thin woman with the baby who had the patchwork cap on its head. She held lightly in her arms the bloodless infant, who kept strangely smiling all over its wizened little face, and continually moving its crooked thumbs.

Nekhlyudov knew the smile to be one of suffering. He asked who the woman was.

'It is that very Anisia I told you about,' said the elder boy.

Nekhlyudov turned to Anisia.

'How do you live?' he asked. 'By what means do you gain your livelihood?'

'How do I live? I go begging,' said Anisia, and began to cry.

Nekhlyudov took out his pocket-book, and gave the woman a ten-rouble note. He had not had time to take two steps before another woman with a baby caught him up, then an old woman, then another young one. All of them spoke of their poverty, and asked for help. Nekhlyudov gave them the sixty roubles – all in small notes – which he had with him, and, terribly sad at heart, turned home, i.e., to the foreman's house.

The foreman met Nekhlyudov with a smile, and informed him that the peasants would come to the meeting in the evening. Nekhlyudov thanked him, and went straight into the garden to stroll along the paths strewn over with the petals of apple-blossom and overgrown with weeds, and to think over all he had seen.

At first all was quiet, but soon Nekhlyudov heard from behind the foreman's house two angry women's voices interrupting each other, and now and then the voice of the ever-smiling foreman. Nekhlyudov listened.

'My strength's at an end. What are you about, dragging the very cross off my neck,'* said an angry woman's voice.

'But she only got in for a moment,' said another voice. 'Give it her back, I tell you. Why do you torment the beast, and the children, too, who want their milk?'

'Pay, then, or work it off,' said the foreman's voice.

Nekhlyudov left the garden and entered the porch, near which stood two dishevelled women – one of them pregnant and evidently near her time. On one of the steps of the porch, with his hands in the pockets of his holland coat, stood the foreman. When they saw the master, the women were silent, and began arranging the kerchiefs on their heads, and the foreman took his hands out of his pockets and began to smile.

This is what had happened. From the foreman's words, it seemed that the peasants were in the habit of letting their calves and even their cows into the meadow belonging to the estate. Two cows belonging to the families of these two women were found in the meadow, and driven into the yard. The foreman demanded from the women thirty copecks for each cow or two days' work. The women, however, maintained that the cows had got into the meadow of their own accord; that they had no money, and asked that the cows, which had stood in the blazing sun since morning without food, piteously lowing, should be returned to them, even if it had to be on the understanding that the price should be worked off later on.

'How often have I not begged of you,' said the smiling foreman, looking back at Nekhlyudov as if calling upon him to be a witness, 'if you drive your cattle home at noon, that you should have an eye on them?'

'I only ran to my little one for a bit, and they got away.'

'Don't run away when you have undertaken to watch the cows.'

'And who's to feed the little one? You'd not give him the breast, I suppose?' said the other woman. 'Now, if they had really damaged the meadow, one would not take it so much to heart; but they only strayed in a moment.'

---

* Those baptized in the Russo-Greek Church always wear a cross round their necks.

'All the meadows are damaged,' the foreman said, turning to Nekhlyudov. 'If I exact no penalty there will be no hay.'

'There, now, don't go sinning like that; my cows have never been caught there before,' shouted the pregnant woman.

'Now that one has been caught, pay up or work it off.'

'All right, I'll work it off; only let me have the cow now, don't torture her with hunger,' she cried, angrily. 'As it is, I have no rest day or night. Mother-in-law is ill, husband taken to drink; I'm all alone to do all the work, and my strength's at an end. I wish you'd choke, you and your working it off.'

Nekhlyudov asked the foreman to let the women take the cows, and went back into the garden to go on thinking out his problem, but there was nothing more to think about.

Everything seemed so clear to him now that he could not stop wondering how it was that everybody did not see it, and that he himself had for such a long while not seen what was so clearly evident. The people were dying out, and had got used to the dying-out process, and had formed habits of life adapted to this process: there was the great mortality among the children, the over-working of the women, the under-feeding, especially of the aged. And so gradually had the people come to this condition that they did not realise the full horrors of it, and did not complain. Therefore, we consider their condition natural and as it should be. Now it seemed as clear as daylight that the chief cause of the people's great want was one that they themselves knew and always pointed out, i.e., that the land which alone could feed them had been taken from them by the landlords.

And how evident it was that the children and the aged died because they had no milk, and they had no milk because there was no pasture land, and no land to grow corn or make hay on. It was quite evident that all the misery of the people or, at least by far the greater part of it, was caused by the fact that the land which should feed them was not in their hands, but in the hands of those who, profiting by their rights to the land, live by the work of these people. The land so much needed by men was tilled by these people, who were on the verge of starvation, so that the corn might be sold abroad and the owners of the land might buy themselves hats and canes, and carriages and bronzes, etc. He understood this as clearly as he understood that horses when they have eaten all the grass in the enclosure where they are kept will have to grow thin and starve unless they are put where they can get food off other land.

This was terrible, and must not go on. Means must be found to alter it, or at least not to take part in it. 'And I will find them,' he thought, as he walked up and down the path under the birch trees.

In scientific circles, government institutions, and in the papers we talk about the causes of the poverty among the people and the means of ameliorating their condition; but we do not talk of the only sure means which would certainly lighten their condition, i.e., giving back to them the land they need so much.

Henry George's fundamental position recurred vividly to his mind and how he had once been carried away by it, and he was surprised that he could have forgotten it. The earth cannot be anyone's property; it cannot be bought or sold any more than water, air, or sunshine. All have an equal right to the advantages it gives to men. And now he knew why he had felt ashamed to remember the transaction at Kousminski. He had been deceiving himself. He knew that no man could have a right to own land, yet he had accepted this right as his, and had given the peasants something which, in the depth of his heart, he knew he had no right to. Now he would not act in this way, and would alter the arrangement in Kousminski also. And he formed a project in his mind to let the land to the peasants, and to acknowledge the rent they paid for it to be their property, to be kept to pay the taxes and for communal uses. This was, of course, not the single-tax system, still it was as near an approach to it as could be had under existing circumstances. His chief consideration, however, was that in this way he would no longer profit by the possession of landed property.

When he returned to the house the foreman, with a specially pleasant smile, asked him if he would not have his dinner now, expressing the fear that the feast his wife was preparing, with the help of the girl with the earrings, might be overdone.

The table was covered with a coarse, unbleached cloth and an embroidered towel was laid on it in lieu of a napkin. A *vieux-saxe* soup tureen with a broken handle stood on the table, full of potato soup, the stock made of the fowl that had put out and drawn in his black leg, and was now cut, or rather chopped, in pieces, which were here and there covered with hairs. After the soup more of the same fowl with the hairs was served roasted, and then curd pasties, very greasy, and with a great deal of sugar. Little appetising as all this was, Nekhlyudov hardly noticed what he was eating; he was occupied with the thought which had in a moment dispersed the sadness with which he had returned from the village.

The foreman's wife kept looking in at the door, whilst the frightened maid with the earrings brought in the dishes; and the foreman smiled more and more joyfully, priding himself on his wife's culinary skill. After dinner, Nekhlyudov succeeded, with some trouble, in making the foreman sit down. In order to revise his own thoughts, and to express them to someone, he explained his project of letting the land to the peasants, and asked the foreman for his opinion. The foreman, smiling as if he had thought all this himself long ago, and was very pleased to hear it, did not really understand it at all. This was not because Nekhlyudov did not express himself clearly, but because according to this project it turned out that Nekhlyudov was giving up his own profit for the profit of others, and the thought that everyone is only concerned about his own profit, to the harm of others, was so deeply rooted in the foreman's conceptions that he imagined he did not understand something when Nekhlyudov said that all the income from the land must be placed to form the communal capital of the peasants.

'Oh, I see; then you, of course, will receive the percentages from that capital,' said the foreman, brightening up.

'Dear me, no. Don't you see, I am giving up the land altogether.'

'But then you will not get any income,' said the foreman, smiling no longer.

'Yes, I am going to give it up.'

The foreman sighed heavily, and then began smiling again. Now he understood. He understood that Nekhlyudov was not quite normal, and at once began to consider how he himself could profit by Nekhlyudov's project of giving up the land, and tried to see this project in such a way that he might reap some advantage from it. But when he saw that this was impossible he grew sorrowful, and the project ceased to interest him, and he continued to smile only in order to please the master.

Seeing that the foreman did not understand him, Nekhlyudov let him go and sat down by the window-sill, that was all cut about and inked over, and began to put his project down on paper.

The sun went down behind the limes, that were covered with fresh green, and the mosquitoes swarmed in, stinging Nekhlyudov. Just as he finished his notes, he heard the lowing of cattle and the creaking of opening gates from the village, and the voices of the peasants gathering together for the meeting. He told the foreman not to call the peasants up to the office, as he meant to go into the village himself and meet the men where they would assemble. Having hurriedly drunk a cup of tea offered him by the foreman, Nekhlyudov went to the village.

Chapter 7

The disinherited

From the crowd assembled in front of the house of the village elder came the sound of voices; but as soon as Nekhlyudov came up the talking ceased, and all the peasants took off their caps, just as those in Kousminski had done. The peasants here were of a much poorer class than those in Kousminski. The men wore shoes made of bark and homespun shirts and coats. Some had come straight from their work in their shirts and with bare feet.

Nekhlyudov made an effort, and began his speech by telling the peasants of his intention to give up his land to them altogether. The peasants were silent, and the expression on their faces did not undergo any change.

'Because I hold,' said Nekhlyudov, 'and believe that everyone has a right to the use of the land.'

'That's certain. That's so, exactly,' said several voices.

Nekhlyudov went on to say that the revenue from the land ought to be divided among all, and that he would therefore suggest that they should rent the land at a price fixed by themselves, the rent to form a communal fund for their own use. Words of approval and agreement were still to be heard, but the serious faces of the peasants grew still more serious, and the eyes that had been fixed on the gentleman dropped, as if they were unwilling to put him to shame by letting him see that everyone had understood his trick, and that no one would be deceived by him.

Nekhlyudov spoke clearly, and the peasants were intelligent, but they did not and could not understand him, for the same reason that the foreman had so long been unable to understand him.

They were fully convinced that it is natural for every man to consider his own interest. The experience of many generations had proved to them that the landlords always considered their own interest to the detriment of the peasants. Therefore, if a landlord called them to a meeting and made them some kind of a new offer, it could evidently only be in order to swindle them more cunningly than before.

'Well, then, what are you willing to rent the land at?' asked Nekhlyudov.

'How can we fix a price? We cannot do it. The land is yours, and the power is in your hands,' answered some voices from among the crowd.

'Oh, not at all. You will yourselves have the use of the money for communal purposes.'

'We cannot do it; the commune is one thing, and this is another.'

'Don't you understand?' said the foreman, with a smile (he had followed Nekhlyudov to the meeting), 'the Prince is letting the land to you for money, and is giving you the money back to form a capital for the commune.'

'We understand very well,' said a cross, toothless old man, without raising his eyes. 'Something like a bank; we should have to pay at a fixed time. We do not wish it; it is hard enough as it is, and that would ruin us completely.'

'That's no go. We prefer to go on the old way,' began several dissatisfied, and even rude, voices.

The refusals grew very vehement when Nekhlyudov mentioned that he would draw up an agreement which would have to be signed by him and by them.

'Why sign? We shall go on working as we have done hitherto. What is all this for? We are ignorant men.'

'We can't agree, because this sort of thing is not what we have been used to. As it was, so let it continue to be. Only the seeds we should like to withdraw.'

This meant that under the present arrangement the seeds had to be provided by the peasants, and they wanted the landlord to provide them.

'Then am I to understand that you refuse to accept the land?' Nekhlyudov asked, addressing a middle-aged, barefooted peasant, with a tattered coat, and a bright look on his face, who was holding his worn cap with his left hand, in a peculiarly straight position, in the same way soldiers hold theirs when commanded to take them off.

'Just so,' said this peasant, who had evidently not yet rid himself of the military hypnotism he had been subjected to while serving his time.

'It means that you have sufficient land,' said Nekhlyudov.

'No, sir, we have not,' said the ex-soldier, with an artificially pleased look, carefully holding his tattered cap in front of him, as if offering it to anyone who liked to make use of it.

'Well, anyhow, you'd better think over what I have said.' Nekhlyudov spoke with surprise, and again repeated his offer.

'We have no need to think about it; as we have said, so it will be,' angrily muttered the morose, toothless old man.

'I shall remain here another day, and if you change your minds, send to let me know.'

The peasants gave no answer.

So Nekhlyudov did not succeed in arriving at any result from this interview.

'If I might make a remark, Prince,' said the foreman, when they got home, 'you will never come to any agreement with them; they are so obstinate. At a meeting these people just stick in one place, and there is no moving them. It is because they are frightened of everything. Why, these very peasants – say that white-haired one, or the dark one, who were refusing, are intelligent peasants. When one of them comes to the office and one makes him sit down to cup of tea it's like in the Palace of Wisdom – he is quite diplomatist,' said the foreman, smiling; 'he will consider everything rightly. At a meeting it's a different man – he keeps repeating one and the same . . . '

'Well, could not some of the more intelligent men be asked to come here?' said Nekhlyudov. 'I would carefully explain it to them.'

'That can be done,' said the smiling foreman.

'Well, then, would you mind calling them here tomorrow?'

'Oh, certainly I will,' said the foreman, and smiled still more joyfully. 'I shall call them tomorrow.'

'Just hear him; he's not artful, not he,' said a blackhaired peasant, with an unkempt beard, as he sat jolting from side to side on a well-fed mare, addressing an old man in a torn coat who rode by his side. The two men were driving a herd of the peasants' horses to graze in the night, alongside the high road and secretly, in the landlord's forest.

'Give you the land for nothing – you need only sign – have they not done the likes of us often enough? No, my friend, none of your humbug. Nowadays we have a little sense,' he added, and began shouting at a colt that had strayed.

He stopped his horse and looked round, but the colt had not remained behind; it had gone into the meadow by the roadside. 'Bother that son of a Turk; he's taken to getting into the landowner's meadows,' said the dark peasant with the unkempt beard, hearing the cracking of the sorrel stalks that the neighing colt was galloping over as he came running back from the scented meadow.

'Do you hear the cracking? We'll have to send the women folk to weed the meadow when there's a holiday,' said the thin peasant with the torn coat, 'or else we'll blunt our scythes.'

'Sign,' he says. The unkempt man continued giving his opinion of the landlord's speech. ' "Sign," indeed, and let him swallow you up.'

'That's certain,' answered the old man. And then they were silent, and the tramping of the horses' feet along the highroad was the only sound to be heard.

Chapter 8

God's peace in the heart

When Nekhlyudov returned he found that the office had been arranged as a bedroom for him. A high bedstead, with a feather bed and two large pillows, had been placed in the room. The bed was covered with a dark red double-bedded silk quilt, which was elaborately and finely quilted, and very stiff. It evidently belonged to the trousseau of the foreman's wife. The foreman offered Nekhlyudov the remains of the dinner, which the latter refused, and excusing himself for the poorness of the fare and the accommodation, he left Nekhlyudov alone.

The peasants' refusal did not at all bother Nekhlyudov. On the contrary, though at Kousminski his offer had been accepted and he had even been thanked for it, and here he was met with suspicion and even enmity, he felt contented and joyful.

It was close and dirty in the office. Nekhlyudov went out into the yard, and was going into the garden, but he remembered: that night, the window of the maid-servant's room, the side porch; and he felt uncomfortable, and did not like to pass the spot desecrated by guilty memories. He sat down on the doorstep, and breathing in the warm air, balmy with the strong scent of fresh birch leaves, he sat for a long time looking into the dark garden and listening to the mill, the nightingales, and some other bird that whistled monotonously in the bush close by. The light disappeared from the foreman's window; in the east, behind the barn, appeared the light of the rising moon, and sheet lightning began to light up the dilapidated house and the blooming, overgrown garden more and more frequently. It began to thunder in the distance, and a black cloud spread over one-third of the sky. The nightingales and the other birds were silent. Above the murmur of the water from the mill came the cackling of geese, and then in the village and in the foreman's yard the first cocks began to crow earlier than usual, as they do on warm, thundery nights. There is a saying that if the cocks crow early the night will be a merry one. For Nekhlyudov the night was more than merry; it was a happy, joyful night. Imagination renewed the impressions of that happy summer which he had spent here as an innocent lad, and he felt himself as he had been not only at that but at all the best moments of his life. He not only remembered but felt as he had felt when, at the age of fourteen, he prayed that God would show him the truth; or when as a child he had wept on his mother's lap, when parting from her, and promising to be always good, and never give her pain; he felt as he did when he and Nikolenka Irteniev resolved always to support each other in living a good life and to try to make everybody happy.

He remembered how he had been tempted in Kousminski, so that he had begun to regret the house and the forest and the farm and the land, and he asked himself if he regretted them now, and it even seemed strange to think that he could regret them. He remembered all he had seen today: the woman with the children, and without her husband, who was in prison for having cut down trees in his (Nekhlyudov's) forest, and the terrible Matrona, who considered, or at least talked as if she considered, that women of her position must give themselves to the gentlefolk; he remembered her relation to the babies, the way in which they were taken to the Foundlings' Hospital, and the unfortunate, smiling, wizened baby with the patchwork cap, dying of starvation. And then he suddenly remembered the prison, the shaved heads, the cells, the disgusting smells, the chains, and, by the side of it all, the madly lavish city life of the rich, himself included.

The bright moon, now almost full, rose above the barn. Dark shadows fell across the yard, and the iron roof of the ruined house shone bright. As if unwilling to waste this light, the nightingales again began their trills.

Nekhlyudov called to mind how he had begun to consider his life in the garden of Kousminski when deciding what he was going to do, and remembered how confused he had become, how he could not arrive at any decision, how many difficulties each question had presented. He asked himself these questions now, and was surprised how simple it all was. It was simple because he was not thinking now of what would be the results for himself, but only thought of what he had to do. And, strange to say, what he had to do for himself he could not decide, but what he had to do for others he knew without any doubt. He had no doubt that he must not leave Katusha, but go on helping her. He had no doubt that he must study, investigate, clear up, understand all this business concerning judgment and punishment, which he felt he saw differently to other people. What would result from it all he did not know, but he knew for certain that he must do it. And this firm assurance gave him joy.

The black cloud had spread all over the sky; the lightning flashed vividly across the yard and the old house with its tumble-down porches, the thunder growled overhead. All the birds were silent, but the leaves rustled and the wind reached the step where Nekhlyudov stood and played with his hair. One drop came down, then another; then they came drumming on the dock leaves and on the iron of the roof, and all the air was filled by a bright flash, and before Nekhlyudov could count three a fearful crash sounded over head and spread pealing all over the sky.

Nekhlyudov went in.

'Yes, yes,' he thought. 'The work that our life accomplishes, the whole of this work, the meaning of it is not, nor can be, intelligible to me. What were my aunts for? Why did Nikolenka Irteniev die? Why am I living? What was Katusha for? And my madness? Why that war? Why my subsequent lawless life? To understand it, to understand the whole of the Master's will is not in my power. But to do His will, that is written down in my conscience, is in my power; that I know for certain. And when I am fulfilling it I have sureness and peace.'

The rain came down in torrents and rushed from the roof into a tub beneath; the lightning lit up the house and yard less frequently. Nekhlyudov went into his room, undressed, and lay down, not without fear of the bugs, whose presence the dirty, torn wall-papers made him suspect.

'Yes, to feel one's self not the master but a servant,' he thought, and rejoiced at the thought. His fears were not vain. Hardly had he put out his candle when the vermin attacked and stung him. 'To give up the land and go to Siberia. Fleas, bugs, dirt! Ah, well; if it must be borne, I shall bear it.' But, in spite of the best of intentions, he could not bear it, and sat down by the open window and gazed with admiration at the retreating clouds and the reappearing moon.

Chapter 9

The land settlement

It was morning before Nekhlyudov could fall asleep, and therefore he woke up late. At noon seven men, chosen from among the peasants at the foreman's invitation, came into the orchard, where the foreman had arranged a table and benches by digging posts into the ground, and fixing boards on the top, under the apple trees. It took some time before the peasants could be persuaded to put on their caps and to sit down on the benches. Especially firm was the ex-soldier, who today had bark shoes on. He stood erect, holding his cap as they do at funerals, according to military regulation. When one of them, a respectable-looking, broad-shouldered old man, with a curly, grizzly beard like that of Michael Angelo's 'Moses', and grey hair that curled round the brown, bald forehead, put on his big cap, and, wrapping his coat round him, got in behind the table and sat down, the rest followed his example. When all had taken their places Nekhlyudov sat down opposite them, and leaning on the table over the paper on which he had drawn up his project, he began explaining it.

Whether it was that there were fewer present, or that he was occupied with the business in hand and not with himself, anyhow, this time Nekhlyudov felt no confusion. He involuntarily addressed the broad-shouldered old man with white ringlets in his grizzly beard, expecting approbation or objections from him. But Nekhlyudov's conjecture was wrong. The respectable-looking old patriarch, though he nodded his handsome head approvingly or shook it, and frowned when the others raised an objection, evidently understood with great difficulty, and only when the others repeated what Nekhlyudov had said in their own words. A little, almost beardless old fellow, blind in one eye, who sat by the side of the patriarch, and had a patched nankeen coat and old boots on, and, as Nekhlyudov found out later, was an oven-builder, understood much better. This man moved his brows quickly, attending to Nekhlyudov's words with an effort, and at once repeated them in his own way. An old, thick-set man with a white beard and intelligent eyes understood as quickly, and took every opportunity to put in an ironical joke, clearly wishing to show off. The ex-soldier seemed also to understand matters, but got mixed, being used to senseless soldiers' talk. A tall man with a small beard, a long nose, and a bass voice, who wore clean, home-made clothes and new bark-plaited shoes, seemed to be the one most seriously interested. This man spoke only when there was need of it. The two other old men, the same toothless one who had shouted a distinct refusal at the meeting the day before to every proposal of Nekhlyudov's, and a tall, white lame old man with a kind face, his thin legs tightly wrapped round with strips of linen, said little, though they listened attentively. First of all Nekhlyudov explained his views in regard to personal property in land. 'The land, according to my idea, can neither he bought nor sold, because if it could be, he who has got the money could buy it all, and exact anything he liked for the use of the land from those who have none.'

'That's true,' said the long-nosed man, in a deep bass.

'Just so,' said the ex-soldier.

'A woman gathers a little grass for her cow; she's caught and imprisoned,' said the white-bearded old man.

'Our own land is five versts away, and as to renting any it's impossible; the price is raised so high that it won't pay,' added the cross, toothless old man. 'They twist us into ropes, worse than during serfdom.'

'I think as you do, and I count it a sin to possess land, so I wish to give it away,' said Nekhlyudov.

'Well, that's a good thing,' said the old man with curls like Angelo's 'Moses', evidently thinking that Nekhlyudov meant to let the land.

'I have come here because I no longer wish to possess any land, and now we must consider the best way of dividing it.'

'Just give it to the peasants, that's all,' said the cross, toothless old man.

Nekhlyudov was abashed for a moment, feeling a suspicion of his not being honest in these words, but he instantly recovered, and made use of the remark in order to express what was in his mind, in reply.

'I should be glad to give it them,' he said, 'but to whom, and how? To which of the peasants? Why, to your commune, and not to that of Deminsk.' (That was the name of a neighbouring village with very little land.) All were silent. Then the ex-soldier said, 'Just so.'

'Now, then, tell me how would you divide the land among the peasants if you had to do it?' said Nekhlyudov.

'We should divide it up equally, so much for every man,' said the oven-builder, quickly raising and lowering his brows.

'How else? Of course, so much per man,' said the good-natured lame man with the white strips of linen round his legs.

Everyone confirmed this statement, considering it satisfactory.

'So much per man? Then are the servants attached to the house also to have a share?' Nekhlyudov asked.

'Oh, no,' said the ex-soldier, trying to appear bold and merry. But the tall, reasonable man would not agree with him.

'If one is to divide, all must share alike,' he said, in his deep bass, after a little consideration.

'It can't be done,' said Nekhlyudov, who had already prepared his reply. 'If all are to share alike, then those who do not work themselves – do not plough – will sell their shares to the rich. The rich will again get at the land. Those who live by working the land will multiply, and land will again be scarce. Then the rich will again get those who need land into their power.'

'Just so,' quickly said the ex-soldier.

'Forbid to sell the land; let only him who ploughs it have it,' angrily interrupted the oven-builder.

To this Nekhlyudov replied that it was impossible to know who was ploughing for himself and who for another.

The tall, reasonable man proposed that an arrangement be made so that they should all plough communally, and those who ploughed should get the produce and those who did not should get nothing.

To this communistic project Nekhlyudov had also an answer ready. He said that for such an arrangement it would be necessary that all should have ploughs, and that all the horses should be alike, so that none should be left behind, and that ploughs and horses and all the implements would have to be communal property, and that in order to get that, all the people would have to agree.

'Our people could not be made to agree in a lifetime,' said the cross old man.

'We should have regular fights,' said the white-bearded old man with the laughing eyes. 'So that the thing is not as simple as it looks,' said Nekhlyudov, 'and this is a thing not only we but many have been considering. There is an American, Henry George. This is what he has thought out, and I agree with him.'

'Why, you are the master, and you give it as you like. What's it to you? The power is yours,' said the cross old man.

This confused Nekhlyudov, but he was pleased to see that not he alone was dissatisfied with this interruption.

'You wait a bit, Uncle Simon; let him tell us about it,' said the reasonable man, in his imposing bass.

This emboldened Nekhlyudov, and he began to explain Henry George's single-tax system 'The earth is no man's; it is God's,' he began.

'Just so; that it is,' several voices replied.

'The land is common to all. All have the same right to it, but there is good land and bad land, and everyone would like to take the good land. How is one to do in order to get it justly divided? In this way: he that will use the good land must pay those who have got no land the value of the land he uses,' Nekhlyudov went on, answering his own question. 'As it would be difficult to say who should pay whom, and money is needed for communal use, it should be arranged that he who uses the good land should pay the amount of the value of his land to the commune for its needs. Then everyone would share equally. If you want to use land pay for it – more for the good, less for the bad land. If you do not wish to use land, don't pay anything, and those who use the land will pay the taxes and the communal expenses for you.'

'Well, he had a head, this George,' said the oven-builder, moving his brows. 'He who has good land must pay more.'

'If only the payment is according to our strength,' said the tall man with the bass voice, evidently foreseeing how the matter would end.

'The payment should be not too high and not too low. If it is too high it will not get paid, and there will be a loss; and if it is too low it will be bought and sold. There would be a trading in land. This is what I wished to arrange among you here.'

'That is just, that is right; yes, that would do,' said the peasants.

'He has a head, this George,' said the broad-shouldered old man with the curls. 'See what he has invented.'

'Well, then, how would it be if I wished to take some land?' asked the smiling foreman.

'If there is an allotment to spare, take it and work it,' said Nekhlyudov.

'What do you want it for? You have sufficient as it is,' said the old man with the laughing eyes.

With this the conference ended.

Nekhlyudov repeated his offer, and advised the men to talk it over with the rest of the commune and to return with the answer.

The peasants said they would talk it over and bring an answer, and left in a state of excitement. Their loud talk was audible as they went along the road, and up to late in the night the sound of voices came along the river from the village.

The next day the peasants did not go to work, but spent it in considering the landlord's offer. The commune was divided into two parties – one which regarded the offer as a profitable one to themselves and saw no danger in agreeing with it, and another which suspected and feared the offer it did not understand. On the third day, however, all agreed, and some were sent to Nekhlyudov to accept his offer. They were influenced in their decision by the explanation some of the old men gave of the landlord's conduct, which did away with all fear of deceit. They thought the gentleman had begun to consider his soul, and was acting as he did for its salvation. The alms which Nekhlyudov had given away while in Panovo made his explanation seem likely. The fact that Nekhlyudov had never before been face to face with such great poverty and so bare a life as the peasants had come to in this place, and was so appalled by it, made him give away money in charity, though he knew that this was not reasonable. He could not help giving the money, of which he now had a great deal, having received a large sum for the forest he had sold the year before, and also the hand money for the implements and stock in Kousminski.

As soon as it was known that the master was giving money in charity, crowds of people, chiefly women, began to come to ask him for help. He did not in the least know how to deal with them, how to decide, how much, and whom to give to. He felt that to refuse to give money, of which he had a great deal, to poor people was impossible, yet to give casually to those who asked was not wise. The last day he spent in Panovo, Nekhlyudov looked over the things left in his aunts' house, and in the bottom drawer of the mahogany wardrobe, with the brass lions' heads with rings through them, he found many letters, and amongst them a photograph of a group consisting of his aunts, Sophia Ivanovna and Mary Ivanovna, a student, and Katusha. Of all the things in the house he took only the letters and the photograph. The rest he left to the miller who, at the smiling foreman's recommendation, had bought the house and all it contained, to be taken down and carried away, at one-tenth of the real value.

Recalling the feeling of regret at the loss of his property which he had felt in Kousminski, Nekhlyudov was surprised how he could have felt this regret. Now he felt nothing but unceasing joy at the deliverance, and a sensation of newness something like that which a traveller must experience when discovering new countries.

Chapter 10

Nekhlyudov returns to town

The town struck Nekhlyudov in a new and peculiar light on his return. He came back in the evening, when the gas was lit, and drove from the railway station to his house, where the rooms still smelt of naphthaline. Agraphena Petrovna and Corney were both feeling tired and dissatisfied, and had even had a quarrel over those things that seemed made only to be aired and packed away. Nekhlyudov's room was empty, but not in order, and the way to it was blocked up with boxes, so that his arrival evidently hindered the business which, owing to a curious kind of inertia, was going on in this house. The evident folly of these proceedings, in which he had once taken part, was so distasteful to Nekhlyudov after the impressions the misery of the life of the peasants had made on him, that he decided to go to a hotel the next day, leaving Agraphena Petrovna to put away the things as she thought fit until his sister should come and finally dispose of everything in the house.

Nekhlyudov left home early and chose a couple of rooms in a very modest and not particularly clean lodging-house within easy reach of the prison, and, having given orders that some of his things should be sent there, he went to see the advocate. It was cold out of doors. After some rainy and stormy weather it had turned out cold, as it often does in spring. It was so cold that Nekhlyudov felt quite chilly in his light overcoat, and walked fast hoping to get warmer. His mind was filled with thoughts of the peasants, the women, children, old men, and all the poverty and weariness which he seemed to have seen for the first time, especially the smiling, old-faced infant writhing with his calf-less little legs, and he could not help contrasting what was going on in the town. Passing by the butchers', fishmongers', and clothiers' shops, he was struck, as if he saw them for the first time, by the appearance of the clean, well-fed shopkeepers, like whom you could not find one peasant in the country. These men were apparently convinced that the pains they took to deceive the people who did not know much about their goods was not a useless but rather an important business. The coachmen with their broad hips and rows of buttons down their sides, and the door-keepers with gold cords on their caps, the servant-girls with their aprons and curly fringes, and especially the smart *isvostchik*s with the nape of their necks clean-shaved, as they sat lolling back in their traps, and examined the passers-by with dissolute and contemptuous air, looked well fed. In all these people Nekhlyudov could not now help seeing some of these very peasants who had been driven into the town by lack of land. Some of the peasants driven to the town had found means of profiting by the conditions of town life and had become like the gentlefolk and were pleased with their position; others were in a worse position than they had been in the country and were more to be pitied than the country people.

Such seemed the bootmakers Nekhlyudov saw in the cellar, the pale, dishevelled washerwomen with their thin, bare, arms ironing at an open window, out of which streamed soapy steam;

such the two house-painters with their aprons, stockingless feet, all bespattered and smeared with paint, whom Nekhlyudov met – their weak, brown arms bared to above the elbows – carrying a pailful of paint, and quarrelling with each other. Their faces looked haggard and cross. The dark faces of the carters jolting along in their carts bore the same expression, and so did the faces of the tattered men and women who stood begging at the street corners. The same kind of faces were to be seen at the open windows of the eating-houses which Nekhlyudov passed. By the dirty tables on which stood tea things and bottles, and between which waiters dressed in white shirts were rushing hither and thither, sat shouting and singing red, perspiring men with stupefied faces. One sat by the window with lifted brows and pouting lips and fixed eyes as if trying to remember something.

'And why are they all gathered here?' Nekhlyudov thought, breathing in together with the dust which the cold wind blew towards him the air filled with the smell of rank oil and fresh paint.

In one street he met a row of carts loaded with something made of iron, that rattled so on the uneven pavement that it made his ears and head ache. He started walking still faster in order to pass the row of carts, when he heard himself called by name. He stopped and saw an officer with sharp pointed moustaches and shining face who sat in the trap of a swell *isvostchik* and waved his hand in a friendly manner, his smile disclosing unusually long, white teeth.

'Nekhlyudov! Can it be you?'

Nekhlyudov's first feeling was one of pleasure. 'Ah, Schönbock!' he exclaimed joyfully; but he knew the next moment that there was nothing to be joyful about.

This was that Schönbock who had been in the house of Nekhlyudov's aunts that day, and whom Nekhlyudov had quite lost out of sight, but about whom he had heard that in spite of his debts he had somehow managed to remain in the cavalry, and by some means or other still kept his place among the rich. His gay, contented appearance corroborated this report.

'What a good thing that I have caught you. There is no one in town. Ah, old fellow; you have grown old,' he said, getting out of the trap and moving his shoulders about. 'I only knew you by your walk. Look here, we must dine together. Is there any place where they feed one decently?'

'I don't think I can spare the time,' Nekhlyudov answered, thinking only of how he could best get rid of his companion without hurting him.

'And what has brought you here?' he asked.

'Business, old fellow. Guardianship business. I am a guardian now. I am managing Samanov's affairs – the millionaire, you know. He has softening of the brain, and he's got fifty-four thousand *desiatins* of land,' he said, with peculiar pride, as if he had himself made all these *desiatins*. 'The affairs were terribly neglected. All the land was let to the peasants. They did not pay anything. There were more than eighty thousand roubles debts. I changed it all in one year, and have got seventy per cent. more out of it. What do you think of that?' he asked proudly.

Nekhlyudov remembered having heard that this Schönbock, just because he had spent all he had, had attained by some special influence the post of guardian to a rich old man who was squandering his property – and was now evidently living by this guardianship.

'How am I to get rid of him without offending him?' thought Nekhlyudov, looking at this full, shiny face with the stiffened moustache and listening to his friendly, good-humoured chatter about where one gets fed best, and his bragging about his doings as a guardian.

'Well, then, where do we dine?'

'Really, I have no time to spare,' said Nekhlyudov, glancing at his watch.

'Then, look here. Tonight, at the races – will you be there?'

'No, I shall not be there.'

'Do come. I have none of my own now, but I back Grisha's horses. You remember; he has a fine stud. You'll come, won't you? And we'll have some supper together.'

'No, I cannot have supper with you either,' said Nekhlyudov with a smile.

'Well, that's too bad! And where are you off to now? Shall I give you a lift?'

'I am going to see an advocate, close to here round the corner.'

'Oh, yes, of course. You have got something to do with the prisons – have turned into a prisoners' mediator, I hear,' said Schönbock, laughing. 'The Korchagins told me. They have left town already. What does it all mean? Tell me.'

'Yes, yes, it is quite true,' Nekhlyudov answered; 'but I cannot tell you about it in the street.'

'Of course; you always were a crank. But you will come to the races?'

'No. I neither can nor wish to come. Please do not be angry with me.'

'Angry? Dear me, no. Where do you live?' And suddenly his face became serious, his eyes fixed, and he drew up his brows. He seemed to be trying to remember something, and Nekhlyudov noticed the same dull expression as that of the man with the raised brows and pouting lips whom he had seen at the window of the eating-house.

'How cold it is! Is it not? Have you got the parcels?' said Schönbock, turning to the *isvostchik*.

'All right. Goodbye. I am very glad indeed to have met you,' and warmly pressing Nekhlyudov's hand, he jumped into the trap and waved his white-gloved hand in front of his shiny face, with his usual smile, showing his exceptionally white teeth.

'Can I have also been like that?' Nekhlyudov thought, as he continued his way to the advocate's. 'Yes, I wished to be like that, though I was not quite like it. And I thought of living my life in that way.'

Chapter 11

An advocate's views on judges and prosecutors

Nekhlyudov was admitted by the advocate before his turn. The advocate at once commenced to talk about the Menshovs' case, which he had read with indignation at the inconsistency of the accusation.

'This case is perfectly revolting,' he said; 'it is very likely that the owner himself set fire to the building in order to get the insurance money, and the chief thing is that there is no evidence to prove the Menshovs' guilt. There are no proofs whatever. It is all owing to the special zeal of the examining magistrate and the carelessness of the prosecutor. If they are tried here, and not in a provincial court, I guarantee that they will be acquitted, and I shall charge nothing. Now then, the next case, that of Theodosia Birukov. The appeal to the Emperor is written. If you go to Petersburg, you'd better take it with you, and hand it in yourself, with a request of your own, or else they will only make a few inquiries, and nothing will come of it. You must try and get at some of the influential members of the Appeal Committee.'

'Well, is this all?'

'No; here I have a letter . . . I see you have turned into a pipe – a spout through which all the complaints of the prison are poured,' said the advocate, with a smile. 'It is too much; you'll not be able to manage it.'

'No, but this is a striking case,' said Nekhlyudov, and gave a brief outline of the case of a peasant who began to read the Gospels to the peasants in the village, and to discuss them with his friends. The priests regarded this as a crime and informed the authorities. The magistrate examined him and the public prosecutor drew up an act of indictment, and the law courts committed him for trial.

'This is really too terrible,' Nekhlyudov said. 'Can it be true?'

'What are you surprised at?'

'Why, everything. I can understand the police-officer, who simply obeys orders, but the prosecutor drawing up an act of that kind. An educated man . . .'

'That is where the mistake lies, that we are in the habit of considering that the prosecutors and the judges in general are some kind of liberal persons. There was a time when they were such, but now it is quite different. They are just officials, only troubled about pay-day. They receive their salaries and want them increased, and there their principles end. They will accuse, judge, and sentence anyone you like.'

'Yes; but do laws really exist that can condemn a man to Siberia for reading the Bible with his friends?'

'Not only to be exiled to the less remote parts of Siberia, but even to the mines, if you can only prove that reading the Bible they took the liberty of explaining it to others not according to orders, and in this way condemned the explanations given by the Church. Blaming the Greek orthodox religion in the presence of the common people means, according to Statute . . . the mines.'

'Impossible!'

'I assure you it is so. I always tell these gentlemen, the judges,' the advocate continued, 'that I cannot look at them without gratitude, because if I am not in prison, and you, and all of us, it is only owing to their kindness. To deprive us of our privileges, and send us all to the less remote parts of Siberia, would be an easy thing for them.'

'Well, if it is so, and if everything depends on the procureur and others who can, at will, either enforce the laws or not, what are the trials for?'

The advocate burst into a merry laugh. 'You do put strange questions. My dear sir, that is philosophy. Well, we might have a talk about that, too. Could you come on Saturday? You will meet men of science, literary men, and artists at my house, and then we might discuss these general questions,' said the advocate, pronouncing the words 'general questions' with ironical pathos. 'You have met my wife? Do come.'

'Thank you; I will try to,' said Nekhlyudov, and felt that he was saying an untruth, and knew that if he tried to do anything it would be to keep away from the advocate's literary evening, and the circle of the men of science, art, and literature.

The laugh with which the advocate met Nekhlyudov's remark that trials could have no meaning if the judges might enforce the laws or not, according to their notion, and the tone with which he pronounced the words 'philosophy' and 'general questions' proved to Nekhlyudov how very differently he and the advocate and, probably, the advocate's friends, looked at things; and he felt that in spite of the distance that now existed between himself and his former companions, Schönbock, etc., the difference between himself and the circle of the advocate and his friends was still greater.

Chapter 12

Why the peasants flock to town

The prison was a long way off and it was getting late, so Nekhlyudov took an *isvostchik*. The *isvostchik*, a middle-aged man with an intelligent and kind face, turned round towards Nekhlyudov as they were driving along one of the streets and pointed to a huge house that was being built there.

'Just see what a tremendous house they have begun to build,' he said, as if he was partly responsible for the building of the house and proud of it. The house was really immense and was being built in a very original style. The strong pine beams of the scaffolding were firmly fixed together with iron bands and a plank wall separated the building from the street.

On the boards of the scaffolding workmen, all bespattered with plaster, moved hither and thither like ants. Some were laying bricks, some hewing stones, some carrying up the heavy hods and pails and bringing them down empty. A fat and finely-dressed gentleman – probably the architect – stood by the scaffolding, pointing upward and explaining something to a contractor, a peasant from the Vladimir government, who was respectfully listening to him. Empty carts were coming out of the gate by which the architect and the contractor were standing, and loaded ones were going in. 'And how sure they all are – those that do the work as well as those that make them do it – that it ought to be; that while their wives at home, who are with child, are labouring beyond their strength, and their children with the patchwork caps, doomed soon to the cold grave, smile with suffering and contort their little legs, they must be building this stupid and useless palace for some stupid and useless person – one of those who spoil and rob them,' Nekhlyudov thought, while looking at the house.

'Yes, it is a stupid house,' he said, uttering his thought out aloud.

'Why stupid?' replied the *isvostchik*, in an offended tone. 'Thanks to it, the people get work; it's not stupid.'

'But the work is useless.'

'It can't be useless, or why should it be done?' said the *isvostchik*. 'The people get bread by it.'

Nekhlyudov was silent, and it would have been difficult to talk because of the clatter the wheels made.

When they came nearer the prison, and the *isvostchik* turned off the paved on to the macadamised road, it became easier to talk, and he again turned to Nekhlyudov.

'And what a lot of these people are flocking to the town nowadays; it's awful,' he said, turning round on the box and pointing to a party of peasant workmen who were coming towards them, carrying saws, axes, sheepskins, coats, and bags strapped to their shoulders.

'More than in other years?' Nekhlyudov asked.

'By far. This year every place is crowded, so that it's just terrible. The employers just fling the workmen about like chaff. Not a job to be got.'

'Why is that?'

'They've increased. There's no room for them.'

'Well, what if they have increased? Why do not they stay in the village?'

'There's nothing for them to do in the village – no land to be had.'

Nekhlyudov felt as one does when touching a sore place. It feels as if the bruised part was always being hit; yet it is only because the place is sore that the touch is felt.

'Is it possible that the same thing is happening everywhere?' he thought, and began questioning the *isvostchik* about the quantity of land in his village, how much land the man himself had, and why he had left the country.

'We have a *desiatin* per man, sir,' he said. 'Our family have three men's shares of the land. My father and a brother are at home, and manage the land, and another brother is serving in the army. But there's nothing to manage. My brother has had thoughts of coming to Moscow, too.'

'And cannot land be rented?'

'How's one to rent it nowadays? The gentry, such as they were, have squandered all theirs. Men of business have got it all into their own hands. One can't rent it from them. They farm it themselves. We have a Frenchman ruling in our place; he bought the estate from our former landlord, and won't let it – and there's an end of it.'

'Who's that Frenchman?'

'Dufour is the Frenchman's name. Perhaps you've heard of him. He makes wigs for the actors in the big theatre; it is a good business, so he's prospering. He bought it from our lady, the whole of the estate, and now he has us in his power; he just rides on us as he pleases. The Lord be thanked, he is a good man himself; only his wife, a Russian, is such a brute that – God have mercy on us. She robs the people. It's awful. Well, here's the prison. Am I to drive you to the entrance? I'm afraid they'll not let us do it, though.'

Chapter 13

Nurse Maslova

When he rang the bell at the front entrance Nekhlyudov's heart stood still with horror as he thought of the state he might find Maslova in today, and at the mystery that he felt to be in her and in the people that were collected in the prison. He asked the jailer who opened the door for Maslova. After making the necessary inquiry the jailer informed him that she was in the hospital. Nekhlyudov went there. A kindly old man, the hospital door-keeper, let him in at once and, after asking Nekhlyudov whom he wanted, directed him to the children's ward. A young doctor saturated with carbolic acid met Nekhlyudov in the passage and asked him severely what he wanted. This doctor was always making all sorts of concessions to the prisoners, and was therefore continually coming into conflict with the prison authorities and even with the head doctor. Fearing lest Nekhlyudov should demand something unlawful, and wishing to show that he made no exceptions for anyone, he pretended to be cross. 'There are no women here; it is the children's ward,' he said.

'Yes, I know; but a prisoner has been removed here to be an assistant nurse.'

'Yes, there are two such here. Then whom do you want?'

'I am closely connected with one of them, named Maslova,' Nekhlyudov answered, 'and should like to speak to her. I am going to Petersburg to hand in an appeal to the Senate about her case and should like to give her this. It is only a photo,' Nekhlyudov said, taking an envelope out of his pocket.

'All right, you may do that,' said the doctor, relenting, and turning to an old woman with a white apron, he told her to call the prisoner – Nurse Maslova.

'Will you take a seat, or go into the waiting-room?'

'Thanks,' said Nekhlyudov, and profiting by the favourable change in the manner of the doctor towards him asked how they were satisfied with Maslova in the hospital.

'Oh, she is all right. She works fairly well, if you take the conditions of her former life into account. But here she is.'

The old nurse came in at one of the doors, followed by Maslova, who wore a blue striped dress, a white apron, a kerchief that quite covered her hair. When she saw Nekhlyudov her face flushed, and she stopped as if hesitating, then frowned, and with downcast eyes went quickly towards him along the strip of carpet in the middle of the passage. When she came up to Nekhlyudov she did not wish to give him her hand, and then gave it, growing redder still. Nekhlyudov had not seen her since the day when she begged forgiveness for having been in a passion, and he expected to find her the same as she was then. But today she was quite different. There was something new in the expression of her face, reserve and shyness, and, as it seemed to him, animosity towards him. He told her what he had already said to the doctor, i.e., that he was going to Petersburg, and he handed her the envelope with the photograph which he had brought from Panovo.

'I found this in Panovo – it's an old photo; perhaps you would like it. Take it.'

Lifting her dark eyebrows, she looked at him with surprise in her squinting eyes, as if asking, 'What is this for?' took the photo silently and put it in the bib of her apron.

'I saw your aunt there,' said Nekhlyudov.

'Did you?' she said, indifferently.

'Are you all right here?' Nekhlyudov asked.

'Oh, yes, it's all right,' she said.

'Not too difficult?'

'Oh, no. But I am not used to it yet.'

'I am glad, for your sake. Anyhow, it is better than there.'

'Than where – there?' she asked, her face flushing again.

'There – in the prison,' Nekhlyudov hurriedly answered.

'Why better?' she asked.

'I think the people are better. Here are none such as there must be there.'

'There are many good ones there,' she said.

'I have been seeing about the Menshovs, and hope they will be liberated,' said Nekhlyudov.

'God grant they may. Such a splendid old woman,' she said, again repeating her opinion of the old woman, and slightly smiling.

'I am going to Petersburg today. Your case will come on soon, and I hope the sentence will be repealed.'

'Whether it is repealed or not won't matter now,' she said.

'Why not now?'

'So,' she said, looking with a quick, questioning glance into his eyes.

Nekhlyudov understood the word and the look to mean that she wished to know whether he still kept firm to his decision or had accepted her refusal.

'I do not know why it does not matter to you,' he said. 'It certainly does not matter as far as I am concerned whether you are acquitted or not. I am ready to do what I told you in any case,' he said decidedly.

She lifted her head and her black squinting eyes remained fixed on him and beyond him, and her face beamed with joy. But the words she spoke were very different from what her eyes said.

'You should not speak like that,' she said.

'I am saying it so that you should know.'

'Everything has been said about that, and there is no use speaking,' she said, with difficulty repressing a smile.

A sudden noise came from the hospital ward, and the sound of a child crying.

'I think they are calling me,' she said, and looked round uneasily.

'Well, goodbye, then,' he said. She pretended not to see his extended hand, and, without taking it, turned away and hastily walked along the strip of carpet, trying to hide the triumph she felt.

'What is going on in her? What is she thinking? What does she feel? Does she mean to prove me, or can she really not forgive me? Is it that she cannot or that she will not express what she feels and thinks? Has she softened or hardened?' he asked himself, and could find no answer. He only knew that she had altered and that an important change was going on in her soul, and this change united him not only to her but also to Him for whose sake that change was being wrought. And this union brought on a state of joyful animation and tenderness.

When she returned to the ward, in which there stood eight small beds, Maslova began, in obedience to the nurse's order, to arrange one of the beds; and, bending over too far with the sheet, she slipped and nearly fell down.

A little convalescent boy with a bandaged neck, who was looking at her, laughed. Maslova could no longer contain herself and burst into loud laughter, and such contagious laughter that several of the children also burst out laughing, and one of the sisters rebuked her angrily.

'What are you giggling at? Do you think you are where you used to be? Go and fetch the food.' Maslova obeyed and went where she was sent; but, catching the eye of the bandaged boy who was not allowed to laugh, she again burst out laughing.

Whenever she was alone Maslova again and again pulled the photograph partly out of the envelope and looked at it admiringly; but only in the evening when she was off duty and alone in the bedroom which she shared with a nurse, did she take it quite out of the envelope and gaze long at the faded yellow photograph, caressing with, her eyes every detail of faces and clothing, the steps of the veranda, and the bushes which served as a background to his and hers and his aunts' faces, and could not cease from admiring especially herself – her pretty young face with the curly hair round the forehead. She was so absorbed that she did not hear her fellow-nurse come into the room.

'What is it that he's given you?' said the good-natured, fat nurse, stooping over the photograph.

'Who's this? You?'

'Who else?' said Maslova, looking into her companion's face with a smile.

'And who's this?'

'Himself.'

'And is this his mother?'

'No, his aunt. Would you not have known me?'

'Never. The whole face is altered. Why, it must be ten years since then.'

'Not years, but a lifetime,' said Maslova. And suddenly her animation went, her face grew gloomy, and a deep line appeared between her brows.

'Why so? Your way of life must have been an easy one.'

'Easy, indeed,' Maslova reiterated, closing her eyes and shaking her head. 'It is hell.'

'Why, what makes it so?'

'What makes it so! From eight till four in the morning, and every night the same!'

'Then why don't they give it up?'

'They can't give it up if they want to. But what's the use of talking?' Maslova said, jumping up and throwing the photograph into the drawer of the table. And with difficulty repressing angry tears, she ran out into the passage and slammed the door.

While looking at the group she imagined herself such as she was there and dreamt of her happiness then and of the possibility of happiness with him now. But her companion's words reminded her of what she was now and what she had been, and brought back all the horrors of that life, which she had felt but dimly, and not allowed herself to realise.

It was only now that the memory of all those terrible nights came vividly back to her, especially one during the carnival when she was expecting a student who had promised to buy her out. She remembered how she – wearing her low-necked silk dress stained with wine, a red bow in her untidy hair, wearied, weak, half tipsy, having seen her visitors off, sat down during an interval in the dancing by the piano beside the bony pianiste with the blotchy face, who played the accompaniments to the violin, and began complaining of her hard fate; and how this pianiste said that she, too, was feeling how heavy her position was and would like to change it; and how Clara suddenly came up to them; and how they all three decided to change their life. They thought that the night was over, and were about to go away, when suddenly the noise of tipsy voices was herd in the ante-room. The violinist played a tune and the pianiste began hammering the first figure of a quadrille on the piano, to the tune of a most merry Russian song. A small, perspiring man, smelling of spirits, with a white tie and swallow-tail coat, which he took off after the first figure, came up to her, hiccoughing, and caught her up, while another fat man, with a beard, and also wearing a dress-coat (they had come straight from a ball) caught Clara up, and for a long time they turned, danced, screamed, drank. . . . And so it went on for another year, and another, and a third. How could she help changing? And he was the cause of it all. And, suddenly, all her former bitterness against him reawoke; she wished to scold, to reproach him. She regretted having neglected the opportunity of repeating to him once more that she knew him, and would not give in to him – would not let him make use of her spiritually as he had done physically.

And she longed for drink in order to stifle the feeling of pity to herself and the useless feeling of reproach to him. And she would have broken her word if she had been inside the prison. Here she could not get any spirits except by applying to the medical assistant, and she was afraid of him because he made up to her, and intimate relations with men were disgusting to her now. After sitting a while on a form in the passage she returned to her little room, and without paying any heed to her companion's words, she wept for a long time over her wrecked life.

Chapter 14

An aristocratic circle

Nekhlyudov had four matters to attend to in Petersburg. The first was the appeal to the Senate in Maslova's case; the second, to hand in Theodosia Birukov's petition to the committee; the third, to comply with Vera Doukhova's requests – i.e., try to get her friend

Shoustova released from prison, and get permission for a mother to visit her son in prison. Vera Doukhova had written to him about this, and he was going to the Gendarmerie Office to attend to these two matters, which he counted as one.

The fourth matter he meant to attend to was the case of some sectarians who had been separated from their families and exiled to the Caucasus because they read and discussed the Gospels. It was not so much to them as to himself he had promised to do all he could to clear up this affair.

Since his last visit to Maslennikov, and especially since he had been in the country, Nekhlyudov had not exactly formed a resolution but felt with his whole nature a loathing for that society in which he had lived till then, that society which so carefully hides the sufferings of millions in order to assure ease and pleasure to a small number of people, so that the people belonging to this society do not and cannot see these sufferings, nor the cruelty and wickedness of their life. Nekhlyudov could no longer move in this society without feeling ill at ease and reproaching himself. And yet all the ties of relationship and friendship, and his own habits, were drawing him back into this society. Besides, that which alone interested him now, his desire to help Maslova and the other sufferers, made it necessary to ask for help and service from persons belonging to that society, persons whom he not only could not respect, but who often aroused in him indignation and a feeling of contempt.

When he came to Petersburg and stopped at his aunt's – his mother's sister, the Countess Tcharsky, wife of a former minister – Nekhlyudov at once found himself in the very midst of that aristocratic circle which had grown so foreign to him. This was very unpleasant, but there was no possibility of getting out of it. To put up at an hotel instead of at his aunt's house would have been to offend his aunt, and, besides, his aunt had important connections and might be extremely useful in all these matters he meant to attend to.

'What is this I hear about you? All sorts of marvels,' said the Countess Katerina Ivanovna Tcharsky, as she gave him his coffee immediately after his arrival. '*Vous posez pour un Howard*. Helping criminals, going the round of prisons, setting things right.'

'Oh, no. I never thought of it.'

'Why not? It is a good thing, only there seems to be some romantic story connected with it. Let us hear all about it.'

Nekhlyudov told her the whole truth about his relations to Maslova.

'Yes, yes, I remember your poor mother telling me about it. That was when you were staying with those old women. I believe they wished to marry you to their ward (the Countess Katerina Ivanovna had always despised Nekhlyudov's aunts on his father's side). So it's she. *Elle est encore jolie?*'

Katerina Ivanovna was a strong, bright, energetic, talkative woman of sixty. She was tall and very stout, and had a decided black moustache on her lip. Nekhlyudov was fond of her and had even as a child been infected by her energy and mirth.

'No, *ma tante*, that's at an end. I only wish to help her, because she is innocently accused. I am the cause of it and the cause of her fate being what it is. I feel it my duty to do all I can for her.'

'But what is this I have heard about your intention of marrying her?'

'Yes, it was my intention, but she does not wish it.'

Katerina Ivanovna looked at her nephew with raised brows and drooping eyeballs, in silent amazement. Suddenly her face changed, and with a look of pleasure she said: 'Well, she is wiser than you. Dear me, you are a fool. And you would have married her?'

'Most certainly.'

'After her having been what she was?'

'All the more, since I was the cause of it.'

'Well, you are a simpleton,' said his aunt, repressing a smile, 'a terrible simpleton; but it is just because you are such a terrible simpleton that I love you.' She repeated the word, evidently liking it, as it seemed to correctly convey to her mind the idea of her nephew's moral state. 'Do you know – what a lucky chance! Aline has a wonderful home – the Magdalene Home. I went there once. They are terribly disgusting. After that I had to pray continually. But Aline is devoted to it, body and soul, so we shall place her there – yours, I mean.'

'But she is condemned to Siberia. I have come on purpose to appeal about it. This is one of my requests to you.'

'Dear me, and where do you appeal to in this case?'

'To the Senate.'

'Ah, the Senate! Yes, my dear Cousin Leo is in the Senate, but he is in the heraldry department, and I don't know any of the real ones. They are all some kind of Germans – Gay, Fay, Day – *tout l'alphabet*, or else all sorts of Ivanovs, Simenovs, Nikitins, or else Ivanenkos, Simonenkos, Nikitenkos, *pour varier*. *Des gens de l'autre monde*. Well, it is all the same. I'll tell my husband, he knows them. He knows all sorts of people. I'll tell him, but you will have to explain, he never understands me. Whatever I may say, he always maintains he does not understand it. *C'est un parti pris*, everyone understands but only not he.'

At this moment a footman with stockinged legs came in with a note on a silver platter.

'There now, from Aline herself. You'll have a chance of hearing Kiesewetter.'

'Who is Kiesewetter?'

'Kiesewetter? Come this evening, and you will find out who he is. He speaks in such a way that the most hardened criminals sink on their knees and weep and repent.'

The Countess Katerina Ivanovna, however strange it may seem, and however little it seemed in keeping with the rest of her character, was a staunch adherent to that teaching which holds that the essence of Christianity lies in the belief in redemption. She went to meetings where this teaching, then in fashion, was being preached, and assembled the 'faithful' in her own house. Though this teaching repudiated all ceremonies, icons, and sacraments, Katerina Ivanovna had icons in every room, and one on the wall above her bed, and she kept all that the Church prescribed without noticing any contradiction in that.

'There now; if your Magdalene could hear him she would be converted,' said the Countess. 'Do stay at home tonight; you will hear him. He is a wonderful man.'

'It does not interest me, *ma tante*.'

'But I tell you that it is interesting, and you must come home. Now you may go. What else do you want of me? *Videz votre sac*.'

'The next is in the fortress.'

'In the fortress? I can give you a note for that to the Baron Kriegsmuth. *Cest un très brave homme*. Oh, but you know him; he was a comrade of your father's. *Il donne dans le spiritisme*. But that does not matter, he is a good fellow. What do you want there?'

'I want to get leave for a mother to visit her son who is imprisoned there. But I was told that this did not depend on Kriegsmuth but on Tcherviansky.'

'I do not like Tcherviansky, but he is Mariette's husband; we might ask her. She will do it for me. *Elle est très gentille.*'

'I have also to petition for a woman who is imprisoned there without knowing what for.'

'No fear; she knows well enough. They all know it very well, and it serves them right, those short-haired ones.'

'We do not know whether it serves them right or not. But they suffer. You are a Christian and believe in the Gospel teaching and yet you are so pitiless.'

'That has nothing to do with it. The Gospels are the Gospels, but what is disgusting remains disgusting. It would be worse if I pretended to love Nihilists, especially short-haired women Nihilists,[*] when I cannot bear them.'

'Why can you not bear them?'

'You ask why, after the First of March?'[†]

'They did not all take part in it on the First of March.'

'Never mind; they should not meddle with what is no business of theirs. It's not women's business.'

'Yet you consider that Mariette may take part in business.'

'Mariette? Mariette is Mariette, and these are goodness knows what. Want to teach everybody.'

'Not to teach but simply to help the people.'

'One knows whom to help and whom not to help without them.'

'But the peasants are in great need. I have just returned from the country. Is it necessary that the peasants should work to the very limits of their strength and never have sufficient to eat while we are living in the greatest luxury?' said Nekhlyudov, involuntarily led on by his aunt's good nature into telling her what he was in his thoughts.

'What do you want, then? That I should work and not eat anything?'

'No, I do not wish you not to eat. I only wish that we should all work and all eat.' He could not help smiling as he said it.

[*] Many advanced women wear their hair short, like men.
[†] The Emperor Alexander II was killed on the First of March, old style.

Again raising her brow and drooping her eyeballs, his aunt looked at him curiously. '*Mon cher, vous finirez mal*,' she said.

Just then the general and former minister, Countess Tcharsky's husband, a tall, broad-shouldered man, came into the room.

'Ah, Dmitri, how d'you do?' he said, turning his freshly-shaved cheek to Nekhlyudov to be kissed. 'When did you get here?' And he silently kissed his wife on the forehead.

'*Non, il est impayable*,' the Countess said, turning to her husband. 'He wants me to go and wash clothes and live on potatoes. He is an awful fool, but all the same do what he is going to ask of you. A terrible simpleton,' she added. 'Have you heard? Kamenskaya is in such despair that they fear for her life,' she said to her husband. 'You should go and call there.'

'Yes; it is dreadful,' said her husband.

'Go along, then, and talk to him. I must write some letters.'

Hardly had Nekhlyudov stepped into the room next to the drawing-room than she called him back.

'Shall I write to Mariette, then?'

'Please, *ma tante*.'

'I shall leave a blank for what you want to say about the short-haired one, and she will give her husband his orders, and he'll do it. Do not think me wicked; they are all so disgusting, your protégées, but *je ne leur veux pas de mal*, bother them. Well, go, but be sure to stay at home this evening to hear Kiesewetter, and we shall have some prayers. And if only you do not resist, *celà vous fera beaucoup de bien*. I know your poor mother and all of you were always very backward in these things.'

Chapter 15

An average statesman

Count Ivan Michaelovitch had been a minister, and was a man of strong convictions. The convictions of Count Ivan Michaelovitch consisted in the belief that, just as it was natural for a bird to feed on worms, to be clothed in feathers and down, and to fly in the air, so it was natural for him to feed on the choicest and most expensive food, prepared by highly-paid cooks, to wear the most comfortable and most expensive clothing, to drive with the best and fastest horses, and that, therefore, all these things should be ready found for him. Besides this, Count Ivan Michaelovitch considered that the more money he could get out of the treasury by all sorts of means, the more orders he had, including different diamond insignia of something or other, and the oftener he spoke to highly-placed individuals of both sexes, so much the better it was.

All the rest Count Ivan Michaelovitch considered insignificant and uninteresting beside these dogmas. All the rest might be as it was, or just the reverse. Count Ivan Michaelovitch lived and acted according to these lights for forty years, and at the end of forty years reached the position of a Minister of State. The chief qualities that enabled Count Ivan Michaelovitch to reach this position were his capacity of understanding the meaning of documents and laws and of drawing up, though clumsily, intelligible State papers, and of spelling them correctly; secondly, his very stately appearance, which enabled him, when necessary, to seem not only extremely proud, but unapproachable and majestic, while at other times he could be abjectly and almost passionately servile; thirdly, the absence of any general principles or rules, either of personal or administrative morality, which made it possible for him either to agree or disagree with anybody according to what was wanted at the time. When acting thus his only endeavour was to sustain the appearance of good breeding and not to seem too plainly inconsistent. As for his actions being moral or not, in themselves, or whether they were going to result in the highest welfare or greatest evil for the whole of the Russian Empire, or even the entire world, that was quite indifferent to him. When he became minister, not only those dependent on him (and there were great many of them) and people connected with him, but many strangers and even he himself were convinced that he was a very clever statesman. But after some time had elapsed and he had done nothing and had nothing to show, and when in accordance with the law of the struggle for existence others, like himself, who had learnt to write and understand documents, stately and unprincipled officials, had displaced him, he turned out to be not only far from clever but very limited and badly educated. Though self-assured, his views hardly reaching the level of those in the leading articles of the Conservative papers, it became apparent that there was nothing in him to distinguish him from those other badly-educated and self-assured officials who had pushed him out, and he himself saw it. But this did not shake his conviction that he had to receive a great deal of money out of the Treasury every year, and new decorations for his dress clothes. This conviction was so firm that no one had the pluck to refuse these things to him, and he received yearly, partly in form of a pension, partly as a salary for being a member in a government institution and chairman of all sorts of committees and councils, several tens of thousands of roubles, besides the right – highly prized by him – of sewing all sorts of new cords to his shoulders and trousers, and ribbons to wear under and enamel stars to fix on to his dress coat. In consequence of this Count Ivan Michaelovitch had very high connections.

Count Ivan Michaelovitch listened to Nekhlyudov as he was wont to listen to the reports of the permanent secretary of his department, and, having heard him, said he would give him two notes, one to the Senator Wolff, of the Appeal Department. 'All sorts of things are reported of him, but *dans tous les cas c'est un homme très comme il faut*,' he said. 'He is indebted to me, and will do all that is possible.' The other note Count Ivan Michaelovitch gave Nekhlyudov was to an influential member of the Petition Committee. The story of Theodosia Birukov as told by Nekhlyudov interested him very much. When Nekhlyudov said that he thought of writing to the Empress, the Count replied that it certainly was a very touching story, and might, if occasion presented itself, be told her, but he could not promise. Let the petition be handed in in due form. Should there be an opportunity, and if a *petit comité* were called on Thursday, he thought he would tell her the story.

As soon as Nekhlyudov had received these two notes, and a note to Mariette from his aunt, he at once set off to these different places.

First he went to Mariette's. He had known her as a half-grown girl, the daughter of an aristocratic but not wealthy family, and had heard how she had married a man who was making a career, whom Nekhlyudov had heard badly spoken of; and, as usual, he felt it hard to ask a favour of a man he did not esteem. In these cases he always felt an inner dissension and dissatisfaction, and wavered whether to ask the favour or not, and always resolved to ask. Besides feeling himself in a false position among those to whose set he no longer regarded himself as belonging, who yet regarded him as belonging to them, he felt himself getting into the old accustomed rut, and in spite of himself fell into the thoughtless and immoral tone that reigned in that circle. He felt that from the first, with his aunt, he involuntarily fell into a bantering tone while talking about serious matters.

Petersburg in general affected him with its usual physically invigorating and mentally dulling effect.

Everything so clean, so comfortably well-arranged, and the people so lenient in moral matters, that life seemed very easy.

A fine, clean, and polite *isvostchik* drove him past fine, clean, polite policemen, along the fine, clean, watered streets, past fine, clean houses to the house in which Mariette lived. At the front door stood a pair of English horses, with English harness, and an English-looking coachman on the box, with the lower part of his face shaved, proudly holding a whip. The doorkeeper, dressed in a wonderfully clean livery, opened the door into the hall, where in still cleaner livery with gold cords stood the footman with his splendid whiskers well combed out, and the orderly on duty in a brand-new uniform. 'The general does not receive, and the generaless does not receive either. She is just going to drive out.'

Nekhlyudov took out Katerina Ivanovna's letter, and going up to a table on which lay a visitors' book, began to write that he was sorry not to have been able to see anyone; when the footman went up the staircase the doorkeeper went out and shouted to the coachman, and the orderly stood up rigid with his arms at his sides following with his eyes a little, slight lady, who was coming down the stairs with rapid steps not in keeping with all the grandeur.

Mariette had a large hat on, with feathers, a black dress and cape, and new black gloves. Her face was covered by a veil.

When she saw Nekhlyudov she lifted the veil off a very pretty face with bright eyes that looked inquiringly at him.

'Ah, Prince Dmitri Ivanovitch Nekhlyudov,' she said, with a soft, pleasant voice. 'I should have known – '

'What! you even remember my name?'

'I should think so. Why, I and my sisters have even been in love with you,' she said, in French. 'But, dear me, how you have altered. Oh, what a pity I have to go out. But let us go up again,' she said and stopped hesitatingly. Then she looked at the clock. 'No, I can't. I am going to Kamenskaya's to attend a Mass for the dead. She is terribly afflicted.'

'Who is this Kamenskaya?'

'Have you not heard? Her son was killed in a duel. He fought Posen. He was the only son. Terrible! The mother is very much afflicted.'

'Yes. I have heard of it.'

'No, I had better go, and you must come again, tonight or tomorrow,' she said, and went to the door with quick, light steps.

'I cannot come tonight,' he said, going out after her; 'but I have a request to make you,' and he looked at the pair of bays that were drawing up to the front door.

'What is this?'

'This is a letter from aunt to you,' said Nekhlyudov, handing her a narrow envelope, with a large crest. 'You'll find all about it in there.'

'I know Countess Katerina Ivanovna thinks I have some influence with my husband in business matters. She is mistaken. I can do nothing and do not like to interfere. But, of course, for you I am willing to be false to my principle. What is this business about?' she said, searching in vain for her pocket with her little black gloved hand.

'There is a girl imprisoned in the fortress, and she is ill and innocent.'

'What is her name?'

'Lydia Shoustova. It's in the note.'

'All right; I'll see what I can do,' she said, and lightly jumped into her little, softly upholstered, open carriage, its brightly-varnished splash-guards glistening in the sunshine, and opened her parasol. The footman got on the box and gave the coachman a sign. The carriage moved, but at that moment she touched the coachman with her parasol and the slim-legged beauties, the bay mares, stopped, bending their beautiful necks and stepping from foot to foot.

'But you must come, only, please, without interested motives,' and she looked at him with a smile, the force of which she well knew, and, as if the performance over and she were drawing the curtain, she dropped the veil over her face again. 'All right,' and she again touched the coachman.

Nekhlyudov raised his hat, and the well-bred bays, slightly snorting, set off, their shoes clattering on the pavement, and the carriage rolled quickly and smoothly on its new rubber tyres, giving a jump only now and then over some unevenness of the road.

Chapter 16

An up-to-date senator

When Nekhlyudov remembered the smiles that had passed between him and Mariette, he shook his head.

'You have hardly time to turn round before you are again drawn into this life,' he thought, feeling that discord and those doubts which the necessity to curry favour from people he did not esteem caused.

After considering where to go first, so as not to have to retrace his steps, Nekhlyudov set off for the Senate. There he was shown into the office where he found a great many very polite and very clean officials in the midst of a magnificent apartment. Maslova's petition was received and handed on to that Wolf, to whom Nekhlyudov had a letter from his uncle, to be examined and reported on.

'There will be a meeting of the Senate this week,' the official said to Nekhlyudov, 'but Maslova's case will hardly come before that meeting.'

'It might come before the meeting on Wednesday, by special request,' one of the officials remarked.

During the time Nekhlyudov waited in the office, while some information was being taken, he heard that the conversation in the Senate was all about the duel, and he heard a detailed account of how a young man, Kaminski, had been killed. It was here he first heard all the facts of the case which was exciting the interest of all

Petersburg. The story was this: Some officers were eating oysters
and, as usual, drinking very much, when one of them said something ill-natured about the regiment to which Kaminski belonged,
and Kaminski called him a liar. The other hit Kaminski. The next
day they fought. Kaminski was wounded in the stomach and died
two hours later. The murderer and the seconds were arrested, but
it was said that though they were arrested and in the guardhouse
they would be set free in a fortnight.

From the Senate Nekhlyudov drove to see an influential member of the petition committee, Baron Vorobiov, who lived in a
splendid house belonging to the Crown. The doorkeeper told
Nekhlyudov in a severe tone that the Baron could not be seen
except on his reception days; that he was with His Majesty the
Emperor today, and the next day he would again have to deliver a
report. Nekhlyudov left his uncle's letter with the doorkeeper and
went on to see the Senator Wolf. Wolf had just had his lunch, and
was as usual helping digestion by smoking a cigar and pacing up and
down the room, when Nekhlyudov came in. Vladimir Vasilievitch
Wolf was certainly *un homme très comme il faut*, and prized this
quality very highly, and from that elevation he looked down at
everybody else. He could not but esteem this quality of his very
highly, because it was thanks to it alone that he had made a brilliant
career, the very career he desired, i.e., by marriage he obtained a
fortune which brought him in eighteen thousand roubles a year,
and by his own exertions the post of a senator. He considered
himself not only *un homme très comme il faut*, but also a man of
knightly honour. By honour he understood not accepting secret
bribes from private persons. But he did not consider it dishonest to
beg money for payment of fares and all sorts of travelling expenses
from the Crown, and to do anything the government might require
of him in return. To ruin hundreds of innocent people, to cause
them to be imprisoned, to be exiled because of their love for their
people and the religion of their fathers, as he had done in one of the
governments of Poland when he was governor there. He did not
consider it dishonourable, but even thought it a noble, manly and
patriotic action. Nor did he consider it dishonest to rob his wife and
sister-in-law, as he had done, but thought it a wise way of arranging
his family life. His family consisted of his commonplace wife, his
sister-in-law, whose fortune he had appropriated by selling

her estate and putting the money to his account, and his meek, frightened, plain daughter, who lived a lonely, weary life, from which she had lately begun to look for relaxation in evangelicism, attending meetings at Aline's, and the Countess Katerina Ivanovna. Wolf's son, who had grown a beard at the age of fifteen, and had at that age begun to drink and lead a depraved life, which he continued to do till the age of twenty, when he was turned out by his father because he never finished his studies, moved in a low set and made debts which committed the father. The father had once paid a debt of two hundred and fifty roubles for his son, then another of six hundred roubles, but warned the son that he did it for the last time, and that if the son did not reform he would be turned out of the house and all further intercourse between him and his family would be put a stop to. The son did not reform, but made a debt of a thousand roubles, and took the liberty of telling his father that life at home was a torment anyhow. Then Wolf declared to his son that he might go where he pleased – that he was no son of his any longer. Since then Wolf pretended he had no son, and no one at home dared speak to him about his son, and Vladimir Vasilievitch Wolf was firmly convinced that he had arranged his family life in the best way. Wolf stopped pacing up and down his study, and greeted Nekhlyudov with a friendly though slightly ironical smile. This was his way of showing how *comme il faut* he was, and how superior to the majority of men. He read the note which Nekhlyudov handed to him.

'Please take a seat, and excuse me if I continue to walk up and down, with your permission,' he said, putting his hands into his coat pockets, and began again to walk with light, soft steps across his large, quietly and stylishly furnished study. 'Very pleased to make your acquaintance and of course very glad to do anything that Count Ivan Michaelovitch wishes,' he said, blowing the fragrant blue smoke out of his mouth and removing his cigar carefully so as not to drop the ash.

'I should only like to ask that the case might come on soon, so that if the prisoner has to go to Siberia she might set off early,' said Nekhlyudov.

'Yes, yes, with one of the first steamers from Nijni. I know,' said Wolf, with his patronising smile, always knowing in advance whatever one wanted to tell him.

'What is the prisoner's name?'

'Maslova.'

Wolf went up to the table and looked at a paper that lay on a piece of cardboard among other business papers.

'Yes, yes. Maslova. All right, I will ask the others. We shall hear the case on Wednesday.'

'Then may I telegraph to the advocate?'

'The advocate! What's that for? But if you like, why not?'

'The causes for appeal may be insufficient,' said Nekhlyudov, 'but I think the case will show that the sentence was passed owing to a misunderstanding.'

'Yes, yes; it may be so, but the Senate cannot decide the case on its merits,' said Wolf, looking seriously at the ash of his cigar. 'The Senate only considers the exactness of the application of the laws and their right interpretation.'

'But this seems to me to be an exceptional case.'

'I know, I know! All cases are exceptional. We shall do our duty. That's all.' The ash was still holding on, but had began breaking, and was in danger of falling.

'Do you often come to Petersburg?' said Wolf, holding his cigar so that the ash should not fall. But the ash began to shake, and Wolf carefully carried it to the ashpan, into which it fell.

'What a terrible thing this is with regard to Kaminski,' he said. 'A splendid young man. The only son. Especially the mother's position,' he went on, repeating almost word for word what everyone in Petersburg was at that time saying about Kaminski. Wolf spoke a little about the Countess Katerina Ivanovna and her enthusiasm for the new religious teaching, which he neither approved nor disapproved of, but which was evidently needless to him who was so *comme il faut*, and then rang the bell.

Nekhlyudov bowed.

'If it is convenient, come and dine on Wednesday, and I will give you a decisive answer,' said Wolf, extending his hand.

It was late, and Nekhlyudov returned to his aunt's.

Chapter 17

Countess Katerina Ivanovna's dinner party

Countess Katerina Ivanovna's dinner hour was half-past seven, and the dinner was served in a new manner that Nekhlyudov had not yet seen anywhere. After they had placed the dishes on the table the waiters left the room and the diners helped themselves. The men would not let the ladies take the trouble of moving, and, as befitted the stronger sex, they manfully took on themselves the burden of putting the food on the ladies' plates and of filling their glasses. When one course was finished, the Countess pressed the button of an electric bell fitted to the table and the waiters stepped in noiselessly and quickly carried away the dishes, changed the plates, and brought in the next course. The dinner was very refined, the wines very costly. A French chef was working in the large, light kitchens, with two white-clad assistants. There were six persons at dinner, the Count and Countess, their son (a surly officer in the Guards who sat with his elbows on the table), Nekhlyudov, a French lady reader, and the Count's chief steward, who had come up from the country. Here, too, the conversation was about the duel, and opinions were given as to how the Emperor regarded the case. It was known that the Emperor was very much grieved for the mother's sake, and all were grieved for her, and as it was also known that the Emperor did not mean to be very severe to the murderer, who defended the honour of his uniform, all were also lenient to the officer who had defended the honour of his uniform. Only the Countess Katerina Ivanovna, with her free thoughtlessness, expressed her disapproval.

'They get drunk, and kill unobjectionable young men. I should not forgive them on any account,' she said.

'Now, that's a thing I cannot understand,' said the Count.

'I know that you never can understand what I say,' the Countess began, and turning to Nekhlyudov, she added:

'Everybody understands except my husband. I say I am sorry for the mother, and I do not wish him to be contented, having killed a man.' Then her son, who had been silent up to then, took the murderer's part, and rudely attacked his mother, arguing that an officer could not behave in any other way, because his fellow-officers would condemn him and turn him out of the regiment. Nekhlyudov listened to the conversation without joining in. Having been an officer himself, he understood, though he did not agree with, young Tcharsky's arguments, and at the same time he could not help contrasting the fate of the officer with that of a beautiful young convict whom he had seen in the prison, and who was condemned to the mines for having killed another in a fight. Both had turned murderers through drunkenness. The peasant had killed a man in a moment of irritation, and he was parted from his wife and family, had chains on his legs, and his head shaved, and was going to hard labour in Siberia, while the officer was sitting in a fine room in the guardhouse, eating a good dinner, drinking good wine, and reading books, and would be set free in a day or two to live as he had done before, having only become more interesting by the affair.

Nekhlyudov said what he had been thinking, and at first his aunt, Katerina Ivanovna, seemed to agree with him, but at last she became silent as the rest had done, and Nekhlyudov felt that he had committed something akin to an impropriety.

In the evening, soon after dinner, the large hall, with high-backed carved chairs arranged in rows as for a meeting, and an armchair next to a little table, with a bottle of water for the speaker, began to fill with people come to hear the foreigner, Kiesewetter, preach.

Elegant equipages stopped at the front entrance. In the hall sat richly-dressed ladies in silks and velvets and lace, with false hair and false busts and drawn-in waists, and among them men in uniform and evening dress, and about five persons of the common class, i.e., two men-servants, a shop-keeper, a footman, and a coachman.

Kiesewetter, a thick-set, grizzled man, spoke English, and a thin young girl, with a pince-nez, translated it into Russian promptly and well.

He was saying that our sins were so great, the punishment for them so great and so unavoidable, that it was impossible to live anticipating such punishment. 'Beloved brothers and sisters, let us for a moment consider what we are doing, how we are living, how we have offended against the all-loving Lord, and how we make Christ suffer, and we cannot but understand that there is no forgiveness possible for us, no escape possible, that we are all doomed to perish. A terrible fate awaits us – everlasting torment,' he said, with tears in his trembling voice. 'Oh, how can we be saved, brothers? How can we be saved from this terrible, unquenchable fire? The house is in flames; there is no escape.'

He was silent for a while, and real tears flowed down his cheeks. It was for about eight years that each time when he got to this part of his speech, which he himself liked so well, he felt a choking in his throat and an irritation in his nose, and the tears came in his eyes, and these tears touched him still more. Sobs were heard in the room. The Countess Katerina Ivanovna sat with her elbows on an inlaid table, leaning her head on her hands, and her shoulders were shaking. The coachman looked with fear and surprise at the foreigner, feeling as if he was about to run him down with the pole of his carriage and the foreigner would not move out of his way. All sat in positions similar to that Katerina Ivanovna had assumed. Wolf's daughter, a thin, fashionably-dressed girl, very like her father, knelt with her face in her hands.

The orator suddenly uncovered his face, and smiled a very real-looking smile, such as actors express joy with, and began again with a sweet, gentle voice:

'Yet there is a way to be saved. Here it is – a joyful, easy way. The salvation is the blood shed for us by the only son of God, who gave himself up to torments for our sake. His sufferings, His blood, will save us. Brothers and sisters,' he said, again with tears in his voice, 'let us praise the Lord, who has given His only begotten son for the redemption of mankind. His holy blood . . .'

Nekhlyudov felt so deeply disgusted that he rose silently, and frowning and keeping back a groan of shame, he left on tiptoe, and went to his room.

Hardly had Nekhlyudov finished dressing the next morning, just as he was about to go down, the footman brought him a card from the Moscow advocate. The advocate had come to St Petersburg on business of his own, and was going to be present when Maslova's case was examined in the Senate, if that would be soon. The telegram sent by Nekhlyudov crossed him on the way. Having found out from Nekhlyudov when the case was going to be heard, and which senators were to be present, he smiled. 'Exactly, all the three types of senators,' he said. 'Wolf is a Petersburg official; Skovorodnikov is a theoretical, and Bay a practical lawyer, and therefore the most alive of them all,' said the advocate. 'There is most hope of him. Well, and how about the Petition Committee?'

'Oh, I'm going to Baron Vorobiov today. I could not get an audience with him yesterday.'

'Do you know why he is *Baron* Vorobiov?' said the advocate, noticing the slightly ironical stress that Nekhlyudov put on this foreign title, followed by so very Russian a surname.

'That was because the Emperor Paul rewarded the grandfather – I think he was one of the Court footmen – by giving him this title. He managed to please him in some way, so he made him a baron. "It's my wish, so don't gainsay me!" And so there's a *Baron* Vorobiov, and very proud of the title. He is a dreadful old humbug.'

'Well, I'm going to see him,' said Nekhlyudov.

'That's good; we can go together. I shall give you a lift.'

As they were going to start, a footman met Nekhlyudov in the ante-room, and handed him a note from Mariette:

Pour vous faire plaisir, j'ai agi tout à fait contre mes principes et j'ai intercédé auprès de mon mari pour votre protégée. Il se trouve que cette personne peut etre relaxée immédiatement. Mon mari à ecrit au commandant. Venez donc disinterestedly. Je vous attends.   M.

'Just fancy!' said Nekhlyudov to the advocate. 'Is this not dreadful? A woman whom they are keeping in solitary confinement for seven months turns out to be quite innocent, and only a word was needed to get her released.'

'That's always so. Well, anyhow, you have succeeded in getting what you wanted.'

'Yes, but this success grieves me. Just think what must be going on there. Why have they been keeping her?'

'Oh, it's best not to look too deeply into it. Well, then, I shall give you a lift, if I may,' said the advocate, as they left the house, and a fine carriage that the advocate had hired drove up to the door. 'It's Baron Vorobiov you are going to see?'

The advocate gave the driver his directions, and the two good horses quickly brought Nekhlyudov to the house in which the Baron lived. The Baron was at home. A young official in uniform, with a long, thin neck, a much protruding Adam's apple, and an extremely light walk, and two ladies were in the first room.

'Your name, please?' the young man with the Adam's apple asked, stepping with extreme lightness and grace across from the ladies to Nekhlyudov.

Nekhlyudov gave his name.

'The Baron was just mentioning you,' said the young man, the Baron's adjutant, and went out through an inner door. He returned, leading a weeping lady dressed in mourning. With her bony fingers the lady was trying to pull her tangled veil over her face in order to hide her tears.

'Come in, please,' said the young man to Nekhlyudov, lightly stepping up to the door of the study and holding it open. When Nekhlyudov came in, he saw before him a thick-set man of medium height, with short hair, in a frock coat, who was sitting in an armchair opposite a large writing-table, and looking gaily in front of himself. The kindly, rosy red face, striking by its contrast with the white hair, moustaches, and beard, turned towards Nekhlyudov with a friendly smile.

'Very glad to see you. Your mother and I were old acquaintances and friends. I have seen you as a boy, and later on as an

officer. Sit down and tell me what I can do for you. Yes, yes,'
he said, shaking his cropped white head, while Nekhlyudov
was telling him Theodosia's story. 'Go on, go on. I quite understand. It is certainly very touching. And have you handed in the
petition?'

'I have got the petition ready,' Nekhlyudov said, getting it out
of his pocket; 'but I thought of speaking to you first in hopes that
the case would then get special attention paid to it.'

'You have done very well. I shall certainly report it myself,' said
the Baron, unsuccessfully trying to put an expression of pity on his
merry face. 'Very touching! It is clear she was but a child; the
husband treated her roughly, this repelled her, but as time went on
they fell in love with each other. Yes I will report the case.'

'Count Ivan Michaelovitch was also going to speak about it.'

Nekhlyudov had hardly got these words out when the Baron's
face changed.

'You had better hand in the petition into the office, after all, and
I shall do what I can,' he said.

At this moment the young official again entered the room,
evidently showing off his elegant manner of walking.

'That lady is asking if she may say a few words more.'

'Well, ask her in. Ah, *mon cher*, how many tears we have to see
shed! If only we could dry them all. One does all that lies within
one's power.'

The lady entered.

'I forgot to ask you that he should not be allowed to give up the
daughter, because he is ready . . .'

'But I have already told you that I should do all I can.'

'Baron, for the love of God! You will save the mother?'

She seized his hand, and began kissing it.

'Everything shall be done.'

When the lady went out Nekhlyudov also began to take leave.

'We shall do what we can. I shall speak about it at the Ministry
of Justice, and when we get their answer we shall do what we
can.'

Nekhlyudov left the study, and went into the office again. Just
as in the Senate office, he saw, in a splendid apartment, a number
of very elegant officials, clean, polite, severely correct and distinguished in dress and in speech.

'How many there are of them; how very many and how well fed they all look! And what clean shirts and hands they all have, and how well all their boots are polished! Who does it for them? How comfortable they all are, as compared not only with the prisoners, but even with the peasants!' These thoughts again involuntarily came to Nekhlyudov's mind.

Chapter 19
An old general of repute

The man on whom depended the easing of the fate of the Petersburg prisoners was an old general of repute – a baron of German descent, who, as it was said of him, had outlived his wits. He had received a profusion of orders, but only wore one of them, the Order of the White Cross. He had received this order, which he greatly valued, while serving in the Caucasus, because a number of Russian peasants, with their hair cropped, and dressed in uniform and armed with guns and bayonets, had killed at his command more than a thousand men who were defending their liberty, their homes, and their families. Later on he served in Poland, and there also made Russian peasants commit many different crimes, and got more orders and decorations for his uniform. Then he served somewhere else, and now that he was a weak, old man he had this position, which ensured him a good house, an income and respect. He strictly observed all the regulations which were prescribed 'from above', and was very zealous in the fulfilment of these regulations, to which he ascribed a special importance, considering that everything else in the world might be changed except the regulations prescribed 'from above'. His duty was to keep political prisoners, men and women, in solitary confinement in such a way that half of them perished in ten years' time, some going out of their minds, some dying of consumption, some committing suicide by starving themselves to death, cutting their veins with bits of glass, hanging, or burning themselves to death.

The old general was not ignorant of this; it all happened within his knowledge; but these cases no more touched his conscience than accidents brought on by thunderstorms, floods, etc. These cases occurred as a consequence of the fulfilment of regulations prescribed 'from above' by His Imperial Majesty. These regulations had to be carried out without fail, and therefore it was absolutely useless to think of the consequences of their fulfilment. The old general did not even allow himself to think of such things, counting it his patriotic duty as a soldier not to think of them for fear of getting weak in the carrying out of these, according to his opinion, very important obligations. Once a week the old general made the round of the cells, one of the duties of his position, and asked the prisoners if they had any requests to make. The prisoners had all sorts of requests. He listened to them quietly, in impenetrable silence, and never fulfilled any of their requests, because they were all in disaccord with the regulations. Just as Nekhlyudov drove up to the old general's house, the high notes of the bells on the belfry clock chimed 'Great is the Lord,' and then struck two. The sound of these chimes brought back to Nekhlyudov's mind what he had read in the notes of the Decembrists* about the way this sweet music repeated every hour re-echoes in the hearts of those imprisoned for life.

Meanwhile the old general was sitting in his darkened drawing-room at an inlaid table, turning a saucer on a piece of paper with the aid of a young artist, the brother of one of his subordinates. The thin, weak, moist fingers of the artist were pressed against the wrinkled and stiff-jointed fingers of the old general, and the hands joined in this manner were moving together with the saucer over a paper that had all the letters of the alphabet written on it. The saucer was answering the questions put by the general as to how souls will recognise each other after death.

When Nekhlyudov sent in his card by an orderly acting as footman, the soul of Joan of Arc was speaking by the aid of the saucer. The soul of Joan of Arc had already spelt letter by letter the words: 'They well knew each other,' and these words had been written down. When the orderly came in the saucer had stopped first on b, then on y, and began jerking hither and thither. This

---

* The Decembrists were a group who attempted, but failed, to put an end to absolutism in Russia at the time of the accession of Nicholas I.

jerking was caused by the general's opinion that the next letter should be b, i.e., Joan of Arc ought to say that the souls will know each other by being cleansed of all that is earthly, or something of the kind, clashing with the opinion of the artist, who thought the next letter should be l, i.e., that the souls should know each other by light emanating from their astral bodies. The general, with his bushy grey eyebrows gravely contracted, sat gazing at the hands on the saucer, and, imagining that it was moving of its own accord, kept pulling the saucer towards b. The pale-faced young artist, with his thin hair combed back behind his ears, was looking with his lifeless blue eyes into a dark corner of the drawing-room, nervously moving his lips and pulling the saucer towards l.

The general made a wry face at the interruption, but after a moment's pause he took the card, put on his pince-nez, and, uttering a groan, rose, in spite of the pain in his back, to his full height, rubbing his numb fingers.

'Ask him into the study.'

'With your excellency's permission I will finish it alone,' said the artist, rising. 'I feel the presence.'

'All right, finish alone,' the general said, severely and decidedly, and stepped quickly, with big, firm and measured strides, into his study.

'Very pleased to see you,' said the general to Nekhlyudov, uttering the friendly words in a gruff tone, and pointing to an armchair by the side of the writing-table. 'Have you been in Petersburg long?'

Nekhlyudov replied that he had only lately arrived.

'Is the Princess, your mother, well?'

'My mother is dead.'

'Forgive me; I am very sorry. My son told me he had met you.'

The general's son was making the same kind of career for himself that the father had done, and, having passed the Military Academy, was now serving in the Inquiry Office, and was very proud of his duties there. His occupation was the management of government spies.

'Why, I served with your father. We were friends – comrades. And you; are you also in the Service?'

'No, I am not.'

The general bent his head disapprovingly.

'I have a request to make, general.'

'Very pleased. In what way can I be of service to you?'

'If my request is out of place pray pardon me. But I am obliged to make it.'

'What is it?'

'There is a certain Gourkevitch imprisoned in the fortress; his mother asks for an interview with him, or at least to be allowed to send him some books.'

The general expressed neither satisfaction nor dissatisfaction at Nekhlyudov's request, but bending his head on one side he closed his eyes as if considering. In reality he was not considering anything, and was not even interested in Nekhlyudov's questions, well knowing that he would answer them according to the law. He was simply resting mentally and not thinking at all.

'You see,' he said at last, 'this does not depend on me. There is a regulation, confirmed by His Majesty, concerning interviews; and as to books, we have a library, and they may have what is permitted.'

'Yes, but he wants scientific books; he wishes to study.'

'Don't you believe it,' growled the general. 'It's not study he wants; it is just only restlessness.'

'But what is to be done? They must occupy their time somehow in their hard condition,' said Nekhlyudov.

'They are always complaining,' said the general. 'We know them.'

He spoke of them in a general way, as if they were all a specially bad race of men. 'They have conveniences here which can be found in few places of confinement,' said the general, and he began to enumerate the comforts the prisoners enjoyed, as if the aim of the institution was to give the people imprisoned there a comfortable home.

'It is true it used to be rather rough, but now they are very well kept here,' he continued. 'They have three courses for dinner – and one of them meat – cutlets, or rissoles; and on Sundays they get a fourth – a sweet dish. God grant every Russian may eat as well as they do.'

Like all old people, the general, having once got on to a familiar topic, enumerated the various proofs he had often given before of the prisoners being exacting and ungrateful.

'They get books on spiritual subjects and old journals. We have a library. Only they rarely read. At first they seem interested, later on the new books remain uncut, and the old ones with their leaves unturned. We tried them,' said the old general, with the dim likeness of a smile. 'We put bits of paper in on purpose, which remained just as they had been placed. Writing is also not forbidden,' he continued. 'A slate is provided, and a slate pencil, so that they can write as a pastime. They can wipe the slate and write again. But they don't write, either. Oh, they very soon get quite tranquil. At first they seem restless, but later on they even grow fat and become very quiet.' Thus spoke the general, never suspecting the terrible meaning of his words.

Nekhlyudov listened to the hoarse old voice, looked at the stiff limbs, the swollen eyelids under the grey brows, at the old, clean-shaved, flabby jaw, supported by the collar of the military uniform, at the white cross that this man was so proud of, chiefly because he had gained it by exceptionally cruel and extensive slaughter, and knew that it was useless to reply to the old man or to explain the meaning of his own words to him.

He made another effort, and asked about the prisoner Shoustova, for whose release, as he had been informed that morning, orders were given.

'Shoustova – Shoustova? I cannot remember all their names, there are so many of them,' he said, as if reproaching them because there were so many. He rang, and ordered the secretary to be called. While waiting for the latter, he began persuading Nekhlyudov to serve, saying that 'honest noblemen', counting himself among the number, 'were particularly needed by the Tsar and – the country,' he added, evidently only to round off his sentence. 'I am old, yet I am serving still, as well as my strength allows.'

The secretary, a dry, emaciated man, with restless, intelligent eyes, came in and reported that Shoustova was imprisoned in some queer, fortified place, and that he had received no orders concerning her.

'When we get the order we shall let her out the same day. We do not keep them; we do not value their visits much,' said the general, with another attempt at a playful smile, which only distorted his old face.

Nekhlyudov rose, trying to keep from expressing the mixed feelings of repugnance and pity which he felt towards this terrible old man. The old man on his part considered that he should not be too severe on the thoughtless and evidently misguided son of his old comrade, and should not leave him without advice.

'Goodbye, my dear fellow; do not take it amiss. It is my affection that makes me say it. Do not keep company with such people as we have at our place here. There are no innocent ones among them. All these people are most immoral. We know them,' he said, in a tone that admitted no possibility of doubt. And he did not doubt, not because the thing was so, but because if it was not so, he would have to admit himself to be not a noble hero living out the last days of a good life, but a scoundrel, who sold, and still continued in his old age to sell, his conscience.

'Best of all, go and serve,' he continued; 'the Tsar needs honest men – and the country,' he added. 'Well, supposing I and the others refused to serve, as you are doing? Who would be left? Here we are, finding fault with the order of things, and yet not wishing to help the government.'

With a deep sigh Nekhlyudov made a low bow, shook the large, bony hand condescendingly stretched out to him and left the room.

The general shook his head reprovingly, and rubbing his back, he again went into the drawing-room where the artist was waiting for him. He had already written down the answer given by the soul of Joan of Arc. The general put on his pince-nez and read, 'Will know one another by light emanating from their astral bodies.'

'Ah,' said the general, with approval, and closed his eyes. 'But how is one to know if the light of all is alike?' he asked, and again crossed fingers with the artist on the saucer.

The *isvostchik* drove Nekhlyudov out of the gate.

'It is dull here, sir,' he said, turning to Nekhlyudov. 'I almost wished to drive off without waiting for you.'

Nekhlyudov agreed. 'Yes, it is dull,' and he took a deep breath, and looked up with a sense of relief at the grey clouds that were floating in the sky, and at the glistening ripples made by the boats and steamers on the Neva.

Chapter 20

Maslova's appeal

The next day Maslova's case was to be examined at the Senate, and Nekhlyudov and the advocate met at the majestic portal of the building, where several carriages were waiting. Ascending the magnificent and imposing staircase to the first floor, the advocate, who knew all the ins and outs of the place, turned to the left and entered through a door which had the date of the introduction of the Code of Laws above it.

After taking off his overcoat in the first narrow room, he found out from the attendant that the senators had all arrived, and that the last had just come in. Fanarin, in his swallow-tail coat, a white tie above the white shirt-front, and a self-confident smile on his lips, passed into the next room. In this room there were to the right a large cupboard and a table, and to the left a winding staircase, which an elegant official in uniform was descending with a portfolio under his arm. In this room an old man with long, white hair and a patriarchal appearance attracted everyone's attention. He wore a short coat and grey trousers. Two attendants stood respectfully beside him. The old man with white hair entered the cupboard and shut himself in.

Fanarin noticed a fellow-advocate dressed in the same way as himself, with a white tie and dress coat, and at once entered into an animated conversation with him.

Nekhlyudov was meanwhile examining the people in the room. The public consisted of about fifteen persons, of whom two were ladies – a young one with a pince-nez, and an old, grey-haired one.

A case of libel was to be heard that day, and therefore the public were more numerous than usual – chiefly persons belonging to the journalistic world.

The usher, a red-cheeked, handsome man in a fine uniform, came up to Fanarin and asked him what his business was. When he heard that it was the case of Maslova, he noted something down and walked away. Then the cupboard door opened and the old man with the patriarchal appearance stepped out, no longer in a short coat but in a gold-trimmed attire, which made him look like a bird, and with metal plates on his breast. This funny costume seemed to make the old man himself feel uncomfortable, and, walking faster than his wont, he hurried out of the door opposite the entrance.

'That is Bay, a most estimable man,' Fanarin said to Nekhlyudov, and then having introduced him to his colleague, he explained the case that was about to be heard, which he considered very interesting.

The hearing of the case soon commenced, and Nekhlyudov, with the public, entered the left side of the Senate Chamber. They all, including Fanarin, took their places behind a grating. Only the Petersburg advocate went up to a desk in front of the grating.

The Senate Chamber was not so big as the Criminal Court; and was more simply furnished, only the table in front of the senators was covered with crimson, gold-trimmed velvet, instead of green cloth; but the attributes of all places of judgment, i.e., the mirror of justice, the icon, the emblem of hypocrisy, and the Emperor's portrait, the emblem of servility, were there.

The usher announced, in the same solemn manner: 'The Court is coming.' Everyone rose in the same way, and the senators entered in their uniforms and sat down on high-backed chairs and leant on the table, trying to appear natural, just in the same way as the judges in the Court of Law. There were four senators present – Nikitin, who took the chair, a clean-shaved man with a narrow face and steely eyes; Wolf, with significantly compressed lips, and little white hands, with which he kept turning over the pages of the business papers; Skovorodnikov, a heavy, fat, pockmarked man – the learned lawyer; and Bay, the patriarchal-looking man who had arrived last.

With the advocates entered the chief secretary and public prosecutor, a lean, clean-shaved young man of medium height, a very dark complexion, and sad, black eyes. Nekhlyudov knew him at once, in spite of his curious uniform and the fact that he had not seen him for six years. He had been one of his best friends in Nekhlyudov's student days.

'The public prosecutor Selenin?' Nekhlyudov asked, turning to the advocate.

'Yes. Why?'

'I know him well. He is a fine fellow.'

'And a good public prosecutor; business-like. Now he is the man you should have interested.'

'He will act according to his conscience in any case,' said Nekhlyudov, recalling the intimate relations and friendship between himself and Selenin, and the attractive qualities of the latter – purity, honesty, and good breeding in its best sense.

'Yes, there is no time now,' whispered Fanarin, who was listening to the report of the case that had commenced.

The Court of Justice was accused of having left a decision of the Court of Law unaltered.

Nekhlyudov listened and tried to make out the meaning of what was going on; but, just as in the Criminal Court, his chief difficulty was that not the evidently chief point, but some side issues, were being discussed. The case was that of a newspaper which had published the account of a swindle arranged by a director of a limited liability company. It seemed that the only important question was whether the director of the company really abused his trust, and how to stop him from doing it. But the questions under consideration were whether the editor had a right to publish this article of his contributor, and what he had been guilty of in publishing it: slander or libel, and in what way slander included libel, or libel included slander, and something rather incomprehensible to ordinary people about all sorts of statutes and resolutions passed by some General Department.

The only thing clear to Nekhlyudov was that, in spite of what Wolf had so strenuously insisted on, the day before, i.e., that the Senate could not try a case on its merits, in this case he was evidently strongly in favour of repealing the decision of the Court of Justice, and that Selenin, in spite of his characteristic reticence, stated the opposite opinion with quite unexpected warmth. The warmth, which surprised Nekhlyudov, evinced by the usually self-controlled Selenin, was due to his knowledge of the director's shabbiness in money matters, and the fact, which had accidentally come to his ears, that Wolf had been to a swell dinner party at the swindler's house only a few days before.

Now that Wolf spoke on the case, guardedly enough, but with evident bias, Selenin became excited, and expressed his opinion with too much nervous irritation for an ordinary business transaction.

It was clear that Selenin's speech had offended Wolf. He grew red, moved in his chair, made silent gestures of surprise, and at last rose, with a very dignified and injured look, together with the other senators, and went out into the debating-room.

'What particular case have you come about?' the usher asked again, addressing Fanarin.

'I have already told you: Maslova's case.'

'Yes, quite so. It is to be heard today, but – '

'But what?' the advocate asked.

'Well, you see, this case was to be examined without taking sides, so that the senators will hardly come out again after passing the resolution. But I will inform them.'

'What do you mean?'

'I'll inform them; I'll inform them.' And the usher again put something down on his paper.

The senators really meant to pronounce their decision concerning the libel case, and then to finish the other business, Maslova's case among it, over their tea and cigarettes, without leaving the debating-room.

Chapter 21

The appeal dismissed

As soon as the senators were seated round the table in the debating-room, Wolf began to bring forward with great animation all the motives in favour of a repeal. The chairman, an ill-natured man at best, was in a particularly bad humour that day. His thoughts were concentrated on the words he had written down in his memoranda on the occasion when not he but Viglanov was appointed to the important post he had long coveted. It was the chairman, Nikitin's, honest conviction that his opinions of the officials of the two upper classes with which he was in connection would furnish valuable material for the historians. He had written a chapter the day before in which the officials of the upper classes got it hot for preventing him, as he expressed it, from averting the ruin towards which the present rulers of Russia were driving it, which simply meant that they had prevented his getting a better salary. And now he was considering what a new light to posterity this chapter would shed on events.

'Yes, certainly,' he said, in reply to the words addressed to him by Wolf, without listening to them.

Bay was listening to Wolf with a sad face and drawing a garland on the paper that lay before him. Bay was a Liberal of the very first water. He held sacred the Liberal traditions of the sixth decade of this century, and if he ever overstepped the limits of strict neutrality it was always in the direction of Liberalism. So in this case; beside the fact that the swindling director, who was prosecuting for libel, was a bad lot, the prosecution of a journalist for libel in itself tending, as it did, to restrict the freedom of the press, inclined Bay to reject the appeal.

When Wolf concluded his arguments Bay stopped drawing his garland and began in a sad and gentle voice (he was sad because he was obliged to demonstrate such truisms) concisely, simply and convincingly to show how unfounded the accusation was, and then, bending his white head, he continued drawing his garland.

Skovorodnikov, who sat opposite Wolf, and, with his fat fingers, kept shoving his beard and moustaches into his mouth, stopped chewing his beard as soon as Bay was silent, and said with a loud, grating voice, that, notwithstanding the fact of the director being a terrible scoundrel, he would have been for the repeal of the sentence if there were any legal reasons for it; but, as there were none, he was of Bay's opinion. He was glad to put this spoke in Wolf's wheel.

The chairman agreed with Skovorodnikov, and the appeal was rejected.

Wolf was dissatisfied, especially because it was like being caught acting with dishonest partiality; so he pretended to be indifferent, and, unfolding the document which contained Maslova's case, he became engrossed in it. Meanwhile the senators rang and ordered tea, and began talking about the event that, together with the duel, was occupying the Petersburgers.

It was the case of the chief of a government department, who was accused of the crime provided for in Statute 995.

'What nastiness,' said Bay, with disgust.

'Why; where is the harm of it? I can show you a Russian book containing the project of a German writer, who openly proposes that it should not be considered a crime,' said Skovorodnikov, drawing in greedily the fumes of the crumpled cigarette, which he held between his fingers close to the palm, and he laughed boisterously.

'Impossible!' said Bay.

'I shall show it you,' said Skovorodnikov, giving the full title of the book, and even its date and the name of its editor.

'I hear he has been appointed governor to some town in Siberia.'

'That's fine. The archdeacon will meet him with a crucifix. They ought to appoint an archdeacon of the same sort,' said Skovorodnikov. 'I could recommend them one,' and he threw the end of his cigarette into his saucer, and again shoved as much of his beard and moustaches as he could into his mouth and began chewing them.

The usher came in and reported the advocate's and Nekhlyudov's desire to be present at the examination of Maslova's case.

'This case,' Wolf said, 'is quite romantic,' and he told them what he knew about Nekhlyudov's relations with Maslova. When they had spoken a little about it and finished their tea and cigarettes, the senators returned into the Senate Chamber and proclaimed their decision in the libel case, and began to hear Maslova's case.

Wolf, in his thin voice, reported Maslova's appeal very fully, but again not without some bias and an evident wish for the repeal of the sentence.

'Have you anything to add?' the chairman said, turning to Fanarin. Fanarin rose, and standing with his broad white chest expanded, proved point by point, with wonderful exactness and persuasiveness, how the Court had in six points strayed from the exact meaning of the law; and besides this he touched, though briefly, on the merits of the case, and on the crying injustice of the sentence. The tone of his speech was one of apology to the senators, who, with their penetration and judicial wisdom, could not help seeing and understanding it all better than he could. He was obliged to speak only because the duty he had undertaken forced him to do so.

After Fanarin's speech one might have thought that there could not remain the least doubt that the Senate ought to repeal the decision of the Court. When he had finished his speech, Fanarin looked round with a smile of triumph, seeing which Nekhlyudov felt certain that the case was won. But when he looked at the senators he saw that Fanarin smiled and triumphed all alone. The senators and the Public Prosecutor did not smile nor triumph, but looked like people wearied, and who were thinking 'We have often heard the like of you; it is all in vain,' and were only too glad when he stopped and ceased uselessly detaining them there. Immediately after the end of the advocate's speech the chairman turned to the Public Prosecutor. Selenin briefly and clearly expressed himself in favour of leaving the decision of the Court unaltered, as he considered all the reasons for appealing inadequate. After this the senators went out into the debating-room. They were divided in their opinions. Wolf was in favour of altering the decision. Bay, when he had understood the case, took up the same side with fervour, vividly presenting the scene at the court to his companions as he clearly saw it himself. Nikitin, who always was on the side of severity and formality, took up the other side. All depended on Skovorodnikov's vote, and he voted for rejecting the appeal, because Nekhlyudov's determination to marry the woman on moral grounds was extremely repugnant to him.

Skovorodnikov was a materialist, a Darwinian, and counted every manifestation of abstract morality, or, worse still, religion, not only as a despicable folly, but as a personal affront to himself. All this bother about a prostitute, and the presence of a celebrated advocate and Nekhlyudov in the Senate were in the highest degree repugnant to him. So he shoved his beard into his mouth and made faces, and very skilfully pretended to know nothing of this case, excepting that the reasons for an appeal were insufficient, and that he, therefore, agreed with the chairman to leave the decision of the Court unaltered.

So the sentence remained unrepealed.

'Terrible,' said Nekhlyudov, as he went out into the waiting-room with the advocate, who was arranging the papers in his portfolio. 'In a matter which is perfectly clear they attach all the importance to the form and reject the appeal. Terrible!'

'The case was spoiled in the Criminal Court,' said the advocate.

'And Selenin, too, was in favour of the rejection. Terrible! terrible!' Nekhlyudov repeated. 'What is to be done now?'

'We will appeal to His Majesty, and you can hand in the petition yourself while you are here. I will write it for you.'

At this moment little Wolf, with his stars and uniform, came out into the waiting-room and approached Nekhlyudov. 'It could not be helped, dear Prince. The reasons for an appeal were not sufficient,' he said, shrugging his narrow shoulders and closing his eyes, and then he went his way.

After Wolf, Selenin came out too, having heard from the senators that his old friend Nekhlyudov was there.

'Well, I never expected to see you here,' he said, coming up to Nekhlyudov, and smiling only with his lips while his eyes remained sad. 'I did not know you were in Petersburg.'

'And I did not know you were Public Prosecutor-in-Chief.'

'How is it you are in the Senate?' asked Selenin. 'I had heard, by the way, that you were in Petersburg. But what are you doing here?'

'Here? I am here because I hoped to find justice and save a woman innocently condemned.'

'What woman?'

'The one whose case has just been decided.'

'Oh! Maslova's case,' said Selenin, suddenly remembering it. 'The appeal had no grounds whatever.'

'It is not the appeal; it's the woman who is innocent, and is being punished.'

Selenin sighed. 'That may well be, but – '

'Not *may be*, but is.'

'How do you know?'

'Because I was on the jury. I know how we made the mistake.'

Selenin became thoughtful. 'You should have made a statement at the time,' he said.

'I did make the statement.'

'It should have been put down in an official report. If this had been added to the petition for the appeal – '

'Yes, but still, as it is, the verdict is evidently absurd.'

'The Senate has no right to say so. If the Senate took upon itself to repeal the decision of the law courts according to its own views as to the justice of the decisions in themselves, the verdict of the jury would lose all its meaning, not to mention that the Senate would have no basis to go upon, and would run the risk of infringing justice rather than upholding it,' said Selenin, calling to mind the case that had just been heard.

'All I know is that this woman is quite innocent, and that the last hope of saving her from an unmerited punishment is gone. The grossest injustice has been confirmed by the highest court.'

'It has not been confirmed. The Senate did not and cannot enter into the merits of the case in itself,' said Selenin. Always busy and rarely going out into society, he had evidently heard nothing of Nekhlyudov's romance. Nekhlyudov noticed it, and made up his mind that it was best to say nothing about his special relations with Maslova.

'You are probably staying with your aunt,' Selenin remarked, apparently wishing to change the subject. 'She told me you were here yesterday, and she invited me to meet you in the evening, when some foreign preacher was to lecture,' and Selenin again smiled only with his lips.

'Yes, I was there, but left in disgust,' said Nekhlyudov angrily, vexed that Selenin had changed the subject.

'Why with disgust? After all, it is a manifestation of religious feeling, though one-sided and sectarian,' said Selenin.

'Why, it's only some kind of whimsical folly.'

'Oh, dear, no. The curious thing is that we know the teaching of our church so little that we see some new kind of revelation in what are, after all, our own fundamental dogmas,' said Selenin, as if hurrying to let his old friend know his new views.

Nekhlyudov looked at Selenin scrutinisingly and with surprise, and Selenin dropped his eyes, in which appeared an expression not only of sadness but also of ill-will.

'Do you, then, believe in the dogmas of the church?' Nekhlyudov asked.

'Of course I do,' replied Selenin, gazing straight into Nekhlyudov's eyes with a lifeless look.

Nekhlyudov sighed. 'It is strange,' he said.

'However, we shall have a talk some other time,' said Selenin. 'I am coming,' he added, in answer to the usher, who had respectfully approached him. 'Yes, we must meet again,' he went on with a sigh. 'But will it be possible for me to find you? You will always find me in at seven o'clock. My address is Nadejdinskaya,' and he gave the number. 'Ah, time does not stand still,' and he turned to go, smiling only with his lips.

'I will come if I can,' said Nekhlyudov, feeling that a man once near and dear to him had, by this brief conversation, suddenly become strange, distant, and incomprehensible, if not hostile to him.

Chapter 23

The Public Prosecutor

When Nekhlyudov knew Selenin as a student, he was a good son, a true friend, and for his years an educated man of the world, with much tact; elegant, handsome, and at the same time truthful and honest. He learned well, without much exertion and with no pedantry, receiving gold medals for his essays. He considered the service of mankind, not only in words but in acts, to be the aim of his young life. He saw no other way of being useful to humanity than by serving the State. Therefore, as soon as he had completed his studies, he systematically examined all the activities to which he might devote his life, and decided to enter the Second Department of the Chancellerie, where the laws are drawn up; and he did so. But, in spite of the most scrupulous and exact discharge of the duties demanded of him, this service gave no satisfaction to his desire of being useful, nor could he awake in himself the consciousness that he was doing 'the right thing'.

This dissatisfaction was so much increased by the friction with his very small-minded and vain fellow officials that he left the Chancellerie and entered the Senate. It was better there, but the same dissatisfaction still pursued him; he felt it to be very different from what he had expected, and from what ought to be.

And now that he was in the Senate his relatives obtained for him the post of Gentleman of the Bedchamber, and he had to go in a carriage, dressed in an embroidered uniform and a white linen apron, to thank all sorts of people for having placed him in the position of a lackey. However much he tried he could find no reasonable explanation for the existence of this post, and felt, more than in the Senate, that it was not 'the right thing', and yet he could not refuse it for fear of hurting those who felt sure they were giving him much pleasure by this appointment, and because it flattered the lowest part of his nature. It pleased him to see himself in a mirror in his gold-embroidered uniform, and to accept the deference paid him by some people because of his position.

Something of the same kind happened when he married. A very brilliant match, from a worldly point of view, was arranged for him, and he married chiefly because by refusing he would have had to hurt the young lady who wished to be married to him, and those who arranged the marriage, and also because a marriage with a nice young girl of noble birth flattered his vanity and gave him pleasure. But this marriage very soon proved to be even less 'the right thing' than the government service and his position at Court.

After the birth of her first child the wife decided to have no more, and began leading that luxurious worldly life in which he now had to participate whether he liked or not.

She was not particularly handsome, and was faithful to him, and she seemed, in spite of all the efforts it cost her, to derive nothing but weariness from the life she led, yet she perseveringly continued to live it, though it was poisoning her husband's life. And all his efforts to alter this life was shattered, as against a stone wall, by her conviction, which all her friends and relatives supported, that all was as it should be.

The child, a little girl with bare legs and long golden curls, was a being perfectly foreign to him, chiefly because she was trained quite otherwise than he wished her to be. There sprung up between the husband and wife the usual misunderstanding, without even the wish to understand each other, and then a silent warfare, hidden from outsiders and tempered by decorum. All this made his life at home a burden, and became even less 'the right thing' than his service and his post.

But it was above all his attitude towards religion which was not 'the right thing'. Like everyone of his set and his time, by the growth of his reason he broke without the least effort the nets of the religious superstitions in which he was brought up, and did not himself exactly know when it was that he freed himself of them. Being earnest and upright, he did not, during his youth and intimacy with Nekhlyudov as a student, conceal his rejection of the State religion. But as years went on and he rose in the service, and especially at the time of the reaction towards conservatism in society, his spiritual freedom stood in his way.

At home, when his father died, he had to be present at the masses said for his soul, and his mother wished him to go to confession or to communion, and it was in a way expected by public opinion, but above all, government service demanded that he should be present at all sorts of services, consecrations, thanksgivings, and the like. Hardly a day passed without some outward religious form having to be observed.

When present at these services he had to pretend that he believed in something which he did not believe in, and being truthful he could not do this. The alternative was, having made up his mind that all these outward signs were deceitful, to alter his life in such a way that he would not have to be present at such ceremonials. But to do what seemed so simple would have cost a great deal. Besides encountering the perpetual hostility of all those who were near to him, he would have to give up the service and his position, and sacrifice his hopes of being useful to humanity by his service, now and in the future. To make such a sacrifice one would have to be firmly convinced of being right.

And he was firmly convinced he was right, as no educated man of our time can help being convinced who knows a little history and how the religions, and especially Church Christianity, originated.

But under the stress of his daily life he, a truthful man, allowed a little falsehood to creep in. He said that in order to do justice to an unreasonable thing one had to study the unreasonable thing. It was a little falsehood, but it sunk him into the big falsehood in which he was now caught.

Before putting to himself the question whether the orthodoxy in which he was born and bred, and which everyone expected him to accept, and without which he could not continue his useful occupation, contained the truth, he had already decided the answer. And to clear up the question he did not read Voltaire, Schopenhauer, Herbert Spencer, or Comte, but the philosophical works of Hegel and the religious works of Vinet and Khomyakov, and naturally found in them what he wanted, i.e., something like peace of mind and a vindication of that religious teaching in which he was educated, which his reason had long ceased to accept, but without which his whole life was filled with unpleasantness which could all be removed by accepting the teaching.

And so he adopted all the usual sophistries which go to prove that a single human reason cannot know the truth, that the truth is only revealed to an association of men, and can only be known by revelation, that revelation is kept by the church, etc. And so he managed to be present at prayers, masses for the dead, to confess, make signs of the cross in front of icons, with a quiet mind, without being conscious of the lie, and to continue in the service which gave him the feeling of being useful and some comfort in his joyless family life. Although he believed this, he felt with his entire being that this religion of his, more than all else, was not 'the right thing', and that is why his eyes always looked sad.

And seeing Nekhlyudov, whom he had known before all these lies had rooted themselves within him, reminded him of what he then was. It was especially after he had hurried to hint at his religious views that he had most strongly felt all this 'not the right thing', and had become painfully sad. Nekhlyudov felt it also after the first joy of meeting his old friend had passed, and therefore, though they promised each other to meet, they did not take any steps towards an interview, and did not again see each other during this stay of Nekhlyudov's in Petersburg.

Chapter 24

Mariette tempts Nekhlyudov

When they left the Senate, Nekhlyudov and the advocate walked on together, the advocate having given the driver of his carriage orders to follow them. The advocate told Nekhlyudov the story of the chief of a government department, about whom the senators had been talking: how the thing was found out, and how the man, who according to law should have been sent to the mines, had been appointed governor of a town in Siberia. Then he related with particular pleasure how several high-placed persons stole a lot of money collected for the erection of the still unfinished monument which they had passed that morning; also, how the mistress of So-and-so got a lot of money at the Stock Exchange, and how So-and-so agreed with So-and-so to sell him his wife. The advocate began another story about a swindle, and all sorts of crimes committed by persons in high places, who instead of being in prison, sat on presidential chairs in all sorts of government institutions. These tales, of which the advocate seemed to have an unending supply, gave him much pleasure, showing as they did, with perfect clearness, that his means of getting money were quite just and innocent compared to the means which the highest officials in Petersburg made use of. The advocate was therefore surprised when Nekhlyudov took an *isvostchik* before hearing the end of the story, said goodbye, and left him. Nekhlyudov felt very sad. It was chiefly the rejection of the appeal by the Senate, confirming the senseless torments that the innocent Maslova was enduring, that saddened him, and also the fact that this rejection made it still harder for him to unite his fate with hers. The stories about existing evils, which the advocate recounted with such relish, heightened his sadness, and so did the cold, unkind look that the once sweet-natured, frank, noble Selenin had given him, and which kept recurring to his mind.

On his return the doorkeeper handed him a note, and said, rather scornfully, that some kind of woman had written it in the hall. It was a note from Shoustova's mother. She wrote that she had come to thank her daughter's benefactor and saviour, and to implore him to come to see them on the Vasilievsky, Sth Line, house No.—— . This was very necessary because of Vera Doukhova. He need not be afraid that they would weary him with expressions of gratitude. They would not speak their gratitude, but be simply glad to see him. Would he not come next morning, if he could?

There was another note from Bogotyrev, a former fellow-officer, aide-de-camp to the Emperor, whom Nekhlyudov had asked to hand personally to the Emperor his petition on behalf of the sectarians. Bogotyrev wrote, in his large, firm hand, that he would put the petition into the Emperor's own hands, as he had promised; but that it had occurred to him that it might be better for Nekhlyudov first to go and see the person on whom the matter depended.

After the impressions received during the last few days, Nekhlyudov felt perfectly hopeless of getting anything done. The plans he had formed in Moscow seemed now something like the dreams of youth, which are inevitably followed by disillusion when life comes to be faced. Still, being now in Petersburg, he considered it his duty to do all he had intended, and he resolved next day, after consulting Bogotyreff, to act on his advice and see the person on whom the case of the sectarians depended.

He got out the sectarians' petition from his portfolio, and began reading it over, when there was a knock at his door, and a footman came in with a message from the Countess Katerina Ivanovna, who asked him to come up and have a cup of tea with her.

Nekhlyudov said he would come at once, and having put the papers back into the portfolio, he went up to his aunt's. He looked out of a window on his way, and saw Mariette's pair of bays standing in front of the house, and he suddenly brightened and felt inclined to smile.

Mariette, with a hat on her head, not in black but with a light dress of many shades, sat with a cup in her hand beside the

Countess's easy chair, prattling about something while her beautiful, laughing eyes glistened. She had said something funny –
something indecently funny – just as Nekhlyudov entered the
room. He knew it by the way she laughed, and by the way
the good-natured Countess Katerina Ivanovna's fat body was
shaking with laughter; while Mariette, her smiling mouth slightly
drawn to one side, her head a little bent, a peculiarly mischiev-
ous expression in her merry, energetic face, sat silently looking
at her companion. From a few words which he overheard,
Nekhlyudov guessed that they were talking of the second piece
of Petersburg news, the episode of the Siberian governor, and
that it was in reference to this subject that Mariette had said
something so funny that the Countess could not control herself
for a long time.

'You will kill me,' she said, coughing.

After saying 'How d'you do?' Nekhlyudov sat down. He was
about to censure Mariette in his mind for her levity when,
noticing the serious and even slightly dissatisfied look in his eyes,
she suddenly, to please him, changed not only the expression of
her face, but also the attitude of her mind; for she felt the wish to
please him as soon as she looked at him. She suddenly turned
serious, dissatisfied with her life, as if seeking and striving after
something; it was not that she pretended, but she really repro-
duced in herself the very same state of mind that he was in,
although it would have been impossible for her to express in
words what was the state of Nekhlyudov's mind at that moment.

She asked him how he had accomplished his tasks. He told her
about his failure in the Senate and his meeting Selenin.

'Oh, what a pure soul! He is, indeed, a *chevalier sans peur et sans
reproche*. A pure soul!' said both ladies, using the epithet commonly
applied to Selenin in Petersburg society.

'What is his wife like?' Nekhlyudov asked.

'His wife? Well, I do not wish to judge, but she does not understand him.'

'Is it possible that he, too, was for rejecting the appeal?' Mariette
asked with real sympathy. 'It is dreadful. How sorry I am for her,'
she added with a sigh.

He frowned, and in order to change the subject began to speak
about Shoustova, who had been imprisoned in the fortress and

was now set free through the influence of Mariette's husband. He thanked her for her trouble, and was going on to say how dreadful he thought it, that this woman and the whole of her family had suffered merely, because no one had reminded the authorities about them, but Mariette interrupted him and expressed her own indignation.

'Say nothing about it to me,' she said. 'When my husband told me she could be set free, it was this that struck me, "What was she kept in prison for if she is innocent?" ' she went on, expressing what Nekhlyudov was about to say.

'It is revolting – revolting.'

Countess Katerina Ivanovna noticed that Mariette was coquetting with her nephew, and this amused her. 'What do you think?' she said, when they were silent. 'Supposing you come to Aline's tomorrow night. Kiesewetter will be there. And you, too,' she said, turning to Mariette. '*Il vous a remarqué*,' she went on to her nephew. 'He told me that what you say (I repeated it all to him) is a very good sign, and that you will certainly come to Christ. You must come absolutely. Tell him to, Mariette, and come yourself.'

'Countess, in the first place, I have no right whatever to give any kind of advice to the Prince,' said Mariette, and gave Nekhlyudov a look that somehow established a full comprehension between them of their attitude in relation to the Countess's words and evangelicalism in general. 'Secondly, I do not much care, you know.'

'Yes, I know you always do things the wrong way round, and according to your own ideas.'

'My own ideas? I have faith like the most simple peasant woman,' said Mariette with a smile. 'And, thirdly, I am going to the French Theatre tomorrow night.'

'Ah! And have you seen that – What's her name?' asked Countess Katerina Ivanovna. Mariette gave the name of a celebrated French actress.

'You must go, most decidedly; she is wonderful.'

'Whom am I to see first, *ma tante* – the actress or the preacher?' Nekhlyudov said with a smile.

'Please don't catch at my words.'

'I should think the preacher first and then the actress, or else the desire for the sermon might vanish altogether,' said Nekhlyudov.

'No; better begin with the French Theatre, and do penance afterwards.'

'Now, then, you are not to hold me up for ridicule. The preacher is the preacher and the theatre is the theatre. One need not weep in order to be saved. One must have faith, and then one is sure to be gay.'

'You, *ma tante*, preach better than any preacher.'

'Do you know what?' said Mariette. 'Come into my box to-morrow.'

'I am afraid I shall not be able to.'

The footman interrupted the conversation by announcing a visitor. It was the secretary of a philanthropic society of which the Countess was president.

'Oh, that is the dullest of men. I think I shall receive him out there, and return to you later on. Mariette, give him his tea,' said the Countess, and left the room, with her quick, wriggling walk.

Mariette took the glove off her firm, rather flat hand, the fourth finger of which was covered with rings.

'Want any?' she said, taking hold of the silver teapot, under which a spirit lamp was burning, and extending her little finger curiously. Her face looked sad and serious.

'It is always terribly painful to me to notice that people whose opinion I value confound me with the position I am placed in.' She seemed ready to cry as she said these last words. And though these words had no meaning, or at any rate a very indefinite meaning, they seemed to be of exceptional depth, meaning, or goodness to Nekhlyudov, so much was he attracted by the look of the bright eyes which accompanied the words of this young, beautiful, and well-dressed woman.

Nekhlyudov looked at her in silence, and could not take his eyes from her face.

'You think I do not understand you and all that goes on in you. Why, everybody knows what you are doing. *C'est le secret de polichinelle*. And I am delighted with your work, and think highly of you.'

'Really, there is nothing to be delighted with; and I have done so little as yet.'

'No matter. I understand your feelings, and I understand her. All right, all right. I will say nothing more about it,' she said, noticing

displeasure on his face. 'But I also understand that after seeing all
the suffering and the horror in the prisons,' Mariette went on, her
only desire that of attracting him, and guessing with her woman's
instinct what was dear and important to him, 'you wish to help the
sufferers, those who are made to suffer so terribly by other men,
and their cruelty and indifference. I understand the willingness to
give one's life, and could give mine in such a cause, but we each
have our own fate.'

'Are you, then, dissatisfied with your fate?'

'I?' she asked, as if struck with surprise that such a question
could be put to her. 'I have to be satisfied, and am satisfied. But
there is a worm that wakes up – '

'And he must not be allowed to fall asleep again. It is a voice that
must be obeyed,' Nekhlyudov said, failing into the trap.

Many a time later on Nekhlyudov remembered with shame
his talk with her. He remembered her words, which were not so
much lies as imitations of his own, and her face, which seemed
looking at him with sympathetic attention when he told her about
the terrors of the prison and of his impressions in the country.

When the Countess returned they were talking not merely like
old, but like exclusive friends who alone understood one another.
They were talking about the injustice of power, of the sufferings
of the unfortunate, the poverty of the people, yet in reality in the
midst of the sound of their talk their eyes, gazing at each other,
kept asking, 'Can you love me?' and answering, 'I can', and the
sex-feeling, taking the most unexpected and brightest forms, drew
them to each other. As she was going away she told him that she
would always he willing to serve him in any way she could, and
asked him to come and see her, if only for a moment, in the
theatre next day, as she had a very important thing to tell him
about.

'Yes, and when shall I see you again?' she added, with a sigh,
carefully drawing the glove over her jewelled hand.

'Say you will come.'

Nekhlyudov promised.

That night, when Nekhlyudov was alone in his room, and lay
down after putting out his candle, he could not sleep. He thought
of Maslova, of the decision of the Senate, of his resolve to follow
her in any case, of his having given up the land. The face of

Mariette appeared to him as if in answer to those thoughts – her look, her sigh, her words, 'When shall I see you again?' and her smile seemed vivid as if he really saw her, and he also smiled. 'Shall I be doing right in going to Siberia? And have I done right in divesting myself of my wealth?' And the answers to the questions on this Petersburg night, on which the daylight streamed into the window from under the blind, were quite indefinite. All seemed mixed in his head. He recalled his former state of mind, and the former sequence of his thoughts, but they had no longer their former power or validity.

'And supposing I have invented all this, and am unable to live it through – supposing I repent of having acted right,' he thought; and unable to answer he was seized with such anguish and despair as he had long not felt. Unable to free himself from his perplexity, he fell into a heavy sleep, such as he had slept after a heavy loss at cards.

Chapter 25

Lydia Shoustova's home

Nekhlyudov awoke next morning feeling as if he had been guilty of some iniquity the day before. He began considering. He could not remember having done anything wrong; he had committed no evil act, but he had had evil thoughts. He had thought that all his present resolutions to marry Katusha and to give up his land were unachievable dreams; that he should be unable to bear it; that it was artificial, unnatural; and that he would have to go on living as he lived.

He had committed no evil action, but, what was far worse than an evil action, he had entertained evil thoughts, whence all evil actions proceed. An evil action may not be repeated, and can be repented of; but evil thoughts generate all evil actions.

An evil action only smooths the path for other evil acts; evil thoughts uncontrollably drag one along that path.

When Nekhlyudov repeated in his mind the thoughts of the day before, he was surprised that he could for a moment have believed these thoughts. However new and difficult that which he had decided to do might be, he knew that it was the only possible way of life for him now, and however easy and natural it might have been to return to his former state, he knew that state to be death.

Yesterday's temptation seemed like the feeling when one awakes from deep sleep, and, without feeling sleepy, wants to lie comfortably in bed a little longer, yet knows that it is time to rise and commence the glad and important work that awaits one.

On that, his last day in Petersburg, he went in the morning to the Vasilievski Ostrov to see Shoustova. Shoustova lived on the second floor, and having been shown the back stairs, Nekhlyudov entered straight into the hot kitchen, which smelt strongly of food. An elderly woman, with turned-up sleeves, with an apron and spectacles, stood by the fire stirring something in a steaming pan.

'Whom do you want?' she asked severely, looking at him over her spectacles.

Before Nekhlyudov had time to answer, an expression of fright and joy appeared on her face.

'Oh, Prince!' she exclaimed, wiping her hands on her apron. 'But why have you come the back way? Our benefactor! I am her mother. They have nearly killed my little girl. You have saved us,' she said, catching hold of Nekhlyudov's hand and trying to kiss it.

'I went to see you yesterday. My sister asked me to. She is here. This way, this way, please,' said Shoustova's mother, as she led the way through a narrow door, and a dark passage, arranging her hair and pulling at her tucked-up skirt. 'My sister's name is Kornilova. You must have heard of her,' she added, stopping before a closed door. 'She was mixed up in a political affair. An extremely clever woman!'

Shoustova's mother opened the door and showed Nekhlyudov into a little room where on a sofa with a table before it sat a plump, short girl with fair hair that curled round her pale, round face, which was very like her mother's. She had a striped cotton blouse on.

Opposite her, in an armchair, leaning forward, so that he was nearly bent double, sat a young fellow with a slight, black beard and moustaches.

'Lydia, Prince Nekhlyudov!' he said.

The pale girl jumped up, nervously pushing back a lock of hair behind her ear, and gazing at the newcomer with a frightened look in her large, grey eyes.

'So you are that dangerous woman whom Vera Doukhova wished me to intercede for?' Nekhlyudov asked, with a smile.

'Yes, I am,' said Lydia Shoustova, her broad, kind, child-like smile disclosing a row of beautiful teeth. 'It was aunt who was so anxious to see you. Aunt!' she called out, in a pleasant, tender voice through a door.

'Your imprisonment grieved Vera Doukhova very much,' said Nekhlyudov.

'Take a seat here, or better here,' said Shoustova, pointing to the battered easy-chair from which the young man had just risen.

'My cousin, Zakharov,' she said, noticing that Nekhlyudov looked at the young man.

The young man greeted the visitor with a smile as kindly as Shoustova's, and when Nekhlyudov sat down he brought himself another chair, and sat by his side. A fair-haired schoolboy of about ten also came into the room and silently sat down on the window-sill.

'Vera Doukhova is a great friend of my aunt's, but I hardly know her,' said Shoustova.

Then a woman with a very pleasant face, with a white blouse and leather belt, came in from the next room.

'How do you do? Thanks for coming,' she began as soon as she had taken the place next to Shoustova's on the sofa.

'Well, and how is Vera. You have seen her? How does she bear her fate?'

'She does not complain,' said Nekhlyudov. 'She says she feels perfectly happy.'

'Ah, that's like Vera. I know her,' said the aunt, smiling and shaking her head. 'One must know her. She has a fine character. Everything for others; nothing for herself.'

'No, she asked nothing for herself, but only seemed concerned about your niece. What seemed to trouble her most was, as she said, that your niece was imprisoned for nothing.'

'Yes, that's true,' said the aunt. 'It is a dreadful business. She suffered, in reality, because of me.'

'Not at all, aunt. I should have taken the papers without you all the same.'

'Allow me to know better,' said the aunt. 'You see,' she went on to Nekhlyudov, 'it all happened because a certain person asked me to keep his papers for a time, and I, having no house at the time, brought them to her. And that very night the police searched her room and took her and the papers, and have kept her up to now, demanding that she should say from whom she had them.'

'But I never told them,' said Shoustova quickly, pulling nervously at a lock that was not even out of place.

'I never said you did' answered the aunt.

'If they took Mitin up it was certainly not through me,' said Shoustova, blushing, and looking round uneasily.

'Don't speak about it, Lydia dear,' said her mother.

'Why not? I should like to relate it,' said Shoustova, no longer smiling nor pulling her lock, but twisting it round her finger and getting redder.

'Don't forget what happened yesterday when you began talking about it.'

'Not at all – Leave me alone, mamma. I did not tell, I only kept quiet. When he examined me about Mitin and about aunt, I said nothing, and told him I would not answer.'

'Then this – Petrov – '

'Petrov is a spy, a gendarme, and a blackguard,' put in the aunt, to explain her niece's words to Nekhlyudov.

'Then he began persuading,' continued Shoustova, excitedly and hurriedly. ' "Anything you tell me," he said, "can harm no one; on the contrary, if you tell me, we may be able to set free innocent people whom we may be uselessly tormenting." Well, I still said I would not tell. Then he said, "All right, don't tell, but do not deny what I am going to say." And he named Mitin.'

'Don't talk about it,' said the aunt.

'Oh, aunt, don't interrupt,' and she went on pulling the lock of hair and looking round. 'And then, only fancy, the next day I hear – they let me know by knocking at the wall – that Mitin is arrested. Well, I think I have betrayed him, and this tormented me so – it tormented me so that I nearly went mad.'

'And it turned out that it was not at all because of you he was taken up?'

'Yes, but I didn't know. I think, "There, now, I have betrayed him." I walk and walk up and down from wall to wall, and cannot help thinking. I think, "I have betrayed him." I lie down and cover myself up, and hear something whispering, "Betrayed! Betrayed Mitin! Mitin betrayed!" I know it is an hallucination, but cannot help listening. I wish to fall asleep, I cannot. I wish not to think, and cannot cease. That is terrible!' and as Shoustova spoke she got more and more excited, and twisted and untwisted the lock of hair round her finger.

'Lydia, dear, be calm,' the mother said, touching her shoulder.

But Shoustova could not stop herself.

'It is all the more terrible – ' she began again, but did not finish, and jumping up with a cry rushed out of the room.

Her mother turned to follow her.

'They ought to be hanged, the rascals!' said the schoolboy who was sitting on the window-sill.

'What's that?' said the mother.

'I only said – Oh, it's nothing,' the schoolboy answered, and taking a cigarette that lay on the table, he began to smoke.

Chapter 26

Lydia's aunt

'Yes, that solitary confinement is terrible for the young,' said the aunt, shaking her head and also lighting a cigarette.

'I should say for everyone,' Nekhlyudov replied.

'No, not for all,' answered the aunt. 'For the real revolutionists, I have been told, it is rest and quiet. A man who is wanted by the police lives in continual anxiety, material want, and fear for himself and others, and for his cause, and at last, when he is taken up and it is all over, and all responsibility is off his shoulders, he can sit and rest. I have been told they actually feel joyful when taken up. But the young and innocent (they always first arrest the innocent, like Lydia), for them the first shock is terrible. It is not that they deprive you of freedom; and the bad food and bad air – all that is nothing. Three times as many privations would be easily borne if it were not for the moral shock when one is first taken.'

'Have you experienced it?'

'I? I was twice in prison,' she answered, with a sad, gentle smile. 'When I was arrested for the first time I had done nothing. I was twenty-two, had a child, and was expecting another. Though the loss of freedom and the parting with my child and husband were hard, they were nothing when compared with what I felt when I found out that I had ceased being a human creature and had become a thing. I wished to say goodbye to my little daughter. I was told to go and get into the trap. I asked where I was being taken to. The answer was that I should know when I got there. I asked what I was accused of, but got no reply. After I had been examined, and after they had undressed me and put numbered prison clothes on me, they led me to a vault, opened a door, pushed me in, and left me alone; a sentinel with a loaded gun paced up and down in front of my door, and every now and then looked in through a crack – I felt terribly depressed. What struck me most at the time was that the gendarme officer who examined me offered me a cigarette. So he knew that people liked smoking, and must know that they liked freedom and light; and that mothers love their children, and children their mothers. Then how could they tear me pitilessly from all that was dear to me, and lock me up in prison like a wild animal? That sort of thing could not be borne without evil effects. Anyone who believes in God and men, and believes that men love one another, will cease to believe it after all that. I have ceased to believe in humanity since then, and have grown embittered,' she finished, with a smile.

Shoustova's mother came in at the door through which her daughter had gone out, and said that Lydia was very much upset, and would not come in again.

'And what has this young life been ruined for?' said the aunt. 'What is especially painful to me is that I am the involuntary cause of it.'

'She will recover in the country, with God's help,' said the mother. 'We shall send her to her father.'

'Yes, if it were not for you she would have perished altogether,' said the aunt. 'Thank you. But what I wished to see you for is this: I wished to ask you to take a letter to Vera Doukhova,' and she got the letter out of her pocket.

'The letter is not closed; you may read and tear it up, or hand it to her, according to how far it coincides with your principles,' she said. 'It contains nothing compromising.'

Nekhlyudov took the letter, and, having promised to give it to Vera Doukhova, he took his leave and went away. He sealed the letter without reading it, meaning to take it to its destination.

Chapter 27

The State Church and the people

The last thing that kept Nekhlyudov in Petersburg was the case of the sectarians, whose petition he intended to get his former fellow-officer, aide-de-camp Bogatyrev, to hand to the Tsar. He came to Bogatyrev in the morning, and found him about to go out, though still at breakfast. Bogatyrev was not tall, but firmly built and wonderfully strong (he could bend a horseshoe), a kind, honest, straight, and even liberal man. In spite of these qualities, he was intimate at Court, and very fond of the Tsar and his family, and by some strange method he managed, while living in that highest circle, to see nothing but the good in it and to take no part in the evil and corruption. He never condemned anybody nor any measure, and either kept silent or spoke in a bold, loud voice, almost shouting what he had to say, and often laughing in the same boisterous manner. And he did not do it for diplomatic reasons, but because such was his character.

'Ah, that's right that you have come. Would you like some breakfast? Sit down, the beefsteaks are fine! I always begin with something substantial – begin and finish, too. Ha! ha! ha! Well, then, have a glass of wine,' he shouted, pointing to a decanter of claret. 'I have been thinking of you. I will hand on the petition. I shall put it into his own hands. You may count on that, only it occurred to me that it would be best for you to call on Toporov.'

Nekhlyudov made a wry face at the mention of Toporov.

'It all depends on him. He will be consulted, anyhow. And perhaps he may himself meet your wishes.'

'If you advise it I shall go.'

'That's right. Well, and how does Petersburg agree with you?' shouted Bogatyrev. 'Tell me. Eh?'

'I feel myself getting hypnotised,' replied Nekhlyudov.

'Hypnotised!' Bogatyrev repeated, and burst out laughing. 'You won't have anything? Well, just as you please,' and he wiped his moustaches with his napkin. 'Then you'll go? Eh? If he does not do it, give the petition to me, and I shall hand it on tomorrow.' Shouting these words, he rose, crossed himself just as naturally as he had wiped his mouth, and began buckling on his sword.

'And now goodbye; I must go. We are both going out,' said Nekhlyudov, and shaking Bogatyrev's strong, broad hand, and with the sense of pleasure which the impression of something healthy and unconsciously fresh always gave him, Nekhlyudov parted from Bogatyrev on the door-steps.

Though he expected no good result from his visit, still Nekhlyudov, following Bogatyrev's advice, went to see Toporov, on whom the sectarians' fate depended.

The position occupied by Toporov, involving as it did an incongruity of purpose, could only be held by a dull man devoid of moral sensibility. Toporov possessed both these negative qualities. The incongruity of the position he occupied was this. It was his duty to keep up and to defend, by external measures, not excluding violence, that Church which, by its own declaration, was established by God Himself and could not be shaken by the gates of hell nor by anything human. This divine and immutable God-established institution had to be sustained and defended by a human institution – the Holy Synod, managed by Toporov and his officials. Toporov did not see this contradiction, nor did he wish to see it, and he was therefore much concerned lest some Romish priest, some pastor, or some sectarian should destroy that Church which the gates of hell could not conquer.

Toporov, like all those who are quite destitute of the fundamental religious feeling that recognises the equality and brotherhood of men, was fully convinced that the common people were creatures entirely different from himself, and that the people needed what he could very well do without, for at the bottom of his heart he believed in nothing, and found such a state very convenient and pleasant. Yet he feared lest the people might also come to such a state, and looked upon it as his sacred duty, as he called it, to save the people therefrom.

A certain cookery book declares that some crabs like to be boiled alive. In the same way he thought and spoke as if the people liked being kept in superstition; only he meant this in a literal sense, whereas the cookery book did not mean its words literally.

His feelings towards the religion he was keeping up were the same as those of the poultry-keeper towards the carrion he fed his fowls on. Carrion was very disgusting, but the fowls liked it; therefore it was right to feed the fowls on carrion. Of course all this worship of the images of the Iberian, Kasan and Smolensk Mothers of God was a gross superstition, but the people liked it and believed in it, and therefore the superstition must be kept up.

Thus thought Toporov, not considering that the people only liked superstition because there always have been, and still are, men like himself who, being enlightened, instead of using their light to help others to struggle out of their dark ignorance, use it to plunge them still deeper into it.

When Nekhlyudov entered the reception-room Toporov was in his study talking with an abbess, a lively and aristocratic lady, who was spreading the Greek orthodox faith in Western Russia among the Uniates (who acknowledge the Pope of Rome), and who have the Greek religion enforced on them. An official who was in the reception-room inquired what Nekhlyudov wanted, and when he heard that Nekhlyudov meant to hand in a petition to the Emperor, he asked him if he would allow the petition to be read first. Nekhlyudov gave it him, and the official took it into the study. The abbess, with her hood and flowing veil and her long train trailing behind, left the study and went out, her white hands (with their well-tended nails) holding a topaz rosary. Nekhlyudov was not immediately asked to come in. Toporov was reading the petition and shaking his head. He was unpleasantly surprised by the clear and emphatic wording of it.

'If it gets into the hands of the Emperor it may cause misunderstandings, and unpleasant questions may be asked,' he thought as he read. Then he put the petition on the table, rang, and ordered Nekhlyudov to be asked in.

He remembered the case of the sectarians; he had had a petition from them before. The case was this: these Christians, fallen away from the Greek Orthodox Church, were first exhorted and then tried by law, but were acquitted. Then the Archdeacon and the Governor arranged, on the plea that their marriages were illegal, to exile these sectarians, separating the husbands, wives, and children. These fathers and wives were now petitioning that they should not be parted. Toporov recollected the first time the case came to his notice: he had at that time hesitated whether he had not better put a stop to it. But then he thought no harm could result from his confirming the decision to separate and exile the different members of the sectarian families, whereas allowing the peasant sect to remain where it was might have a bad effect on the rest of the inhabitants of the place and cause them to fall away from Orthodoxy. And then the affair also proved the zeal of the Archdeacon, and so he let the case proceed along the lines it had taken. But now that they had a defender such as Nekhlyudov, who had some influence in Petersburg, the case might be specially pointed out to the Emperor as something cruel, or it might get into the foreign papers. Therefore he at once took an unexpected decision.

'How do you do?' he said, with the air of a very busy man, receiving Nekhlyudov standing, and at once starting on the business. 'I know this case. As soon as I saw the names I recollected this unfortunate business,' he said, taking up the petition and showing it to Nekhlyudov. 'And I am much indebted to you for reminding me of it. It is the over-zealousness of the provincial authorities.'

Nekhlyudov stood silent, looking with no kindly feelings at the immovable, pale mask of a face before him.

'And I shall give orders that these measures should be revoked and the people reinstated in their homes.'

'So that I need not make use of this petition?'

'I promise you most assuredly,' answered Toporov, laying a stress on the word I, as if quite convinced that his honesty, his word was the best guarantee. 'It will be best if I write at once. Take a seat, please.'

He went up to the table and began to write. As Nekhlyudov sat down he looked at the narrow, bald skull, at the fat, blue-veined hand that was swiftly guiding the pen, and wondered why this evidently indifferent man was doing what he did and why he was doing it with such care.

'Well, here you are,' said Toporov, sealing the envelope; 'you may let your clients know,' and he stretched his lips to imitate a smile.

'Then what did these people suffer for?' Nekhlyudov asked, as he took the envelope.

Toporov raised his head and smiled, as if Nekhlyudov's question gave him pleasure. 'That I cannot tell. All I can say is that the interests of the people guarded by us are so important that too great a zeal in matters of religion is not so dangerous or so harmful as the indifference which is now spreading – '

'But how is it that in the name of religion the very first demands of righteousness are violated – families are separated?'

Toporov continued to smile patronisingly, evidently thinking what Nekhlyudov said very pretty. Anything that Nekhlyudov could say he would have considered very pretty and very one-sided, from the height of what he considered his far-reaching office in the State.

'It may seem so from the point of view of a private individual,' he said, 'but from an administrative point of view it appears in a rather different light. However, I must bid you goodbye, now,' said Toporov, bowing his head and holding out his hand, which Nekhlyudov pressed.

'The interests of the people! Your interests is what you mean!' thought Nekhlyudov as he went out. And he ran over in his mind the people in whom is manifested the activity of the institutions that uphold religion and educate the people. He began with the woman punished for the illicit sale of spirits, the boy for theft, the tramp for tramping, the incendiary for setting a house on fire, the banker for fraud, and that unfortunate Lydia Shoustova imprisoned only because they hoped to get such information as they required from her. Then he thought of the sectarians punished for violating Orthodoxy, and Gourkevitch for wanting constitutional government, and Nekhlyudov clearly saw that all these people were arrested, locked up, exiled, not really because they transgressed against justice or behaved unlawfully, but only because they were an obstacle hindering the officials and the rich from enjoying the property they had taken away from the people. And the woman who sold wine without having a licence, and the thief knocking about the town, and Lydia Shoustova hiding proclamations, and the sectarians upsetting superstitions, and Gourkevitch desiring a constitution, were a real hindrance. It seemed perfectly clear to Nekhlyudov that all these officials, beginning with his aunt's husband, the senators, and Toporov, down to those clean and correct gentlemen who sat at the tables in the Ministry Office, were not at all troubled by the fact that that in such a state of things the innocent had to suffer, but were only concerned how to get rid of the really dangerous, so that the rule that ten guilty should escape rather than that one innocent should be condemned was not observed, but, on the contrary, for the sake of getting rid of one really dangerous person, ten who seemed dangerous were punished, as, when cutting a rotten piece out of anything, one has to cut away some that is good.

This explanation seemed very simple and clear to Nekhlyudov; but its very simplicity and clearness made him hesitate to accept it. Was it possible that so complicated a phenomenon could have so simple and terrible an explanation? Was it possible that all these words about justice, law, religion, and God, and so on, were mere words, hiding the coarsest cupidity and cruelty?

Chapter 28

The meaning of Mariette's attraction

Nekhlyudov would have left Petersburg on the evening of the same day, but he had promised Mariette to meet her at the theatre, and though he knew that he ought not to keep that promise, he deceived himself into the belief that it would not be right to break his word.

'Am I capable of withstanding these temptations?' he asked himself not quite honestly. 'I shall try for the last time.'

He dressed in his evening clothes, and arrived at the theatre during the second act of the eternal *Dame aux Camélias*, in which a foreign actress once again, and in a novel manner, showed how women die of consumption.

The theatre was quite full. Mariette's box was at once, and with great deference, shown to Nekhlyudov at his request. A liveried servant stood in the corridor outside; he bowed to Nekhlyudov as to one whom he knew, and opened the door of the box.

All the people who sat and stood in the boxes on the opposite side, those who sat near and those who were in the *parterre*, with their grey, grizzly, bald, or curly heads – all were absorbed in watching the thin, bony actress who, dressed in silks and laces, was wriggling before them, and speaking in an unnatural voice.

Someone called 'Hush!' when the door opened, and two streams, one of cool, the other of hot, air touched Nekhlyudov's face.

Mariette and a lady whom he did not know, with a red cape and a big, heavy head-dress, were in the box, and two men also, Mariette's husband, the general, a tall, handsome man with a severe, inscrutable countenance, a Roman nose, and a uniform padded round the chest, and a fair man, with a bit of shaved chin between pompous whiskers.

Mariette, graceful, slight, elegant, her low-necked dress showing her firm, shapely, slanting shoulders, with a little black mole where they joined her neck, immediately turned, and pointed with her face to a chair behind her in an engaging manner, and smiled a smile that seemed full of meaning to Nekhlyudov.

The husband looked at him in the quiet way in which he did everything, and bowed. In the look he exchanged with his wife, the master, the owner of a beautiful woman, was to be seen at once.

When the monologue was over the theatre resounded with the clapping of hands. Mariette rose, and holding up her rustling silk skirt, went into the back of the box and introduced Nekhlyudov to her husband.

The general, without ceasing to smile with his eyes, said he was very pleased, and then sat inscrutably silent.

'I ought to have left today, had I not promised,' said Nekhlyudov to Mariette.

'If you do not care to see me,' said Mariette, in answer to what his words implied, 'you will see a wonderful actress. Was she not splendid in the last scene?' she asked, turning to her husband.

The husband bowed his head.

'This sort of thing does not touch me,' said Nekhlyudov. 'I have seen so much real suffering lately that – '

'Yes, sit down and tell me.'

The husband listened, his eyes smiling more and more ironically. 'I have been to see that woman whom they have set free, and who has been kept in prison for so long; she is quite broken down.'

'That is the woman I spoke to you about,' Mariette said to her husband.

'Oh, yes, I was very pleased that she could be set free,' said the husband quietly, nodding and smiling under his moustache with evident irony, so it seemed to Nekhlyudov. 'I shall go and have a smoke.'

Nekhlyudov sat waiting to hear what the something was that Mariette had to tell him. She said nothing, and did not even try to say anything, but joked and spoke about the performance, which she thought ought to touch Nekhlyudov. Nekhlyudov saw that she had nothing to tell, but only wished to show herself to him in all the splendour of her evening toilet, with her shoulders and little mole; and this was pleasant and yet repulsive to him.

The charm that had veiled all this sort of thing from Nekhlyudov was not removed, but it was as if he could see what lay beneath. Looking at Mariette, he admired her, and yet he knew that she was a liar, living with a husband who was making his career by means of the tears and lives of hundreds and hundreds of people, and that she was quite indifferent about it, and that all she had said the day before was untrue. What she wanted – neither he nor she knew why – was to make him fall in love with her. This both attracted and disgusted him. Several times, on the point of going away, he took up his hat, and then stayed on.

But at last, when the husband returned with a strong smell of tobacco in his thick moustache, and looked at Nekhlyudov with a patronising, contemptuous air, as if not recognising him, Nekhlyudov left the box before the door was closed again, found his overcoat, and went out of the theatre. As he was walking home along the Nevsky, he could not help noticing a well-shaped and aggressively finely-dressed woman, who was quietly walking in front of him along the broad asphalt pavement. The consciousness of her detestable power was noticeable in her face and the whole of her figure. All who met or passed that woman looked at her. Nekhlyudov walked faster than she did and, involuntarily, also looked her in the face. The face, which was probably painted, was handsome, and the woman looked at him with a smile and her eyes sparkled. And, curiously enough, Nekhlyudov was suddenly reminded of Mariette, because he again felt both attracted and disgusted just as when in the theatre.

Having hurriedly passed her, Nekhlyudov turned off on to the Morskaya, and passed on to the embankment, where, to the surprise of a policeman, he began pacing up and down the pavement.

'The other one gave me just such a smile when I entered the theatre,' he thought, 'and the meaning of the smile was the same. The only difference is, that this one said plainly, "If you want me, take me; if not, go your way," and the other one pretended that she was not thinking of this, but living in some high and refined state, while this was really at the root. Besides, this one was driven to it by necessity, while the other amused herself by playing with that enchanting, disgusting, frightful passion. This woman of the street was like stagnant, smelling water offered to those whose thirst was greater than their disgust; that other one in the theatre was like the poison which, unnoticed, poisons everything it gets into.'

Nekhlyudov recalled his liaison with the *Maréchal*'s wife, and shameful memories rose before him.

'The animalism of the brute nature in man is disgusting,' thought he, 'but as long as it remains in its naked form we observe it from the height of our spiritual life and despise it; and – whether one has fallen or resisted – one remains what one was before. But when that same animalism hides under a cloak of poetry and aesthetic feeling and demands our worship – then we are swallowed up by it completely, and worship animalism, no longer distinguishing good from evil. Then it is awful.'

Nekhlyudov perceived all this now as clearly as he saw the palace, the sentinels, the fortress, the river, the boats, and the Stock Exchange. And just as on this northern summer night there was no restful darkness on the earth, but only a dismal, dull light coming from an invisible source, so in Nekhlyudov's soul there was no longer the restful darkness, ignorance. Everything seemed clear. It was clear that everything considered important and good was insignificant and repulsive, and that all the glamour and luxury hid the old, well-known crimes, which not only remained unpunished but were adorned with all the splendour which men were capable of inventing.

Nekhlyudov wished to forget all this, not to see it, but he could no longer help seeing it. Though he could not see the source of the light which revealed it to him any more than he could see the source of the light which lay over Petersburg; and though the light appeared to him dull, dismal, and unnatural, yet he could not help seeing what it revealed, and he felt both joyful and anxious.

Chapter 29

For her sake and for God's

On his return to Moscow Nekhlyudov went at once to the prison hospital to bring Maslova the sad news that the Senate had confirmed the decision of the Court, and that she must prepare to go to Siberia. He had little hope of the success of his petition to the Emperor, which the advocate had written for him, and which he now brought with him for Maslova to sign. And, strange to say, he did not at present even wish to succeed; he had got used to the thought of going to Siberia and living among the exiled and the convicts, and he could not easily picture to himself how his life and Maslova's would shape if she were acquitted. He remembered the thought of the American writer, Thoreau, who at the time when slavery existed in America said that 'under a government that imprisons any unjustly the true place for a just man is also a prison.' Nekhlyudov, especially after his visit to Petersburg and all he discovered there, thought in the same way.

'Yes, the only place befitting an honest man in Russia at the present time is a prison,' he thought, and even felt that this applied to him personally, when he drove up to the prison and entered its walls.

The doorkeeper recognised Nekhlyudov, and told him at once that Maslova was no longer there.

'Where is she, then?'

'In the cell again.'

'Why has she been removed?' Nekhlyudov asked.

'Oh, your excellency, what are such people?' said the door-keeper, contemptuously. 'She's been carrying on with the medical assistant, so the head doctor ordered her back.'

Nekhlyudov had had no idea how near Maslova and the state of her mind were to him. He was stunned by the news.

He felt as one feels at the news of a great and unforeseen misfortune, and his pain was very severe. His first feeling was one of shame. He, with his joyful idea of the change that he imagined was going on in her soul, now seemed ridiculous in his own eyes. He thought that all her pretence of not wishing to accept his sacrifice, all the reproaches and tears, were only the devices of a depraved woman, who wished to use him to the best advantage. He seemed to remember having seen signs of obduracy at his last interview with her. All this flashed through his mind as he instinctively put on his hat and left the hospital.

'What am I to do now? Am I still bound to her? Has this action of hers not set me free?' And as he put these questions to himself he knew at once that if he considered himself free, and threw her up, he would be punishing himself, and not her, which was what he wished to do, and he was seized with fear.

'No, what has happened cannot alter – it can only strengthen my resolve. Let her do what flows from the state her mind is in. If it is carrying on with the medical assistant, let her carry on with the medical assistant; that is her business. I must do what my conscience demands of me. And my conscience expects me to sacrifice my freedom. My resolution to marry her, if only in form, and to follow wherever she may be sent, remains unalterable.' Nekhlyudov said all this to himself with vicious obstinacy as he left the hospital and walked with resolute steps towards the big gates of the prison. He asked the warder on duty at the gate to inform the inspector that he wished to see Maslova. The warder knew Nekhlyudov, and told him of an important change that had taken place in the prison. The old inspector had been discharged, and a new, very severe official appointed in his place.

'They are so strict nowadays, it's just awful,' said the jailer. 'He is in here; they will let him know directly.'

The new inspector was in the prison and soon came to Nekhlyudov. He was a tall, angular man, with high cheek bones, morose, and very slow in his movements.

'Interviews are allowed in the visiting room on the appointed days,' he said, without looking at Nekhlyudov.

'But I have a petition to the Emperor, which I want signed.'

'You can give it to me.'

'I must see the prisoner myself. I was always allowed to before.'

'That was so, before,' said the inspector, with a furtive glance at Nekhlyudov.

'I have a permission from the governor,' insisted Nekhlyudov, and took out his pocket-book.

'Allow me,' said the inspector, taking the paper from Nekhlyudov with his long, dry, white fingers, on the first of which was a gold ring, still without looking him in the eyes. He read the paper slowly. 'Step into the office, please.'

This time the office was empty. The inspector sat down by the table and began sorting some papers that lay on it, evidently intending to be present at the interview.

When Nekhlyudov asked whether he might see the political prisoner, Doukhova, the inspector answered, shortly, that he could not. 'Interviews with political prisoners are not permitted,' he said, and again fixed his attention on his papers. With a letter to Doukhova in his pocket, Nekhlyudov felt as if he had committed some offence, and his plans had been discovered and frustrated.

When Maslova entered the room the inspector raised his head, and, without looking at either her or Nekhlyudov, remarked, 'You may talk,' and went on sorting his papers. Maslova had again the white jacket, petticoat and kerchief on. When she came up to Nekhlyudov and saw his cold, hard look, she blushed scarlet, and crumbling the hem of her jacket with her hand, she cast down her eyes. Her confusion, so it seemed to Nekhlyudov, confirmed the hospital doorkeeper's words.

Nekhlyudov had meant to treat her in the same way as before, but could not bring himself to shake hands with her, so disgusting was she to him now.

'I have brought you bad news,' he said, in a monotonous voice, without looking at her or taking her hand. 'The Senate has refused.'

'I knew it would,' she said, in a strange tone, as if she were gasping for breath.

Formerly Nekhlyudov would have asked why she said she knew it would; now he only looked at her. Her eyes were full of tears. But this did not soften him; it roused his irritation against her even more.

The inspector rose and began pacing up and down the room.

In spite of the disgust Nekhlyudov was feeling at the moment, he considered it right to express his regret at the Senate's decision.

'You must not despair,' he said. 'The petition to the Emperor may meet with success, and I hope – '

'I'm not thinking of that,' she said, looking piteously at him with her wet, squinting eyes.

'What is it, then?'

'You have been to the hospital, and they have most likely told you about me – '

'What of that? That is your affair,' said Nekhlyudov coldly, and frowned. The cruel feeling of wounded pride that had quieted down rose with renewed force when she mentioned the hospital.

'He, a man of the world, whom any girl of the best families would think it happiness to marry, offered himself as a husband to this woman, and she could not even wait, but began intriguing with the medical assistant,' thought he, with a look of hatred.

'Here, sign this petition,' he said, taking a large envelope from his pocket, and laying the paper on the table. She wiped the tears with a corner of her kerchief, and asked what to write and where.

He showed her, and she sat down and arranged the cuff of her right sleeve with her left hand; he stood behind her, and silently looked at her back, which shook with suppressed emotion, and evil and good feelings were fighting in his breast – feelings of wounded pride and of pity for her who was suffering – and the last feeling was victorious.

He could not remember which came first; did the pity for her first enter his heart, or did he first remember his own sins – his own repulsive actions, the very same for which he was condemning her? Anyhow, he both felt himself guilty and pitied her.

Having signed the petition and wiped her inky finger on her petticoat, she got up and looked at him.

'Whatever happens, whatever comes of it, my resolve remains unchanged,' said Nekhlyudov. The thought that he had forgiven her heightened his feeling of pity and tenderness for her, and he wished to comfort her. 'I will do what I have said; wherever they take you I shall be with you.'

'What's the use?' she interrupted hurriedly, though her whole face lighted up.

'Think what you will want on the way – '

'I don't know of anything in particular, thank you.'

The inspector came up, and without waiting for a remark from him Nekhlyudov took leave, and went out with peace, joy, and love towards everybody in his heart such as he had never felt before. The certainty that no action of Maslova could change his love for her filled him with joy and raised him to a level which he had never before attained. Let her intrigue with the medical assistant; that was her business. He loved her not for his own but for her sake and for God's.

And this intrigue, for which Maslova was turned out of the hospital, and of which Nekhlyudov believed she was really guilty, consisted of the following:

Maslova was sent by the head nurse to get some herb tea from the dispensary at the end of the corridor, and there, all alone, she found the medical assistant, a tall man, with a blotchy face, who had for a long time been bothering her. In trying to get away from him Maslova gave him such a push that he knocked his head against a shelf, from which two bottles fell and broke. The head doctor, who was passing at that moment, heard the sound of breaking glass, and saw Maslova run out, quite red, and shouted to her:

'Ah, my good woman, if you start intriguing here, I'll send you about your business. What is the meaning of it?' he went on, addressing the medical assistant, and looking at him over his spectacles.

The assistant smiled, and began to justify himself. The doctor gave no heed to him, but, lifting his head so that he now looked through his spectacles, he entered the ward. He told the inspector the same day to send another more sedate assistant-nurse in Maslova's place. And this was her 'intrigue' with the medical assistant.

Being turned out for a love intrigue was particularly painful to Maslova, because the relations with men, which had long been repulsive to her, had become specially disgusting after meeting Nekhlyudov. The thought that, judging her by her past and present position, every man, the blotchy assistant among them, considered he had a right to offend her, and was surprised at her refusal, hurt her deeply, and made her pity herself and brought tears to her eyes.

When she went out to Nekhlyudov this time she wished to clear herself of the false charge which she knew he would certainly have heard about. But when she began to justify herself she felt he did not believe her, and that her excuses would only strengthen his suspicions; tears choked her, and she was silent.

Maslova still thought and continued to persuade herself that she had never forgiven him, and hated him, as she told him at their second interview, but in reality she loved him again, and loved him so that she did all he wished her to do; left off drinking, smoking, coquetting, and entered the hospital because she knew he wished it. And if every time he reminded her of it, she refused so decidedly to accept his sacrifice and marry him, it was because she liked repeating the proud words she had once uttered, and because she knew that a marriage with her would be a misfortune for him.

She had resolutely made up her mind that she would not accept his sacrifice, and yet the thought that he despised her and believed that she still was what she had been, and did not notice the change that had taken place in her, was very painful. That he could still think she had done wrong while in the hospital tormented her more than the news that her sentence was confirmed.

Chapter 30

The astonishing institution called Criminal Law

Maslova might be sent off with the first gang of prisoners, therefore Nekhlyudov got ready for his departure. But there was so much to be done that he felt that he could not finish it, however much time he might have. It was quite different now from what it

had been. Formerly he used to be obliged to look for an occupation, the interest of which always centred in one person, i.e.,
Dmitri Ivanovitch Nekhlyudov, and yet, though every interest of
his life was thus centred, all these occupations were very weari-
some. Now all his occupations related to other people and not to
Dmitri Ivanovitch, and they were all interesting and attractive,
and there was no end to them. Nor was this all. Formerly Dmitri
Ivanovitch Nekhlyudov's occupations always made him feel vexed
and irritable; now they produced a joyful state of mind. The
business at present occupying Nekhlyudov could be divided under
three headings. He himself, with his usual pedantry, divided it in
that way, and accordingly kept the papers referring to it in three
different portfolios. The first referred to Maslova, and was chiefly
that of taking steps to get her petition to the Emperor attended to,
and preparing for her probable journey to Siberia.

The second was about his estates. In Panovo he had given the
land to the peasants on condition of their paying rent to be put to
their own communal use. But he had to confirm this transaction
by a legal deed, and to make his will, in accordance with it. In
Kousminski the state of things was still as he had first arranged it,
i.e., he was to receive the rent; but the terms had to be fixed, and
also how much of the money he would use to live on, and how
much he would leave for the peasants' use. As he did not know
what his journey to Siberia would cost him, he could not decide
to lose this revenue altogether, though he reduced the income
from it by half.

The third part of his business was to help the convicts, who
applied more and more often to him. At first when he came in
contact with the prisoners, and they appealed to him for help, he
at once began interceding for them, hoping to lighten their fate,
but he soon had so many applications that he felt the impossibility
of attending to all of them, and that naturally led him to take up
another piece of work, which at last roused his interest even more
than the three first. This new part of his business was finding an
answer to the following questions: What was this astonishing
institution called criminal law, of which the results were that in
the prison, with some of the inmates of which he had lately
become acquainted, and in all those other places of confinement,
from the Peter and Paul Fortress in Petersburg to the island of

Sakhalin, hundreds and thousands of victims were pining? What did this strange criminal law exist for? How had it originated?

From his personal relations with the prisoners, from notes by some of those in confinement, and by questioning the advocate and the prison priest, Nekhlyudov came to the conclusion that the convicts, the so-called criminals, could be divided into five classes. The first were quite innocent people, condemned by judicial blunder. Such were the Menshovs, supposed to be incendiaries, Maslova, and others. There were not many of these; according to the priest's words, only seven per cent., but their condition excited particular interest.

To the second class belong persons condemned for actions done under peculiar circumstances, i.e., in a fit of passion, jealousy, or drunkenness, circumstances under which those who judged them would surely have committed the same actions.

The third class consisted of people punished for having committed actions which, according to their understanding, were quite natural, and even good, but which those other people, the men who made the laws, considered to be crimes. Such were the persons who sold spirits without a licence, smugglers, those who gathered grass and wood on large estates and in the forests belonging to the Crown; the thieving miners; and those unbelieving people who robbed churches.

To the fourth class belonged those who were imprisoned only because they stood morally higher than the average level of society. Such were the Sectarians, the Poles, the Circassians rebelling in order to regain their independence, the political prisoners, the Socialists, the strikers condemned for withstanding the authorities. There was, according to Nekhlyudov's observations, a very large percentage belonging to this class; among them some of the best of men.

The fifth class consisted of persons who had been far more sinned against by society than they had sinned against it. These were castaways, stupefied by continual oppression and temptation, such as the boy who had stolen the rugs, and hundreds of others whom Nekhlyudov had seen in the prison and out of it. The conditions under which they lived seemed to lead on systematically to those actions which are termed crimes. A great many thieves and murderers with whom he had lately come in contact, according to Nekhlyudov's estimate, belonged to this class. To this class Nekhlyudov also reckoned those depraved, demoralised creatures whom the new school of criminology classify as the criminal type, and the existence of which is considered to be the chief proof of the necessity of criminal law and punishment. This demoralised, depraved, abnormal type was, according to Nekhlyudov, exactly the same as that against whom society had sinned, only here society had sinned not directly against them, but against their parents and forefathers.

Among this latter class Nekhlyudov was specially struck by one Okhotin, an inveterate thief, the illegitimate son of a prostitute, brought up in a doss-house, who, up to the age of thirty, had apparently never met with anyone whose morality was above that of a policeman, and who had got into a band of thieves when quite young. He was gifted with an extraordinary sense of humour, by means of which he made himself very attractive. He asked Nekhlyudov for protection, at the same time making fun of himself, the lawyers, the prison, and laws human and divine.

Another was the handsome Fedorov, who, with a band of robbers, of whom he was the chief, had robbed and murdered an old man, an official. Fedorov was a peasant, whose father had been unlawfully deprived of his house, and who, later on, when serving as a soldier, had suffered much because he had fallen in love with an officer's mistress. He had a fascinating, passionate nature, that longed for enjoyment at any cost. He had never met anybody who restrained himself for any cause whatever, and had never heard a word about any aim in life other than enjoyment.

Nekhlyudov distinctly saw that both these men were richly endowed by nature, but had been neglected and crippled like uncared-for plants.

He had also met a tramp and a woman who had repelled him by their dullness and seeming cruelty, but even in them he could find no trace of the criminal type written about by the Italian school, but only saw in them people who were repulsive to him personally, just in the same way as some he had met outside the prison, in swallow-tail coats wearing epaulettes, or bedecked with lace. And so the investigation of the reasons why all these very different persons were put in prison, while others just like them were going about free and even judging them, formed a fourth task for Nekhlyudov.

He hoped to find an answer to this question in books, and bought all that referred to it. He got the works of Lombroso, Garofalo, Ferry, List, Maudsley, Tard, and read them carefully. But as he read he became more and more disappointed. It happened to him as it always happens to those who turn to science not in order to play a part in it, nor to write, nor to dispute, nor to teach, but simply for an answer to an every-day question of life. Science answered thousands of different very subtle and ingenious questions touching criminal law, but not the one he was trying to solve. He asked a very simple question: 'Why, and with what right, do some people lock up, torment, exile, flog, and kill others, while they are themselves just like those whom they torment, flog, and kill?' And in answer he got deliberations as to whether human beings had free will or not. Whether signs of criminality could be detected by measuring the skulls or not. What part heredity played in crime. Whether immorality could be inherited. What madness is, what degeneration is, and what temperament is. How climate, food, ignorance, imitativeness, hypnotism, or passion act. What society is. What are its duties, etc., etc.

These disquisitions reminded him of the answer he once got from a little boy whom he met coming home from school. Nekhlyudov asked him if he had learned his spelling.

'I have,' answered the boy.

'Well, then, tell me, how do you spell "leg"?'

'A dog's leg, or what kind of leg?' the boy answered, with a sly look.

Answers in the form of new questions, like the boy's, was all Nekhlyudov got in reply to his one primary question. He found much that was clever, learned much that was interesting, but what he did not find was an answer to the principal question: By what right some people punish others?

Not only did he not find any answer, but all the arguments were brought forward in order to explain and vindicate punishment, the necessity of which was taken as an axiom.

Nekhlyudov read much, but only in snatches, and putting down his failure to this superficial way of reading, hoped to find the answer later on. He would not allow himself to believe in the truth of the answer which began, more and more often, to present itself to him.

Chapter 31

Nekhlyudov's sister and her husband

The gang of prisoners, with Maslova among them, was to start on the 5th July. Nekhlyudov arranged to start on the same day.

The day before, Nekhlyudov's sister and her husband came to town to see him.

Nekhlyudov's sister, Nathalie Ivanovna Rogozhinsky, was ten years older than her brother. She had been very fond of him when he was a boy, and later on, just before her marriage, they grew very close to each other, as if they were equals, she being a young woman of twenty-five, he a lad of fifteen. At that time she was in love with his friend, Nikolenka Irteniev, since dead. They both loved Nikolenka, and loved in him and in themselves that which is good, and which unites all men. Since then they had both been depraved, he by military service and a vicious life, she by marriage with a man whom she loved with a sensual love, who did not care for the things that had once been so dear and holy to her and to her brother, nor even understand the meaning of those aspirations towards moral perfection and the service of mankind, which once constituted her life, and put them down to ambition and the wish to show off; that being the only explanation comprehensible to him.

Nathalie's husband had been a man without a name and without means, but cleverly steering towards Liberalism or Conservatism, according to which best suited his purpose, he managed to make a comparatively brilliant judicial career. Some peculiarity which made him attractive to women assisted him when he was no longer in his first youth. While travelling abroad he made Nekhlyudov's acquaintance, and managed to make Nathalie, who was also no longer a girl, fall in love with him, rather against her mother's wishes, who considered a marriage with him to be a misalliance for her daughter. Nekhlyudov, though he tried to hide it from himself, though he fought against it, hated his brother-in-law.

Nekhlyudov had a strong antipathy towards him because of the vulgarity of his feelings, his assurance and narrowness, but chiefly because of Nathalie, who managed to love him in spite of the narrowness of his nature, and loved him so selfishly, so sensually, and stifled for his sake all the good that had been in her.

It always hurt Nekhlyudov to think of Nathalie as the wife of that hairy, self-assured man with the shiny, bald patch on his head. He could not even master a feeling of revulsion towards their children, and when he heard that she was again going to have a baby, he felt something like sorrow that she had once more been infected with something bad by this man who was so foreign to him. The Rogozhinskys had come to Moscow alone, having left their two children – a boy and a girl – at home, and stopped in the best rooms of the best hotel. Nathalie at once went to her mother's old house, but hearing from Agraphena Petrovna that her brother had left, and was living in a lodging-house, she drove there. The dirty servant met her in the stuffy passage, dark but for a lamp which burnt there all day. He told her that the Prince was not in.

Nathalie asked to be shown into his rooms, as she wished to leave a note for him, and the man took her up.

Nathalie carefully examined her brother's two little rooms. She noticed in everything the love of cleanliness and order she knew so well in him, and was struck by the novel simplicity of the surroundings. On his writing-table she saw the paper-weight with the bronze dog on the top which she remembered; the tidy way in which his different portfolios and writing utensils were placed on the table was also familiar, and so was the large, crooked ivory paper knife which marked the place in a French book by Tard, which lay with other volumes on punishment and a book in English by Henry George. She sat down at the table and wrote a note asking him to be sure to come that same day, and shaking her head in surprise at what she saw, she returned to her hotel.

Two questions regarding her brother now interested Nathalie: his marriage with Katusha, which she had heard spoken about in their town – for everybody was speaking about it – and his giving away the land to the peasants, which was also known, and struck many as something of a political nature, and dangerous. The marriage with Katusha pleased her in a way. She admired that resoluteness which was so like him and herself as they used to be

in those happy times before her marriage. And yet she was horrified when she thought her brother was going to marry such a
dreadful woman. The latter was the stronger feeling of the two,
and she decided to use all her influence to prevent him from doing
it, though she knew how difficult this would be.

The other matter, the giving up of the land to the peasants, did
not touch her so nearly, but her husband was very indignant about
it, and expected her to influence her brother against it.

Rogozhinsky said that such an action was the height of inconsistency, flightiness, and pride, the only possible explanation of
which was the desire to appear original, to brag, to make oneself
talked about.

'What sense could there be in letting the land to the peasants, on
condition that they pay the rent to themselves?' he said. 'If he was
resolved to do such a thing, why not sell the land to them through
the Peasants' Bank? There might have been some sense in that. In
fact, this act verges on insanity.'

And Rogozhinsky began seriously thinking about putting Nekhlyudov under guardianship, and demanded of his wife that she
should speak seriously to her brother about his curious intention.

Chapter 32

Nekhlyudov's anarchism

As soon as Nekhlyudov returned that evening and saw his sister's
note on the table he started to go and see her. He found Nathalie
alone, her husband having gone to take a rest in the next room.
She wore a tightly-fitting black silk dress, with a red bow in front.
Her black hair was crimped and arranged according to the latest
fashion.

The pains she took to appear young, for the sake of her husband, whose equal she was in years, were very obvious.

When she saw her brother she jumped up and hurried towards
him, with her silk dress rustling. They kissed, and looked smilingly at each other. There passed between them that mysterious
exchange of looks, full of meaning, in which all was true, and

which cannot be expressed in words. Then came words which were not true. They had not met since their mother's death.

'You have grown stouter and younger,' he said, and her lips puckered up with pleasure.

'And you have grown thinner.'

'Well, and how is your husband?' Nekhlyudov asked.

'He is taking a rest; he did not sleep all night.' There was much to say, but it was not said in words; only their looks expressed what their words failed to say.

'I went to see you.'

'Yes, I know. I moved because the house is too big for me. I was lonely there, and dull. I want nothing of all that is there, so that you had better take it all – the furniture, I mean, and things.'

'Yes, Agraphena Petrovna told me. I went there. Thanks, very much. But – '

At this moment the hotel waiter brought in a silver tea-set. While he set the table they were silent. Then Nathalie sat down at the table and made the tea, still in silence. Nekhlyudov also said nothing.

At last Nathalie began resolutely. 'Well, Dmitri, I know all about it.' And she looked at him.

'What of that? I am glad you know.'

'How can you hope to reform her after the life she has led?' she asked.

He sat quite straight on a small chair, and listened attentively, trying to understand her and to answer rightly. The state of mind called forth in him by his last interview with Maslova still filled his soul with quiet joy and good will to all men.

'It is not her but myself I wish to reform,' he replied.

Nathalie sighed.

'There are other means besides marriage to do that.'

'But I think it is the best. Besides, it leads me into that world in which I can be of use.'

'I cannot believe you will be happy,' said Nathalie.

'It's not my happiness that is the point.'

'Of course, but if she has a heart she cannot be happy – cannot even wish it.'

'She does not wish it.'

'I understand; but life – '

'Yes – life?'

'Demands something different.'

'It demands nothing but that we should do what is right,' said Nekhlyudov, looking into her face, still handsome, though slightly wrinkled round eyes and mouth.

'I do not understand,' she said, and sighed.

'Poor darling; how could she change so?' he thought, calling back to his mind Nathalie as she had been before her marriage, and feeling towards her a tenderness woven out of innumerable memories of childhood. At that moment Rogozhinsky entered the room, with head thrown back and expanded chest, and stepping lightly and softly in his usual manner, his spectacles, his bald patch, and his black beard all glistening.

'How do you do? How do you do?' he said, laying an unnatural and intentional stress on his words. (Though, soon after the marriage, they had tried to be more familiar with each other, they had never succeeded.)

They shook hands, and Rogozhinsky sank softly into an easy-chair.

'Am I not interrupting your conversation?'

'No, I do not wish to hide what I am saying or doing from anyone.'

As soon as Nekhlyudov saw the hairy hands, and heard the patronising, self-assured tones, his meekness left him in a moment.

'Yes, we were talking about his intentions,' said Nathalie. 'Shall I give you a cup of tea?' she added, taking the teapot.

'Yes, please. What particular intentions do you mean?'

'That of going to Siberia with the gang of prisoners, among whom is the woman I consider myself to have wronged,' uttered Nekhlyudov.

'I hear not only to accompany her, but more than that.'

'Yes, and to marry her if she wishes it.'

'Dear me! But if you do not object I should like to ask you to explain your motives. I do not understand them.'

'My motives are that this woman – that this woman's first step on her way to degradation – ' Nekhlyudov got angry with himself, and was unable to find the right expression. 'My motives are that I am the guilty one, and she gets the punishment.'

'If she is being punished she cannot be innocent, either.'

'She is quite innocent.' And Nekhlyudov related the whole incident with unnecessary warmth.

'Yes, that was a case of carelessness on the part of the president, the result of which was a thoughtless answer on the part of the jury; but there is the Senate for cases like that.'

'The Senate has rejected the appeal.'

'Well, if the Senate has rejected it, there cannot have been sufficient reasons for an appeal,' said Rogozhinsky, evidently sharing the prevailing opinion that truth is the product of judicial decrees. 'The Senate cannot enter into the question on its merits. If there is a real mistake, the Emperor should be petitioned.'

'That has been done, but there is no probability of success. They will apply to the Department of the Ministry, the Department will consult the Senate, the Senate will repeat its decision, and, as usual, the innocent will get punished.'

'In the first place, the Department of the Ministry won't consult the Senate,' said Rogozhinsky, with a condescending smile; 'it will give orders for the original deeds to be sent from the Law Court, and if it discovers a mistake it will decide accordingly. And, secondly, the innocent are never punished, or at least in very rare, exceptional cases. It is the guilty who are punished,' Rogozhinsky said deliberately, and smiled self-complacently.

'And I have become fully convinced that most of those condemned by law are innocent.'

'How's that?'

'Innocent in the literal sense. Just as this woman is innocent of poisoning anyone; as innocent as a peasant I have just come to know, of the murder he never committed; as a mother and son who were on the point of being condemned for incendiarism, which was committed by the owner of the house that was set on fire.'

'Well, of course there always have been and always will be judicial errors. Human institutions cannot be perfect.'

'And, besides, there are a great many people convicted who are innocent of doing anything considered wrong by the society they have grown up in.'

'Excuse me, this is not so; every thief knows that stealing is wrong, and that we should not steal; that it is immoral,' said Rogozhinsky, with his quiet, self-assured, slightly contemptuous smile, which specially irritated Nekhlyudov.

'No, he does not know it; they say to him "don't steal", and he knows that the master of the factory steals his labour by keeping back his wages; that the government, with its officials, robs him continually by taxation.'

'Why, this is anarchism,' Rogozhinsky said, quietly defining his brother-in-law's words.

'I don't know what it is; I am only telling you the truth,' Nekhlyudov continued. 'He knows that the government is robbing him, knows that we landed proprietors have robbed him long since, robbed him of the land which should be the common property of all, and then, if he picks up dry wood to light his fire on that land stolen from him, we put him in jail, and try to persuade him that he is a thief. Of course he knows that not he but those who robbed him of the land are thieves, and that to get any restitution of what has been robbed is his duty towards his family.'

'I don't understand, or if I do I cannot agree with it. The land must be somebody's property,' began Rogozhinsky quietly, and, convinced that Nekhlyudov was a Socialist, and that Socialism demands that all the land should be divided equally, that such a division would be very foolish, and that he could easily prove it to be so, he said. 'If you divided it equally today, it would tomorrow be again in the hands of the most industrious and clever.'

'Nobody is thinking of dividing the land equally. The land must not be anybody's property; must not be a thing to be bought and sold or rented.'

'The rights of property are inborn in man; without them the cultivation of land would present no interest. Destroy the rights of property and we lapse into barbarism.' Rogozhinsky uttered this authoritatively, repeating the usual argument in favour of private ownership of land which is supposed to be irrefutable, based on the assumption that people's desire to possess land proves that they need it.

'On the contrary, only when the land is nobody's property will it cease to lie idle, as it does now, while the landlords, like dogs in the manger, unable themselves to put it to use, will not let those use it who are able.'

'But, Dmitri Ivanovitch, what you are saying is sheer madness. Is it possible to abolish property in land in our age? I know it is your old hobby. But allow me to tell you straight,' and Rogozhinsky grew pale, and his voice trembled. It was evident that this question touched him very nearly. 'I should advise you to consider this question well before attempting to solve it practically.'

'Are you speaking of my personal affairs?'

'Yes, I hold that we who are placed in special circumstances should bear the responsibilities which spring from those circumstances, should uphold the conditions in which we were born, and which we have inherited from our predecessors, and which we ought to pass on to our descendants.'

'I consider it my duty – '

'Wait a bit,' said Rogozhinsky, not permitting the interruption. 'I am not speaking for myself or my children. The position of my children is assured, and I earn enough for us to live comfortably, and I expect my children will live so too, so that my interest in your action – which, if you will allow me to say so, is not well considered – is not based on personal motives; it is on principle that I cannot agree with you. I should advise you to think it well over, to read – ?'

'Please allow me to settle my affairs, and to choose what to read and what not to read, myself,' said Nekhlyudov, turning pale. Feeling his hands grow cold, and that he was no longer master of himself, he stopped, and began drinking his tea.

Chapter 33

The aim of the Law

'Well, and how are the children?' Nekhlyudov asked his sister when he was calmer. The sister told him about the children. She said they were staying with their grandmother (their father's mother), and, pleased that his dispute with her husband had come to an end, she began telling him how her children played that they were travelling, just as he used to do with his three dolls, one of them a negro and another which he called the French lady.

'Can you really remember it all?' said Nekhlyudov, smiling.

'Yes, and just fancy, they play in the very same way.'

The unpleasant conversation had been brought to an end, and Nathalie was quieter, but she did not care to talk in her husband's presence of what could be comprehensible only to her brother, so, wishing to start a general conversation, she began talking about the sorrow of Kamenski's mother at losing her only son, who had fallen in a duel, for this Petersburg topic of the day had now reached Moscow. Rogozhinsky expressed disapproval at the state of things that excluded murder in a duel from the ordinary criminal offences. This remark evoked a rejoinder from Nekhlyudov, and a new dispute arose on the subject. Nothing was fully explained, neither of the antagonists expressed all he had in his mind, each keeping to his conviction, which condemned the other. Rogozhinsky felt that Nekhlyudov condemned him and despised his activity, and he wished to show him the injustice of his opinions.

Nekhlyudov, on the other hand, felt provoked by his brother-in-law's interference in his affairs concerning the land. And knowing in his heart of hearts that his sister, her husband, and their children, as his heirs, had a right to do so, was indignant that this narrow-minded man persisted with calm assurance to regard as just and lawful what Nekhlyudov no longer doubted was folly and crime.

This man's arrogance annoyed Nekhlyudov.

'What could the law do?' he asked.

'It could sentence one of the two duellists to the mines like an ordinary murderer.'

Nekhlyudov's hands grew cold.

'Well, and what good would that be?' he asked, hotly.

'It would be just.'

'As if justice were the aim of the law,' said Nekhlyudov.

'What else?'

'The upholding of class interests! I think the law is only an instrument for upholding the existing order of things beneficial to our class.'

'This is a perfectly new view,' said Rogozhinsky with a quiet smile; 'the law is generally supposed to have a totally different aim.'

'Yes, so it has in theory but not in practice, as I have found out. The law aims only at preserving the present state of things, and therefore it persecutes and executes those who stand above the ordinary level and wish to raise it – the so-called political prisoners – as well as those who are below the average, the so-called criminal types.'

'I do not agree with you. In the first place, I cannot admit that the criminals classed as political are punished because they are above the average. In most cases they are the refuse of society, just as much perverted, though in a different way, as the criminal types whom you consider below the average.'

'But I happen to know men who are morally far above their judges; all the sectarians are moral, from – '

But Rogozhinsky, a man not accustomed to be interrupted when he spoke, did not listen to Nekhlyudov, but went on talking at the same time, thereby irritating him still more.

'Nor can I admit that the object of the law is the upholding of the present state of things. The law aims at reforming – '

'A nice kind of reform, in a prison!' Nekhlyudov put in.

'Or removing,' Rogozhinsky went on, persistently, 'the perverted and brutalised persons that threaten society.'

'That's just what it doesn't do. Society has not the means of doing either the one thing or the other.'

'How is that? I don't understand,' said Rogozhinsky with a forced smile.

'I mean that only two reasonable kinds of punishment exist: those used in the old days – corporal and capital punishment, which, as human nature gradually softens, come more and more into disuse,' said Nekhlyudov.

'There, now, this is quite new and very strange to hear from your lips.'

'Yes, it is reasonable to hurt a man so that he should not do in future what he is hurt for doing, and it is also quite reasonable to cut a man's head off when he is injurious or dangerous to society. These punishments have a reasonable meaning. But what sense is there in locking up in a prison a man perverted by want of occupation and bad example; to place him in a position where he is provided for, where laziness is imposed on him, and where he is in company with the most perverted of men? What reason is there to take a man at public cost (it comes to more than five hundred roubles per head) from the Tula to the Irkutsk government, or from Kursk – '

'Yes, but all the same, people are afraid of those journeys at public cost, and if it were not for such journeys and the prisons, you and I would not be sitting here as we are.'

'The prisons cannot ensure our safety, because these people do not stay there for ever, but are set free again. On the contrary, in those establishments men are brought to the greatest vice and degradation, so that the danger is increased.'

'You mean to say that the penitentiary system should be improved.'

'It cannot be improved. Improved prisons would cost more than all that is being now spent on the people's education, and would lay a still heavier burden on the people.'

'The shortcomings of the penitentiary system in nowise invalidate the law itself,' Rogozhinsky continued again, without heeding his brother-in-law.

'There is no remedy for these shortcomings,' said Nekhlyudov, raising his voice.

'What of that? Shall we therefore go and kill, or, as a certain statesman proposed, go putting out people's eyes?' Rogozhinsky remarked.

'Yes; that would be cruel, but it would be effective. What is done now is cruel, and not only ineffective, but so stupid that one cannot understand how people in their senses can take part in so absurd and cruel a business as criminal law.'

'But I happen to take part in it,' said Rogozhinsky, growing pale.

'That is your business. But to me it is incomprehensible.'

'I think there are a good many things incomprehensible to you,' said Rogozhinsky, with a trembling voice.

'I have seen how one public prosecutor did his very best to get an unfortunate boy condemned, who could have evoked nothing but sympathy in an unperverted mind. I know how another cross-examined a sectarian and put down the reading of the Gospels as a criminal offence; in fact, the whole business of the Law Courts consists in senseless and cruel actions of that sort.'

'I should not serve if I thought so,' said Rogozhinsky, rising.

Nekhlyudov noticed a peculiar glitter under his brother-in-law's spectacles. 'Can it be tears?' he thought. And they were really tears of injured pride. Rogozhinsky went up to the window, got out his handkerchief, coughed and rubbed his spectacles, took them off, and wiped his eyes.

When he returned to the sofa he lit a cigar, and did not speak any more.

Nekhlyudov felt pained and ashamed of having offended his brother-in-law and his sister to such a degree, especially as he was going away the next day.

He parted with them in confusion, and drove home.

'All I have said may be true – anyhow he did not reply. But it was not said in the right way. How little I must have changed if I could be carried away by ill-feeling to such an extent as to hurt and wound poor Nathalie in such a way!' he thought.

Chapter 34

The prisoners start for Siberia

The gang of prisoners, among whom was Maslova, was to leave Moscow by rail at 3 p.m.; therefore, in order to see the gang start, and walk to the station with the prisoners Nekhlyudov meant to reach the prison before 12 o'clock.

The night before, as he was packing up and sorting his papers, he came upon his diary, and read some bits here and there. The last bit written before he left for Petersburg ran thus: 'Katusha does not wish to accept my sacrifice; she wishes to make a sacrifice herself. She has conquered, and so have I. She makes me happy by the inner change, which seems to me, though I fear to believe it, to be going on in her. I fear to believe it, yet she seems to be coming back to life.' Then further on he read. 'I have lived through something very hard and very joyful. I learnt that she has behaved very badly in the hospital, and I suddenly felt great pain. I never expected that it could be so painful. I spoke to her with loathing and hatred, then all of a sudden I called to mind how many times I have been, and even still am, though but in thought, guilty of the thing that I hated her for, and immediately I became disgusting to myself, and pitied her and felt happy again. If only we could manage to see the beam in our own eye in time, how kind we should be.' Then he wrote: 'I have been to see Nathalie, and again self-satisfaction made me unkind and spiteful, and a heavy feeling remains. Well, what is to be done? Tomorrow a new life will begin. A final goodbye to the old! Many new impressions have accumulated, but I cannot yet bring them to unity.'

When he awoke the next morning Nekhlyudov's first feeling was regret about the affair between him and his brother-in-law.

'I cannot go away like this,' he thought. 'I must go and make it up with them.' But when he looked at his watch he saw that he had not time to go, but must hurry so as not to be too late for the departure of the gang. He hastily got everything ready, and sent the things to the station with a servant and Taras, Theodosia's husband, who was going with them. Then he took the first *isvostchik* he could find and drove off to the prison.

The prisoners' train started two hours before the train by which he was going, so Nekhlyudov paid his bill in the lodgings and left for good.

It was July, and the weather was unbearably hot. From the stones, the walls, the iron of the roofs, which the sultry night had not cooled, the heat streamed into the motionless air. When at rare intervals a slight breeze did arise, it brought but a whiff of hot air filled with dust and smelling of oil paint.

There were few people in the streets, and those who were out tried to keep on the shady side. Only the sunburnt peasants, with their bronzed faces and bark shoes on their feet, who were mending the road, sat hammering the stones into the burning sand in the sun; while the policemen, in their holland blouses, with revolvers fastened with orange cords, stood melancholy and depressed in the middle of the road, changing from foot to foot; and the tramcars, the horses of which wore holland hoods on their heads, with slits for the ears, kept passing up and down the sunny road with ringing bells.

When Nekhlyudov drove up to the prison the gang had not left the yard. The work of delivering and receiving the prisoners that had commenced at 4 a.m. was still going on. The gang was to consist of six hundred and twenty-three men and sixty-four women; they had all to be received according to the registry lists.

The sick and the weak to be sorted out, and all to be delivered to the convoy. The new inspector, with two assistants, the doctor and medical assistant, the officer of the convoy, and the clerk, were sitting in the prison yard at a table covered with writing materials and papers, which was placed in the shade of a wall. They called the prisoners one by one, examined and questioned them, and took notes. The rays of the sun had gradually reached the table, and it was growing very hot and oppressive for want of air and because of the breathing crowd of prisoners that stood close by.

'Good gracious, will this never come to an end!' the convoy officer, a tall, fat, red-faced man with high shoulders, who kept puffing the smoke of his cigarette into his thick moustache, asked, as he drew in a long puff. 'You are killing me. From where have you got them all? Are there many more?' the clerk inquired.

'Twenty-four men and the women.'

'What are you standing there for? Come on,' shouted the convoy officer to the prisoners who had not yet passed the revision, and who stood crowded one behind the other. The prisoners had been standing there more than three hours, packed in rows in the full sunlight, waiting their turns.

While this was going on in the prison yard, outside the gate, besides the sentinel who stood there as usual with a gun, were drawn up about twenty carts, to carry the luggage of the prisoners and such prisoners as were too weak to walk, and a group of relatives and friends waiting to see the prisoners as they came out and to exchange a few words if a chance presented itself, and to give them a few things. Nekhlyudov took his place among the group. He had stood there about an hour when the clanking of chains, the noise of footsteps, authoritative voices, the sound of coughing, and the low murmur of a large crowd became audible.

This continued for about five minutes, during which several jailers went in and out of the gateway. At last the word of command was given. The gate opened with a thundering noise, the clattering of the chains became louder, and the convoy soldiers, dressed in white blouses and carrying guns, came out into the street and took their places in a large, exact circle in front of the gate; this was evidently a usual, often-practised manoeuvre. Then another command was given, and the prisoners began coming out in couples, with flat, pancake-shaped caps on their shaved heads and sacks over their shoulders, dragging their chained legs and swinging one arm, while the other held up a sack.

First came the men condemned to hard labour, all dressed alike in grey trousers and cloaks with marks on the back. All of them – young and old, thin and fat, pale and red, dark and bearded and beardless, Russians, Tartars, and Jews – came out, clattering with their chains and briskly swinging their arms as if prepared to go a long distance, but stopped after having taken ten steps, and obediently took their places behind each other, four abreast. Then without interval streamed out more shaved men, dressed in the same manner but with chains only on their legs. These were condemned to exile. They came out as briskly and stopped as suddenly, taking their places four in a row. Then came those exiled by their communes. Then the women in the same order: first those condemned to hard labour, with grey cloaks and kerchiefs; then the exiled women, and those following their husbands of their own free will, dressed in their own town or village clothing. Some of the women were carrying babies wrapped in the fronts of their grey cloaks.

With the women came the children, boys and girls, who like colts in a herd of horses, pressed in among the prisoners.

The men took their places silently, only coughing now and then, or making short remarks.

The women talked without intermission. Nekhlyudov thought he saw Maslova as they were coming out, but she was at once lost in the large crowd, and he could only see grey creatures, seemingly devoid of all that was human, or at any rate of all that was womanly, with sacks on their backs and children round them, taking their places behind the men.

Though all the prisoners had been counted inside the prison walls, the convoy counted them again, comparing the numbers with the list. This took very long, especially as some of the prisoners moved and changed places, which confused the convoy.

The convoy soldiers shouted and pushed the prisoners (who complied obediently, but angrily) and counted them over again. When all had been counted, the convoy officer gave a command, and the crowd became agitated. The weak men and women and children rushed, racing each other, towards the carts, and began placing their bags on the carts and climbing up themselves. Women with crying babies, merry children quarrelling for places, and dull, careworn prisoners got into the carts.

Several of the prisoners took off their caps and came up to the convoy officer with some request. Nekhlyudov found out later that they were asking for places on the carts. Nekhlyudov saw how the officer, without looking at the prisoners, drew in a whiff from his cigarette, and then suddenly waved his short arm in front of one of the prisoners, who quickly drew his shaved head back between his shoulders as if afraid of a blow, and sprang back.

'I will give you a lift such that you'll remember. You'll get there on foot right enough,' shouted the officer. Only one of the men was granted his request – an old man with chains on his legs; and Nekhlyudov saw the old man take off his pancake-shaped cap, and go up to the cart crossing himself. He could not manage to get up on the cart because of the chains that prevented his lifting his old legs, and a woman who was sitting in the cart at last pulled him in by the arm.

When all the sacks were in the carts, and those who were allowed to get in were seated, the officer took off his cap, wiped his forehead, his bald head and fat, red neck, and crossed himself.

'March,' commanded the officer. The soldiers' guns gave a click; the prisoners took off their caps and crossed themselves, those who were seeing them off shouted something, the prisoners shouted in answer, a row arose among the women, and the gang, surrounded by the soldiers in their white blouses, moved forward, raising the dust with their chained feet. The soldiers went in front; then came the convicts condemned to hard labour, clattering with their chains; then the exiled and those exiled by the communes, chained in couples by their wrists; then the women. After them, on the carts loaded with sacks, came the weak. High up on one of the carts sat a woman closely wrapped up, and she kept shrieking and sobbing.

Chapter 35

Not men but strange and terrible creatures?

The procession was such a long one that the carts with the luggage and the weak started only when those in front were already out of sight. When the last of the carts moved, Nekhlyudov got into the trap that stood waiting for him and told the *isvostchik* to catch up the prisoners in front, so that he could see if he knew any of the men in the gang, and then try and find out Maslova among the women and ask her if she had received the things he sent.

It was very hot, and a cloud of dust that was raised by a thousand tramping feet stood all the time over the gang that was moving down the middle of the street. The prisoners were walking quickly, and the slow-going *isvostchik*'s horse was some time in catching them up. Row upon row they passed, those strange and terrible-looking creatures, none of whom Nekhlyudov knew.

On they went, all dressed alike, moving a thousand feet all shod alike, swinging their free arms as if to keep up their spirits. There were so many of them, they all looked so much alike, and they were all placed in such unusual, peculiar circumstances, that they seemed to Nekhlyudov to be not men but some sort of strange and terrible creatures. This impression passed when he recognised in the crowd of convicts the murderer Fedorov, and among the exiles Okhotin the wit, and another tramp who had appealed to him for assistance. Almost all the prisoners turned and looked at the trap that was passing them and at the gentleman inside. Fedorov tossed his head backwards as a sign that he had recognised Nekhlyudov, Okhotin winked, but neither of them bowed, considering it not the thing.

As soon as Nekhlyudov came up to the women he saw Maslova; she was in the second row. The first in the row was a short-legged, black-eyed, hideous woman, who had her cloak tucked up in her girdle. This was Koroshavka. The next was a pregnant woman, who dragged herself along with difficulty. The third was Maslova; she was carrying her sack on her shoulder, and looking straight before her. Her face looked calm and determined. The fourth in the row was a young, lovely woman who was walking along briskly, dressed in a short cloak, her kerchief tied in peasant fashion. This was Theodosia.

Nekhlyudov got down and approached the women, meaning to ask Maslova if she had got the things he had sent her, and how she was feeling, but the convoy sergeant, who was walking on that side, noticed him at once, and ran towards him.

'You must not do that, sir. It is against the regulations to approach the gang,' shouted the sergeant as he came up.

But when he recognised Nekhlyudov (everyone in the prison knew Nekhlyudov) the sergeant raised his fingers to his cap, and, stopping in front of Nekhlyudov, said: 'Not now; wait till we get to the railway station; here it is not allowed.'

'Don't lag behind; march!' he shouted to the convicts, and putting on a brisk air, he ran back to his place at a trot, in spite of the heat and the elegant new boots on his feet.

Nekhlyudov went on to the pavement and told the *isvostchik* to follow him; himself walking, so as to keep the convicts in sight. Wherever the gang passed it attracted attention mixed with horror and compassion. Those who drove past leaned out of the vehicles and followed the prisoners with their eyes. Those on foot stopped and looked with fear and surprise at the terrible sight. Some came up and gave alms to the prisoners. The alms were received by the convoy. Some, as if they were hypnotised, followed the gang, but then stopped, shook their heads, and followed the prisoners only with their eyes. Everywhere the people came out of the gates and doors, and called others to come out, too, or leaned out of the windows looking, silent and immovable, at the frightful procession. At a cross-road a fine carriage was stopped by the gang. A fat coachman, with a shiny face and two rows of buttons on his back, sat on the box; a married couple sat facing the horses: the wife a pale, thin woman with a light-coloured bonnet on her head and a bright sunshade in her hand; the husband with a top-hat and a well-cut light-coloured overcoat. On the seat in front sat their children – a well-dressed little girl, with loose, fair hair, and as fresh as a flower, who also held a bright parasol, and an eight-year-old boy, with a long, thin neck and sharp collarbones, a sailor hat with long ribbons on his head.

The father was angrily scolding the coachman because he had not passed in front of the gang when he had a chance, and the mother frowned and half closed her eyes with a look of disgust, shielding herself from the dust and the sun with her silk sunshade, which she held close to her face.

The fat coachman frowned angrily at the unjust rebukes of his master – who had himself given the order to drive along that street – and with difficulty held in the glossy, black horses, foaming under their harness and impatient to go on.

The policeman wished with all his soul to please the owner of the fine equipage by stopping the gang, yet felt that the dismal solemnity of the procession could not be broken even for so rich a gentleman. He only raised his fingers to his cap to show his respect for riches, and looked severely at the prisoners as if promising in any case to protect the owners of the carriage from them. So the carriage had to wait till the whole of the procession had passed, and could only move on when the last of the carts, laden with sacks and prisoners, rattled by. The hysterical woman who sat on one of the carts, and had grown calm, again began shrieking and sobbing when she saw the elegant carriage. Then the coachman tightened the reins with a slight touch, and the black trotters, their shoes ringing against the paving stones, drew the carriage, softly swaying on its rubber tires, towards the country house where the husband, the wife, the girl, and the boy with the sharp collar-bones were going to amuse themselves. Neither the father nor the mother gave the girl and boy any explanation of what they had seen, so that the children had themselves to find out the meaning of this curious sight. The girl, taking the expression of her father's and mother's faces into consideration, solved the problem by assuming that these people were quite another kind of men and women than her father and mother and their acquaintances, that they were bad people, and that they had therefore to be treated in the manner they were being treated.

Therefore the girl felt nothing but fear, and was glad when she could no longer see those people.

But the boy with the long, thin neck, who looked at the procession of prisoners without taking his eyes off them, solved the question differently.

He still knew, firmly and without any doubt, for he had it from God, that these people were just the same kind of people as he was, and like all other people, and therefore someone had done these people some wrong, something that ought not to have been done, and he was sorry for them, and felt no horror either of those who were shaved and chained or of those who had shaved and chained them. And so the boy's lips pouted more and more, and he made greater and greater efforts not to cry, thinking it a shame to cry in such a case.

Chapter 36

The tender mercies of the Lord

Nekhlyudov kept up with the quick pace of the convicts. Though lightly clothed he felt dreadfully hot, and it was hard to breathe in the stifling, motionless, burning air filled with dust.

When he had walked about a quarter of a mile he again got into the trap, but it felt still hotter in the middle of the street. He tried to recall last night's conversation with his brother-in-law, but the recollections no longer excited him as they had done in the morning. They were dulled by the impressions made by the starting and procession of the gang, and chiefly by the intolerable heat.

On the pavement, in the shade of some trees overhanging a fence, he saw two schoolboys standing over a kneeling man who sold ices. One of the boys was already sucking a pink spoon and enjoying his ices, the other was waiting for a glass that was being filled with something yellowish.

'Where could I get a drink?' Nekhlyudov asked his *isvostchik*, feeling an insurmountable desire for some refreshment.

'There is a good eating-house close by,' the *isvostchik* answered, and turning a corner, drove up to a door with a large signboard. The plump clerk in a Russian shirt, who stood behind the counter, and the waiters in their once white clothing who sat at the tables (there being hardly any customers) looked with curiosity at the unusual visitor and offered him their services. Nekhlyudov asked for a bottle of seltzer water and sat down some way from the window at a small table covered with a dirty cloth. Two men sat at another table with tea-things and a white bottle in front of them, mopping their foreheads, and calculating something in a friendly manner. One of them was dark and bald, and had just such a border of hair at the back as Rogozhinsky. This sight again reminded Nekhlyudov of yesterday's talk with his brother-in-law and his wish to see him and Nathalie.

'I shall hardly be able to do it before the train starts,' he thought; 'I'd better write.' He asked for paper, an envelope, and a stamp, and as he was sipping the cool, effervescent water he considered what he should say. But his thoughts wandered, and he could not manage to compose a letter.

> My dear Nathalie – I cannot go away with the heavy impress-
> ion that yesterday's talk with your husband has left. [he began]
> What next? Shall I ask him to forgive me what I said yester-
> day? But I only said what I felt, and he will think that I am
> taking it back. Besides, this interference of his in my private
> matters. . . . No, I cannot,

and again he felt hatred rising in his heart towards that man so foreign to him. He folded the unfinished letter and put it in his pocket, paid, went out, and again got into the trap to catch up the gang. It had grown still hotter. The stones and the walls seemed to be breathing out hot air. The pavement seemed to scorch the feet, and Nekhlyudov felt a burning sensation in his hand when he touched the lacquered splashguard of his trap.

The horse was jogging along at a weary trot, beating the uneven, dusty road monotonously with its hoofs, the *isvostchik* kept falling into a doze, Nekhlyudov sat without thinking of anything.

At the bottom of a street, in front of a large house, a group of people had collected, and a convoy soldier stood by.

'What has happened?' Nekhlyudov asked of a porter.

'Something the matter with a convict.'

Nekhlyudov got down and came up to the group. On the rough stones, where the pavement slanted down to the gutter, lay a broadly-built, red-bearded, elderly convict, with his head lower than his feet, and very red in the face. He had a grey cloak and grey trousers on, and lay on his back with the palms of his freckled hands downwards, and at long intervals his broad, high chest heaved, and he groaned, while his bloodshot eyes were fixed on the sky. By him stood a cross-looking policeman, a pedlar, a postman, a clerk, an old woman with a parasol, and a short-haired boy with an empty basket.

'They are weak. Having been locked up in prison they've got weak, and then they lead them through the most broiling heat,' said the clerk, addressing Nekhlyudov, who had just come up.

'He'll die, most likely,' said the woman with the parasol, in a doleful tone.

'His shirt should be untied,' said the postman.

The policeman began, with his thick, trembling fingers, clumsily to untie the tapes that fastened the shirt round the red, sinewy neck. He was evidently excited and confused, but still thought it necessary to address the crowd.

'What have you collected here for? It is hot enough without your keeping the wind off.'

'They should have been examined by a doctor, and the weak ones left behind,' said the clerk, showing off his knowledge of the law.

The policeman, having undone the tapes of the shirt, rose and looked round.

'Move on, I tell you. It is not your business, is it? What's there to stare at?' he said, and turned to Nekhlyudov for sympathy, but not finding any in his face he turned to the convoy soldier.

But the soldier stood aside, examining the trodden-down heel of his boot, and was quite indifferent to the policeman's perplexity.

'Those whose business it is don't care. Is it right to do men to death like this? A convict is a convict, but still he is a man,' different voices were heard saying in the crowd.

'Put his head up higher, and give him some water,' said Nekhlyudov.

'Water has been sent for,' said the policeman, and taking the prisoner under the arms he with difficulty pulled his body a little higher up.

'What's this gathering here?' said a decided, authoritative voice, and a police officer, with a wonderfully clean, shiny blouse, and still more shiny top-boots, came up to the assembled crowd.

'Move on. No standing about here,' he shouted to the crowd, before he knew what had attracted it.

When he came near and saw the dying convict, he made a sign of approval with his head, just as if he had quite expected it, and, turning to the policeman, said, 'How is this?'

The policeman said that, as a gang of prisoners was passing, one of the convicts had fallen down, and the convoy officer had ordered him to be left behind.

'Well, that's all right. He must be taken to the police station. Call an *isvostchik*.'

'A porter has gone for one,' said the policeman, with his fingers raised to his cap.

The shopman began something about the heat.

'Is it your business, eh? Move on,' said the police officer, and looked so severely at him that the clerk was silenced.

'He ought to have a little water,' said Nekhlyudov. The police officer looked severely at Nekhlyudov also, but said nothing. When the porter brought a mug full of water, he told the policeman to offer some to the convict. The policeman raised the drooping head, and tried to pour a little water down the mouth; but the prisoner could not swallow it, and it ran down his beard, wetting his jacket and his coarse, dirty linen shirt.

'Pour it on his head,' ordered the officer; and the policeman took off the pancake-shaped cap and poured the water over the red curls and bald part of the prisoner's head. His eyes opened wide as if in fear, but his position remained unchanged.

Streams of dirt trickled down his dusty face, but the mouth continued to gasp in the same regular way, and his whole body shook.

'And what's this? Take this one,' said the police officer, pointing to Nekhlyudov's *isvostchik*. 'You, there, drive up.'

'I am engaged,' said the *isvostchik*, dismally, and without looking up.

'It is my *isvostchik*; but take him. I will pay you,' said Nekhlyudov, turning to the *isvostchik*.

'Well, what are you waiting for?' shouted the officer. 'Catch hold.'

The policeman, the porter, and the convoy soldier lifted the dying man and carried him to the trap, and put him on the seat.

But he could not sit up; his head fell back, and the whole of his body glided off the seat.

'Make him lie down,' ordered the officer.

'It's all right, your honour; I'll manage him like this,' said the policeman, sitting down by the dying man, and clasping his strong, right arm round the body under the arms. The convoy soldier lifted the stockingless feet, in prison shoes, and put them into the trap.

The police officer looked around, and noticing the pancake-shaped hat of the convict lifted it up and put it on the wet, drooping head.

'Go on,' he ordered.

The *isvostchik* looked angrily round, shook his head, and, accompanied by the convoy soldier, drove back to the police station. The policeman, sitting beside the convict, kept dragging up the body that was continually sliding down from the seat, while the head swung from side to side.

The convoy soldier, who was walking by the side of the trap, kept putting the legs in their place. Nekhlyudov followed the trap.

Chapter 37

Spilled like water on the ground

The trap passed the fireman who stood sentinel at the entrance,[*] drove into the yard of the police station, and stopped at one of the doors. In the yard several firemen with their sleeves tucked up were washing some kind of cart and talking loudly. When the trap stopped, several policemen surrounded it, and taking the lifeless body of the convict under the arms, took him out of the trap, which creaked under him. The policeman who had brought the body got down, shook his numbed arm, took off his cap, and crossed himself. The body was carried through the door and up the stairs. Nekhlyudov followed. In the small, dirty room where the body was taken there stood four beds. On two of them sat a

---

[*] The headquarters of the fire brigade and the police station are generally together in Moscow.

couple of sick men in dressing-gowns, one with a crooked mouth, whose neck was bandaged, the other one in consumption. Two of the beds were empty; the convict was laid on one of them. A little man, with glistening eyes and continually moving brows, with only his underclothes and stockings on, came up with quick, soft steps, looked at the convict and then at Nekhlyudov, and burst into loud laughter. This was a madman who was being kept in the police hospital.

'They wish to frighten me, but no, they won't succeed,' he said.

The policemen who carried the corpse were followed by a police officer and a medical assistant. The medical assistant came up to the body and touched the freckled hand, already growing cold, which, though still soft, was deadly pale. He held it for a moment, and then let it go. It fell lifelessly on the stomach of the dead man.

'He's ready,' said the medical assistant, but, evidently to be quite in order, he undid the wet, brown shirt, and tossing back the curls from his ear, put it to the yellowish, broad, immovable chest of the convict. All were silent. The medical assistant raised himself again, shook his head, and touched with his fingers first one and then the other lid over the open, fixed blue eyes.

'I'm not frightened, I'm not frightened.' The madman kept repeating these words, and spitting in the direction of the medical assistant.

'Well?' asked the police officer.

'Well! He must he put into the mortuary.'

'Are you sure? Mind,' said the police officer.

'It's time I should know,' said the medical assistant, drawing the shirt over the body's chest. 'However, I will send for Mathew Ivanovitch. Let him have a look. Petrov, call him,' and the medical assistant stepped away from the body.

'Take him to the mortuary,' said the police officer. 'And then you must come into the office and sign,' he added to the convoy soldier, who had not left the convict for a moment.

'Yes, sir,' said the soldier.

The policemen lifted the body and carried it down again. Nekhlyudov wished to follow, but the madman kept him back.

'You are not in the plot! Well, then, give me a cigarette,' he said. Nekhlyudov got out his cigarette case and gave him one.

The madman, quickly moving his brows all the time, began relating how they tormented him by thought-suggestion.

'Why, they are all against me, and torment and torture me through their mediums.'

'I beg your pardon,' said Nekhlyudov, and without listening any further he left the room and went out into the yard, wishing to know where the body would be put.

The policemen with their burden had already crossed the yard, and were coming to the door of a cellar. Nekhlyudov wished to go up to them, but the police officer stopped him.

'What do you want?'

'Nothing.'

'Nothing? Then go away.'

Nekhlyudov obeyed, and went back to his *isvostchik*, who was dozing. He awoke him, and they drove back towards the railway station.

They had not made a hundred steps when they met a cart accompanied by a convoy soldier with a gun. On the cart lay another convict, who was already dead. The convict lay on his back in the cart, his shaved head, from which the pancake-shaped cap had slid over the black-bearded face down to the nose, shaking and thumping at every jolt. The driver, in his heavy boots, walked by the side of the cart, holding the reins; a policeman followed on foot. Nekhlyudov touched his *isvostchik*'s shoulder.

'Just look what they are doing,' said the *isvostchik*, stopping his horse.

Nekhlyudov got down and, following the cart, again passed the sentinel and entered the gate of the police station. By this time the firemen had finished washing the cart, and a tall, bony man, the chief of the fire brigade, with a coloured band round his cap, stood in their place, and with his hands in his pockets, was severely looking at a fat-necked, well-fed bay stallion that was being led up and down before him by a fireman. The stallion was lame on one of his fore feet, and the chief of the firemen was angrily saying something to a veterinary who stood by.

The police officer was also present. When he saw the cart he went up to the convoy soldier.

'Where did you bring him from?' he asked, shaking his head disapprovingly.

'From the Gorbatovskaya,' answered the policeman.

'A prisoner?' asked the chief of the fire brigade.

'Yes. It's the second today.'

'Well, I must say they've got some queer arrangements. Though of course it's a broiling day,' said the chief of the fire brigade; then, turning to the fireman who was leading the lame stallion, he shouted: 'Put him into the corner stall. And as to you, you hound, I'll teach you how to cripple horses which are worth more than you are, you scoundrel.'

The dead man was taken from the cart by the policemen just in the same way as the first had been, and carried upstairs into the hospital. Nekhlyudov followed them as if he were hypnotised.

'What do you want?' asked one of the policemen. But Nekhlyudov did not answer, and followed where the body was being carried. The madman, sitting on a bed, was smoking greedily the cigarette Nekhlyudov had given him.

'Ah, you've come back,' he said, and laughed. When he saw the body he made a face, and said, 'Again! I am sick of it. I am not a boy, am I, eh?' and he turned to Nekhlyudov with a questioning smile.

Nekhlyudov was looking at the dead man, whose face, which had been hidden by his cap, was now visible. This convict was as handsome in face and body as the other was hideous. He was a man in the full bloom of life. Notwithstanding that he was disfigured by the half of his head being shaved, the straight, rather low forehead, raised a bit over the black, lifeless eyes, was very fine, and so was the nose above the thin, black moustaches. There was a smile on the lips that were already growing blue, a small beard outlined the lower part of the face, and on the shaved side of the head a firm, well-shaped ear was visible.

One could see what possibilities of a higher life had been destroyed in this man. The fine bones of his hands and shackled feet, the strong muscles of all his well-proportioned limbs, showed what a beautiful, strong, agile human animal this had been. As an animal merely he had been a far more perfect one of his kind than the bay stallion, about the laming of which the fireman was so angry.

Yet he had been done to death, and no one was sorry for him as a man, nor was anyone sorry that so fine a working animal had perished. The only feeling evinced was that of annoyance because of the bother caused by the necessity of getting this body, threatening putrefaction, out of the way. The doctor and his assistant entered the hospital, accompanied by the inspector of the police station. The doctor was a thick-set man, dressed in pongee silk coat and trousers of the same material, closely fitting his muscular thighs. The inspector was a little fat fellow, with a red face, round as a ball, which he made still broader by a habit he had of filling his cheeks with air, and slowly letting it out again. The doctor sat down on the bed by the side of the dead man, and touched the hands in the same way as his assistant had done, put his ear to the heart, rose, and pulled his trousers straight. 'Could not be more dead,' he said.

The inspector filled his mouth with air and slowly blew it out again.

'Which prison is he from?' he asked the convoy soldier.

The soldier told him, and reminded him of the chains on the dead man's feet.

'I'll have them taken off; we have got a smith about, the Lord be thanked,' said the inspector, and blew up his cheeks again; he went towards the door, slowly letting out the air.

'Why has this happened?' Nekhlyudov asked the doctor.

The doctor looked at him through his spectacles.

'Why has what happened? Why they die of sunstroke, you mean? This is why: they sit all through the winter without exercise and without light, and suddenly they are taken out into the sunshine, and on a day like this, and they march in a crowd so that they get no air, and sunstroke is the result.'

'Then why are they sent out?'

'Oh, as to that, go and ask those who send them. But may I ask who are you?'

'I am a stranger.'

'Ah, well, good-afternoon; I have no time.' The doctor was vexed; he gave his trousers a downward pull, and went towards the beds of the sick.

'Well, how are you getting on?' he asked the pale man with the crooked mouth and bandaged neck.

Meanwhile the madman sat on a bed, and having finished his cigarette, kept spitting in the direction of the doctor.

Nekhlyudov went down into the yard and out of the gate past the firemen's horses and the hens and the sentinel in his brass helmet, and got into the trap, the driver of which had again fallen asleep.

Chapter 38

The convict train

When Nekhlyudov came to the station, the prisoners were all seated in railway carriages with grated windows. Several persons, come to see them off, stood on the platform, but were not allowed to come up to the carriages.

The convoy was much troubled that day. On the way from the prison to the station, besides the two Nekhlyudov had seen, three other prisoners had fallen and died of sunstroke. One was taken to the nearest police station like the first two, and the other two died at the railway station.* The convoy men were not troubled because five men who might have been alive died while in their charge. This did not trouble them, but they were concerned lest anything that the law required in such cases should be omitted. To convey the bodies to the places appointed, to deliver up their papers, to take them off the lists of those to be conveyed to Nijni – all this was very troublesome, especially on so hot a day.

It was this that occupied the convoy men, and before it could all be accomplished Nekhlyudov and the others who asked for leave to go up to the carriages were not allowed to do so. Nekhlyudov, however, was soon allowed to go up, because he tipped the convoy sergeant. The sergeant let Nekhlyudov pass, but asked him to be quick and get his talk over before any of the authorities noticed. There were fifteen carriages in all, and except one carriage for the officials, they were full of prisoners. As Nekhlyudov passed the carriages he listened to what was going on in them. In all the

---

* In Moscow, in the beginning of the eighth decade of this century, five convicts died of sunstroke in one day on their way from the Boutyrki prison to the Nijni railway station.

carriages was heard the clanging of chains, the sound of bustle, mixed with loud and senseless language, but not a word was being said about their dead fellow-prisoners. The talk was all about sacks, drinking water, and the choice of seats.

Looking into one of the carriages, Nekhlyudov saw convoy soldiers taking the manacles off the hands of the prisoners. The prisoners held out their arms, and one of the soldiers unlocked the manacles with a key and took them off; the other collected them.

After he had passed all the other carriages, Nekhlyudov came up to the women's carriages. From the second of these he heard a woman's groans: 'Oh, oh, oh! O God! Oh, oh! O God!'

Nekhlyudov passed this carriage and went up to a window of the third carriage, which a soldier pointed out to him. When he approached his face to the window, he felt the hot air, filled with the smell of perspiration, coming out of it, and heard distinctly the shrill sound of women's voices. All the seats were filled with red, perspiring, loudly-talking women, dressed in prison cloaks and white jackets. Nekhlyudov's face at the window attracted their attention. Those nearest ceased talking and drew closer. Maslova, in her white jacket and her head uncovered, sat by the opposite window. The white-skinned, smiling Theodosia sat a little nearer. When she recognised Nekhlyudov, she nudged Maslova and pointed to the window. Maslova rose hurriedly, threw her kerchief over her black hair, and with a smile on her hot, red face came up to the window and took hold of one of the bars.

'Well, it is hot,' she said, with a glad smile.

'Did you get the things?'

'Yes, thank you.'

'Is there anything more you want?' asked Nekhlyudov, while the air came out of the hot carriage as out of an oven.

'I want nothing, thank you.'

'If we could get a drink?' said Theodosia.

'Yes, if we could get a drink,' repeated Maslova.

'Why, have you not got any water?'

'They put some in, but it is all gone.'

'Directly, I will ask one of the convoy men. Now we shall not see each other till we get to Nijni.'

'Why? Are you going?' said Maslova, as if she did not know it, and looked joyfully at Nekhlyudov.

'I am going by the next train.'

Maslova said nothing, but only sighed deeply.

'Is it true, sir, that twelve convicts have been done to death?' said a severe-looking old prisoner with a deep voice like a man's.

It was Korableva.

'I did not hear of twelve; I have seen two,' said Nekhlyudov.

'They say there were twelve they killed. And will nothing be done to them? Only think! The fiends!'

'And have none of the women fallen ill?' Nekhlyudov asked.

'Women are stronger,' said another of the prisoners – a short little woman – and laughed; 'only there's one that has taken it into her head to be delivered. There she goes,' she said, pointing to the next carriage, whence proceeded the groans.

'You ask if we want anything,' said Maslova, trying to keep the smile of joy from her lips; 'could not this woman be left behind. suffering as she is? There, now, if you would tell the authorities.'

'Yes, I will.'

'And one thing more; could she not see her husband, Taras?' she added, pointing with her eyes to the smiling Theodosia.

'He is going with you, is he not?'

'Sir, you must not talk,' said a convoy sergeant, not the one who had let Nekhlyudov come up. Nekhlyudov left the carriage and went in search of an official to whom he might speak for the woman in travail and about Taras, but could not find him, nor get an answer from any of the convoy for a long time. They were all in a bustle; some were leading a prisoner somewhere or other, others running to get themselves provisions, some were placing their things in the carriages or attending on a lady who was going to accompany the convoy officer, and they answered Nekhlyudov's questions unwillingly. Nekhlyudov found the convoy officer only after the second bell had been rung. The officer with his short arm was wiping the moustaches that covered his mouth and shrugging his shoulders, reproving the corporal for something or other.

'What is it you want?' he asked Nekhlyudov.

'You've got a woman there who is being confined, so I thought best – '

'Well, let her be confined; we shall see later on,' and briskly swinging his short arms, he ran up to his carriage. At the moment the guard passed with a whistle in his hand, and from the people on the platform and from the women's carriages there arose a sound of weeping and words of prayer.

Nekhlyudov stood on the platform by the side of Taras, and looked how, one after the other, the carriages glided past him, with the shaved heads of the men at the grated windows. Then the first of the women's carriages came up, with women's heads at the windows, some covered with kerchiefs and some uncovered, then the second, whence proceeded the same groans, then the carriage where Maslova was. She stood with the others at the window, and looked at Nekhlyudov with a pathetic smile.

Chapter 39

Brother and sister

There were still two hours before the passenger train by which Nekhlyudov was going would start. He had thought of using this interval to see his sister again; but after the impressions of the morning he felt much excited and so done up that, sitting down on a sofa in the first-class refreshment-room, he suddenly grew so drowsy that he turned over on to his side, and, laying his face on his hand, fell asleep at once. A waiter in a dress coat with a napkin in his hand woke him.

'Sir, sir, are you not Prince Nekhlyudov? There's a lady looking for you.'

Nekhlyudov started up and recollected where he was and all that had happened in the morning.

He saw in his imagination the procession of prisoners, the dead bodies, the railway carriages with barred windows, and the women locked up in them, one of whom was groaning in travail with no one to help her, and another who was pathetically smiling at him through the bars.

The reality before his eyes was very different, i.e., a table with vases, candlesticks and crockery, and agile waiters moving round the table, and in the background a cupboard and a counter laden with fruit and bottles, behind it a barman, and in front the backs of

passengers who had come up for refreshments. When Nekhlyudov had risen and sat gradually collecting his thoughts, he
noticed that everybody in the room was inquisitively looking at
something that was passing by the open doors.

He also looked, and saw a group of people carrying a chair on
which sat a lady whose head was wrapped in a kind of airy fabric.

Nekhlyudov thought he knew the footman who was supporting
the chair in front. And also the man behind, and a doorkeeper with
gold cord on his cap, seemed familiar. A lady's maid with a fringe
and an apron, who was carrying a parcel, a parasol, and something
round in a leather case, was walking behind the chair. Then came
Prince Korchagin, with his thick lips, apoplectic neck, and a
travelling cap on his head; behind him Missy, her cousin Misha,
and an acquaintance of Nekhlyudov's – the long-necked diplomat
Osten, with his protruding Adam's apple and his unvarying merry
mood and expression. He was saying something very emphatically,
though jokingly, to the smiling Missy. The Korchagins were
moving from their estate near the city to the estate of the Princess's
sister on the Nijni railway. The procession – the men carrying the
chair, the maid, and the doctor – vanished into the ladies' waiting-
room, evoking a feeling of curiosity and respect in the onlookers.
But the old Prince remained and sat down at the table, called a
waiter, and ordered food and drink. Missy and Osten also remained
in the refreshment-room and were about to sit down, when they
saw an acquaintance in the doorway, and went up to her. It was
Nathalie Rogozhinsky. Nathalie came into the refreshment-room
accompanied by Agraphena Petrovna, and both looked round the
room. Nathalie noticed at one and the same moment both her
brother and Missy. She first went up to Missy, only nodding to her
brother; but, having kissed her, at once turned to him.

'At last I have found you,' she said. Nekhlyudov rose to greet
Missy, Misha, and Osten, and to say a few words to them. Missy
told him about their house in the country having been burnt
down, which necessitated their moving to her aunt's. Osten began
relating a funny story about a fire. Nekhlyudov paid no attention,
and turned to his sister.

'How glad I am that you have come.'

'I have been here a long time,' she said. 'Agraphena Petrovna is
with me.' And she pointed to Agraphena Petrovna, who, in a

waterproof and with a bonnet on her head, stood some way off, and bowed to him with kindly dignity and some confusion, not wishing to intrude.

'We looked for you everywhere.'

'And I had fallen asleep here. How glad I am that you have come,' repeated Nekhlyudov. 'I had begun to write to you.'

'Really?' she said, looking frightened. 'What about?'

Missy and the gentleman, noticing that an intimate conversation was about to commence between the brother and sister, went away. Nekhlyudov and his sister sat down by the window on a velvet-covered sofa, on which lay a plaid, a box, and a few other things.

'Yesterday, after I left you, I felt inclined to return and express my regret, but I did not know how he would take it,' said Nekhlyudov. 'I spoke hastily to your husband, and this tormented me.'

'I knew,' said his sister, 'that you did not mean to. Oh, you know!' and the tears came to her eyes, and she touched his hand. The sentence was not clear, but he understood it perfectly, and was touched by what it expressed. Her words meant that, besides the love for her husband which held her in its sway, she prized and considered important the love she had for him, her brother, and that every misunderstanding between them caused her deep suffering.

'Thank you, thank you. Oh! what I have seen today!' he said, suddenly recalling the second of the dead convicts. 'Two prisoners have been done to death.'

'Done to death? How?'

'Yes, done to death. They led them in this heat, and two died of sunstroke.'

'Impossible! What, today? Just now?'

'Yes, just now. I have seen their bodies.'

'But why done to death? Who killed them?' asked Nathalie.

'They who forced them to go killed them,' said Nekhlyudov, with irritation, feeling that she looked at this, too, with her husband's eyes.

'Oh, Lord!' said Agraphena Petrovna, who had come up to them.

'Yes, we have not the slightest idea of what is being done to these unfortunate beings. But it ought to be known,' added

Nekhlyudov, and looked at old Korchagin, who sat with a napkin tied round him and a bottle before him, and who looked round at Nekhlyudov.

'Nekhlyudov,' he called out, 'won't you join me and take some refreshment? It is excellent before a journey.'

Nekhlyudov refused, and turned away.

'But what are you going to do?' Nathalie continued.

'What I can. I don't know, but I feel I must do something. And I shall do what I am able to.'

'Yes, I understand. And how about them?' she continued, with a smile and a look towards Korchagin. 'Is it possible that it is all over?'

'Completely, and I think without any regret on either side.'

'It is a pity. I am sorry. I am fond of her. However, it's all right. But why do you wish to bind yourself?' she added shyly. 'Why are you going?'

'I go because I must,' answered Nekhlyudov, seriously and dryly, as if wishing to stop this conversation. But he felt ashamed of his coldness towards his sister at once. 'Why not tell her all I am thinking?' he thought, 'and let Agraphena Petrovna also hear it,' he thought, with a look at the old servant, whose presence made the wish to repeat his decision to his sister even stronger.

'You mean my intention to marry Katusha? Well, you see, I made up my mind to do it, but she refuses definitely and firmly,' he said, and his voice shook, as it always did when he spoke of it. 'She does not wish to accept my sacrifice, but is herself sacrificing what in her position means much, and I cannot accept this sacrifice, if it is only a momentary impulse. And so I am going with her, and shall be where she is, and shall try to lighten her fate as much as I can.'

Nathalie said nothing. Agraphena Petrovna looked at her with a questioning look, and shook her head. At this moment the former procession issued from the ladies' room. The same handsome footman (Philip) and the doorkeeper were carrying the Princess Korchagin. She stopped the men who were carrying her, and motioned to Nekhlyudov to approach, and, with a pitiful, languishing air, she extended her white, ringed hand, expecting the firm pressure of his hand with a sense of horror.

'*Épouvantable*!' she said, meaning the heat. 'I cannot stand it! *Ce climat me tue*!' And, after a short talk about the horrors of the Russian climate, she gave the men a sign to go on.

'Be sure and come,' she added, turning her long face towards Nekhlyudov as she was borne away.

The procession with the Princess turned to the right towards the first-class carriages. Nekhlyudov, with the porter who was carrying his things, and Taras with his bag, turned to the left.

'This is my companion,' said Nekhlyudov to his sister, pointing to Taras, whose story he had told her before.

'Surely not third class?' said Nathalie, when Nekhlyudov stopped in front of a third-class carriage, and Taras and the porter with the things went in.

'Yes; it is more convenient for me to be with Taras,' he said. 'One thing more,' he added; 'up to now I have not given the Kousminski land to the peasants; so that, in case of my death, your children will inherit it.'

'Dmitri, don't!' said Nathalie.

'If I do give it away, all I can say is that the rest will be theirs, as it is not likely I shall marry; and if I do marry I shall have no children, so that – '

'Dmitri, don't talk like that!' said Nathalie. And yet Nekhlyudov noticed that she was glad to hear him say it.

Higher up, by the side of a first-class carriage, there stood a group of people still looking at the carriage into which the Princess Korchagin had been carried. Most of the passengers were already seated. Some of the latecomers hurriedly clattered along the boards of the platform, the guard was closing the doors and asking the passengers to get in and those who were seeing them off to come out.

Nekhlyudov entered the hot, smelly carriage, but at once stepped out again on to the small platform at the back of the carriage. Nathalie stood opposite the carriage, with her fashionable bonnet and cape, by the side of Agraphena Petrovna, and was evidently trying to find something to say.

She could not even say '*Écrivez*'. because they had long ago laughed at this word, habitually spoken by those about to part. The short conversation about money matters had in a moment destroyed the tender brotherly and sisterly feelings that had taken hold of them. They felt estranged, so that Nathalie was glad when the train moved; and she could only say, nodding her head with a sad and tender look, 'Goodbye, goodbye, Dmitri.' But as soon as the carriage had passed her she thought of how she should repeat her conversation with her brother to her husband, and her face became serious and troubled.

Nekhlyudov, too, though he had nothing but the kindest feelings for his sister, and had hidden nothing from her, now felt depressed and uncomfortable with her, and was glad to part. He felt that the Nathalie who was once so near to him no longer existed, and in her place was only a slave of that hairy, unpleasant husband, who was so foreign to him. He saw it clearly when her face lit up with peculiar animation as he spoke of what would peculiarly interest her husband, i.e., the giving up of the land to the peasants and the inheritance.

And this made him sad.

Chapter 40

The fundamental law of human life

The heat in the large third-class carriage, which had been standing in the burning sun all day, was so great that Nekhlyudov did not go in, but stopped on the little platform behind the carriage which formed a passage to the next one. But there was not a breath of fresh air here either, and Nekhlyudov breathed freely only when the train had passed the buildings and the draught blew across the platform.

'Yes, killed,' he repeated to himself, the words he had used to his sister. And in his imagination in the midst of all other impressions there arose with wonderful clearness the beautiful face of the second dead convict, with the smile of the lips, the severe expression of the brows, and the small, firm ear below the shaved bluish skull.

And what seemed terrible was that he had been murdered, and no one knew who had murdered him. Yet he had been murdered. He was led out like all the rest of the prisoners by Maslennikov's orders. Maslennikov had probably given the order in the usual manner, had signed with his stupid flourish the paper with the printed heading, and most certainly would not consider himself guilty. Still less would the careful doctor who examined the convicts consider himself guilty. He had performed his duty accurately, and had separated the weak. How could he have foreseen this terrible heat, or the fact that they would start so late in the day and in such crowds? The prison inspector? But the inspector had only carried into execution the order that on a given day a certain number of exiles and convicts – men and women – had to be sent off. The convoy officer could not be guilty either, for his business was to receive a certain number of persons in a certain place, and to deliver up the same number. He conducted them in the usual manner, and could not foresee that two such strong men as those Nekhlyudov saw would not be able to stand it and would die. No one is guilty, and yet the men have been murdered by these people who are not guilty of their murder.

'All this comes,' Nekhlyudov thought, 'from the fact that all these people, governors, inspectors, police officers, and men, consider that there are circumstances in which human relations are not necessary between human beings. All these men, Maslennikov, and the inspector, and the convoy officer, if they were not *governor, inspector, officer,* would have considered twenty times before sending people in such heat in such a mass – would have stopped twenty times on the way, and, seeing that a man was growing weak, gasping for breath, would have led him into the shade, would have given him water and let him rest, and if an accident had still occurred they would have expressed pity. But they not only did not do it, but hindered others from doing it, because they considered not men and their duty towards them but only the office they themselves filled, and held what that office demanded of them to be above human relations. That's what it is,' Nekhlyudov went on in his thoughts. 'If one acknowledges but for a single hour that anything can be more important than love for one's fellow-men, even in some one exceptional case, any crime can be committed without a feeling of guilt.'

Nekhlyudov was so engrossed by his thoughts that he did not notice how the weather changed. The sun was covered over by a low-hanging, ragged cloud. A compact, light grey cloud was rapidly coming from the west, and was already falling in heavy, driving rain on the fields and woods far in the distance. Moisture, coming from the cloud, mixed with the air. Now and then the cloud was rent by flashes of lightning, and peals of thunder mingled more and more often with the rattling of the train. The cloud came nearer and nearer, the rain-drops driven by the wind began to spot the platform and Nekhlyudov's coat; and he stepped to the other side of the little platform, and, inhaling the fresh, moist air – filled with the smell of corn and wet earth that had long been waiting for rain – he stood looking at the gardens, the woods, the yellow rye fields, the green oatfields, the dark-green strips of potatoes in bloom, that glided past. Everything looked as if covered over with varnish – the green turned greener, the yellow yellower, the black blacker.

'More! more!' said Nekhlyudov, gladdened by the sight of gardens and fields revived by the beneficent shower. The shower did not last long. Part of the cloud had come down in rain, part passed over, and the last fine drops fell straight on to the earth. The sun reappeared, everything began to glisten, and in the east – not very high above the horizon – appeared a bright rainbow, with the violet tint very distinct and broken only at one end.

'Why, what was I thinking about?' Nekhlyudov asked himself when all these changes in nature were over, and the train ran into a cutting between two high banks.

'Oh! I was thinking that all those people (inspector, convoy men, all those in the service) are for the greater part kind people – cruel only because they are serving.' He recalled Maslennikov's indifference when he told him about what was being done in the prison, the inspector's severity, the cruelty of the convoy officer when he refused places on the carts to those who asked for them, and paid no attention to the fact that there was a woman in travail in the train. All these people were evidently invulnerable and impregnable to the simplest feelings of compassion only because they held offices. 'As officials they were impermeable to the feelings of humanity, as this paved ground is impermeable to the rain.' Thus thought Nekhlyudov as he looked at the railway embankment paved with stones of different colours, down which the water was running in streams instead of soaking into the earth. 'Perhaps it is necessary to pave the banks with stones, but it is sad to look at the ground, which might be yielding corn, grass, bushes, or trees in the same way as the ground visible up there is doing – deprived of vegetation, and so it is with men,' thought Nekhlyudov. 'Perhaps these governors, inspectors, policemen, are needed, but it is terrible to see men deprived of the chief human attribute, that of love and sympathy for one another. The thing is,' he continued, 'that these people consider lawful what is not lawful, and do not consider the eternal, immutable law, written in the hearts of men by God, as law. That is why I feel so depressed when I am with these people. I am simply afraid of them, and really they are terrible, more terrible than robbers. A robber might, after all, feel pity, but they can feel no pity, they are inured against pity as these stones are against vegetation. That is what makes them terrible. It is said that the Pugatchevs, the Razins * are terrible. These are a thousand times more terrible,' he continued, in his thoughts. 'If a psychological problem were set to find means of making men of our time – Christian, humane, simple, kind people – perform the most horrible crimes without feeling guilty, only one solution could be devised: to go on doing what is being done. It is only necessary that these people should be governors, inspectors, policemen; that they should be fully convinced that there is a kind of business, called government service, which allows men to treat other men as things, without human brotherly relations with them, and also that these people should be so linked together by this government service that the responsibility for the results of their actions should not fall on any one of them separately. Without these conditions, the terrible acts I witnessed today would be impossible in our times. It all lies in the fact that men think there are circumstances in which one may deal with human beings without love; and there are no such circumstances. One may deal with things without love. One may cut down trees, make bricks, hammer iron without love; but you cannot deal with men without it, just as one cannot deal with bees without being careful. If you deal carelessly with bees you will injure them, and will yourself be injured. And so with men. It cannot be otherwise, because natural love is the fundamental law of human life. It is true that a man cannot force another to love

---

* Leaders of rebellions in Russia: Stonka Razin in the 17th and Pugatchev in the 18th century.

him, as he can force him to work for him; but it does not follow that a man may deal with men without love, especially to demand anything from them. If you feel no love, sit still,' Nekhlyudov thought; 'occupy yourself with things, with yourself, with anything you like, only not with men. You can only eat without injuring yourself when you feel inclined to eat, so you can only deal with men usefully when you love. Only let yourself deal with a man without love, as I did yesterday with my brother-in-law, and there are no limits to the suffering you will bring on yourself, as all my life proves. Yes, yes, it is so,' thought Nekhlyudov; 'it is good; yes, it is good,' he repeated, enjoying the freshness after the torturing heat, and conscious of having attained to the fullest clearness on a question that had long occupied him.

Chapter 41

Taras's story

The carriage in which Nekhlyudov had taken his place was half filled with people. There were in it servants, working men, factory hands, butchers, Jews, shopmen, workmen's wives, a soldier, two ladies, a young one and an old one with bracelets on her arm, and a severe-looking gentleman with a cockade on his black cap. All these people were sitting quietly; the bustle of taking their places was long over; some sat cracking and eating sunflower seeds, some smoking, some talking.

Taras sat, looking very happy, opposite the door, keeping a place for Nekhlyudov, and carrying on an animated conversation with a man in a cloth coat who sat opposite to him, and who was, as Nekhlyudov afterwards found out, a gardener going to a new situation. Before reaching the place where Taras sat Nekhlyudov stopped between the seats near a reverend-looking old man with a white beard and nankeen coat, who was talking with a young woman in peasant dress. A little girl of about seven, dressed in a new peasant costume, sat, her little legs dangling above the floor, by the side of the woman, and kept cracking seeds.

The old man turned round, and, seeing Nekhlyudov, he moved the lappets of his coat off the varnished seat next to him, and said, in a friendly manner:

'Please, here's a seat.'

Nekhlyudov thanked him, and took the seat. As soon as he was seated the woman continued the interrupted conversation.

She was returning to her village, and related how her husband, whom she had been visiting, had received her in town.

'I was there during the carnival, and now, by the Lord's help, I've been again,' she said. 'Then, God willing, at Christmas I'll go again.'

'That's right,' said the old man, with a look at Nekhlyudov, 'it's the best way to go and see him, else a young man can easily go to the bad, living in a town.'

'Oh, no, sir, mine is not such a man. No nonsense of any kind about him; his life is as good as a young maiden's. The money he earns he sends home all to a copeck. And, as to our girl here, he was so glad to see her, there are no words for it,' said the woman, and smiled.

The little girl, who sat cracking her seeds and spitting out the shells, listened to her mother's words, and, as if to confirm them, looked up with calm, intelligent eyes into Nekhlyudov's and the old man's faces.

'Well, if he's good, that's better still,' said the old man. 'And none of that sort of thing?' he added, with a look at a couple, evidently factory hands, who sat at the other side of the carriage. The husband, with his head thrown back, was pouring vodka down his throat out of a bottle, and the wife sat holding a bag, out of which they had taken the bottle, and watched him intently.

'No, mine neither drinks nor smokes,' said the woman who was conversing with the old man, glad of the opportunity of praising her husband once more. 'No, sir, the earth does not hold many such.' And, turning to Nekhlyudov, she added, 'That's the sort of man he is.'

'What could be better?' said the old man, looking at the factory worker, who had had his drink and had passed the bottle to his wife. The wife laughed, shook her head, and also raised the bottle to her lips.

Noticing Nekhlyudov's and the old man's look directed towards them, the factory worker addressed the former.

'What is it, sir? That we are drinking? Ah, no one sees how we work, but everyone sees how we drink. I have earned it, and I am drinking and treating my wife, and no one else.'

'Yes, yes,' said Nekhlyudov, not knowing what to say.

'True, sir. My wife is a steady woman. I am satisfied with my wife, because she can feel for me. Is it right what I'm saying, Mavra?'

'There you are, take it, I don't want any more,' said the wife, returning the bottle to him. 'And what are you jawing for like that?' she added.

'There now! She's good – that good; and suddenly she'll begin squeaking like a wheel that's not greased. Mavra, is it right what I'm saying?'

Mavra laughed and moved her hand with a tipsy gesture.

'Oh, my, he's at it again.'

'There now, she's that good – that good; but let her get her tail over the reins, and you can't think what she'll be up to. . . . Is it right what I'm saying? You must excuse me, sir, I've had a drop! What's to be done?' said the factory worker, and, preparing to go to sleep, put his head in his wife's lap.

Nekhlyudov sat a while with the old man, who told him all about himself. The old man was a stove builder, who had been working for fifty-three years, and had built so many stoves that he had lost count, and now he wanted to rest, but had no time. He had been to town and found employment for the young ones, and was now going to the country to see the people at home. After hearing the old man's story, Nekhlyudov went to the place that Taras was keeping for him.

'It's all right, sir; sit down; we'll put the bag here,' said the gardener, who sat opposite Taras, in a friendly tone, looking up into Nekhlyudov's face.

'Rather a tight fit, but no matter since we are friends,' said Taras, smiling, and lifting the bag, which weighed more than five stone, as if it were a feather, he carried it across to the window.

'Plenty of room; besides, we might stand up a bit; and even under the seat it's as comfortable as you could wish. What's the good of humbugging?' he said, beaming with friendliness and kindness.

Taras spoke of himself as being unable to utter a word when quite sober; but drink, he said, helped him to find the right words, and then he could express everything. And in reality, when he was sober Taras kept silent; but when he had been drinking, which happened rarely and only on special occasions, he became very pleasantly talkative. Then he spoke a great deal, spoke well and very simply and truthfully, and especially with great kindliness, which shone in his gentle, blue eyes and in the friendly smile that never left his lips. He was in such a state today. Nekhlyudov's approach interrupted the conversation; but when he had put the bag in its place, Taras sat down again, and with his strong hands folded in his lap, and looking straight into the gardener's face, continued his story. He was telling his new acquaintance about his wife and giving every detail: what she was being sent to Siberia for, and why he was now following her. Nekhlyudov had never heard a detailed account of this affair, and so he listened with interest. When he came up, the story had reached the point when the attempt to poison was already an accomplished fact, and the family had discovered that it was Theodosia's doing.

'It's about my troubles that I'm talking,' said Taras, addressing Nekhlyudov with cordial friendliness. 'I have chanced to come across such a hearty man, and we've got into conversation, and I'm telling him all.'

'I see,' said Nekhlyudov.

'Well, then in this way, my friend, the business became known. Mother, she takes that cake. "I'm going," says she, "to the police officer." My father is a just old man. "Wait, wife," says he, "the little woman is a mere child, and did not herself know what she was doing. We must have pity. She may come to her senses." But, dear me, mother would not hear of it. "While we keep her here," she says, "she may destroy us all like cockroaches." Well, friend, so she goes off for the police officer. He bounces in upon us at once. Calls for witnesses.'

'Well, and you?' asked the gardener.

'Well, I, you see, friend, roll about with the pain in my stomach, and vomit. All my inside is turned inside out; I can't even speak. Well, so father he goes and harnesses the mare, and puts Theodosia into the cart, and is off to the police-station, and then to the magistrate's. And she, you know, just as she had done from the first, so also there, confesses all to the magistrate – where she got the arsenic, and how she kneaded the cake. "Why did you do it?" says he. "Why," says she, "because he's hateful to me. I prefer Siberia to a life with him." That's me,' and Taras smiled.

'Well, so she confessed all. Then, naturally – the prison, and father returns alone. And harvest time just coming, and mother the only woman at home, and she no longer strong. So we think what we are to do. Could we not bail her out? So father went to see an official. No go. Then another. I think he went to five of them, and we thought of giving it up. Then we happened to come across a clerk – such an artful one as you don't often find. "You give me five roubles, and I'll get her out," says he. He agreed to do it for three. Well, and what do you think, friend? I went and pawned the linen she herself had woven, and gave him the money. As soon as he had written that paper,' drawled out Taras, just as if he were speaking of a shot being fired, 'we succeeded at once. I went to fetch her myself. Well, friend, so I got to town, put up the mare, took the paper, and went to the prison. "What do you want?" "This is what I want," say I, "you've got my wife here in prison." "And have you got a paper?" I gave him the paper. He gave it a look. "Wait," says he. So I sat down on a bench. It was already past noon by the sun. An official comes out. "You are Vargushov?" "I am." "Well, you may take her." The gates opened, and they led her out in her own clothes quite all right. "Well, come along. Have you come on foot?" "No, I have the horse here." So I went and paid the ostler, and harnessed, put in all the hay that was left, and covered it with sacking for her to sit on. She got in and wrapped her shawl round her, and off we drove. She says nothing and I say nothing. Just as we were coming up to the house she says, "And how's mother; is she alive?" "Yes, she's alive." "And father; is he alive?" "Yes, he is.' "Forgive me, Taras," she says, "for my folly. I did not myself know what I was doing." So I say, "Words won't mend matters. I have forgiven you long ago," and I said no more. We got home, and she just fell at mother's feet. Mother says, "The Lord will forgive you." And father said, "How d'you do?" and "What's past is past. Live as best you can. Now," says he, "is not the time for all that; there's the harvest to be gathered in down at Skorodino," he says. "Down on the manured acre, by the Lord's help, the ground has borne such rye that the sickle can't tackle it. It's all interwoven and heavy, and has sunk beneath its weight; that must be reaped. You and Taras had better go and see to it tomorrow." Well, friend, from that moment she took to the work and worked so that everyone wondered. At that time we rented three *desiatins*, and by God's help we had a wonderful crop both of oats and rye. I mow and she binds the sheaves, and sometimes we both of us reap. I am good at work and not afraid of it, but she's better still at whatever she takes up. She's a smart woman, young, and full of life; and as to work, friend, she'd grown that eager that I had to stop her. We get home, our fingers swollen, our arms aching, and she, instead of resting, rushes off to the barn to make binders for the sheaves for next day. Such a change!'

'Well, and to you? Was she kinder, now?' asked the gardener.

'That's beyond question. She clings to me as if we were one soul. Whatever I think she understands. Even mother, angry as she was, could not help saying: "It's as if our Theodosia had been transformed; she's quite a different woman now!" We were once going to cart the sheaves with two carts. She and I were in the first, and I say, "How could you think of doing that, Theodosia?" and she says, "How could I think of it? Just so, I did not wish to live with you. I thought I'd rather die than live with you!" I say, "And now?" and she says, "Now you're in my heart!" ' Taras stopped, and smiled joyfully, shook his head as if surprised. 'Hardly had we got the harvest home when I went to soak the hemp, and when I got home there was a summons, she must go to be tried, and we had forgotten all about the matter that she was to be tried for.'

'It can only be the evil one,' said the gardener. 'Could any man of himself think of destroying a living soul? We had a fellow once – ' and the gardener was about to commence his tale when the train began to stop.

'It seems we are coming to a station,' he said. 'I'll go and have a drink.'

The conversation stopped, and Nekhlyudov followed the gardener out of the carriage on to the wet platform of the station.

Chapter 42

Le vrai Grand Monde

Before Nekhlyudov got out he had noticed in the station yard several elegant equipages, some with three, some with four, well-fed horses, with tinkling bells on their harness. When he stepped out on the wet, dark-coloured boards of the platform, he saw a group of people in front of the first-class carriage, among whom were conspicuous a stout lady with costly feathers on her hat, and a waterproof, and a tall, thin-legged young man in a cycling suit. The young man had by his side an enormous, well-fed dog, with a valuable collar. Behind them stood footmen, holding wraps and umbrellas, and a coachman, who had also come to meet the train.

On the whole of the group, from the fat lady down to the coachman who stood holding up his long coat, there lay the stamp of wealth and quiet self-assurance. A curious and servile crowd rapidly gathered round this group – the station-master, in his red cap, a gendarme, a thin young lady in a Russian costume, with beads round her neck, who made a point of seeing the trains come in all through the summer, a telegraph clerk, and passengers, men and women.

In the young man with the dog Nekhlyudov recognised young Korchagin, a *gymnasium* student. The fat lady was the Princess's sister, to whose estate the Korchagins were now moving. The guard, with his gold cord and shiny top-boots, opened the carriage door and stood holding it as a sign of deference, while Philip and a porter with a white apron carefully carried out the long-faced Princess in her folding chair. The sisters greeted each other, and French sentences began flying about. Would the Princess go in a closed or an open carriage? At last the procession started towards the exit, the lady's maid, with her curly fringe, parasol and leather case, in the rear.

Nekhlyudov, not wishing to meet them and to have to take leave over again, stopped before he got to the door, waiting for the procession to pass.

The Princess, her son, Missy, the doctor, and the maid went out first, the old Prince and his sister-in-law remained behind. Nekhlyudov was too far to catch anything but a few disconnected French sentences of their conversation One of the sentences uttered by the Prince, as it often happens, for some unaccountable reason remained in his memory with all its intonations and the sound of the voice.

'*Oh, il est du vrai grand monde, du vrai grand monde,*' said the Prince in his loud, self-assured tone as he went out of the station with his sister-in-law, accompanied by the respectful guards and porters.

At this moment from behind the corner of the station suddenly appeared a crowd of workmen in bark shoes, wearing sheepskin coats and carrying bags on their backs. The workmen went up to the nearest carriage with soft yet determined steps, and were about to get in, but were at once driven away by a guard. Without stopping, the workmen passed on, hurrying and jostling one another, to the next carriage and began getting in, catching their bags against the corners and door of the carriage, but another guard caught sight of them from the door of the station, and shouted at them severely. The workmen, who had already got in, hurried out again and went on, with the same soft and firm steps, still further towards Nekhlyudov's carriage. A guard was again going to stop them, but Nekhlyudov said there was plenty of room inside, and that they had better get in. They obeyed and got in, followed by Nekhlyudov.

The workmen were about to take their seats, when the gentleman with the cockade and the two ladies, looking at this attempt to settle in their carriage as a personal insult to themselves, indignantly protested and wanted to turn them out. The workmen – there were twenty of them, old men and quite young ones, all of them wearied, sunburnt, with haggard faces – began at once to move on through the carriage, catching the seats, the walls, and the doors with their bags. They evidently felt they had offended in some way, and seemed ready to go on indefinitely wherever they were ordered to go.

'Where are you pushing to, you fiends? Sit down here,' shouted another guard they met.

'*Voilà encore des nouvelles*,' exclaimed the younger of the two ladies, quite convinced that she would attract Nekhlyudov's notice by her good French.

The other lady with the bracelets kept sniffing and making faces, and remarked something about how pleasant it was to sit with smelly peasants.

The workmen, who felt the joy and calm experienced by people who have escaped some kind of danger, threw off their heavy bags with a movement of their shoulders and stowed them away under the seats.

The gardener had left his own seat to talk with Taras, and now went back, so that there were two unoccupied seats opposite and one next to Taras. Three of the workmen took these seats, but when Nekhlyudov came up to them, in his gentleman's clothing, they got so confused that they rose to go away, but Nekhlyudov asked them to stay, and himself sat down on the arm of the seat, by the passage down the middle of the carriage.

One of the workmen, a man of about fifty, exchanged a surprised and even frightened look with a young man. That Nekhlyudov, instead of scolding and driving them away, as was natural to a gentleman, should give up his seat to them, astonished and perplexed them. They even feared that this might have some evil result for them.

However, they soon noticed that there was no underlying plot when they heard Nekhlyudov talking quite simply with Taras, and they grew quiet and told one of the lads to sit down on his bag and give his seat to Nekhlyudov. At first the elderly workman who sat opposite Nekhlyudov shrank and drew back his legs for fear of touching the gentleman, but after a while he grew quite friendly, and in talking to him and Taras even slapped Nekhlyudov on the knee when he wanted to draw special attention to what he was saying.

He told them all about his position and his work in the peat bogs, whence he was now returning home. He had been working there for two and a half months, and was bringing home his wages, which only came to ten roubles, since part had been paid beforehand when he was hired. They worked, as he explained, up to their knees in water from sunrise to sunset, with two hours' interval for dinner.

'Those who are not used to it find it hard, of course,' he said; 'but when one's hardened it doesn't matter, if only the food is right. At first the food was bad. Later the people complained, and they got good food, and it was easy to work.'

Then he told them how for twenty-eight years he went out to work, and sent all his earnings home. First to his father, then to his eldest brother, and now to his nephew, who was at the head of the household. On himself he spent only two or three roubles of the fifty or sixty he earned a year, just for luxuries – tobacco and matches.

'I'm a sinner, when tired I even drink a little vodka sometimes,' he added, with a guilty smile.

Then he told them how the women did the work at home, and how the contractor had treated them to half a pail of vodka before they started today, how one of them had died, and another was returning home ill. The sick workman he was talking about was in a corner of the same carriage. He was a young lad, with a pale, sallow face and bluish lips. He was evidently tormented by inter-mittent fever. Nekhlyudov went up to him, but the lad looked up with such a severe and suffering expression that Nekhlyudov did not care to bother him with questions, but advised the elder man to give him quinine, and wrote down the name of the medicine. He wished to give him some money, but the old workman said he would pay for it himself.

'Well, much as I have travelled, I have never met such a gentleman before. Instead of punching your head, he actually gives up his place to you,' said the old man to Taras. 'It seems there are all sorts of gentlefolk, too.'

'Yes, this is quite a new and different world,' thought Nekh-lyudov, looking at these spare, sinewy, limbs, coarse, home-made garments, and sunburnt, kindly, though weary-looking faces, and feeling himself surrounded on all sides with new people and the serious interests, joys, and sufferings of a life of labour.

'Here is *le vrai grand monde*,' thought Nekhlyudov, remembering the words of Prince Korchagin and all that idle, luxurious world to which the Korchagins belonged, with their petty, mean interests. And he felt the joy of a traveller on discovering a new, unknown, and beautiful world.

Part 3

Chapter 1

Maslova makes new friends

The gang of prisoners to which Maslova belonged had walked about three thousand three hundred miles. She and the other prisoners condemned for criminal offences had travelled by rail and by steamboats as far as the town of Perm. It was only here that Nekhlyudov succeeded in obtaining a permission for her to continue the journey with the political prisoners, as Vera Doukhova, who was among the latter, advised him to do. The journey up to Perm had been very trying to Maslova both morally and physically. Physically, because of the overcrowding, the dirt, and the disgusting vermin, which gave her no peace; morally, because of the equally disgusting men. The men, like the vermin, though they changed at each halting-place, were everywhere alike importunate; they swarmed round her, giving her no rest. Among the women prisoners and the men prisoners, the jailers and the convoy soldiers, the habit of a kind of cynical debauch was so firmly established that unless a female prisoner was willing to utilise her position as a woman she had to be constantly on the watch. To be continually in a state of fear and strife was very trying. And Maslova was specially exposed to attacks, her appearance being attractive and her past known to everyone. The decided resistance with which she now met the importunity of all the men seemed offensive to them, and awakened another feeling, that of ill-will towards her. But her position was made a little easier by her intimacy with Theodosia, and Theodosia's husband, who, having heard of the molestations his wife was subject to, had in Nijni been arrested at his own desire in order to be able to protect her, and was now travelling with the gang as a prisoner. Maslova's position became much more bearable when she was allowed to join the political prisoners, who were provided with better accomodations, better food, and were treated less rudely, but besides all

this Maslova's condition was much improved because among
the political prisoners she was no longer molested by the men,
and could live without being reminded of that past which she was
so anxious to forget. But the chief advantage of the change lay in
the fact that she made the acquaintance of several persons who
exercised a decided and most beneficial influence on her character. Maslova was allowed to stop with the political prisoners at all
the halting-places, but being a strong and healthy woman she was
obliged to march with the criminal convicts. In this way she
walked all the way from Tomsk. Two political prisoners also
marched with the gang, Mary Pavlovna Schetinina, the girl with
the hazel eyes who had attracted Nekhlyudov's attention when he
had been to visit Doukhova in prison, and one Simonson, who
was on his way to the Takoutsk district, the dishevelled dark
young fellow with deep-lying eyes, whom Nekhlyudov had also
noticed during that visit. Mary Pavlovna was walking because she
had given her place on the cart to one of the criminals, a woman
expecting to be confined, and Simonson because he did not dare
to avail himself of a class privilege.

These three always started early in the morning before the rest
of the political prisoners, who followed later on in the carts.

They were ready to start in this way just outside a large town,
where a new convoy officer had taken charge of the gang.

It was early on a dull September morning. It kept raining and
snowing alternately, and the cold wind blew in sudden gusts. The
whole gang of prisoners, consisting of four hundred men and fifty
women, was already assembled in the court of the halting station.
Some of them were crowding round the chief of the convoy, who
was giving to specially appointed prisoners money for two days'
keep to distribute among the rest, while others were purchasing
food from women who had been let into the courtyard. One
could hear the voices of the prisoners counting their money and
making their purchases, and the shrill voices of the women with
the food.

Simonson, in his rubber jacket and rubber overshoes fastened
with a string over his worsted stockings (he was a vegetarian and
would not wear the skin of slaughtered animals), was also in the
courtyard waiting for the gang to start. He stood by the porch and
jotted down in his notebook a thought that had occurred to him.

This was what he wrote: 'If a bacterium watched and examined a human nail it would pronounce it inorganic matter, and thus we, examining our globe and watching its crust, pronounce it to be inorganic. This is incorrect.'

Katusha and Mary Pavlovna, both wearing top-boots and with shawls tied round their heads, came out of the building into the courtyard where the women sat sheltered from the wind by the northern wall of the court, and vied with one another, offering their goods, hot meat pie, fish, vermicelli, buckwheat porridge, liver, beef, eggs, milk. One had even a roast pig to offer.

Having bought some eggs, bread, fish, and some rusks, Maslova was putting them into her bag, while Mary Pavlovna was paying the women, when a movement arose among the convicts. All were silent and took their places. The officer came out and began giving the last orders before starting. Everything was done in the usual manner. The prisoners were counted, the chains on their legs examined, and those who were to march in couples linked together with manacles. But suddenly the angry, authoritative voice of the officer shouting something was heard, also the sound of a blow and the crying of a child. All was silent for a moment and then came a hollow murmur from the crowd. Maslova and Mary Pavlovna advanced towards the spot whence the noise proceeded.

Chapter 2

An incident of the march

This is what Mary Pavlovna and Katusha saw when they came up to the scene whence the noise proceeded. The officer, a sturdy fellow, with fair moustaches, stood uttering words of foul and coarse abuse, and rubbing with his left the palm of his right hand, which he had hurt in hitting a prisoner on the face. In front of him a thin, tall convict, with half his head shaved and dressed in a cloak too short for him and trousers much too short, stood wiping his bleeding face with one hand, and holding a little shrieking girl wrapped in a shawl with the other.

'I'll give it you' (foul abuse); 'I'll teach you to reason' (more abuse); 'you're to give her to the women!' shouted the officer. 'Now, then, on with them.'

The convict, who was exiled by the commune, had been carrying his little daughter all the way from Tomsk, where his wife had died of typhus, and now the officer ordered him to be manacled. The exile's explanation that he could not carry the child if he was manacled irritated the officer, who happened to be in a bad temper, and he gave the troublesome prisoner a beating.[*] Before the injured convict stood a convoy soldier, and a black-bearded prisoner with manacles on one hand and a look of gloom on his face, which he turned now to the officer, now to the prisoner with the little girl.

The officer repeated his orders for the soldiers to take away the girl. The murmur among the prisoners grew louder.

'All the way from Tomsk they were not put on,' came a hoarse voice from someone in the rear. 'It's a child, and not a puppy.'

'What's he to do with the lassie? That's not the law,' said someone else.

'Who's that?' shouted the officer as if he had been stung, and rushed into the crowd.

'I'll teach you the law. Who spoke. You? You?'

'Everybody says so, because – ' said a short, broad-faced prisoner. Before he had finished speaking the officer hit him in the face.

'Mutiny, is it? I'll show you what mutiny means. I'll have you all shot like dogs, and the authorities will be only too thankful. Take the girl.'

The crowd was silent. One convoy soldier pulled away the girl, who was screaming desperately, while another manacled the prisoner, who now submissively held out his hand.

'Take her to the women,' shouted the officer, arranging his sword belt.

The little girl, whose face had grown quite red, was trying to disengage her arms from under the shawl, and screamed unceasingly. Mary Pavlovna stepped out from among the crowd and came up to the officer.

'Will you allow me to carry the little girl?' she said.

'Who are you?' asked the officer.

* A fact described by Linev in his *Transportation*.

'A political prisoner.'

Mary Pavlovna's handsome face, with the beautiful prominent eyes (he had noticed her before when the prisoners were given into his charge), evidently produced an effect on the officer. He looked at her in silence as if considering, then said: 'I don't care; carry her if you like. It is easy for you to show pity; if he ran away who would have to answer?'

'How could he run away with the child in his arms?' said Mary Pavlovna.

'I have no time to talk with you. Take her if you like.'

'Shall I give her?' asked the soldier.

'Yes, give her.'

'Come to me,' said Mary Pavlovna, trying to coax the child to come to her.

But the child in the soldier's arms stretched herself towards her father and continued to scream, and would not go to Mary Pavlovna.

'Wait a bit, Mary Pavlovna,' said Maslova, getting a rusk out of her bag; 'she will come to me.'

The little girl knew Maslova, and when she saw her face and the rusk she let her take her. All was quiet. The gates were opened, and the gang stepped out, the convoy counted the prisoners over again, the bags were packed and tied on to the carts, the weak seated on the top. Maslova with the child in her arms took her place among the women next to Theodosia. Simonson, who had all the time been watching what was going on, stepped with large, determined strides up to the officer, who, having given his orders, was just getting into a trap, and said, 'You have behaved badly.'

'Get to your place; it is no business of yours.'

'It is my business to tell you that you have behaved badly and I have said it,' said Simonson, looking intently into the officer's face from under his bushy eyebrows.

'Ready? March!' the officer called out, paying no heed to Simonson, and, taking hold of the driver's shoulder, he got into the trap. The gang started and spread out as it stepped on to the muddy high road with ditches on each side, which passed through a dense forest.

Chapter 3

Mary Pavlovna

In spite of the hard conditions in which they were placed, life among the political prisoners seemed very good to Katusha after the depraved, luxurious and effeminate life she had led in town for the last six years, and after two months' imprisonment with criminal prisoners. The fifteen to twenty miles they did per day, with one day's rest after two days' marching, strengthened her physically, and the fellowship with her new companions opened out to her a life full of interests such as she had never dreamed of. People so wonderful (as she expressed it) as those whom she was now going with she had not only never met but could not even have imagined.

'There now, and I cried when I was sentenced,' she said. 'Why, I must thank God for it all the days of my life. I have learned to know what I never should have found out else.'

The motives she understood easily and without effort that guided these people, and, being of the people, fully sympathised with them. She understood that these persons were for the people and against the upper classes, and though themselves belonging to the upper classes had sacrificed their privileges, their liberty and their lives for the people. This especially made her value and admire them. She was charmed with all the new companions, but particularly with Mary Pavlovna, and she was not only charmed with her, but loved her with a peculiar, respectful and rapturous love. She was struck by the fact that this beautiful girl, the daughter of a rich general, who could speak three languages, gave away all that her rich brother sent her, and lived like the simplest working girl, and dressed not only simply, but poorly, paying no heed to her appearance. This trait and a complete absence of coquetry was particularly surprising and therefore attractive to Maslova. Maslova could see that Mary Pavlovna knew, and was even pleased to know, that she was handsome, and yet the effect her appearance had on men was not at all pleasing to her; she was even afraid of it, and felt an absolute disgust to all love affairs. Her men companions knew it, and if they felt attracted by her never permitted themselves to show it to her, but treated her as they would a man; but with strangers, who often molested her, the great physical strength on which she prided herself stood her in good stead.

'It happened once,' she said to Katusha, 'that a man followed me in the street and would not leave me on any account. At last I gave him such a shaking that he was frightened and ran away.'

She became a revolutionary, as she said, because she felt a dislike to the life of the well-to-do from childhood up, and loved the life of the common people, and she was always being scolded for spending her time in the servants' hall, in the kitchen or the stables instead of the drawing-room.

'And I found it amusing to be with cooks and the coachmen, and dull with our gentlemen and ladies,' she said. 'Then when I came to understand things I saw that our life was altogether wrong; I had no mother and I did not care for my father, and so when I was nineteen I left home, and went with a girl friend to work as a factory hand.'

After she left the factory she lived in the country, then returned to town and lived in a lodging, where they had a secret printing press. There she was arrested and sentenced to hard labour. Mary Pavlovna said nothing about it herself, but Katusha heard from others that Mary Pavlovna was sentenced because, when the lodging was searched by the police and one of the revolutionists fired a shot in the dark, she pleaded guilty.

As soon as she had learned to know Mary Pavlovna, Katusha noticed that, whatever the conditions she found herself in, Mary Pavlovna never thought of herself, but was always anxious to serve, to help someone, in matters small or great. One of her present companions, Novodvorov, said of her that she devoted herself to philanthropic amusements. And this was true. The interest of her whole life lay in the search for opportunities of serving others. This kind of amusement had become the habit, the business of her life. And she did it all so naturally that those who knew her no longer valued but simply expected it of her.

When Maslova first came among them, Mary Pavlovna felt repulsed and disgusted. Katusha noticed this, but she also noticed that, having made an effort to overcome these feelings, Mary Pavlovna became particularly tender and kind to her. The tenderness and kindness of so uncommon a being touched Maslova so much that she gave her whole heart, and unconsciously accepting her views, could not help imitating her in everything.

This devoted love of Katusha touched Mary Pavlovna in her turn, and she learned to love Katusha.

These women were also united by the repulsion they both felt to sexual love. The one loathed that kind of love, having experienced all its horrors, the other, never having experienced it, looked on it as something incomprehensible and at the same time as something repugnant and offensive to human dignity.

Chapter 4

Simonson

Mary Pavlovna's influence was one that Maslova submitted to because she loved Mary Pavlovna. Simonson influenced her because he loved her.

Everybody lives and acts partly according to his own, partly according to other people's, ideas. This is what constitutes one of the great differences among men. To some, thinking is a kind of mental game; they treat their reason as if it were a fly-wheel without a connecting strap, and are guided in their actions by other people's ideas, by custom or laws; while others look upon their own ideas as the chief motive power of all their actions, and always listen to the dictates of their own reason and submit to it, accepting other people's opinions only on rare occasions and after weighing them critically. Simonson was a man of the latter sort; he settled and verified everything according to his own reason and acted on the decisions he arrived at. When a schoolboy he made up his mind that his father's income, made as a paymaster in government office, was dishonestly gained, and he told his father that it ought to be given to the people. When his father, instead of listening to him, gave him a scolding, he left his father's house and would not make use of his father's means. Having come to the conclusion that all the existing misery was a result of the people's ignorance, he joined the socialists, who carried on propaganda among the people, as soon as he left the university and got a place as a village schoolmaster. He taught and explained to his pupils and to the peasants what he considered to be just, and openly blamed what he thought unjust. He was arrested and tried. During his trial he determined to tell his judges that his was a just cause, for which he ought not to be tried or punished. When the judges paid no heed to his words, but went on with the trial, he decided not to answer them and kept resolutely silent when they questioned him. He was exiled to the government of Archangel. There he formulated a religious teaching which was founded on the theory that everything in the world was alive, that nothing is lifeless, and that all the objects we consider to be without life or inorganic are only parts of an enormous organic body which we cannot compass. A man's task is to sustain the life of that huge organism and all its animate parts. Therefore he was against war, capital punishment and every kind of killing, not only of human beings, but also of animals. Concerning marriage, too, he had a peculiar idea of his own; he thought that increase was a lower function of man, the highest function being to serve the already existing lives. He found a confirmation of his theory in the fact that there were phagocytes in the blood. Celibates, according to his opinion, were the same as phagocytes, their function being to help the weak and the sickly particles of the organism. From the moment he came to this conclusion he began to consider himself as well as Mary Pavlovna as phagocytes, and to live accordingly, though as a youth he had been addicted to vice. His love for Katusha did not infringe this conception, because he loved her platonically, and such love he considered could not hinder his activity as a phagocyte, but acted, on the contrary, as an inspiration.

Not only moral, but also most practical questions he decided in his own way. He applied a theory of his own to all practical business, had rules relating to the number of hours for rest and for work, to the kind of food to eat, the way to dress, to heat and light up the rooms. With all this Simonson was very shy and modest; and yet when he had once made up his mind nothing could make him waver. And this man had a decided influence on Maslova through his love for her. With a woman's instinct Maslova very soon found out that he loved her. And the fact that she could awaken love in a man of that kind raised her in her own estimation. It was Nekhlyudov's magnanimity and what had been in the past that made him offer to marry her, but Simonson loved her such as she was now, loved her simply because of the love he bore her. And she felt that Simonson considered her to be an exceptional woman, having peculiarly high moral qualities. She did not quite know what the qualities he attributed to her were, but in order to be on the safe side and that he should not be disappointed in her, she tried with all her might to awaken in herself all the highest qualities she could conceive, and she tried to be as good as possible. This had begun while they were still in prison, when on a common visiting day she had noticed his kindly dark blue eyes gazing fixedly at her from under his projecting brow. Even then she had noticed that this was a peculiar man, and that he was looking at her in a peculiar manner, and had also noticed the striking combination of sternness – the unruly hair and the frowning forehead gave him this appearance – with the child-like kindness and innocence of his look. She saw him again in Tomsk, where she joined the political prisoners. Though they had not uttered a word, their looks told plainly that they had understood one another. Even after that they had had no serious conversation with each other, but Maslova felt that when he spoke in her presence his words were addressed to her, and that he spoke for her sake, trying to express himself as plainly as he could; but it was when he started walking with the criminal prisoners that they grew specially near to one another.

Chapter 5

The political prisoners

Until they left Perm Nekhlyudov only twice managed to see Katusha, once in Nijni, before the prisoners were embarked on a barge surrounded with a wire netting, and again in Perm in the prison office. At both these interviews he found her reserved and unkind. She answered his questions as to whether she was in want of anything, and whether she was comfortable, evasively and bashfully, and, as he thought, with the same feeling of hostile reproach which she had shown several times before. Her depressed state of mind, which was only the result of the molestations from the men that she was undergoing at the time, tormented Nekhlyudov. He feared lest, influenced by the hard and degrading circumstances in which she was placed on the journey, she should again get into that state of despair and discord with her own self which formerly made her irritable with him, and which had caused her to drink and smoke excessively to gain oblivion. But he was unable to help her in any way during this part of the journey, as it was impossible for him to be with her. It was only when she joined the political prisoners that he saw how unfounded his fears were, and at each interview he noticed that inner change he so strongly desired to see in her becoming more and more marked. The first time they met in Tomsk she was again just as she had been when leaving Moscow. She did not frown or become confused when she saw him, but met him joyfully and simply, thanking him for what he had done for her, especially for bringing her among the people with whom she now was.

After two months' marching with the gang, the change that had taken place within her became noticeable in her appearance. She grew sunburned and thinner, and seemed older; wrinkles appeared on her temples and round her mouth. She had no ringlets on her forehead now, and her hair was covered with the kerchief; in the way it was arranged, as well as in her dress and her manners, there was no trace of coquetry left. And this change, which had taken place and was still progressing in her, made Nekhlyudov very happy.

He felt for her something he had never experienced before. This feeling had nothing in common with his first poetic love for her, and even less with the sensual love that had followed, nor even with the satisfaction of a duty fulfilled, not unmixed with self-admiration, with which he decided to marry her after the trial. The present feeling was simply one of pity and tenderness. He had felt it when he met her in prison for the first time, and then again when, after conquering his repugnance, he forgave her the imagined intrigue with the medical assistant in the hospital (the injustice done her had since been discovered); it was the same feeling he now had, only with this difference, that formerly it was momentary, and that now it had become permanent. Whatever he was doing, whatever he was thinking now, a feeling of pity and tenderness dwelt with him, and not only pity and tenderness for her, but for everybody. This feeling seemed to have opened the floodgates of love, which had found no outlet in Nekhlyudov's soul, and the love now flowed out to everyone he met.

During this journey Nekhlyudov's feelings were so stimulated that he could not help being attentive and considerate to everybody, from the coachman and the convoy soldiers to the prison inspectors and governors whom he had to deal with. Now that Maslova was among the political prisoners, Nekhlyudov could not help becoming acquainted with many of them, first in Ekaterinburg, where they had a good deal of freedom and were kept altogether in a large cell, and then on the road when Maslova was marching with three of the men and four of the women. Coming in contact with political exiles in this way made Nekhlyudov completely change his mind concerning them.

From the very beginning of the revolutionary movement in Russia, but especially since that First of March, when Alexander II was murdered, Nekhlyudov regarded the revolutionists with dislike and contempt. He was repulsed by the cruelty and secrecy of the methods they employed in their struggles against the government, especially the cruel murders they committed, and their arrogance also disgusted him. But having learned more intimately to know them and all they had suffered at the hands of the government, he saw that they could not be other than they were.

Terrible and endless as were the torments which were inflicted on the criminals, there was at least some semblance of justice shown them before and after they were sentenced, but in the case of the political prisoners there was not even that semblance, as Nekhlyudov saw in the case of Sholostova and that of many and many of his new acquaintances. These people were dealt with like fish caught with a net; everything that gets into the nets is pulled ashore, and then the big fish which are required are sorted out and the little ones are left to perish unheeded on the shore. Having captured hundreds that were evidently guiltless, and that could not be dangerous to the government, they left them imprisoned for years, where they became consumptive, went out of their minds or committed suicide; and kept them only because they had no inducement to set them free, while they might be of use to elucidate some question at a judicial inquiry, safe in prison. The fate of these persons, often innocent even from the government point of view, depended on the whim, the humour of, or the amount of leisure at the disposal of, some police officer or spy, or public prosecutor, or magistrate, or governor, or minister. Some one of these officials feels dull, or inclined to distinguish himself, and makes a number of arrests, and imprisons or sets free, according to his own fancy or that of the higher authorities. And the higher official, actuated by like motives, according to whether he is inclined to distinguish himself, or to what his relations to the minister are, exiles men to the other side of the world or keeps them in solitary confinement, condemns them to Siberia, to hard labour, to death, or sets them free at the request of some lady.

They were dealt with as in war, and they naturally employed the means that were used against them. And as the military men live in an atmosphere of public opinion that not only conceals from them the guilt of their actions, but sets these actions up as feats of heroism, so these political offenders were also constantly surrounded by an atmosphere of public opinion which made the cruel actions they committed, in the face of danger and at the risk of liberty and life, and all that is dear to men, seem not wicked but glorious actions. Nekhlyudov found in this the explanation of the surprising phenomenon that men with the mildest characters, who seemed incapable of witnessing the sufferings of any living creature, much less of inflicting pain, quietly prepared to murder men, nearly all of them considering murder lawful and just on certain occasions as a means for self-defence, for the attainment of higher aims or for the general welfare.

The importance they attributed to their cause, and consequently to themselves, flowed naturally from the importance the government attached to their actions, and the cruelty of the punishments it inflicted on them. When Nekhlyudov came to know them better he became convinced that they were not the right-down villains that some imagined them to be, nor the complete heroes that others thought them, but ordinary people, just the same as others, among whom there were some good and some bad, and some mediocre, as there are everywhere.

There were some among them who had turned revolutionists because they honestly considered it their duty to fight the existing evils, but there were also those who chose this work for selfish, ambitious motives; the majority, however, was attracted to the revolutionary idea by the desire for danger, for risks, the enjoyment of playing with one's life, which, as Nekhlyudov knew from his military experiences, is quite common to the most ordinary people while they are young and full of energy. But wherein they differed from ordinary people was that their moral standard was a higher one than that of ordinary men. They considered not only self-control, hard living, truthfulness, but also the readiness to sacrifice everything, even life, for the common welfare as their duty. Therefore the best among them stood on a moral level that is not often reached, while the worst were far below the ordinary level, many of them being untruthful, hypocritical and at the same time self-satisfied and proud. So that Nekhlyudov learned not only to respect but to love some of his new acquaintances, while he remained more than indifferent to others.

Chapter 6

Kryltzov's story

Nekhlyudov grew especially fond of Kryltzov, a consumptive young man condemned to hard labour, who was going with the same gang as Katusha. Nekhlyudov had made his acquaintance already in Ekaterinburg, and talked with him several times on the road after that. Once, in summer, Nekhlyudov spent nearly the whole of a day with him at a halting station, and Kryltzov, having once started talking, told him his story and how he had become a revolutionist. Up to the time of his imprisonment his story was soon told. He lost his father, a rich landed proprietor in the south of Russia, when still a child. He was the only son, and his mother brought him up. He learned easily in the university, as well as the gymnasium, and was first in the mathematical faculty in his year. He was offered a choice of remaining in the university or going abroad. He hesitated. He loved a girl and was thinking of marriage, and taking part in the rural administration. He did not like giving up either offer, and could not make up his mind. At this time his fellow-students at the university asked him for money for a common cause. He did not know that this common cause was revolutionary, which he was not interested in at that time, but gave the money from a sense of comradeship and vanity, so that it should not be said that he was afraid. Those who received the money were caught, a note was found which proved that the money had been given by Kryltzov. he was arrested, and first kept at the police station, then imprisoned.

'The prison where I was put,' Kryltzov went on to relate (he was sitting on the high shelf bedstead, his elbows on his knees, with sunken chest, the beautiful, intelligent eyes with which he looked at Nekhlyudov glistening feverishly) 'they were not specially strict in that prison. We managed to converse, not only by tapping the wall, but could walk about the corridors, share

our provisions and our tobacco, and in the evenings we even sang
in chorus. I had a fine voice – yes, if it had not been for mother it
would have been all right, even pleasant and interesting. Here I
made the acquaintance of the famous Petrov – he afterwards killed
himself with a piece of glass at the fortress – and also of others. But
I was not yet a revolutionary. I also became acquainted with my
neighbours in the cells next to mine. They were both caught with
Polish proclamations and arrested in the same cause, and were
tried for an attempt to escape from the convoy when they were
being taken to the railway station. One was a Pole, Lozinsky;
the other a Jew, Rozovsky. Yes. Well, this Rozovsky was quite
a boy. He said he was seventeen, but he looked fifteen – thin,
small, active, with black, sparkling eyes, and, like most Jews, very
musical. His voice was still breaking, and yet he sang beautifully.
Yes. I saw them both taken to be tried. They were taken in the
morning. They returned in the evening, and said they were
condemned to death. No one had expected it. Their case was so
unimportant; they only tried to get away from the convoy, and
had not even wounded anyone. And then it was so unnatural to
execute such a child as Rozovsky. And we in prison all came to the
conclusion that it was only done to frighten them, and would not
be confirmed. At first we were excited, and then we comforted
ourselves, and life went on as before. Yes. Well, one evening, a
watchman comes to my door and mysteriously announces to me
that carpenters had arrived, and were putting up the gallows. At
first I did not understand. What's that? What gallows? But the
watchman was so excited that I saw at once it was for our two. I
wished to tap and communicate with my comrades, but was afraid
those two would hear. The comrades were also silent. Evidently
everybody knew. In the corridors and in the cells everything was
as still as death all that evening. They did not tap the wall nor sing.
At ten the watchman came again and announced that a hangman
had arrived from Moscow. He said it and went away. I began
calling him back. Suddenly I hear Rozovsky shouting to me across
the corridor: "What's the matter? Why do you call him?" I
answered something about asking him to get me some tobacco,
but he seemed to guess, and asked me: "Why did we not sing
tonight, why did we not tap the walls?" I do not remember what I
said, but I went away so as not to speak to him. Yes. It was a

terrible night. I listened to every sound all night. Suddenly,
towards morning, I hear doors opening and somebody walking –
many persons. I went up to my window. There was a lamp
burning in the corridor. The first to pass was the inspector. He
was stout, and seemed a resolute, self-satisfied man, but he looked
ghastly pale, downcast, and seemed frightened; then his assistant,
frowning but resolute; behind them the watchman. They passed
my door and stopped at the next, and I hear the assistant calling
out in a strange voice: "Lozinsky, get up and put on clean linen."
Yes. Then I hear the creaking of the door; they entered into his
cell. Then I hear Lozinsky's steps going to the opposite side of the
corridor. I could only see the inspector. He stood quite pale, and
buttoned and unbuttoned his coat, shrugging his shoulders. Yes.
Then, as if frightened of something, he moved out of the way.
It was Lozinsky, who passed him and came up to my door. A
handsome young fellow he was, you know, of that nice Polish
type: broad-shouldered, his head covered with fine, fair, curly hair
as with a cap, and with beautiful blue eyes. So blooming, so fresh,
so healthy. He stopped in front of my window, so that I could see
the whole of his face. A dreadful, gaunt, livid face. "Kryltzov,
have you any cigarettes?" I wished to pass him some, but the
assistant hurriedly pulled out his cigarette case and passed it to
him. He took out one, the assistant struck a match, and he lit the
cigarette and began to smoke and seemed to be thinking. Then, as
if he had remembered something, he began to speak. "It is cruel
and unjust. I have committed no crime. I – " I saw something
quiver in his white young throat, from which I could not take my
eyes, and he stopped. Yes. At that moment I hear Rozovsky
shouting in his fine, Jewish voice. Lozinsky threw away the
cigarette and stepped from the door. And Rozovsky appeared at
the window. His childish face, with the limpid black eyes, was
red and moist. He also had clean linen on, the trousers were too
wide, and he kept pulling them up and trembled all over. He
approached his pitiful face to my window. "Kryltzov, it's true that
the doctor has prescribed cough mixture for me, is it not? I am not
well. I'll take some more of the mixture." No one answered, and
he looked inquiringly, now at me, now at the inspector. What he
meant to say I never made out. Yes. Suddenly the assistant again
put on a stern expression, and called out in a kind of squeaking

tone: "Now, then, no nonsense. Let us go." Rozovsky seemed incapable of understanding what awaited him, and hurried, almost ran, in front of him all along the corridor. But then he drew back, and I could hear his shrill voice and his cries, then the trampling of feet, and general hubbub. He was shrieking and sobbing. The sounds came fainter and fainter, and at last the door rattled and all was quiet. Yes. And so they hanged them. Throttled them both with a rope. A watchman, another one, saw it done, and told me that Lozinsky did not resist, but Rozovsky struggled for a long time, so that they had to pull him up on to the scaffold and to force his head into the noose. Yes. This watchman was a stupid fellow. He said: "They told me, sir, that it would be frightful, but it was not at all frightful. After they were hanged they only shrugged their shoulders twice, like this." He showed how the shoulders convulsively rose and fell. "Then the hangman pulled a bit so as to tighten the noose, and it was all up, and they never budged." ' And Kryltzov repeated the watchman's words, 'Not at all frightful', and tried to smile, but burst into sobs instead.

For a long time after that he kept silent, breathing heavily, and repressing the sobs that were choking him.

'From that time I became a revolutionist. Yes,' he said, when he was quieter and finished his story in a few words. He belonged to the Narodovoltzy party, and was even at the head of the disorganising group, whose object was to terrorise the government so that it should give up its power of its own accord. With this object he travelled to Petersburg, to Kiev, to Odessa and abroad, and was everywhere successful. A man in whom he had full confidence betrayed him. He was arrested, tried, kept in prison for two years, and condemned to death, but the sentence was mitigated to one of hard labour for life.

He went into consumption while in prison, and in the conditions he was now placed he had scarcely more than a few months longer to live. This he knew, but did not repent of his action, but said that if he had another life he would use it in the same way to destroy the conditions in which such things as he had seen were possible.

This man's story and his intimacy with him explained to Nekhlyudov much that he had not previously understood.

Chapter 7

Nekhlyudov seeks an interview with Maslova

On the day when the convoy officer had the encounter with the prisoners at the halting station about the child, Nekhlyudov, who had spent the night at the village inn, woke up late, and was some time writing letters to post at the next government town, so that he left the inn later than usual, and did not catch up with the gang on the road as he had done previously, but came to the village where the next halting station was as it was growing dusk.

Having dried himself at the inn, which was kept by an elderly woman who had an extraordinarily fat, white neck, he had his tea in a clean room decorated with a great number of icons and pictures and then hurried away to the halting station to ask the officer for an interview with Katusha. At the last six halting stations he could not get the permission for an interview from any of the officers. Though they had been changed several times, not one of them would allow Nekhlyudov inside the halting stations, so that he had not seen Katusha for more than a week. This strictness was occasioned by the fact that an important prison official was expected to pass that way. Now this official had passed without looking in at the gang, after all, and Nekhlyudov hoped that the officer who had taken charge of the gang in the morning would allow him an interview with the prisoners, as former officers had done.

The landlady offered Nekhlyudov a trap to drive him to the halting station, situated at the farther end of the village, but Nekhlyudov preferred to walk. A young labourer, a broad-shouldered young fellow of herculean dimensions, with enormous top-boots freshly blackened with strongly smelling tar, offered himself as a guide.

A dense mist obscured the sky, and it was so dark that when the young fellow was three steps in advance of him Nekhlyudov could not see him unless the light of some window happened to fall on the spot, but he could hear the heavy boots wading through the deep, sticky slush. After passing the open place in front of the church and the long street, with its rows of windows shining brightly in the darkness, Nekhlyudov followed his guide to the outskirts of the village, where it was pitch dark. But soon here, too, rays of light, streaming through the mist from the lamps in the front of the halting station, became discernible through the darkness. The reddish spots of light grew bigger and bigger; at last the stakes of the palisade, the moving figure of the sentinel, a post painted with white and black stripes and the sentinel's box became visible.

The sentinel called his usual 'Who goes there?' as they approached, and seeing they were strangers treated them with such severity that he would not allow them to wait by the palisade; but Nekhlyudov's guide was not abashed by this severity.

'Hallo, lad! why so fierce? You go and rouse your boss while we wait here?'

The sentinel gave no answer, but shouted something in at the gate and stood looking at the broad-shouldered young labourer scraping the mud off Nekhlyudov's boots with a chip of wood by the light of the lamp. From behind the palisade came the hum of male and female voices. In about three minutes more something rattled, the gate opened, and a sergeant, with his cloak thrown over his shoulders, stepped out of the darkness into the lamplight.

The sergeant was not as strict as the sentinel, but he was extremely inquisitive. He insisted on knowing what Nekhlyudov wanted the officer for, and who he was, evidently scenting his booty and anxious not to let it escape. Nekhlyudov said he had come on special business, and would show his gratitude, and would the sergeant take a note for him to the officer. The sergeant took the note, nodded, and went away. Some time after the gate rattled again, and women carrying baskets, boxes, jugs and sacks came out, loudly chattering in their peculiar Siberian dialect as they stepped over the threshold of the gate. None of them wore peasant costumes, but were dressed town fashion, wearing jackets and fur-lined cloaks. Their skirts were tucked up high, and their heads wrapped up in shawls. They examined Nekhlyudov and his guide curiously by the light of the lamp. One of them showed evident pleasure at the sight of the broad-shouldered fellow, and affectionately administered to him a dose of Siberian abuse.

'You demon, what are you doing here? The devil take you,' she said, addressing him.

'I've been showing this traveller here the way,' answered the young fellow. 'And what have you been bringing here?'

'Dairy produce, and I am to bring more in the morning.'

The guide said something in answer that made not only the women but even the sentinel laugh, and, turning to Nekhlyudov, he said:

'You'll find your way alone? Won't get lost, will you?'

'I shall find it all right.'

'When you have passed the church it's the second from the two-storeyed house. Oh, and here, take my staff,' he said, handing the stick he was carrying, and which was longer than himself, to Nekhlyudov; and splashing through the mud with his enormous boots, he disappeared in the darkness, together with the women.

His voice mingling with the voices of the women was still audible through the fog, when the gate again rattled, and the sergeant appeared and asked Nekhlyudov to follow him to the officer.

Chapter 8

Nekhlyudov and the officer

This halting station, like all such stations along the Siberian road, was surrounded by a courtyard, fenced in with a palisade of sharp-pointed stakes, and consisted of three one-storeyed houses. One of them, the largest, with grated windows, was for the prisoners, another for the convoy soldiers, and the third, in which the office was, for the officers.

There were lights in the windows of all the three houses, and, like all such lights, they promised, here in a specially deceptive manner, something cosy inside the walls. Lamps were burning before the porches of the houses and about five lamps more along the walls lit up the yard.

The sergeant led Nekhlyudov along a plank which lay across the yard up to the porch of the smallest of the houses.

When he had gone up the three steps of the porch he let Nekhlyudov pass before him into the ante-room, in which a small lamp was burning, and which was filled with smoky fumes. By the stove a soldier in a coarse shirt with a necktie and black trousers, and with one top-boot on, stood blowing the charcoal in a samovar, using the other boot as bellows.* When he saw Nekhlyudov, the soldier left the samovar and helped him off with his waterproof; then went into the inner room.

'He has come, your honour.'

'Well, ask him in,' came an angry voice.

'Go in at the door,' said the soldier, and went back to the samovar.

In the next room an officer with fair moustaches and a very red face, dressed in an Austrian jacket that closely fitted his broad chest and shoulders, sat at a covered table, on which were the remains of his dinner and two bottles; there was a strong smell of tobacco and some very strong, cheap scent in the warm room. On seeing Nekhlyudov the officer rose and gazed ironically and suspiciously, as it seemed, at the newcomer.

'What is it you want?' he asked, and, not waiting for a reply, he shouted through the open door:

'Bernov, the samovar! What are you about?'

'Coming at once.'

'You'll get it "at once" so that you'll remember it,' shouted the officer, and his eyes flashed.

'I'm coming,' shouted the soldier, and brought in the samovar. Nekhlyudov waited while the soldier placed the samovar on the table. When the officer had followed the soldier out of the room with his cruel little eyes looking as if they were aiming where best to hit him, he made the tea, got the four-cornered decanter out of his travelling case and some Albert biscuits, and having placed all this on the cloth he again turned to Nekhlyudov. 'Well, how can I he of service to you?'

'I should like to be allowed to visit a prisoner,' said Nekhlyudov, without sitting down.

---

* The long boots worn in Russia have concertina-like sides, and when held to the chimney of the somovar can be used instead of bellows to make the charcoal inside burn up.

'A political one? That's forbidden by the law,' said the officer.

'The woman I mean is not a political prisoner,' said Nekhlyudov.

'Yes. But pray take a seat,' said the officer. Nekhlyudov sat down.

'She is not a political one, but at my request she has been allowed by the higher authorities to join the political prisoners – '

'Oh, yes, I know,' interrupted the other; 'a little dark one? Well, yes, that can be managed. Won't you smoke?' He moved a box of cigarettes towards Nekhlyudov, and, having carefully poured out two tumblers of tea, he passed one to Nekhlyudov. 'If you please,' he said.

'Thank you; I should like to see – '

'The night is long. You'll have plenty of time. I shall order her to be sent out to you.'

'But could I not see her where she is? Why need she be sent for?' Nekhlyudov said.

'In to the political prisoners? It is against the law.'

'I have been allowed to go in several times. If there is any danger of my passing anything in to them I could do it through her just as well.'

'Oh, no; she would be searched,' said the officer, and laughed in an unpleasant manner.

'Well, why not search me?'

'All right; we'll manage without that,' said the officer, opening the decanter, and holding it out towards Nekhlyudov's tumbler of tea. 'May I? No? Well, just as you like. When you are living here in Siberia you are too glad to meet an educated person. Our work, as you know, is the saddest, and when one is used to better things it is very hard. The idea they have of us is that convoy officers are coarse, uneducated men, and no one seems to remember that we may have been born for a very different position.'

This officer's red face, his scents, his rings, and especially his unpleasant laughter disgusted Nekhlyudov very much, but today, as during the whole of his journey, he was in that serious, attentive state which did not allow him to behave slightingly or disdainfully towards any man, but made him feel the necessity of speaking to everyone 'entirely', as he expressed to himself this relation to men. When he had heard the officer and understood his state of mind, he said in a serious manner:

'I think that in your position, too, some comfort could be found in helping the suffering people,' he said.

'What are their sufferings? You don't know what these people are.'

'They are not special people,' said Nekhlyudov; 'they are just such people as others, and some of them are quite innocent.'

'Of course, there are all sorts among them, and naturally one pities them. Others won't let anything off, but I try to lighten their condition where I can. It's better that I should suffer, but not they. Others keep to the law in every detail, even as far as to shoot, but I show pity. May I? – Take another,' he said, and poured out another tumbler of tea for Nekhlyudov.

'And who is she, this woman that you want to see?' he asked.

'It is an unfortunate woman who got into a brothel, and was there falsely accused of poisoning, and she is a very good woman,' Nekhlyudov answered.

The officer shook his head. 'Yes, it does happen. I can tell you about a certain Emma who lived in Kasan. She was a Hungarian by birth, but she had quite Persian eyes,' he continued, unable to restrain a smile at the recollection; 'there was so much chic about her that a countess – '

Nekhlyudov interrupted the officer and returned to the former topic of conversation.

'I think that you could lighten the condition of the people while they are in your charge. And in acting that way I am sure you would find great joy!' said Nekhlyudov, trying to pronounce as distinctly as possible, as he might if talking to a foreigner or a child.

The officer looked at Nekhlyudov impatiently, waiting for him to stop so as to continue the tale about the Hungarian with Persian eyes, who evidently presented herself very vividly to his imagination and quite absorbed his attention.

'Yes, of course, this is all quite true,' he said, 'and I do pity them; but I should like to tell you about Emma. What do you think she did – ?'

'It does not interest me,' said Nekhlyudov, 'and I will tell you straight, that though I was myself very different at one time, I now hate that kind of relation to women.'

The officer gave Nekhlyudov a frightened look.

'Won't you take some more tea?' he said.

'No, thank you.'

'Bernov!' the officer called, 'take the gentleman to Vakoulov. Tell him to let him into the separate political room. He may remain there till the inspection.'

Chapter 9

The political prisoners

Accompanied by the orderly, Nekhlyudov went out into the courtyard, which was dimly lit up by the red light of the lamps.

'Where to?' asked the convoy sergeant, addressing the orderly.

'Into the separate cell, No. 5.'

'You can't pass here; the boss has gone to the village and taken the keys.'

'Well, then, pass this way.'

The soldier led Nekhlyudov along a board to another entrance. While still in the yard Nekhlyudov could hear the din of voices and general commotion going on inside as in a beehive when the bees are preparing to swarm; but when he came nearer and the door opened the din grew louder, and changed into distinct sounds of shouting, abuse and laughter. He heard the clatter of chairs and smelt the well-known foul air. This din of voices and the clatter of the chairs, together with the close smell, always flowed into one tormenting sensation, and produced in Nekhlyudov a feeling of moral nausea which grew into physical sickness, the two feelings mingling with and heightening each other.

The first thing Nekhlyudov saw, on entering, was a large, stinking tub. A corridor into which several doors opened led from the entrance. The first was the family room, then the bachelors' room, and at the very end two small rooms were set apart for the political prisoners.

The buildings, which were arranged to hold one hundred and fifty prisoners, now that there were four hundred and fifty inside, were so crowded that the prisoners could not all get into the rooms, but filled the passage, too. Some were sitting or lying on the floor, some were going out with empty teapots, or bringing them back filled with boiling water. Among the latter was Taras. He overtook Nekhlyudov and greeted him affectionately. The kind face of Taras was disfigured by dark bruises on his nose and under his eye.

'What has happened to you?' asked Nekhlyudov.

'Yes, something did happen,' Taras said, with a smile.

'All because of the woman,' added a prisoner, who followed Taras; 'he's had a row with Blind Fedka.'

'And how's Theodosia?'

'She's all right. Here I am bringing her the water for her tea,' Taras answered, and went into the family room.

Nekhlyudov looked in at the door. The room was crowded with women and men, some of whom were on and some under the bedsteads; it was full of steam from the wet clothes that were drying, and the chatter of women's voices was unceasing. The next door led into the bachelors' room. This room was still more crowded; even the doorway and the passage in front of it were blocked by a noisy crowd of men in wet garments, busy doing or deciding something or other.

The convoy sergeant explained that it was the prisoner appointed to buy provisions, paying off out of the food money what was owing to a sharper who had won from or lent money to the prisoners, and receiving back little tickets made of playing cards. When they saw the convoy soldier and a gentleman, those who were nearest became silent, and followed them with looks of ill-will. Among them Nekhlyudov noticed the criminal Fedorov, whom he knew, and who always kept a miserable lad with a swelled appearance and raised eyebrows beside him, and also a disgusting, noseless, pock-marked tramp, who was notorious among the prisoners because he killed his comrade in the marshes while trying to escape, and had, as it was rumoured, fed on his flesh. The tramp stood in the passage with his wet cloak thrown over one shoulder, looking mockingly and boldly at Nekhlyudov, and did not move out of the way. Nekhlyudov passed him by.

Though this kind of scene had now become quite familiar to him, though he had during the last three months seen these four hundred criminal prisoners over and over again in many different circumstances: in the heat; enveloped in clouds of dust which they raised as they dragged their chained feet along the road; and at the resting places by the way, where the most horrible scenes of barefaced debauchery had occurred; yet every time he came among them, and felt their attention fixed upon him as it was now, shame and consciousness of his sin against them tormented him. To this sense of shame and guilt was added an unconquerable feeling of loathing and horror. He knew that, placed in a position such as theirs, they could not be other than they were, and yet he was unable to stifle his disgust.

'It's well for them do-nothings,' Nekhlyudov heard someone say in a hoarse voice as he approached the room of the political prisoners. Then followed a word of obscene abuse, and spiteful, mocking laughter.

Chapter 10

Makar Devkin

When they had passed the bachelors' room the sergeant who accompanied Nekhlyudov left him, promising to come for him before the inspection would take place. As soon as the sergeant was gone a prisoner, quickly stepping with his bare feet and holding up the chains, came close up to Nekhlyudov, enveloping him in the strong, acid smell of perspiration, and said in a mysterious whisper:

'Help the lad, sir; he's got into an awful mess. Been drinking. Today he's given his name as Karmanov at the inspection. Take his part, sir. We dare not, or they'll kill us,' and looking uneasily round he turned away.

This is what had happened. The criminal Karmanov had persuaded a young fellow who resembled him in appearance and was sentenced to exile to change names with him and go to the mines instead of him, while he only went to exile. Nekhlyudov knew all this. Some convict had told him about this exchange the week before. He nodded as a sign that he understood and would do what was in his power, and continued his way without looking round.

Nekhlyudov knew this convict, and was surprised by his action. When in Ekaterinburg the convict had asked Nekhlyudov to get a permission for his wife to follow him. The convict was a man of medium size and of the most ordinary peasant type, about thirty years old. He was condemned to hard labour for an attempt to murder and rob. His name was Makar Devkin. His crime was a very curious one. In the account he gave of it to Nekhlyudov, he said it was not his but his devil's doing. He said that a traveller had come to his father's house and hired his sledge to drive him to a village thirty miles off for two roubles. Makar's father told him to drive the stranger. Makar harnessed the horse, dressed, and sat down to drink tea with the stranger. The stranger related at the tea-table that he was going to be married and had five hundred roubles, which he had earned in Moscow, with him. When he had heard this, Makar went out into the yard and put an axe into the sledge under the straw. 'And I did not myself know why I was taking the axe,' he said. ' "Take the axe", says *he*, and I took it. We got in and started. We drove along all right; I even forgot about the axe. Well, we were getting near the village; only about four miles more to go. The way from the cross-road to the high road was up hill, and I got out. I walked behind the sledge and *he* whispers to me, "What are you thinking about? When you get to the top of the hill you will meet people along the highway, and then there will be the village. He will carry the money away. If you mean to do it, now's the time." I stooped over the sledge as if to arrange the straw, and the axe seemed to jump into my hand of itself. The man turned round. "What are you doing?" I lifted the axe and tried to knock him down, but he was quick, jumped out, and took hold of my hands. "What are you doing, you villain?" He threw me down into the snow, and I did not even struggle, but gave in at once. He bound my arms with his girdle, and threw me into the sledge, and took me straight to the police station. I was imprisoned and tried. The commune gave me a good character, said that I was a good man, and that nothing wrong had been noticed about me. The masters for whom I worked also spoke well of me, but we had no money to engage a lawyer, and so I was condemned to four years' hard labour.'

It was this man who, wishing to save a fellow-villager, knowing that he was risking his life thereby, told Nekhlyudov the prisoner's secret, for doing which (if found out) he should certainly be throttled.

Chapter 11

Maslova and her companions

The political prisoners were kept in two small rooms, the doors of which opened into a part of the passage partitioned off from the rest. The first person Nekhlyudov saw on entering into this part of the passage was Simonson in his rubber jacket and with a log of pine wood in his hands, crouching in front of a stove, the door of which trembled, drawn in by the heat inside.

When he saw Nekhlyudov he looked up at him from under his protruding brow, and gave him his hand without rising.

'I am glad you have come; I want to speak to you,' he said, looking Nekhlyudov straight in the eyes with an expression of importance.

'Yes; what is it?' Nekhlyudov asked.

'It will do later on; I am busy just now,' and Simonson turned again towards the stove, which he was heating according to a theory of his own, so as to lose as little heat energy as possible.

Nekhlyudov was going to enter in at the first door, when Maslova, stooping and pushing a large heap of rubbish and dust towards the stove with a handleless birch broom, came out of the other. She had a white jacket on, her skirt was tucked up, and a kerchief, drawn down to her eyebrows, protected her hair from the dust. When she saw Nekhlyudov, she drew herself up, flushing and animated, put down the broom, wiped her hands on her skirt, and stopped right in front of him. 'You are tidying up the apartments, I see,' said Nekhlyudov, shaking hands.

'Yes; my old occupation,' and she smiled. 'But the dirt! You can't imagine what it is. We have been cleaning and cleaning. Well, is the plaid dry?' she asked, turning to Simonson.

'Almost,' Simonson answered, giving her a strange look, which struck Nekhlyudov.

'All right, I'll come for it, and will bring the cloaks to dry. Our people are all in here,' she said to Nekhlyudov, pointing to the first door as she went out of the second.

Nekhlyudov opened the door and entered a small room dimly lit by a little metal lamp, which was standing low down on the shelf bedstead. It was cold in the room, and there was a smell of the dust, which had not had time to settle, damp and tobacco smoke.

Only those who were close to the lamp were clearly visible, the bedsteads were in the shade and wavering shadows glided over the walls. Two men, appointed as caterers, who had gone to fetch boiling water and provisions, were away; most of the political prisoners were gathered together in the small room. There was Nekhlyudov's old acquaintance, Vera Doukhova, with her large, frightened eyes, and the swollen vein on her forehead, in a grey jacket with short hair, and thinner and yellower than ever. She had a newspaper spread out in front of her, and sat rolling cigarettes with a jerky movement of her hands.

Emily Rintzeva, whom Nekhlyudov considered to be the pleasantest of the political prisoners, was also here. She looked after the housekeeping, and managed to spread a feeling of home comfort even in the midst of the most trying surroundings. She sat beside the lamp, with her sleeves rolled up, wiping cups and mugs, and placing them, with her deft, red and sunburnt hands, on a cloth that was spread on the bedstead. Rintzeva was a plain-looking young woman, with a clever and mild expression of face, which, when she smiled, had a way of suddenly becoming merry, animated and captivating. It was with such a smile that she now welcomed Nekhlyudov.

'Why, we thought you had gone back to Russia,' she said.

Here in a dark corner was also Mary Pavlovna, busy with a little, fair-haired girl, who kept prattling in her sweet, childish accents.

'How nice that you have come,' she said to Nekhlyudov.

'Have you seen Katusha? And we have a visitor here,' and she pointed to the little girl.

Here was also Anatole Kryltzov with felt boots on, sitting in a far corner with his feet under him, doubled up and shivering, his arms folded in the sleeves of his cloak, and looking at Nekhlyudov with feverish eyes. Nekhlyudov was going up to him, but to the right of the door a man with spectacles and reddish curls, dressed in a rubber jacket, sat talking to the pretty, smiling Grabetz. This was the celebrated revolutionist Novodvorov. Nekhlyudov hastened to greet him. He was in a particular hurry about it, because this man was the only one among all the political prisoners whom he disliked. Novodvorov's eyes glistened through his spectacles as he looked at Nekhlyudov and held his narrow hand out to him.

'Well, are you having a pleasant journey?' he asked, with apparent irony.

'Yes, there is much that is interesting,' Nekhlyudov answered, as if he did not notice the irony, but took the question for politeness, and passed on to Kryltzov.

Though Nekhlyudov appeared indifferent, he was really far from indifferent, and these words of Novodvorov, showing his evident desire to say or do something unpleasant, interfered with the state of kindness in which Nekhlyudov found himself, and he felt depressed and sad.

'Well, how are you?' he asked, pressing Kryltzov's cold and trembling hand.

'Pretty well, only I cannot get warm; I got wet through,' Kryltzov answered, quickly replacing his hands into the sleeves of his cloak. 'And here it is also beastly cold. There, look, the window-panes are broken,' and he pointed to the broken panes behind the iron bars. 'And how are you? Why did you not come?'

'I was not allowed to, the authorities were so strict, but today the officer is lenient.'

'Lenient indeed!' Kryltzov remarked. 'Ask Mary what she did this morning.'

Mary Pavlovna from her place in the corner related what had happened about the little girl that morning when they left the halting station.

'I think it is absolutely necessary to make a collective protest,' said Vera Doukhova, in a determined tone, and yet looking now at one, now at another, with a frightened, undecided look. 'Valdemar Simonson did protest, but that is not sufficient.'

'What protest!' muttered Kryltzov, cross and frowning. Her want of simplicity, artificial tone and nervousness had evidently been irritating him for a long time.

'Are you looking for Katusha?' he asked, addressing Nekhlyudov. 'She is working all the time. She has cleaned this, the men's room, and now she has gone to clean the women's! Only it is not possible to clean away the fleas. And what is Mary doing there?' he asked, nodding towards the corner where Mary Pavlovna sat.

'She is combing out her adopted daughter's hair,' replied Rint-zeva.

'But won't she let the insects loose on us?' asked Kryltzov.

'No, no; I am very careful. She is a clean little girl now. You take her,' said Mary, turning to Rintzeva, 'while I go and help Katusha, and I will also bring him his plaid.'

Rintzeva took the little girl on her lap, pressing her plump, bare, little arms to her bosom with a mother's tenderness, and gave her a bit of sugar. As Mary Pavlovna left the room, two men came in with boiling water and provisions.

Chapter 12

Nabatov and Markel

One of the men who came in was a short, thin young man, who had a cloth-covered sheepskin coat on, and high top-boots. He stepped lightly and quickly, carrying two steaming teapots, and holding a loaf wrapped in a cloth under his arm.

'Well, so our prince has put in an appearance again,' he said, as he placed the teapot beside the cups, and handed the bread to Rintzeva. 'We have bought wonderful things,' he continued, as he took off his sheepskin, and flung it over the heads of the others into the corner of the bedstead. 'Markel has bought milk and eggs. Why, we'll have a regular ball today. And Rintzeva is spreading out her aesthetic cleanliness,' he said, and looked with a smile at Rintzeva, 'and now she will make the tea.'

The whole presence of this man – his motion, his voice, his look – seemed to breathe vigour and merriment. The other newcomer was just the reverse of the first. He looked despondent and sad. He was short, bony, had very prominent cheek bones, a sallow complexion, thin lips and beautiful, greenish eyes, rather far apart. He wore an old wadded coat, top-boots and goloshes, and was carrying two pots of milk and two round boxes made of birch bark, which he placed in front of Rintzeva. He bowed to Nekhlyudov, bending only his neck, and with his eyes fixed on him. Then, having reluctantly given him his damp hand to shake, he began to take out the provisions.

Both these political prisoners were of the people; the first was Nabatov, a peasant; the second, Markel Kondratiev, a factory hand. Markel did not come among the revolutionists till he was quite a man, Nabatov only eighteen. After leaving the village school, owing to his exceptional talents Nabatov entered the gymnasium, and maintained himself by giving lessons all the time he studied there, and obtained the gold medal. He did not go to the university because, while still in the seventh class of the gymnasium, he made up his mind to go among the people and enlighten his neglected brethren. This he did, first getting the place of a government clerk in a large village. He was soon arrested because he read to the peasants and arranged a co-operative industrial association among them. They kept him imprisoned for eight months and then set him free, but he remained under police supervision. As soon as he was liberated he went to another village, got a place as schoolmaster, and did the same as he had done in the first village. He was again taken up and kept fourteen months in prison, where his convictions became yet stronger.

After that he was exiled to the Perm government, from where he escaped. Then he was put to prison for seven months and after that exiled to Archangel. There he refused to take the oath of allegiance that was required of them and was condemned to be exiled to the Yakutsk Govern-ment, so that half his life since he reached manhood was passed in prison and exile. All these adventures did not embitter him nor weaken his energy, but rather stimulated it. He was a lively young fellow, with a splendid digestion, always active, gay and vigorous. He never repented of anything, never looked far ahead, and used all his powers, his cleverness, his practical knowledge to act in the present. When free, he worked towards the aim he had set himself, the enlightening and the uniting of the working men, especially the country labourers. When in prison he was just as energetic and practical in finding means to come in contact with the outer world, and in arranging his own life and the life of his group as comfortably as the conditions would allow. Above all things he was a communist. He wanted, as it seemed to him, nothing for himself and contented himself with very little, but demanded very much for the group of his comrades, and could work for it either physically or mentally day and night, without sleep or food. As a peasant he had been industrious, observant, clever at his work, and naturally self-controlled, polite without any effort, and attentive not only to the wishes but also the opinions of others. His widowed mother, an illiterate, superstitious old peasant woman, was still living, and Nabatov helped her and went to see her while he was free. During the time he spent at home he entered into all the interests of his mother's life, helped her in her work, and continued his intercourse with former playfellows; smoked cheap tobacco with them in so-called 'dog's feet',* took part in their fist fights, and explained to them how they were all being deceived by the State, and how they ought to disentangle themselves out of the deception they were kept in. When he thought or spoke of what a revolution would do for the people he always imagined this people from whom he had sprung himself left in very nearly the same conditions as they were in, only with sufficient land and without the gentry and without officials. The revolution, according to him, and in this he differed from Novodvorov and Novodvorov's follower, Markel Kondratiev, should not alter the elementary forms of the life of the people, should not break down the whole edifice, but should only alter the inner walls of the beautiful, strong, enormous old structure he loved so dearly.

He was also a typical peasant in his views on religion, never thinking about metaphysical questions, about the origin of all origins, or the future life. God was to him, as also to Arago, an hypothesis which he had had no need of up to now. He had

---

* A kind of cigarette that the peasants smoke, made of a bit of paper and bent at one end into a hook.

no business with the origin of the world, whether Moses or Darwin was right. Darwinism, which seemed so important to his fellows, was only the same kind of plaything of the mind as the creation in six days.

The question how the world had originated did not interest him, just because the question how it would be best to live in this world was ever before him. He never thought about future life, always bearing in the depth of his soul the firm and quiet conviction inherited from his forefathers, and common to all labourers on the land, that just as in the world of plants and animals nothing ceases to exist, but continually changes its form, the manure into grain, the grain into a food, the tadpole into a frog, the caterpillar into a butterfly, the acorn into an oak, so man also does not perish, but only undergoes a change. He believed in this, and therefore always looked death straight in the face, and bravely bore the sufferings that led towards it, but did not care and did not know how to speak about it. He loved work, was always employed in some practical business, and put his comrades in the way of the same kind of practical work.

The other political prisoner from among the people, Markel Kondratiev, was a very different kind of man. He began to work at the age of fifteen, and took to smoking and drinking in order to stifle a dense sense of being wronged. He first realised he was wronged one Christmas when they, the factory children, were invited to a Christmas tree, got up by the employer's wife, where he received a farthing whistle, an apple, a gilt walnut and a fig, while the employer's children had presents given them which seemed gifts from fairyland, and had cost more than fifty roubles, as he afterwards heard.

When he was twenty a celebrated revolutionist came to their factory to work as a working girl, and noticing his superior qualities began giving books and pamphlets to Kondratiev and to talk and explain his position to him, and how to remedy it. When the possibility of freeing himself and others from their oppressed state rose clearly in his mind, the injustice of this state appeared more cruel and more terrible than before, and he longed passionately not only for freedom, but also for the punishment of those who had arranged and who kept up this cruel injustice. Kondratiev devoted himself with passion to the acquirement of knowledge. It was not clear to him how knowledge should bring about the realisation of the social ideal, but he believed that the knowledge that had shown him the injustice of the state in which he lived would also abolish that injustice itself. Besides knowledge would, in his opinion, raise him above others. Therefore he left off drinking and smoking, and devoted all his leisure time to study. The revolutionist gave him lessons, and his thirst for every kind of knowledge, and the facility with which he took it in, surprised her. In two years he had mastered algebra, geometry, history – which he was specially fond of – and made acquaintance with artistic and critical, and especially socialistic literature. The revolutionist was arrested, and Kondratiev with her, forbidden books having been found in their possession, and they were imprisoned and then exiled to the Vologda government. There Kondratiev became acquainted with Novodvorov, and read a great deal more revolutionary literature, remembered it all, and became still firmer in his socialistic views. While in exile he became leader in a large strike, which ended in the destruction of a factory and the murder of the director. He was again arrested and condemned to Siberia.

His religious views were of the same negative nature as his views of the existing economic conditions. Having seen the absurdity of the religion in which he was brought up, and having gained with great effort, and at first with fear, but later with rapture, freedom from it, he did not tire of viciously and with venom ridiculing priests and religious dogmas, as if wishing to revenge himself for the deception that had been practised on him.

He was ascetic through habit, contented himself with very little, and, like all those used to work from childhood and whose muscles have been developed, he could work much and easily, and was quick at any manual labour; but what he valued most was the leisure in prisons and halting stations, which enabled him to continue his studies. He was now studying the first volume of Karl Marx's, and carefully hid the book in his sack as if it were a great treasure. He behaved with reserve and indifference to all his comrades, except Novodvorov, to whom he was greatly attached, and whose arguments on all subjects he accepted as unanswerable truths.

He had an indefinite contempt for women, whom he looked upon as a hindrance in all necessary business. But he pitied

Maslova and was gentle with her, for he considered her an example of the way the lower are exploited by the upper classes. The same reason made him dislike Nekhlyudov, so that he talked little with him, and never pressed Nekhlyudov's hand, but only held out his own to be pressed when greeting him.

Chapter 13

Love affairs of the exiles

The stove had burned up and got warm, the tea was made and poured out into mugs and cups, and milk was added to it; rusks, fresh rye and wheat bread, hard-boiled eggs, butter, and calf's head and feet were placed on the cloth. Everybody moved towards the part of the shelf beds which took the place of the table and sat eating and talking. Rintzeva sat on a box pouring out the tea. The rest crowded round her, apart from Kryltzov, who had taken off his wet cloak and wrapped himself in his dry plaid and lay in his own place talking to Nekhlyudov.

After the cold and damp march and the dirt and disorder they had found here, and after the pains they had taken to get it tidy, after having drunk hot tea and eaten, they were all in the best and brightest of spirits.

The fact that the tramp of feet, the screams and abuse of the criminals, reached them through the wall, reminding them of their surroundings, seemed only to increase the sense of cosiness. As on an island in the midst of the sea, these people felt themselves for a brief interval not swamped by the degradation and sufferings which surrounded them; this made their spirits rise, and excited them. They talked about everything except their present position and that which awaited them. Then, as it generally happens among young men, and women especially, if they are forced to remain together, as these people were, all sorts of agreements and disagreements and attractions, curiously blended, had sprung up among them. Almost all of them were in love. Novodvorov was in love with the pretty, smiling Grabetz. This Grabetz was a

young, thoughtless girl who had gone in for a course of study,
perfectly indifferent to revolutionary questions, but succumbing
to the influence of the day, she compromised herself in some way
and was exiled. The chief interest of her life during the time of her
trial in prison and in exile was her success with men, just as it had
been when she was free. Now on the way she comforted herself
with the fact that Novodvorov had taken a fancy to her, and she
fell in love with him. Vera Doukhova, who was very prone to fall
in love herself, but did not awaken love in others, though she was
always hoping for mutual love, was sometimes drawn to Nabatov,
then to Novodvorov. Kryltzov felt something like love for Mary
Pavlovna. He loved her with a man's love, but knowing how
she regarded this sort of love, hid his feelings under the guise
of friendship and gratitude for the tenderness with which she
attended to his wants. Nabatov and Rintzeva were attached to
each other by very complicated ties. Just as Mary Pavlovna was a
perfectly chaste maiden, in the same way Rintzeva was perfectly
chaste as her own husband's wife. When only a schoolgirl of
sixteen she fell in love with Rintzev, a student of the Petersburg
University, and married him before he left the university, when
she was only nineteen years old. During his fourth year at the
university her husband had become involved in the students'
rows, was exiled from Petersburg, and turned revolutionist. She
left the medical courses she was attending, followed him, and also
turned revolutionist. If she had not considered her husband the
cleverest and best of men she would not have fallen in love with
him; and if she had not fallen in love would not have married; but
having fallen in love and married him whom she thought the best
and cleverest of men, she naturally looked upon life and its aims in
the way the best and cleverest of men looked at them. At first he
thought the aim of life was to learn, and she looked upon study as
the aim of life. He became a revolutionist, and so did she. She
could demonstrate very clearly that the existing state of things
could not go on, and that it was everybody's duty to fight this state
of things and to try to bring about conditions in which the
individual could develop freely, etc. And she imagined that she
really thought and felt all this, but in reality she only regarded
everything her husband thought as absolute truth, and only sought
for perfect agreement, perfect identification of her own soul with

his, which alone could give her full moral satisfaction. The parting with her husband and their child, whom her mother had taken, was very hard to bear; but she bore it firmly and quietly, since it was for her husband's sake and for that cause which she had not the slightest doubt was true, since he served it. She was always with her husband in thought, and did not love and could not love any other any more than she had done before. But Nabatov's devoted and pure love touched and excited her. This moral, firm man, her husband's friend, tried to treat her as a sister, but something more appeared in his behaviour to her, and this something frightened them both, and yet gave colour to their life of hardship.

So that in all this circle only Mary Pavlovna and Kondratiev were quite free from love affairs.

Chapter 14

Conversations in prison

Expecting to have a private talk with Katusha, as usual, after tea, Nekhlyudov sat by the side of Kryltzov, conversing with him. Among other things he told him the story of Makar's crime and about his request to him. Kryltzov listened attentively, gazing at Nekhlyudov with glistening eyes.

'Yes,' said Kryltzov suddenly, 'I often think that here we are going side by side with them, and who are they? The same for whose sake we are going, and yet we not only do not know them, but do not even wish to know them. And they, even worse than that, they hate us and look upon us as enemies. This is terrible.'

'There is nothing terrible about it,' broke in Novodvorov. 'The masses always worship power only. The government is in power, and they worship it and hate us. Tomorrow we shall have the power, and they will worship us,' he said with his grating voice. At that moment a volley of abuse and the rattle of chains sounded from behind the wall, something was heard thumping against it and screaming and shrieking, someone was being beaten, and someone was calling out, 'Murder! help!'

'Hear them, the beasts! What intercourse can there be between us and such as them?' quietly remarked Novodvorov.

'You call them beasts, and Nekhlyudov was just telling me about such an action!' irritably retorted Kryltzov, and went on to say how Makar was risking his life to save a fellow-villager. 'That is not the action of a beast, it is heroism.'

'Sentimentality!' Novodvorov ejaculated ironically; 'it is difficult for us to understand the emotions of these people and the motives on which they act. You see generosity in the act, and it may be simply jealousy of that other criminal.'

'How is it that you never wish to see anything good in another?' Mary Pavlovna said suddenly, flaring up.

'How can one see what does not exist?'

'How does it not exist, when a man risks dying a terrible death?'

'I think,' said Novodvorov, 'that if we mean to do our work, the first condition is that' (here Kondratiev put down the book he was reading by the lamplight and began to listen attentively to his master's words) 'we should not give way to fancy, but look at things as they are. We should do all in our power for the masses, and expect nothing in return. The masses can only be the object of our activity, but cannot be our fellow-workers as long as they remain in that state of inertia they are in at present,' he went on, as if delivering a lecture. 'Therefore, to expect help from them before the process of development – that process which we are preparing them for – has taken place is an illusion.'

'What process of development?' Kryltzov began, flushing all over. 'We say that we are against arbitrary rule and despotism, and is this not the most awful despotism?'

'No despotism whatever,' quietly rejoined Novodvorov. 'I am only saying that I know the path that the people must travel, and can show them that path.'

'But how can you be sure that the path you show is the true path? Is this not the same kind of despotism that lay at the bottom of the Inquisition, of all persecutions, and the great revolution? They, too, knew the one true way, by means of their science.'

'Their having erred is no proof of my going to err; besides, there is a great difference between the ravings of ideologues and the facts based on sound, economic science.' Novodvorov's voice filled the room; he alone was speaking, all the rest were silent.

'They are always disputing,' Mary Pavlovna said, when there was a moment's silence.

'And you yourself, what do you think about it?' Nekhlyudov asked her.

'I think Kryltzov is right when he says we should not force our views on the people.'

'And you, Katusha?' asked Nekhlyudov with a smile, waiting anxiously for her answer, fearing she would say something awkward.

'I think the common people are wronged,' she said, and blushed scarlet. 'I think they are dreadfully wronged.'

'That's right, Maslova, quite right,' cried Nabatov. 'They are terribly wronged, the people, and they must not be wronged, and therein lies the whole of our task.'

'A curious idea of the object of revolution,' Novodvorov remarked crossly, and began to smoke.

'I cannot talk to him,' said Kryltzov in a whisper, and was silent.

'And it is much better not to talk,' Nekhlyudov said.

Chapter 15

Novodvorov

Although Novodvorov was highly esteemed of all the revolutionists, though he was very learned, and considered very wise, Nekhlyudov reckoned him among those of the revolutionists who, being below the average moral level, were very far below it.

His inner life was of a nature directly opposite to that of Simonson's. Simonson was one of those people (of an essentially masculine type) whose actions follow the dictates of their reason, and are determined by it. Novodvorov belonged, on the contrary, to the class of people of a feminine type, whose reason is directed partly towards the attainment of aims set by their feelings, partly to the justification of acts suggested by their feelings.

The whole of Novodvorov's revolutionary activity, though he could explain it very eloquently and very convincingly, appeared to Nekhlyudov to be founded on nothing but ambition and the desire for supremacy. At first his capacity for assimilating the thoughts of others, and of expressing them correctly, had given him a position of supremacy among pupils and teachers in the *gymnasium* and the university, where qualities such as his are highly prized, and he was satisfied. When he had finished his studies and received his diploma he suddenly altered his views, and from a modern liberal he turned into a rabid Narodovoletz, in order (so Kryltzov, who did not like him, said) to gain supremacy in another sphere.

As he was devoid of those moral and aesthetic qualities which call forth doubts and hesitation, he very soon acquired a position in the revolutionary world which satisfied him – that of the leader of a party. Having once chosen a direction, he never doubted or hesitated, and was therefore certain that he never made a mistake. Everything seemed quite simple, clear and certain. And the narrowness and one-sidedness of his views did make everything seem simple and clear. One only had to be logical, as he said. His self-assurance was so great that it either repelled people or made them submit to him. As he carried on his work among very young people, his boundless self-assurance led them to believe him very profound and wise; the majority did submit to him, and he had a great success in revolutionary circles. His activity was directed to the preparation of a rising in which he was to usurp the power and call together a council. A programme, composed by him, should be proposed before the council, and he felt sure that this programme of his solved every problem, and that it would be impossible not to carry it out.

His comrades respected but did not love him. He did not love anyone, looked upon all men of note as upon rivals, and would have willingly treated them as old male monkeys treat young ones if he could have done it. He would have torn all mental power, every capacity, from other men, so that they should not interfere with the display of his talents. He behaved well only to those who bowed before him. Now, on the journey he behaved well to Kondratiev, who was influenced by his propaganda; to Vera Doukhova and pretty little Grabetz, who were both in love with him. Although in principle he was in favour of the woman's movement, yet in the depth of his soul he considered all women stupid and insignificant except those whom he was sentimentally in love with (as he was now in love with Grabetz), and such women he considered to be exceptions, whose merits he alone was capable of discerning.

The question of the relations of the sexes he also looked upon as thoroughly solved by accepting free union. He had one nominal and one real wife, from both of whom he was separated, having come to the conclusion that there was no real love between them, and now he thought of entering on a free union with Grabetz. He despised Nekhlyudov for 'playing the fool', as Novodvorov termed it, with Maslova, but especially for the freedom Nekhlyudov took of considering the defects of the existing system and the methods of correcting those defects in a manner which was not only not exactly the same as Novodvorov's, but was Nekhlyudov's own – a prince's, that is, a fool's manner. Nekhlyudov felt this relation of Novodvorov's towards him, and knew to his sorrow that in spite of the state of good will in which he found himself on this journey he could not help paying this man in his own coin, and could not stifle the strong antipathy he felt for him.

Chapter 16

Simonson speaks to Nekhlyudov

The voices of officials sounded from the next room. All the prisoners were silent, and a sergeant, followed by two convoy soldiers, entered. The time of the inspection had come. The sergeant counted everyone, and when Nekhlyudov's turn came he addressed him with kindly familiarity.

'You must not stay any longer, Prince, after the inspection; you must go now.'

Nekhlyudov knew what this meant, went up to the sergeant and shoved a three-rouble note into his hand.

'Ah, well, what is one to do with you? Stay a bit longer, if you like.' The sergeant was about to go when another sergeant, followed by a convict, a spare man with a thin beard and a bruise under his eye, came in.

'It's about the girl I have come,' said the convict.

'Here's daddy come,' came the ringing accents of a child's voice, and a flaxen head appeared from behind Rintzeva, who, with Katusha's and Mary Pavlovna's help, was making a new garment for the child out of one of Rintzeva's own petticoats.

'Yes, daughter, it's me,' Busovkin, the prisoner, said softly.

'She is quite comfortable here,' said Mary Pavlovna, looking with pity at Busovkin's bruised face. 'Leave her with us.'

'The ladies are making me new clothes,' said the girl, pointing to Rintzeva's sewing – 'nice red ones,' she went on, prattling.

'Do you wish to sleep with us?' asked Rintzeva, caressing the child.

'Yes, I wish. And daddy, too.'

'No, daddy can't. Well, leave her then,' she said, turning to the father.

'Yes, you may leave her,' said the first sergeant, and went out with the other.

As soon as they were out of the room Nabatov went up to Busovkin, slapped him on the shoulder, and said: 'I say, old fellow, is it true that Karmanov wishes to exchange?'

Busovkin's kindly, gentle face turned suddenly sad and a veil seemed to dim his eyes.

'We have heard nothing – hardly,' he said, and with the same dimness still over his eyes he turned to the child.

'Well, Aksutka, it seems you're to make yourself comfortable with the ladies,' and he hurried away.

'It's true about the exchange, and he knows it very well,' said Nabatov.

'What are you going to do?'

'I shall tell the authorities in the next town. I know both prisoners by sight,' said Nekhlyudov.

All were silent, fearing a recommencement of the dispute.

Simonson, who had been lying with his arms thrown back behind his head, and not speaking, rose, and determinedly walked up to Nekhlyudov, carefully passing round those who were sitting.

'Could you listen to me now?'

'Of course,' and Nekhlyudov rose and followed him.

Katusha looked up with an expression of suspense, and meeting Nekhlyudov's eyes, she blushed and shook her head.

'What I want to speak to you about is this,' Simonson began, when they had come out into the passage. In the passage the din of the criminal's voices and shouts sounded louder. Nekhlyudov made a face, but Simonson did not seem to take any notice.

'Knowing of your relations to Katerina Maslova,' he began seriously and frankly, with his kind eyes looking straight into Nekhlyudov's face, 'I consider it my duty' – He was obliged to stop because two voices were heard disputing and shouting, both at once, close to the door.

'I tell you, blockhead, they are not mine,' one voice shouted.

'May you choke, you devil,' snorted the other.

At this moment Mary Pavlovna came out into the passage.

'How can one talk here?' she said; 'go in, Vera is alone there,' and she went in at the second door, and entered a tiny room, evidently meant for a solitary cell, which was now placed at the disposal of the political women prisoners, Vera Doukhova lay covered up, head and all, on the bed.

'She has got a headache, and is asleep, so she cannot hear you, and I will go away,' said Mary Pavlovna.

'On the contrary, stay here,' said Simonson; 'I have no secrets from anyone, certainly none from you.'

'All right,' said Mary Pavlovna, and moving her whole body from side to side, like a child, so as to get farther back on to the bed, she settled down to listen, her beautiful hazel eyes seeming to look somewhere far away.

'Well, then, this is my business,' Simonson repeated. 'Knowing of your relations to Katerina Maslova, I consider myself bound to explain to you my relations to her.'

Nekhlyudov could not help admiring the simplicity and truthfulness with which Simonson spoke to him.

'What do you mean?'

'I mean that I should like to marry Katerina Maslova – '

'How strange!' said Mary Pavlovna, fixing her eyes on Simonson.

' – And so I made up my mind to ask her to be my wife,' Simonson continued.

'What can I do? It depends on her,' said Nekhlyudov.

'Yes; but she will not come to any decision without you.'

'Why?'

'Because as long as your relations with her are unsettled she cannot make up her mind.'

'As far as I am concerned, it is finally settled. I should like to do what I consider to be my duty and also to lighten her fate, but on no account would I wish to put any restraint on her.'

'Yes, but she does not wish to accept your sacrifice.'

'It is no sacrifice.'

'And I know that this decision of hers is final.'

'Well, then, there is no need to speak to me,' said Nekhlyudov.

'She wants you to acknowledge that you think as she does.'

'How can I acknowledge that I must not do what I consider to be my duty? All I can say is that I am not free, but she is.'

Simonson was silent; then, after thinking a little, he said: 'Very well, then, I'll tell her. You must not think I am in love with her,' he continued; 'I love her as a splendid, unique, human being who has suffered much. I want nothing from her. I have only an awful longing to help her, to lighten her posi– '

Nekhlyudov was surprised to hear the trembling in Simonson's voice.

' – to lighten her position,' Simonson continued. 'If she does not wish to accept your help, let her accept mine. If she consents, I shall ask to be sent to the place where she will be imprisoned. Four years are not an eternity. I would live near her, and perhaps might lighten her fate – ' and he again stopped, too agitated to continue.

'What am I to say?' said Nekhlyudov. 'I am very glad she has found such a protector as you – '

'That's what I wanted to know,' Simonson interrupted.

'I wanted to know if, loving her and wishing her happiness, you would consider it good for her to marry me?'

'Oh, yes,' said Nekhlyudov decidedly.

'It all depends on her; I only wish that this suffering soul should find rest,' said Simonson, with such childlike tenderness as no one could have expected from so morose-looking a man.

Simonson rose, and stretching his lips out to Nekhlyudov, smiled shyly and kissed him.

'So I shall tell her,' and he went away.

Chapter 17

'I have nothing more to say'

'What do you think of that?' said Mary Pavlovna. 'In love – quite in love. Now, that's a thing I never should have expected, that Valdemar Simonson should be in love, and in the silliest, most boyish manner. It is strange, and, to say the truth, it is sad,' and she sighed.

'But she? Katusha? How does she look at it, do you think?' Nekhlyudov asked.

'She?' Mary Pavlovna waited, evidently wishing to give as exact an answer as possible. 'She? Well, you see, in spite of her past she has one of the most moral natures – and such fine feelings. She loves you – loves you well, and is happy to be able to do you even the negative good of not letting you get entangled with her. Marriage with you would be a terrible fall for her, worse than all that's past, and therefore she will never consent to it. And yet your presence troubles her.'

'Well, what am I to do? Ought I to vanish?'

Mary Pavlovna smiled her sweet, childlike smile, and said, 'Yes, partly.'

'How is one to vanish partly?'

'I am talking nonsense. But as for her, I should like to tell you that she probably sees the silliness of this rapturous kind of love (he has not spoken to her), and is both flattered and afraid of it. I am not competent to judge in such affairs, you know, still I believe that on his part it is the most ordinary man's feeling, though it is masked. He says that this love arouses his energy and is Platonic, but I know that even if it is exceptional, still at the bottom it is degrading.'

Mary Pavlovna had wandered from the subject, having started on her favourite theme.

'Well, but what am I to do?' Nekhlyudov asked.

'I think you should tell her everything; it is always best that everything should be clear. Have a talk with her; I shall call her. Shall I?' said Mary Pavlovna.

'If you please,' said Nekhlyudov, and Mary Pavlovna went.

A strange feeling overcame Nekhlyudov when he was alone in the little room with the sleeping Vera Doukhova, listening to her soft breathing, broken now and then by moans, and to the incessant dirt that came through the two doors that separated him from the criminals. What Simonson had told him freed him from the self-imposed duty, which had seemed hard and strange to him in his weak moments, and yet now he felt something that was not merely unpleasant but painful.

He had a feeling that this offer of Simonson's destroyed the exceptional character of his sacrifice, and thereby lessened its value in his own and others' eyes; if so good a man who was not bound to her by any kind of tie wanted to join his fate to hers, then this sacrifice was not so great. There may have also been an admixture of ordinary jealousy. He had got so used to her love that he did not like to admit that she loved another.

Then it also upset the plans he had formed of living near her while she was doing her term. If she married Simonson his presence would be unnecessary, and he would have to form new plans.

Before he had time to analyse his feelings the loud din of the prisoners' voices came in with a rush (something special was going on among them today) as the door opened to let Katusha in.

She stepped briskly close up to him and said, 'Mary Pavlovna has sent me.'

'Yes, I must have a talk with you. Sit down. Valdemar Simonson has been speaking to me.'

She sat down and folded her hands in her lap and seemed quite calm, but hardly had Nekhlyudov uttered Simonson's name when she flushed crimson.

'What did he say?' she asked.

'He told me he wanted to marry you.'

Her face suddenly puckered up with pain, but she said nothing and only cast down her eyes.

'He is asking for my consent or my advice. I told him that it all depends entirely on you – that you must decide.'

'Ah, what does it all mean? Why?' she muttered, and looked in his eyes with that peculiar squint that always strangely affected Nekhlyudov.

They sat silent for a few minutes looking into each other's eyes, and this look told much to both of them.

'You must decide,' Nekhlyudov repeated.

'What am I to decide? Everything has long been decided.'

'No; you must decide whether you will accept Mr Simonson's offer,' said Nekhlyudov.

'What sort of a wife can I be – I, a convict? Why should I ruin Mr Simonson, too?' she said, with a frown.

'Well, but if the sentence should be mitigated.'

'Oh, leave me alone. I have nothing more to say,' she said, and rose to leave the room.

Chapter 18

Neverov's fate

When, following Katusha, Nekhlyudov returned to the men's room, he found everyone there in agitation. Nabatov, who went about all over the place, and who got to know everybody, and noticed everything, had just brought news which staggered them all. The news was that he had discovered a note on a wall, written by the revolutionist Petlin, who had been sentenced to hard labour, and who, everyone thought, had long since reached the Kara; and now it turned out that he had passed this way quite recently, the only political prisoner among criminal convicts.

'On the 17th of August,' so ran the note, 'I was sent off alone with the criminals. Neverov was with me, but hanged himself in the lunatic asylum in Kasan. I am well and in good spirits and hope for the best.'

All were discussing Petlin's position and the possible reasons of Neverov's suicide. Only Kryltzov sat silent and preoccupied, his glistening eyes gazing fixedly in front of him.

'My husband told me that Neverov had a vision while still in the Petropavlovski prison,' said Rintzeva.

'Yes, he was a poet, a dreamer; this sort of people cannot stand solitary confinement,' said Novodvorov. 'Now, I never gave my imagination vent when in solitary confinement, but arranged my days most systematically, and in this way always bore it very well.'

'What is there unbearable about it? Why, I used to be glad when they locked me up,' said Nabatov cheerfully, wishing to dispel the general depression.

'A fellow's afraid of everything; of being arrested himself and entangling others, and of spoiling the whole business, and then he gets locked up, and all responsibility is at an end, and he can rest; he can just sit and smoke.'

'You knew him well?' asked Mary Pavlovna, glancing anxiously at the altered, haggard expression of Kryltzov's face.

'Neverov a dreamer?' Kryltzov suddenly began, panting for breath as if he had been shouting or singing for a long time. 'Neverov was a man "such as the earth bears few of", as our doorkeeper used to express it. Yes, he had a nature like crystal, you could see him right through; he could not lie, he could not dissemble; not simply thin-skinned, but with all his nerves laid bare, as if he were flayed. Yes, his was a complicated, rich nature, not such a – but where is the use of talking?' he added, with a vicious frown. 'Shall we first educate the people and then change the forms of life, or first change the forms and then struggle, using peaceful propaganda or terrorism? So we go on disputing while *they* kill; *they* do not dispute – they know their business; they don't care whether dozens, hundreds of men perish – and what men! No; that the best should perish is just what they want. Yes, Herzen said that when the Decembrists were withdrawn from circulation the average level of our society sank. I should think so, indeed. Then Herzen himself and his fellows were withdrawn; now is the turn of the Neverovs.'

'They can't all be got rid of,' said Nabatov, in his cheerful tones. 'There will always be left enough to continue the breed.'

'No, there won't, if we show any pity to *them* there,' Kryltzov said, raising his voice; and not letting himself be interrupted, 'Give me a cigarette.'

'Oh, Anatole, it is not good for you,' said Mary Pavlovna. 'Please do not smoke.'

'Oh, leave me alone,' he said angrily, and lit a cigarette, but at once began to cough and to retch, as if he were going to be sick. Having cleared his throat though, he went on:

'What we have been doing is not the thing at all. Not to argue, but for all to unite – to destroy them – that's it.'

'But *they* are also human beings,' said Nekhlyudov.

'No, *they* are not human, they who can do what they are doing – no – there now, I heard that some kind of bombs and balloons have been invented. Well, one ought to go up in such a balloon and sprinkle bombs down on *them* as if *they* were bugs, until *they* are all exterminated – yes, because – ' he was going to continue, but, flushing all over, he began coughing worse than before, and a stream of blood rushed from his mouth.

Nabatov ran to get ice. Mary Pavlovna brought valerian drops and offered them to him, but he, breathing quickly and heavily, pushed her away with his thin, white hand, and kept his eyes closed. When the ice and cold water had eased Kryltzov a little, and he had been put to bed, Nekhlyudov, having said good-night to everybody, went out with the sergeant, who had been waiting for him some time.

The criminals were now quiet, and most of them were asleep. Though the people were lying on and under the bed shelves and in the space between, they could not all be placed inside the rooms, and some of them lay in the passage with their sacks under their heads and covered with their cloaks. The moans and sleepy voices came through the open doors and sounded through the passage. Everywhere lay compact heaps of human beings covered with prison cloaks. Only a few men who were sitting in the bachelors' room by the light of a candle end, which they put out when they noticed the sergeant, were awake, and an old man who sat naked under the lamp in the passage picking the vermin off his shirt. The foul air in the political prisoners' rooms seemed pure compared to the stinking closeness here. The smoking lamp shone dimly as through a mist, and it was difficult to breathe. Stepping along the passage, one had to look carefully for an empty space, and having put down one foot had to find place for the other. Three persons, who had evidently found no room even in the passage, lay in the anteroom, close to the stinking and leaking tub. One of these was an old idiot, whom Nekhlyudov had often seen marching with the gang; another was a boy about twelve; he lay between the two other convicts, with his head on the leg of one of them.

When he had passed out of the gate Nekhlyudov took a deep breath and long continued to breathe in deep draughts of frosty air.

Chapter 19

Why is it done?

It had cleared up and was starlight. Except in a few places the mud was frozen hard when Nekhlyudov returned to his inn and knocked at one of its dark windows. The broad-shouldered labourer came barefooted to open the door for him and let him in. Through a door on the right, leading to the back premises, came the loud snoring of the carters, who slept there, and the sound of many horses chewing oats came from the yard. The front room, where a red lamp was burning in front of the icons, smelt of wormwood and perspiration, and someone with mighty lungs was snoring behind a partition. Nekhlyudov undressed, put his leather travelling pillow on the oilcloth sofa, spread out his rug and lay down, thinking over all he had seen and heard that day; the boy sleeping on the liquid that oozed from the stinking tub, with his head on the convict's leg, seemed more dreadful than all else.

Unexpected and important as his conversation with Simonson and Katusha that evening had been, he did not dwell on it; his situation in relation to that subject was so complicated and indefinite that he drove the thought from his mind. But the picture of those unfortunate beings, inhaling the noisome air, and lying in the liquid oozing out of the stinking tub, especially that of the boy, with his innocent face asleep on the leg of a criminal, came all the more vividly to his mind, and he could not get it out of his head.

To know that somewhere far away there are men who torture other men by inflicting all sorts of humiliations and inhuman

degradation and sufferings on them, or for three months incessantly to look on while men were inflicting these humiliations and
sufferings on other men is a very different thing. And Nekhlyudov
felt it. More than once during these three months he asked himself, 'Am I mad because I see what others do not, or are they mad
that do these things that I see?'

Yet they (and there were many of them) did what seemed so
astonishing and terrible to him with such quiet assurance that what
they were doing was necessary and was important and useful work
that it was hard to believe they were mad; nor could he, conscious
of the clearness of his thoughts, believe he was mad; and all this
kept him continually in a state of perplexity.

This is how the things he saw during these three months
impressed Nekhlyudov: from among the people who were free,
those were chosen, by means of trials and the administration,
who were the most nervous, the most hot-tempered, the most
excitable, the most gifted and the strongest, but the least careful
and cunning. These people, not a wit more dangerous than
many of those who remained free, were first locked in prisons,
transported to Siberia, where they were provided for and kept
months and years in perfect idleness, and away from nature, their
families, and useful work – that is, away from the conditions
necessary for a natural and moral life. This firstly. Secondly, these
people were subjected to all sorts of unnecessary indignity in
these different places – chains, shaved heads, shameful clothing –
that is, they were deprived of the chief motives that induce the
weak to live good lives, the regard for public opinion, the sense
of shame and the consciousness of human dignity. Thirdly, they
were continually exposed to dangers, such as the epidemics so
frequent in places of confinement, exhaustion, flogging, not to
mention accidents, such as sunstrokes, drowning or conflag-
rations, when the instinct of self-preservation makes even the
kindest, most moral men commit cruel actions, and excuse such
actions when committed by others.

Fourthly, these people were forced to associate with others who
were particularly depraved by life, and especially by these very
institutions – rakes, murderers and villains – who act on those who
are not yet corrupted by the measures inflicted on them as leaven
acts on dough.

And fifthly, the fact that all sorts of violence, cruelty, inhumanity, are not only tolerated, but even permitted by the government, when it suits its purposes, was impressed on them most forcibly by the inhuman treatment they were subjected to: by the sufferings inflicted on children, women and old men; by floggings with rods and whips; by rewards offered for bringing a fugitive back, dead or alive; by the separation of husbands and wives, and the uniting them with the wives and husbands of others for sexual intercourse; by shooting or hanging them. To those who were deprived of their freedom, who were in want and misery, acts of violence were evidently still more permissible. All these institutions seemed purposely invented for the production of depravity and vice, condensed to such a degree that no other conditions could produce it, and for the spreading of this condensed depravity and vice broadcast among the whole population.

'Just as if a problem had been set to find the best, the surest means of depraving the greatest number of persons,' thought Nekhlyudov, while investigating the deeds that were being done in the prisons and halting stations. Every year hundreds of thousands were brought to the highest pitch of depravity, and when completely depraved they were set free to carry the depravity they had caught in prison among the people. In the prisons of Tamen, Ekaterinburg, Tomsk and at the halting stations Nekhlyudov saw how successfully the object society seemed to have set itself was attained.

Ordinary, simple men with a conception of the demands of the social and Christian Russian peasant morality lost this conception, and found a new one, founded chiefly on the idea that any outrage or violence was justifiable if it seemed profitable. After living in a prison those people became conscious with the whole of their being that, judging by what was happening to themselves, all the moral laws, the respect and the sympathy for others which church and the moral teachers preach, was really set aside, and that therefore, they too need not keep the laws. Nekhlyudov noticed the effects of prison life on all the convicts he knew – on Fedorov, on Makar, and even on Taras, who, after two months among the convicts, struck Nekhlyudov by the want of morality in his arguments. Nekhlyudov found out during his journey how tramps, escaping into the marshes, persuade a comrade to escape with them, and then kill him and feed on his flesh. (He saw a living man who was accused of this and acknowledged the fact.) And the most terrible part was that this was not a solitary, but a recurring case.

Only by a special cultivation of vice, such as was perpetrated in these establishments, could a Russian be brought to the state of this tramp, who excelled Nietzsche's newest teaching, and held that everything was possible and nothing forbidden, and who spread this teaching first among the convicts and then among the people in general.

The only explanation of all that was being done was the wish to put a stop to crime by fear, by correction, by lawful vengeance as it was written in the books. But in reality nothing in the least resembling any of these results came to pass. Instead of vice being put a stop to, it only spread further; instead of being frightened, the criminals were encouraged (many a tramp returned to prison of his own free will). Instead of being corrected, every kind of vice was systematically instilled, while the desire for vengeance did not weaken by the measures of the government, but was bred in the people who had none of it.

'Then why is it done?' Nekhlyudov asked himself, but could find no answer. And what seemed most surprising was that all this was not being done accidentally, not by mistake, not once, but that it had continued for centuries, with this difference only, that at first the people's nostrils used to be torn and their ears cut off; then they were branded, and now they were manacled and transported by steam instead of on the old carts. The arguments brought forward by those in government service, who said that the things which aroused his indignation were simply due to the imperfect arrangements of the places of confinement, and that they could all be put to rights if prisons of a modern type were built, did not satisfy Nekhlyudov, because he knew that what revolted him was not the consequence of a better or worse arrangement of the prisons. He had read of model prisons with electric bells, of executions by electricity, recommended by Tard; but this refined kind of violence revolted him even more.

But what revolted Nekhlyudov most was that there were men in the law courts and in the ministry who received large salaries, taken from the people, for referring to books written by men like themselves and with like motives, and sorting actions that violated laws made by themselves according to different statutes; and, in obedience to these statutes, sending those guilty of such actions to places where they were completely at the mercy of cruel, hardened inspectors, jailers, convoy soldiers, where millions of them perished body and soul.

Now that he had a closer knowledge of prisons, Nekhlyudov found out that all those vices which developed among the prisoners – drunkenness, gambling, cruelty, and all these terrible crimes, even cannibalism – were not casual, or due to degeneration or to the existence of monstrosities of the criminal type, as science, going hand in hand with the government, explained it, but an unavoidable consequence of the incomprehensible delusion that men may punish one another. Nekhlyudov saw that cannibalism did not commence in the marshes, but in the ministry. He saw that his brother-in-law, for example, and, in fact, all the lawyers and officials, from the usher to the minister, do not care in the least for justice or the good of the people about whom they spoke, but only for the roubles they were paid for doing the things that were the source whence all this degradation and suffering flowed. This was quite evident.

'Can it be, then, that all this is done simply through misapprehension? Could it not be managed that all these officials should have their salaries secured to them, and a premium paid them, besides, so that they should leave off doing all that they were doing now?' Nekhlyudov thought; and in spite of the fleas, that seemed to spring up round him like water from a fountain whenever he moved, he fell fast asleep.

Chapter 20

The journey resumed

The carters had left the inn long before Nekhlyudov awoke. The landlady had had her tea, and came in wiping her fat, perspiring neck with her handkerchief, and said that a soldier had brought a note from the halting station. The note was from Mary Pavlovna. She wrote that Kryltzov's attack was more serious than they had imagined. 'We wished him to be left behind and to remain with him, but this has not been allowed, so that we shall take him on; but we fear the worst. Please arrange so that if he should be left in the next town, one of us might remain with him. If in order to get the permission to stay I should be obliged to get married to him, I am of course ready to do so.'

Nekhlyudov sent the young labourer to the post station to order horses and began packing up hurriedly. Before he had drunk his second tumbler of tea the three-horsed postcart drove up to the porch with ringing bells, the wheels rattling on the frozen mud as on stones. Nekhlyudov paid the fat-necked landlady, hurried out and got into the cart, and gave orders to the driver to go on as fast as possible, so as to overtake the gang. Just past the gates of the commune pasture ground they did overtake the carts, loaded with sacks and the sick prisoners, as they rattled over the frozen mud, that was just beginning to be rolled smooth by the wheels (the officer was not there, he had gone in advance). The soldiers, who had evidently been drinking, followed by the side of the road, chatting merrily. There were a great many carts. In each of the first carts sat six invalid criminal convicts, close-packed. On each of the last two were three political prisoners. Novodvorov, Grabetz and Kondratiev sat on one, Rintzeva, Nabatov and the woman to whom Mary Pavlovna had given up her own place on the other, and on one of the carts lay Kryltzov on a heap of hay, with a pillow under his head, and Mary Pavlovna sat by him on the edge of the cart. Nekhlyudov ordered his driver to stop, got out and went up to Kryltzov. One of the tipsy soldiers waved his hand towards Nekhlyudov, but he paid no attention and started walking by Kryltzov's side, holding on to the side of the cart with his hand. Dressed in a sheepskin coat, with a fur cap on his head and his mouth bound up with a handkerchief, he seemed paler and thinner than ever. His beautiful eyes looked very large and brilliant. Shaken from side to side by the jottings of the cart, he lay with his eyes fixed on Nekhlyudov; but when asked about his health, he only closed his eyes and angrily shook his head. All his energy seemed to be needed in order to bear the jolting of the cart. Mary Pavlovna was on the other side. She exchanged a significant glance with Nekhlyudov, which expressed all her anxiety about Kryltzov's state, and then began to talk at once in a cheerful manner.

'It seems the officer is ashamed of himself,' she shouted, so as to be heard above the rattle of the wheels. 'Busovkin's manacles have been removed, and he is carrying his little girl himself. Katusha and Simonson are with him, and Vera, too. She has taken my place.'

Kryltzov said something that could not be heard because of the noise, and frowning in the effort to repress his cough shook his head. Then Nekhlyudov stooped towards him, so as to hear, and Kryltzov, freeing his mouth of the handkerchief, whispered:

'Much better now. Only not to catch cold.'

Nekhlyudov nodded in acquiescence, and again exchanged a glance with Mary Pavlovna.

'How about the problem of the three bodies?' whispered Kryltzov, smiling with great difficulty. 'The solution is difficult.'

Nekhlyudov did not understand, but Mary Pavlovna explained that he meant the well-known mathematical problem which defined the position of the sun, moon and earth, which Kryltzov compared to the relations between Nekhlyudov, Katusha and Simonson. Kryltzov nodded, to show that Mary Pavlovna had explained his joke correctly.

'The decision does not lie with me,' Nekhlyudov said.

'Did you get my note? Will you do it?' Mary Pavlovna asked.

'Certainly,' answered Nekhlyudov; and noticing a look of displeasure on Kryltzov's face, he returned to his conveyance, and holding with both hands to the sides of the cart, got in, which jolted with him over the ruts of the rough road. He passed the gang, which, with its grey cloaks and sheepskin coats, chains and manacles, stretched over three-quarters of a mile of the road. On the opposite side of the road Nekhlyudov noticed Katusha's blue shawl, Vera Doukhova's black coat, and Simonson's crochet cap, white worsted stockings, with bands, like those of sandals, tied round him. Simonson was walking with the woman and carrying on a heated discussion.

When they saw Nekhlyudov they bowed to him, and Simonson raised his hat in a solemn manner. Nekhlyudov, having nothing to say, did not stop, and was soon ahead of the carts. Having got again on to a smoother part of the road, they drove still more quickly, but they had continually to turn aside to let pass long rows of carts that were moving along the road in both directions.

The road, which was cut up by deep ruts, lay through a thick pine forest, mingled with birch trees and larches, bright with yellow leaves they had not yet shed. By the time Nekhlyudov had passed about half the gang he reached the end of the forest. Fields now lay stretched along both sides of the road, and the crosses and cupolas of a monastery appeared in the distance. The clouds had dispersed, and it had cleared up completely; the leaves, the frozen puddles and the gilt crosses and cupolas of the monastery glittered brightly in the sun that had risen above the forest. A little to the right mountains began to gleam white in the blue-grey distance, and the trap entered a large village. The village street was full of people, both Russians and other nationalities, wearing peculiar caps and cloaks. Tipsy men and women crowded and chattered round booths, traktirs, public houses and carts. The vicinity of a town was noticeable. Giving a pull and a lash of the whip to the horse on his right, the driver sat down sideways on the right edge of the seat, so that the reins hung over that side, and with evident desire of showing off, he drove quickly down to the river, which had to be crossed by a ferry. The raft was coming towards them, and had reached the middle of the river. About twenty carts were waiting to cross. Nekhlyudov had not long to wait. The raft, which had been pulled far up the stream, quickly approached the landing, carried by the swift waters. The tall, silent, broad-shouldered, muscular ferryman, dressed in sheepskins, threw the ropes and moored the raft with practised hand, landed the carts that were on it, and put those that were waiting on the bank on board. The whole raft was filled with vehicles and horses shuffling at the sight of the water. The broad, swift river splashed against the sides of the ferryboats, tightening their moorings.

When the raft was full, and Nekhlyudov's cart, with the horses taken out of it, stood closely surrounded by other carts on the side of the raft, the ferryman barred the entrance, and, paying no heed to the prayers of those who had not found room in the raft, unfastened the ropes and set off.

All was quiet on the raft; one could hear nothing but the tramp of the ferryman's boots and the horses changing from foot to foot.

Chapter 21

'Just a worthless tramp'

Nekhlyudov stood on the edge of the raft looking at the broad river. Two pictures kept rising up in his mind. One, that of Kryltzov, unprepared for death and dying, made a heavy, sorrowful impression on him. The other, that of Katusha, full of energy, having gained the love of such a man as Simonson, and found a true and solid path towards righteousness, should have been pleasant, yet it also created a heavy impression on Nekhlyudov's mind, and he could not conquer this impression.

The vibrating sounds of a big brass bell reached them from the town. Nekhlyudov's driver, who stood by his side, and the other men on the raft raised their caps and crossed themselves, all except a short, dishevelled old man, who stood close to the railway and whom Nekhlyudov had not noticed before. He did not cross himself, but raised his head and looked at Nekhlyudov. This old man wore a patched coat, cloth trousers and worn and patched shoes. He had a small wallet on his back, and a high fur cap with the fur much rubbed on his head.

'Why don't you pray, old chap?' asked Nekhlyudov's driver as he replaced and straightened his cap. 'Are you unbaptized?'

'Who's one to pray to?' asked the old man quickly, in a determinedly aggressive tone.

'To whom? To God, of course,' said the driver sarcastically.

'And you just show me where he is, that god.' There was something so serious and firm in the expression of the old man, that the driver felt that he had to do with a strong-minded man, and was a bit abashed. And trying not to show this, not to be silenced, and not to be put to shame before the crowd that was observing them, he answered quickly.

'Where? In heaven, of course.'

'And have you been up there?'

'Whether I've been or not, everyone knows that you must pray to God.'

'No one has ever seen God at any time. The only begotten Son who is in the bosom of the Father he hath declared him,' said the old man in the same rapid manner, and with a severe frown on his brow.

'It's clear you are not a Christian, but a hole-worshipper. You pray to a hole,' said the driver, shoving the handle of his whip into his girdle, pulling straight the harness on one of the horses.

Someone laughed.

'What is your faith, Dad?' asked a middle-aged man, who stood by his cart on the same side of the raft.

'I have no kind of faith, because I believe no one – no one but myself,' said the old man as quickly and decidedly as before.

'How can you believe yourself?' Nekhlyudov asked, entering into a conversation with him. 'You might make a mistake.'

'Never in your life,' the old man said decidedly, with a toss of his head.

'Then why are there different faiths?' Nekhlyudov asked.

'It's just because men believe others and do not believe themselves that there are different faiths. I also believed others, and lost myself as in a swamp – lost myself so that I had no hope of finding my way out. Old Believers and New Believers and Judaisers and Khlysty and Popovitzy, and Bespopovitzy and Avstriaks and Molokans and Skoptzy – every faith praises itself only, and so they all creep about like blind puppies. There are many faiths, but the spirit is one – in me and in you and in him. So that if everyone believes himself all will be united. Everyone be himself, and all will be as one.'

The old man spoke loudly and often looked round, evidently wishing that as many as possible should hear him.

'And have you long held this faith?'

'I? A long time. This is the twenty-third year that they persecute me.'

'Persecute you? How?'

'As they persecuted Christ, so they persecute me. They seize me, and take me before the courts and before the priests, the Scribes and the Pharisees. Once they put me into a madhouse; but they can do nothing because I am free. They say, "What is your name?" thinking I shall name myself. But I do not give myself a name. I have given up everything: I have no name, no place, no country, nor anything. I am just myself. "What is your name?" "Man." "How old are you?" I say, "I do not count my years and cannot count them, because I always was, I always shall be." "Who are your parents?" "I have no parents except God and Mother Earth. God is my father." "And the Tsar? Do you recognise the Tsar?" they say. I say, "Why not? He is his own Tsar, and I am my own Tsar." "Where's the good of talking to him?" they say; and I say, "I do not ask you to talk to me." And so they begin tormenting me.'

'And where are you going now?' asked Nekhlyudov.

'Where God will lead me. I work when I can find work, and when I can't I beg.' The old man noticed that the raft was approaching the bank and stopped, looking round at the bystanders with a look of triumph.

Nekhlyudov got out his purse and offered some money to the old man, but he refused, saying:

'I do not accept this sort of thing – bread I do accept.'

'Well, then, excuse me.'

'There is nothing to excuse, you have not offended me. And it is not possible to offend me.' And the old man put the wallet he had taken off again on his back. Meanwhile, the post-cart had been landed and the horses harnessed.

'I wonder you should care to talk to him, sir,' said the driver, when Nekhlyudov, having tipped the bowing ferryman, got into the cart again. 'He is just a worthless tramp.'

Chapter 22

Nekhlyudov sees the general

When they got to the top of the hill bank the driver turned to Nekhlyudov.

'Which hotel am I to drive to?'

'Which is the best?'

'Nothing could be better than the Siberian, but Dukov's is also good.'

'Drive to whichever you like.'

The driver again seated himself sideways and drove faster. The town was like all such towns. The same kind of houses with attic windows and green roofs, the same kind of cathedral, the same kind of shops and stores in the principal street, and even the same kind of policemen. Only the houses were almost all of them wooden, and the streets were not paved. In one of the chief streets the driver stopped at the door of an hotel, but there was no room to be had, so he drove to another. And here Nekhlyudov, after two months, found himself once again in surroundings such as he had been accustomed to as far as comfort and cleanliness went. Though the room he was shown to was simple enough, yet Nekhlyudov felt greatly relieved to be there after two months of post-carts, country inns and halting stations. His first business was to clean himself of the lice which he had never been able to get thoroughly rid of after visiting a halting station. When he had unpacked he went to the Russian bath, after which he made himself fit to be seen in a town, put on a starched shirt, trousers that had got rather creased along the seams, a frock-coat and an overcoat, and drove to the governor of the district. The hotel-keeper called an *isvostchik*, whose well-fed Kirghiz horse and vibrating trap soon brought Nekhlyudov to the large porch of a big building, in front of which stood sentinels and a policeman. The house had a garden in front, and at the back, among the naked branches of aspen and birch trees, there grew thick and dark green pines and firs.

The general was not well, and did not receive; but Nekhlyudov asked the footman to hand in his card all the same, and the footman came back with a favourable reply.

'You are asked to come in.'

The hall, the footman, the orderly, the staircase, the dancing-room, with its well-polished floor, were very much the same as in Petersburg, only more imposing and rather dirtier. Nekhlyudov was shown into the cabinet.

The general, a bloated, potato-nosed man, with a sanguine disposition, large bumps on his forehead, bald head, and puffs under his eyes, sat wrapped in a Tartar silk dressing-gown smoking a cigarette and sipping his tea out of a tumbler in a silver holder.

'How do you do, sir? Excuse my dressing-gown; it is better
so than if I had not received you at all,' he said, pulling up his
dressing-gown over his fat neck with its deep folds at the nape. 'I
am not quite well, and do not go out. What has brought you to
our remote region?'

'I am accompanying a gang of prisoners, among whom there is a
person closely connected with me, said Nekhlyudov, and now I
have come to see your Excellency partly in behalf of this person,
and partly about another business.' The general took a whiff and a
sip of tea, put his cigarette into a malachite ashpan, with his
narrow eyes fixed on Nekhlyudov, listening seriously. He only
interrupted him once to offer him a cigarette.

The general belonged to the learned type of military men who
believed that liberal and humane views can be reconciled with
their profession. But being by nature a kind and intelligent man,
he soon felt the impossibility of such a reconciliation; so as not to
feel the inner discord in which he was living, he gave himself up
more and more to the habit of drinking, which is so widely spread
among military men, and was now suffering from what doctors
term alcoholism. He was imbued with alcohol, and if he drank
any kind of liquor it made him tipsy. Yet strong drink was an
absolute necessity to him, he could not live without it, so he was
quite drunk every evening; but had grown so used to this state that
he did not reel nor talk any special nonsense. And if he did talk
nonsense, it was accepted as words of wisdom because of the
important and high position which he occupied. Only in the
morning, just at the time Nekhlyudov came to see him, he was
like a reasonable being, could understand what was said to him,
and fulfil more or less aptly a proverb he was fond of repeating:
'He's tipsy, but he's wise, so he's pleasant in two ways.'

The higher authorities knew he was a drunkard, but he was
more educated than the rest, though his education had stopped at
the spot where drunkenness had got hold of him. He was bold,
adroit, of imposing appearance, and showed tact even when tipsy;
therefore, he was appointed, and was allowed to retain so public
and responsible an office.

Nekhlyudov told him that the person he was interested in was a
woman, that she was sentenced, though innocent, and that a
petition had been sent to the Emperor in her behalf.

'Yes, well?' said the general.

'I was promised in Petersburg that the news concerning her fate should be sent to me not later than this month and to this place–'

The general stretched his hand with its stumpy fingers towards the table, and rang a bell, still looking at Nekhlyudov and puffing at his cigarette.

'So I would like to ask you that this woman should be allowed to remain here until the answer to her petition comes.'

The footman, an orderly in uniform, came in.

'Ask if Anna Vasilievna is up,' said the general to the orderly, 'and bring some more tea.' Then, turning to Nekhlyudov, 'Yes, and what else?'

'My other request concerns a political prisoner who is with the same gang.'

'Dear me,' said the general, with a significant shake of the head.

'He is seriously ill – dying, and he will probably be left here in the hospital, so one of the women prisoners would like to stay behind with him.'

'She is no relation of his?'

'No, but she is willing to marry him if that will enable her to remain with him.'

The general looked fixedly with twinkling eyes at his interlocutor, and, evidently with a wish to discomfit him, listened, smoking in silence.

When Nekhlyudov had finished, the general took a book off the table, and, wetting his finger, quickly turned over the pages and found the statute relating to marriage.

'What is she sentenced to?' he asked, looking up from the book.

'She? To hard labour.'

'Well, then, the position of one sentenced to that cannot be bettered by marriage.'

'Yes, but – '

'Excuse me. Even if a free man should marry her, she would have to serve her term. The question in such cases is, whose is the heavier punishment, hers or his?'

'They are both sentenced to hard labour.'

'Very well; so they are quits,' said the general, with a laugh. 'She's got what he has, only as he is sick he may be left behind, and of course what can be done to lighten his fate shall be done.

But as for her, even if she did marry him, she could not remain behind.'

'The generaless is having her coffee,' the footman announced.

The general nodded and continued:

'However, I shall think about it. What are their names? Put them down here.'

Nekhlyudov wrote down the names.

Nekhlyudov's request to be allowed to see the dying man the general answered by saying, 'Neither can I do that. Of course I do not suspect you, but you take an interest in him and in the others, and you have money, and here with us anything can be done with money. I have been told to put down bribery. But how can I put down bribery when everybody takes bribes? And the lower their rank the more ready they are to be bribed. How can one find it out across more than three thousand miles? There any official is a little Tsar, just as I am here,' and he laughed. 'You have in all likelihood been to see the political prisoners; you gave money and got permission to see them,' he said, with a smile. 'Is it not so?'

'Yes, it is.'

'I quite understand that you had to do it. You pity a political prisoner and wish to see him. And the inspector or the convoy soldier accepts, because he has a salary of twice twenty copecks and a family, and he can't help accepting it. In his place and yours I should have acted in the same way as you and he did. But in my position I do not permit myself to swerve an inch from the letter of the law, just because I am a man, and might be influenced by pity. But I am a member of the executive, and I have been placed in a position of trust on certain conditions, and these conditions I must carry out. Well, so this business is finished. And now let us hear what is going on in the metropolis.' And the general began questioning with the evident desire to hear the news and to show how very human he was.

Chapter 23

The sentence commuted

'By-the-way, where are you staying?' asked the general as he was taking leave of Nekhlyudov. 'At Dukov's? Well, it's horrid enough there. Come and dine with us at five o'clock. You speak English?'

'Yes, I do.'

'That's good. You see, an English traveller has just arrived here. He is studying the question of transportation and examining the prisons of Siberia. Well, he is dining with us tonight, and you come and meet him. We dine at five, and my wife expects punctuality. Then I shall also give you an answer what to do about that woman, and perhaps it may be possible to leave someone behind with the sick prisoner.'

Having made his bow to the general, Nekhlyudov drove to the post-office, feeling himself in an extremely animated and energetic frame of mind.

The post-office was a low-vaulted room. Several officials sat behind a counter serving the people, of whom there was quite a crowd. One official sat with his head bent to one side and kept stamping the envelopes, which he slipped dexterously under the stamp. Nekhlyudov had not long to wait. As soon as he had given his name, everything that had come for him by post was at once handed to him. There was a good deal: letters, and money, and books, and the last number of *Fatherland Notes*. Nekhlyudov took all these things to a wooden bench, on which a soldier with a book in his hand sat waiting for something, took the seat by his side, and began sorting the letters. Among them was one registered letter in a fine envelope, with a distinctly stamped bright red seal. He broke the seal, and seeing a letter from Selenin and some official paper inside the envelope, he felt the blood rush to his face, and his heart stood still. It was the answer to

Katusha's petition. What would that answer be? Nekhlyudov glanced hurriedly through the letter, written in an illegibly small, hard, and cramped hand, and breathed a sigh of relief. The answer was a favourable one.

Dear friend [wrote Selenin], our last talk has made a profound impression on me. You were right concerning Maslova. I looked carefully through the case, and see that shocking injustice has been done her. It could be remedied only by the Committee of Petitions before which you laid it. I managed to assist at the examination of the case, and I enclose herewith the copy of the mitigation of the sentence. Your aunt, the Countess Katerina Ivanovna, gave me the address which I am sending this to. The original document has been sent to the place where she was imprisoned before her trial, and will from there be probably sent at once to the principal government office in Siberia. I hasten to communicate this glad news to you and warmly press your hand.

Yours,
Selenin

The document ran thus: 'His Majesty's office for the reception of petitions, addressed to his Imperial name' – here followed the date – 'by order of the chief of his Majesty's office for the reception of petitions addressed to his Imperial name. The meschanka Katerina Maslova is hereby informed that his Imperial Majesty, with reference to her most loyal petition, condescending to her request, deigns to order that her sentence to hard labour should be commuted to one of exile to the less distant districts of Siberia.'

This was joyful and important news; all that Nekhlyudov could have hoped for Katusha, and for himself also, had happened. It was true that the new position she was in brought new complications with it. While she was a convict, marriage with her could only be fictitious, and would have had no meaning except that he would have been in a position to alleviate her condition. And now there was nothing to prevent their living together, and Nekhlyudov had not prepared himself for that. And, besides, what of her relations to Simonson? What was the meaning of her words yesterday? If she consented to a union with Simonson, would it be well? He could not unravel all these questions, and gave up thinking about it. 'It will all clear itself up later on,' he thought; 'I must not think about it now, but convey the glad news to her as soon as possible, and set her free.' He thought that the copy of the document he had received would suffice, so when he left the post-office he told the *isvostchik* to drive him to the prison.

Though he had received no order from the governor to visit the prison that morning, he knew by experience that it was easy to get from the subordinates what the higher officials would not grant, so now he meant to try and get into the prison to bring Katusha the joyful news, and perhaps to get her set free, and at the same time to inquire about Kryltzov's state of health, and tell him and Mary Pavlovna what the general had said. The prison inspector was a tall, imposing-looking man, with moustaches and whiskers that twisted towards the corners of his mouth. He received Nekhlyudov very gravely, and told him plainly that he could not grant an outsider the permission to interview the prisoners without a special order from his chief. To Nekhlyudov's remark that he had been allowed to visit the prisoners even in the cities he answered:

'That may be so, but I do not allow it,' and his tone implied, 'You city gentlemen may think to surprise and perplex us, but we in Eastern Siberia also know what the law is, and may even teach it you.' The copy of a document straight from the Emperor's own office did not have any effect on the prison inspector either. He decidedly refused to let Nekhlyudov come inside the prison walls. He only smiled contemptuously at Nekhlyudov's naive conclusion, that the copy he had received would suffice to set Maslova free, and declared that a direct order from his own superiors would be needed before anyone could be set at liberty. The only things he agreed to do were to communicate to Maslova that a mitigation had arrived for her, and to promise that he would not detain her an hour after the order from his chief to liberate her would arrive. He would also give no news of Kryltzov, saying he could not even tell if there was such a prisoner; and so Nekhlyudov, having accomplished next to nothing, got into his trap and drove back to his hotel.

The strictness of the inspector was chiefly due to the fact that an epidemic of typhus had broken out in the prison, owing to twice the number of persons that it was intended for being crowded in it. The *isvostchik* who drove Nekhlyudov said, 'Quite a lot of people are dying in the prison every day, some kind of disease having sprung up among them, so that as many as twenty were buried in one day.'

Chapter 24

The general's household

In spite of his ineffectual attempt at the prison, Nekhlyudov, still in the same vigorous, energetic frame of mind, went to the governor's office to see if the original of the document had arrived for Maslova. It had not arrived, so Nekhlyudov went back to the hotel and wrote without delay to Selenin and the advocate about it. When he had finished writing he looked at his watch and saw it was time to go to the general's dinner party.

On the way he again began wondering how Katusha would receive the news of the mitigation of her sentence. Where she would be settled? How he should live with her? What about Simonson? What would his relations to her be? He remembered the change that had taken place in her, and this reminded him of her past. 'I must forget it for the present,' he thought, and again hastened to drive her out of his mind. 'When the time comes I shall see,' he said to himself, and began to think of what he ought to say to the general.

The dinner at the general's, with the luxury habitual to the lives of the wealthy and those of high rank, to which Nekhlyudov had been accustomed, was extremely enjoyable after he had been so long deprived not only of luxury but even of the most ordinary comforts. The mistress of the house was a Petersburg *grande dame* of the old school, a maid of honour at the court of Nicholas I, who spoke French quite naturally and Russian very unnaturally. She held herself very erect and, moving her hands, she kept her elbows close to her waist. She was quietly and somewhat sadly considerate of her husband, and extremely kind to all her visitors, though with a tinge of difference in her behaviour according to their position.

She received Nekhlyudov as if he were one of them, and her fine, almost imperceptible flattery made him once again aware of his virtues and gave him a feeling of satisfaction. She made him feel that she knew of that honest though rather singular step of his which had brought him to Siberia, and held him to be an exceptional man. This refined flattery and the elegance and luxury of the general's house had the effect of making Nekhlyudov succumb to the enjoyment of the handsome surroundings, the delicate dishes and the ease and pleasure of intercourse with educated people of his own class, so that the surroundings in the midst of which he had lived for the last months seemed a dream from which he had awakened to reality. Besides those of the household, the general's daughter and her husband and an aide-de-camp, there were an Englishman, a merchant interested in gold mines, and the governor of a distant Siberian town. All these people seemed pleasant to Nekhlyudov. The Englishman, a healthy man with a rosy complexion, who spoke very bad French, but whose command of his own language was very good and oratorically impressive, who had seen a great deal, was very interesting to listen to when he spoke about America, India, Japan and Siberia.

The young merchant interested in the gold mines, the son of a peasant, whose evening dress was made in London, who had diamond studs to his shirt, possessed a fine library, contributed freely to philanthropic work, and held liberal European views, seemed pleasant to Nekhlyudov as a sample of a quite new and good type of civilised European culture, grafted on a healthy, uncultivated peasant stem.

The governor of the distant Siberian town was that same man who had been so much talked about in Petersburg at the time Nekhlyudov was there. He was plump, with thin, curly hair, soft blue eyes, carefully-tended white hands, with rings on the fingers, a pleasant smile, and very big in the lower part of his body. The master of the house valued this governor because of all the officials he was the only one who would not be bribed. The mistress of the house, who was very fond of music and a very good pianist herself, valued him because he was a good musician and played duets with her.

Nekhlyudov was in such good humour that even this man was not unpleasant to him, in spite of what he knew of his vices. The bright, energetic aide-de-camp, with his bluey grey chin, who was continually offering his services, pleased Nekhlyudov by his good nature. But it was the charming young couple, the general's daughter and her husband, who pleased Nekhlyudov best. The daughter was a plain-looking, simple-minded young woman, wholly absorbed in her two children. Her husband, whom she had fallen in love with and married after a long struggle with her parents, was a Liberal, who had taken honours at the Moscow University, a modest and intellectual young man in government service, who made up statistics and studied chiefly the foreign tribes, which he liked and tried to save from dying out.

All of them were not only kind and attentive to Nekhlyudov, but evidently pleased to see him, as a new and interesting acquaintance. The general, who came in to dinner in uniform and with a white cross round his neck, greeted Nekhlyudov as a friend, and asked the visitors to the side table to take a glass of vodka and something to whet their appetites. The general asked Nekhlyudov what he had been doing since he left that morning, and Nekhlyudov told him he had been to the post-office and received the news of the mitigation of that person's sentence that he had spoken of in the morning, and again asked for a permission to visit the prison.

The general, apparently displeased that business should be mentioned at dinner, frowned and said nothing.

'Have a glass of vodka' he said, addressing the Englishman, who had just come up to the table. The Englishman drank a glass, and said he had been to see the cathedral and the factory, but would like to visit the great transportation prison.

'Oh, that will just fit in,' said the general to Nekhlyudov. 'You will be able to go together. Give them a pass,' he added, turning to his aide-de-camp.

'When would you like to go?' Nekhlyudov asked.

'I prefer visiting the prisons in the evening,' the Englishman answered. 'All are indoors and there is no preparation; you find them all as they are.'

'Ah, he would like to see it in all its glory! Let him do so. I have written about it and no attention has been paid to it. Let him find out from foreign publications,' the general said, and went up to the dinner table, where the mistress of the house was showing the visitors their places. Nekhlyudov sat between his hostess and the

Englishman. In front of him sat the general's daughter and the ex-director of the government department in Petersburg. The conversation at dinner was carried on by fits and starts: now it was India that the Englishman talked about, now the Tonkin expedition that the general strongly disapproved of, now the universal bribery and corruption in Siberia. All these topics did not interest Nekhlyudov much.

But after dinner, over their coffee, Nekhlyudov and the Englishman began a very interesting conversation about Gladstone, and Nekhlyudov thought he had said many clever things which were noticed by his interlocutor. And Nekhlyudov felt it more and more pleasant to be sipping his coffee seated in an easy-chair among amiable, well-bred people. And when at the Englishman's request the hostess went up to the piano with the ex-director of the government department, and they began to play in well-practised style Beethoven's fifth symphony, Nekhlyudov fell into a mental state of perfect self-satisfaction to which he had long been a stranger, as though he had only just found out what a good fellow he was.

The grand piano was a splendid instrument, the symphony was well performed. At least, so it seemed to Nekhlyudov, who knew and liked that symphony. Listening to the beautiful *andante*, he felt a tickling in his nose, he was so touched by his many virtues.

Nekhlyudov thanked his hostess for the enjoyment that he had been deprived of for so long, and was about to say goodbye and go when the daughter of the house came up to him with a determined look and said, with a blush, 'You asked about my children. Would you like to see them?'

'She thinks that everybody wants to see her children,' said her mother, smiling at her daughter's winning tactlessness. 'The Prince is not at all interested.'

'On the contrary, I am very much interested,' said Nekhlyudov, touched by this overflowing, happy mother-love. 'Please let me see them.'

'She's taking the Prince to see her babies,' the general shouted, laughing from the card-table, where he sat with his son-in-law, the mine owner and the aide-de-camp. 'Go, go, pay your tribute.'

The young woman, visibly excited by the thought that judgment was about to be passed on her children, went quickly towards the inner apartments, followed by Nekhlyudov. In the third, a lofty room, papered with white and lit up by a shaded lamp, stood two small cots, and a nurse with a white cape on her shoulders sat between the cots. She had a kindly, true Siberian face, with its high cheek-bones.

The nurse rose and bowed. The mother stooped over the first cot, in which a two-year-old little girl lay peacefully sleeping with her little mouth open and her long, curly hair tumbled over the pillow.

'This is Katie,' said the mother, straightening the white and blue crochet coverlet, from under which a little white foot pushed itself languidly out.

'Is she not pretty? She's only two years old, you know.'

'Lovely.'

'And this is Vassuk, as "grandpapa" calls him. Quite a different type. A Siberian, is he not?'

'A splendid boy,' said Nekhlyudov, as he looked at the little fatty lying asleep on his stomach.

'Yes,' said the mother, with a smile full of meaning.

Nekhlyudov recalled to his mind chains, shaved heads, fighting debauchery, the dying Kryltzov, Katusha and the whole of her past, and he began to feel envious and to wish for what he saw here, which now seemed to him pure and refined happiness.

After having repeatedly expressed his admiration of the children, thereby at least partially satisfying their mother, who eagerly drank in this praise, he followed her back to the drawing-room, where the Englishman was waiting for him to go and visit the prison, as they had arranged. Having taken leave of their hosts, the old and the young ones, the Englishman and Nekhlyudov went out into the porch of the general's house.

The weather had changed. It was snowing, and the snow fell densely in large flakes, and already covered the road, the roof and the trees in the garden, the steps of the porch, the roof of the trap and the back of the horse.

The Englishman had a trap of his own, and Nekhlyudov, having told the coachman to drive to the prison, called his *isvostchik* and got in with the heavy sense of having to fulfil an unpleasant duty, and followed the Englishman over the soft snow, through which the wheels turned with difficulty.

Chapter 25

Maslova's decision

The dismal prison house, with its sentinel and lamp burning under the gateway, produced an even more dismal impression, with its long row of lighted windows, than it had done in the morning, in spite of the white covering that now lay over everything – the porch, the roof and the walls.

The imposing inspector came up to the gate and read the pass that had been given to Nekhlyudov and the Englishman by the light of the lamp, shrugged his fine shoulders in surprise, but, in obedience to the order, asked the visitors to follow him in. He led them through the courtyard and then in at a door to the right and up a staircase into the office. He offered them a seat and asked what he could do for them, and when he heard that Nekhlyudov would like to see Maslova at once, he sent a jailer to fetch her. Then he prepared himself to answer the questions which the Englishman began to put to him, Nekhlyudov acting as interpreter.

'How many persons is the prison built to hold?' the Englishman asked. 'How many are confined in it? How many men? How many women? Children? How many sentenced to the mines? How many exiles? How many sick persons?'

Nekhlyudov translated the Englishman's and the inspector's words without paying any attention to their meaning, and felt an awkwardness he had not in the least expected at the thought of the impending interview. When, in the midst of a sentence he was translating for the Englishman, he heard the sound of approaching footsteps, and the office door opened, and, as had happened many times before, a jailer came in, followed by Katusha, and he saw her with a kerchief tied round her head and in a prison jacket, a heavy sensation came over him. 'I wish to live, I want a family, children, I want a human life.' These thoughts flashed through his mind as she entered the room with rapid steps and blinking her eyes.

He rose and made a few steps to meet her, and her face appeared hard and unpleasant to him. It was again as it had been at the time when she reproached him. She flushed and turned pale, her fingers nervously twisting a corner of her jacket. She looked up at him, then cast down her eyes.

'You know that a mitigation has come?'

'Yes, the jailer told me.'

'So that as soon as the original document arrives you may come away and settle where you like. We shall consider – '

She interrupted him hurriedly. 'What have I to consider? Where Valdemar Simonson goes, there I shall follow.' In spite of the excitement she was in she raised her eyes to Nekhlyudov's and pronounced these words quickly and distinctly, as if she had prepared what she had to say.

'Indeed!'

'Well, Dmitri Ivanovitch, you see he wishes me to live with him – ' and she stopped, quite frightened, and corrected herself. 'He wishes me to be near him. What more can I desire? I must look upon it as happiness. What else is there for me – '

'One of two things,' thought he. 'Either she loves Simonson and does not in the least require the sacrifice I imagined I was bringing her, or she still loves me and refuses me for my own sake, and is burning her ships by uniting her fate with Simonson.' And Nekhlyudov felt ashamed and knew that he was blushing.

'And you yourself, do you love him?' he asked.

'Loving or not loving, what does it matter? I have given up all that. And then Valdemar Simonson is quite an exceptional man.'

'Yes, of course,' Nekhlyudov began. 'He is a splendid man, and I think – '

But she again interrupted him, as if afraid that he might say too much or that she should not say all. 'No, Dmitri Ivanovitch, you must forgive me if I am not doing what you wish,' and she looked at him with those unfathomable, squinting eyes of hers. 'Yes, it evidently must be so. You must live, too.'

She said just what he had been telling himself a few moments before, but he no longer thought so now and felt very differently. He was not only ashamed, but felt sorry to lose all he was losing with her. 'I did not expect this,' he said.

'Why should you live here and suffer? You have suffered enough.'

'I have not suffered. It was good for me, and I should like to go on serving you if I could.'

'We do not want anything,' she said, and looked at him. 'You have done so much for me as it is. If it had not been for you – ' She wished to say more, but her voice trembled.

'You certainly have no reason to thank me,' Nekhlyudov said.

'Where is the use of our reckoning? God will make up our accounts,' she said, and her black eyes began to glisten with the tears that filled them.

'What a good woman you are,' he said.

'I good?' she said through her tears, and a pathetic smile lit up her face.

'Are you ready?' the Englishman asked.

'Directly,' replied Nekhlyudov and asked her about Kryltzov. She got over her emotion and quietly told him all she knew. Kryltzov was very weak and had been sent into the infirmary. Mary Pavlovna was very anxious, and had asked to be allowed to go to the infirmary as a nurse, but could not get the permission.

'Am I to go?' she asked, noticing that the Englishman was waiting.

'I will not say goodbye; I shall see you again,' said Nekhlyudov, holding out his hand.

'Forgive me,' she said so low that he could hardly hear her. Their eyes met, and Nekhlyudov knew by the strange look of her squinting eyes and the pathetic smile with which she said not 'Goodbye' but 'Forgive me,' that of the two reasons that might have led to her resolution, the second was the real one. She loved him, and thought that by uniting herself to him she would be spoiling his life. By going with Simonson she thought she would be setting Nekhlyudov free, and felt glad that she had done what she meant to do, and yet she suffered at parting from him.

She pressed his hand, turned quickly and left the room.

Nekhlyudov was ready to go, but saw that the Englishman was noting something down, and did not disturb him, but sat down on a wooden seat by the wall, and suddenly a feeling of terrible weariness came over him. It was not a sleepless night that had tired him, not the journey, not the excitement, but he felt terribly tired of living. He leaned against the back of the bench, shut his eyes and in a moment fell into a deep, heavy sleep.

'Well, would you like to look round the cells now?' the inspector asked.

Nekhlyudov looked up and was surprised to find himself where he was. The Englishman had finished his notes and expressed a wish to see the cells.

Nekhlyudov, tired and indifferent, followed him.

Chapter 26

The English visitor

When they had passed the anteroom and the sickening, stinking corridor, the Englishman and Nekhlyudov, accompanied by the inspector, entered the first cell, where those sentenced to hard labour were confined. The beds took up the middle of the cell and the prisoners were all in bed. There were about seventy of them. When the visitors entered all the prisoners jumped up and stood beside the beds, excepting two, a young man who was in a state of high fever, and an old man who did nothing but groan.

The Englishman asked if the young man had long been ill. The inspector said that he was taken ill in the morning, but that the old man had long been suffering with pains in the stomach, but could not be removed, as the infirmary had been overfilled for a long time. The Englishman shook his head disapprovingly, said he would like to say a few words to these people, asking Nekhlyudov to interpret. It turned out that besides studying the places of exile and the prisons of Siberia, the Englishman had another object in view, that of preaching salvation through faith and by the redemption.

'Tell them,' he said, 'that Christ died for them. If they believe in this they shall be saved.' While he spoke, all the prisoners stood silent with their arms at their sides. 'This book, tell them,' he continued, 'says all about it. Can any of them read?'

There were more than twenty who could.

The Englishman took several bound Testaments out of a hang-bag, and many strong hands with their hard, black nails stretched out from beneath the coarse shirt-sleeves towards him. He gave away two Testaments in this cell.

The same thing happened in the second cell. There was the same foul air, the same icon hanging between the windows, the same tub to the left of the door, and they were all lying side by side close to one another, and jumped up in the same manner and stood stretched full length with their arms by their sides, all but three, two of whom sat up and one remained lying, and did not even look at the newcomers; these three were also ill. The Englishman made the same speech and again gave away two books.

In the third room four were ill. When the Englishman asked why the sick were not put all together into one cell, the inspector said that they did not wish it themselves, that their diseases were not infectious, and that the medical assistant watched them and attended to them.

'He has not set foot here for a fortnight,' muttered a voice.

The inspector did not say anything and led the way to the next cell. Again the door was unlocked, and all got up and stood silent. Again the Englishman gave away Testaments. It was the same in the fifth and sixth cells, in those to the right and those to the left.

From those sentenced to hard labour they went on to the exiles.

From the exiles to those evicted by the commune and those who followed of their own free will.

Everywhere men, cold, hungry, idle, infected, degraded, imprisoned, were shown off like wild beasts.

The Englishman, having given away the appointed number of Testaments, stopped giving any more, and made no speeches. The oppressing sight, and especially the stifling atmosphere, quelled even his energy, and he went from cell to cell, saying nothing but 'All right' to the inspector's remarks about what prisoners there were in each cell.

Nekhlyudov followed as in a dream, unable either to refuse to go on or to go away, and with the same feelings of weariness and hopelessness.

In one of the exiles' cells Nekhlyudov, to his surprise, recognised the strange old man he had seen crossing the ferry that morning. This old man was sitting on the floor by the beds, barefooted, with only a dirty cinder-coloured shirt on, torn on one shoulder, and similar trousers. He looked severely and enquiringly at the new-comers. His emaciated body, visible through the holes of his shirt, looked miserably weak, but in his face was even more concentrated seriousness and animation than when Nekhlyudov saw him crossing the ferry. As in all the other cells, so here also the prisoners jumped up and stood erect when the official entered, but the old man remained sitting. His eyes glittered and his brows frowned with wrath.

'Get up,' the inspector called out to him.

The old man did not rise and only smiled contemptuously.

'Thy servants are standing before thee. I am not thy servant. Thou bearest the seal – ' The old man pointed to the inspector's forehead.

'Wha-a-t?' said the inspector threateningly, and made a step towards him.

'I know this man,' Nekhlyudov hastened to say; 'what is he imprisoned for?'

'The police have sent him here because he has no passport. We ask them not to send such, but they will do it,' said the inspector, casting an angry side look at the old man.

'And so it seems thou, too, art one of Antichrist's army?' the old man said to Nekhlyudov.

'No, I am a visitor,' said Nekhlyudov.

'What, hast thou come to see how Antichrist tortures men? There, look, he has locked them up in a cage, a whole army of them. Men should eat bread in the sweat of their brow. And he has locked them up with no work to do, and feeds them like swine, so that they should turn into beasts.'

'What is he saying?' asked the Englishman.

Nekhlyudov told him the old man was blaming the inspector for keeping men imprisoned.

'Ask him how he thinks one should treat those who do not keep to the laws,' said the Englishman.

Nekhlyudov translated the question. The old man laughed in a strange manner, showing his teeth.

'The laws?' he repeated with contempt. 'He first robbed everybody, took all the earth, all the rights away from men, killed all those who were against him, and then wrote laws, forbidding robbery and murder. He should have written these laws before.'

Nekhlyudov translated. The Englishman smiled. 'Well, anyhow, ask him how one should treat thieves and murderers at present?'

Nekhlyudov again translated his question.

'Tell him he should take the seal of Antichrist off himself,' the old man said, frowning severely; 'then there will be no thieves and murderers. Tell him so.'

'He is crazy,' said the Englishman, when Nekhlyudov had translated the old man's words, and, shrugging his shoulders, he left the cell.

'Do thy business and leave them alone. Everyone for himself. God knows whom to execute, whom to forgive, and we do not know,' said the old man. 'Every man be his own chief, then the chiefs will not be wanted. Go, go!' he added, angrily frowning and looking with glittering eyes at Nekhlyudov, who lingered in the cell. 'Hast thou not looked on long enough how the servants of Antichrist feed lice on men? Go, go!'

When Nekhlyudov went out he saw the Englishman standing by the open door of an empty cell with the inspector, asking what the cell was for. The inspector explained that it was the mortuary.

'Oh,' said the Englishman when Nekhlyudov had translated, and expressed the wish to go in.

The mortuary was an ordinary cell, not very large. A small lamp hung on the wall and dimly lit up sacks and logs of wood that were piled up in one corner, and four dead bodies lay on the bedshelves to the right. The first body had a coarse linen shirt and trousers on; it was that of a tall man with a small beard and half his head shaved. The body was quite rigid; the bluish hands, that had evidently been folded on the breast, had separated; the legs were also apart and the bare feet were sticking out. Next to him lay a bare-footed old woman in a white petticoat, her head, with its thin plait of hair, uncovered, with a little, pinched yellow face and a sharp nose. Beyond her was another man with something lilac on. This colour reminded Nekhlyudov of something. He came nearer and looked at the body. The small, pointed beard sticking upwards, the firm, well-shaped nose, the high, white forehead, the thin, curly hair; he recognised the familiar features and could hardly believe his eyes. Yesterday he had seen this face angry, excited, and full of suffering; now it was quiet, motionless, and terribly beautiful. Yes, it was Kryltzov, or at any rate the trace that his material existence had left behind. 'Why had he suffered? Why had he lived? Does he now understand?' Nekhlyudov thought, and there seemed to be no answer, seemed to be nothing but death, and he felt faint. Without taking leave of the Englishman, Nekhlyudov asked the inspector to lead him out into the yard, and feeling the absolute necessity of being alone to think over all that had happened that evening, he drove back to his hotel.

Chapter 28

A new life dawns for Nekhlyudov

Nekhlyudov did not go to bed, but went up and down his room for a long time. His business with Katusha was at an end. He was not wanted, and this made him sad and ashamed. His other business was not only unfinished, but troubled him more than ever and demanded his activity.

All this horrible evil that he had seen and learned to know lately, and especially today in that awful prison, this evil which had killed that dear Kryltzov, ruled and was triumphant, and he could foresee no possibility of conquering or even knowing how to conquer it.

Those hundreds and thousands of degraded human beings locked up in the noisome prisons by indifferent generals, procureurs, inspectors, rose up in his imagination; he remembered the strange, free old man accusing the officials, and therefore considered mad, and among the corpses the beautiful, waxen face of Kryltzov, who had died in anger. And again the question as to whether he was mad or those who considered they were in their right minds while they committed all these deeds stood before him with renewed force and demanded an answer.

Tired of pacing up and down, tired of thinking, he sat down on the sofa near the lamp and mechanically opened the Testament which the Englishman had given him as a remembrance, and which he had thrown on the table when he emptied his pockets on coming in.

'It is said one can find an answer to everything here,' he thought, and opened the Testament at random and began reading Matt. xviii. 1–4:

> In that hour came the disciples unto Jesus, saying, Who then is greatest in the Kingdom of Heaven? And He called to Him a little child, and set him in the midst of them, and said, Verily I say unto you, Except ye turn and become as little children, ye shall in nowise enter into the kingdom of heaven. Whosoever therefore shall humble himself as this little child the same is the greatest in the kingdom of heaven.

'Yes, yes, that is true,' he said, remembering that he had known the peace and joy of life only when he had humbled himself.

> And whosoever shall receive one such little child in My name receiveth Me, but whoso shall cause one of these little ones to stumble, it is more profitable for him that a great millstone should be hanged about his neck and that he should be sunk in the depths of the sea. (*Matt.* xviii. 5, 6.)

'What is this for, "Whosoever shall receive?" Receive where? And what does "in My name" mean?' he asked, feeling that these words did not tell him anything. 'And why "the millstone round his neck and the depths of the sea"? No, that is not it: it is not clear,' and he remembered how more than once in his life he had taken to reading the Gospels, and how want of clearness in these passages had repulsed him. He went on to read the seventh, eighth, ninth, and tenth verses about the occasions of stumbling, and that they must come, and about punishment by casting men into hell fire, and some kind of angels who see the face of the Father in Heaven. 'What a pity that this is so incoherent,' he thought, 'yet one feels that there is something good in it.'

For the Son of Man came to save that which was lost [he continued to read] How think ye? If any man have a hundred sheep and one of them go astray, doth he not leave the ninety and nine and go into the mountains and seek that which goeth astray? And if so be that he find it, verily I say unto you, he rejoiceth over it more than over the ninety and nine which have not gone astray. Even so it is not the will of your Father which is in Heaven that one of these little ones should perish.

'Yes, it is not the will of the Father that they should perish, and here they are perishing by hundreds and thousands. And there is no possibility of saving them,' he thought.

Then came Peter and said to him, How oft shall my brother offend me and I forgive him? Until seven times? Jesus saith unto him, I say not unto thee until seven times, but until seventy times seven. Therefore is the Kingdom of Heaven likened unto a certain king which made a reckoning with his servants. And when he had begun to reckon, one was brought unto him which owed him ten thousand talents. But forasmuch as he had not wherewith to pay, his lord commanded him to be sold, and his wife and children, and all that he had, and payment to be made. The servant therefore fell down and worshipped him, saying, Lord, have patience with me; I will pay thee all. And the lord of that servant, being moved with compassion, released him and forgave him the debt. But that servant went out, and found one of his fellow-servants which owed him a hundred pence; and he laid hold on him and took him by the throat, saying, Pay what thou owest. So his fellow-servant fell down and besought him, saying, Have patience with me and I will pay thee. And he would not, but went and cast him into prison till he should pay that which was due. So when his fellow-servants saw what was done, they were exceeding sorry, and came and told unto their lord all that was done. Then his lord called him unto him and saith to him, Thou wicked servant, I forgave thee all that debt because

thou besought me; shouldst not thou also have mercy on thy
fellow-servant as I had mercy on thee?

'And is this all?' Nekhlyudov suddenly exclaimed aloud, and
the inner voice of the whole of his being said, 'Yes, it is all.' And
it happened to Nekhlyudov, as it often happens to men who are
living a spiritual life. The thought that seemed strange at first and
paradoxical or even to be only a joke, being confirmed more
and more often by life's experience, suddenly appeared as the
simplest, truest certainty. In this way the idea that the only
certain means of salvation from the terrible evil from which men
were suffering was that they should always acknowledge themselves to be sinning against God, and therefore unable to punish
or correct others, because they were dear to Him. It became clear
to him that all the dreadful evil he had been witnessing in prisons
and jails, and the quiet self-satisfaction of the perpetrators of this
evil, were the consequences of men trying to do what was
impossible; trying to correct evil while being evil themselves;
vicious men were trying to correct other vicious men, and
thought they could do it by using mechanical means, and the
only consequence of all this was that the needs and the cupidity
of some men induced them to take up this so-called punishment
and correction as a profession, and become themselves utterly
corrupt, and go on unceasingly depraving those whom they
torment. Now he saw clearly what all the terrors he had seen
came from, and what ought to be done to put a stop to them.
The answer he could not find was the same that Christ gave to
Peter. It was that we should forgive always an infinite number of
times because there are no men who have not sinned themselves,
and therefore none can punish or correct others.

'But surely it cannot be so simple,' thought Nekhlyudov, and
yet he saw with certainty, strange as it had seemed at first, that it
was not only a theoretical but also a practical solution of the
question. The usual objection, 'What is one to do with the evil
doers? Surely not let them go unpunished?' no longer confused
him. This objection might have a meaning if it were proved that
punishment lessened crime, or improved the criminal, but when
the contrary was proved, and it was evident that it was not in
people's power to correct each other, the only reasonable thing to

do is to leave off doing the things which are not only useless, but harmful, immoral and cruel.

For many centuries people who were considered criminals have been tortured. Well, and have they ceased to exist? No; their numbers have been increased not alone by the criminals corrupted by punishment but also by those lawful criminals, the judges, procureurs, magistrates and jailers, who judge and punish men. Nekhlyudov now understood that society and order in general exists not because of these lawful criminals who judge and punish others, but because in spite of men being thus depraved, they still pity and love one another.

In hopes of finding a confirmation of this thought in the Gospel, Nekhlyudov began reading it from the beginning. When he had read the Sermon on the Mount, which had always touched him, he saw in it for the first time today not beautiful abstract thoughts, setting forth for the most part exaggerated and impossible demands, but simple, clear, practical laws. If these laws were carried out in practice (and this was quite possible) they would establish perfectly new and surprising conditions of social life, in which the violence that filled Nekhlyudov with such indignation would cease of itself. Not only this, but the greatest blessing that is obtainable to men, the kingdom of heaven on earth would be established.

There were five of these laws.

The first (*Matt.* v. 21–26), that man should not only do no murder, but not even be angry with his brother, should not consider anyone worthless: '*Raca*', and if he has quarrelled with anyone he should make it up with him before bringing his gift to God – i.e., before praying.

The second (*Matt.* v. 27–32), that man should not only not commit adultery but should not even seek for enjoyment in a woman's beauty, and if he has once come together with a woman he should never be faithless to her.

The third (*Matt.* 33–37), that man should never bind himself by oath.

The fourth (*Matt.* 38–42), that man should not only not demand an eye for an eye, but when struck on one cheek should hold out the other, should forgive an offence and bear it humbly, and never refuse the service others demand of him.

The fifth (*Matt.* 43–48), that man should not only not hate his enemy and not fight him, but love him, help him, serve him.

Nekhlyudov sat staring at the lamp and his heart stood still. Recalling the monstrous confusion of the life we lead, he distinctly saw what that life could be if men were brought up to obey these rules, and rapture such as he had long not felt filled his soul, just as if after long days of weariness and suffering he had suddenly found ease and freedom.

He did not sleep all night, and as it happens to many and many a man who reads the Gospels, he understood for the first time the full meaning of the words read so often before but passed by unnoticed. He imbibed all these necessary, important and joyful revelations as a sponge imbibes water. And all he read seemed so familiar and seemed to confirm, to form into a conception, what he had known long ago, but had never realised and never quite believed. Now he realised and believed it, and not only realised and believed that if men would obey these laws they would obtain the highest blessing they can attain to; he also realised and believed that the only duty of every man is to fulfil these laws; that in this lies the only reasonable meaning of life, that every stepping aside from these laws is a mistake which is immediately followed by retribution. This flowed from the whole of the teaching, and was most strongly and clearly illustrated in the parable of the vineyard.

The husbandman imagined that the vineyard in which they were sent to work for their master was their own, that all that was in was made for them, and that their business was to enjoy life in this vineyard, forgetting the Master and killing all those who reminded them of his existence. 'Are we do not doing the same,' Nekhlyudov thought, 'when we imagine ourselves to be masters of our lives, and that life is given us for enjoyment? This evidently is an incongruity. We were sent here by someone's will and for some reason. And we have concluded that we live only for our own joy, and of course we feel unhappy as labourers do when not fulfilling their Master's orders. The Master's will is expressed in these commandments. If men will only fulfil these laws, the kingdom of heaven will be established on earth, and men will receive the greatest good that they can attain to.

' "Seek ye first the kingdom and His righteousness, and all these things shall be added unto you."

'And so here it is, the business of my life. Scarcely have I finished one and another has commenced.' And a perfectly new life dawned that night for Nekhlyudov, not because he had entered into new conditions of life, but because everything he did after that night had a new and quite different significance than before. How this new period of his life will end time alone will prove.